Dear Romance Reader:

This year Avon Books is celebrating the sixth anniversary of "The Avon Romance"—six years of historical romances of the highest quality by both new and established writers. Thanks to our terrific authors, our "ribbon books" are stronger and more exciting than ever before. And thanks to you, our loyal readers, our books continue to be a spectacular success!

"The Avon Romances" are just some of the fabulous novels in Avon Books' dazzling *Year of Romance*, bringing you month after month of top-notch romantic entertainment. How wonderful it is to escape for a few hours with romances by your favorite "leading ladies"—Shirlee Busbee, Karen Robards, and Johanna Lindsey. And how satisfying it is to discover in a new writer the talent that will make her a rising star.

Every month in 1988, Avon Books' *Year of Romance*, will be special because Avon Books believes that romance—the readers, the writers, and the books—deserves it!

Sweet Reading,

Susanne Jaffe
Editor-in-Chief

Ellen Edwards
Senior Editor

STOLEN HEART

BARBARA DAWSON SMITH

AVON BOOKS ◆ NEW YORK

AVON BOOKS
A division of
The Hearst Corporation
105 Madison Avenue
New York, New York 10016

First Avon Books Printing: November 1988

AVON TRADEMARK REG. U.S. PAT. OFF. AND IN OTHER COUNTRIES, MARCA REGISTRADA, HECHO EN U.S.A.

Printed in the U.S.A.

K-R 10 9 8 7 6 5 4 3 2 1

With heartfelt thanks to
Joyce Bell, Alice Borchardt, Arnette Lamb,
and Susan Wiggs.
And, as always, to my husband.

Chapter 1

That cowboy was still staring at her.

Annoyed by his rudeness, Kristy Donovan tightened her black-gloved hands around the worn reticule in her lap. The dark stranger had the coldest blue eyes she'd ever seen. He was tall and lean and exuded an air of confidence bordering on arrogance. She tipped her chin up to challenge his insolent gaze until a tardy sense of propriety reminded her that ladies didn't stare.

Flashing him a final scathing look, Kristy turned her attention toward the lobby of the Capitol National Bank of Denver. The vast, high-ceilinged room somehow reminded her of a church, with its marble floor and dignified decor. The quiet was broken only by the hushed murmur of voices from the scattering of customers at the iron-barred tellers' booths.

For the past ten minutes, she'd been sitting outside the bank president's office, awaiting her one o'clock appointment and trying to quell the rolling sensation in her stomach. Kristy wasn't sure if her faint queasiness was caused by tension about the imminent meeting or by the greasy meal she'd lunched on at a nearby boardinghouse. But for whatever reason, her insides felt as restless as a cat in a cage.

And that cowboy wasn't helping matters any.

She stole another glance at him through the inky veil of her eyelashes. The damned polecat was still watching her!

He was lounging against the wall several yards away, a long, denim-covered leg crooked so that his boot pointed at the floor. In one hand he held his Stetson hat; the thumb of the other hand was hooked casually in the gun belt that

1

rode low on his hips. All Kristy could see of his weapons were the finely tooled ivory butts, but the sight was enough to make her suppress a shudder. A reckless gun in a barroom brawl had ended her father's life.

Quickly she lifted her gaze to the crisp white shirt that stretched across the cowboy's broad chest, and then up to his face, where his clean-shaven skin was weathered dark by the sun. The careless combing of his midnight black hair bespoke an absence of male vanity. Something about his indolent posture and rugged good looks brought to mind secret, sinful pleasures, something Kristy viewed with wary disdain. She had seen men like him along the Mississippi, men who made a living preying on lonely women of means. The only thing different about this man was the insulting stare of those glacial blue eyes.

She saw his gaze wander down to her bosom, where he appeared to be fascinated by the rise and fall of the black bombazine that hugged her breasts. Despite the modesty of her high-necked gown, Kristy felt herself blush with a warmth that had nothing to do with the sultry August day. He had the manners of a river rat, gawking that way at a lady in widow's weeds!

Maybe he can tell you aren't a real lady, an inner voice whispered.

Kristy tried to brush away the thought, yet it lingered. Could the stranger see the unladylike trace of fiery red in her brown hair? Did he notice her creamy complexion still held a few stubborn freckles despite her attempts to bleach them out with lemon juice and buttermilk? Nonsense, she scolded herself. Even that sharp-eyed cowboy couldn't guess her demure exterior hid a rebellious spirit and a blazing temper.

Kristy sat up straighter. After years spent working for the upper class, her manners were well-bred, her speech impeccable. No one here in Colorado had questioned her claim that she was from an impoverished but genteel family back in St. Louis. Only her ten-year-old brother Jeremy knew of the disreputable upbringing they'd shared as the children of a riverboat gambler. And Jeremy was no more inclined to volunteer that fact than she was.

"Excuse me—are you Mrs. Donovan?"

Kristy realized that a slight, sandy-haired gentleman was standing before her. She opened her mouth to correct his form of address but caught herself. Knowing a seventeen-year-old girl would have trouble getting a loan, she was posing as a widow to appear more mature. The banker needn't know she was really James Donovan's daughter, she reasoned.

"Yes, I'm Mrs. Donovan."

"Sheldon Arbuckle, at your service," he said, inclining his head in a deferential bow. "I'm Mr. Barnes's secretary. I'm terribly sorry, but it appears he's late returning from his luncheon appointment."

"That's quite all right. I don't mind waiting," Kristy said graciously, although she was hot and worried and anxious to bring the interview to a successful conclusion.

"Might I fetch you some refreshment, Mrs. Donovan? A cup of tea, perhaps, or some water?"

"Nothing, thank you." Though her mouth was parched, she didn't dare try to hold a glass in her shaky fingers.

"I'll let you know the moment Mr. Barnes returns," promised Arbuckle. He scurried across to a modest desk against the wall near the spot where the cowboy still lounged, watching Kristy with those hard blue eyes.

The look of courteous respect on Arbuckle's thin face turned into a frosty frown. "You, there," he said, addressing the dark stranger. "Have you business to conduct here?"

His haughty tone might have intimidated another man, but the cowboy seemed unaffected. Kristy heard the faint jangle of spurs as the stranger straightened with an unhurried movement and surveyed the smaller man, his face bland.

"Matter of fact, I do." His voice was low and vibrant to Kristy's ears, but she turned her gaze down to her reticule, pretending not to listen.

"And what might that be?" Arbuckle demanded.

"You're holding some papers for a friend of mine, name of Brett Jordan."

"Ah, yes . . . Mr. Barnes told me someone would be by for them." Paper rustled as he added with a trace of suspicion, "Here they are, Mr. . . . what did you say your name was?"

"I didn't."

The cowboy's rudeness failed to surprise Kristy. Hearing the heavy tread of his boots and the musical jangle of his spurs, she couldn't resist taking a peek as he walked over to the desk to fetch the documents. Without so much as a by-your-leave, he settled himself into an armchair beside the secretary's station, crossing his long legs and shuffling through the papers.

Sheldon Arbuckle opened his mouth as if to protest. Then his disapproving expression vanished as he glanced toward the lobby, where a portly man with graying, muttonchop whiskers was walking toward them at a dignified pace. Arbuckle hurried to greet him. "Good afternoon, Mr. Barnes. Mrs. Donovan is here to see you." Discreetly he indicated Kristy.

The man bowed formally to her. "I'm Franklin Barnes."

Her stomach lurched as Kristy recalled the purpose of their meeting. Everything would work out, she tried to assure herself.

With outward calm, she rose. "It's a pleasure to meet you, Mr. Barnes," she said, her voice well modulated.

"The pleasure is all mine," he said with a hearty smile. "I understand you own the Bar S ranch, up near Painted Rock?"

"Yes, that's correct."

"And you need a loan."

"Yes, sir, I do."

"How large an amount did you have in mind?"

Kristy glanced at the cowboy who sat within earshot. The crude boor was staring at her again, making no attempt to hide the fact that he was eavesdropping. Incensed, she jerked her eyes back to the bank president. Why was Barnes conducting this interview in so public a place?

"Is there somewhere we might discuss this matter in private?" she asked, careful to keep her tone soft and apologetic, her green eyes wide and appealing. Nothing worked better on a man than a show of frail femininity.

This time was no exception.

Barnes darted a dismayed frown at the cowboy. For an instant Kristy had the oddest impression of some wordless exchange between the two men. She scoffed at her vivid imagination. What possible connection could there be between that disreputable drifter and the president of a bank?

Barnes cleared his throat. "Oh . . . er . . . of course, Mrs. Donovan. Forgive my lack of manners. We can talk in my office."

Taking her by the elbow, he led her toward a door in the mahogany-paneled wall. She couldn't resist giving the cowboy a disdainful glare as she passed him, her chin lifted regally and her black silk skirts swishing around her high-buttoned shoes.

The office was somewhat somber, with a marble-topped desk dominating the room. The aroma of stale cigar smoke hung in the air. Maroon draperies blocked the hot rays of afternoon sun and rendered the room dim and stuffy.

Tension twisted Kristy's stomach as she settled into a leather guest chair. Beneath the prison of her corset, a rivulet of sweat trickled between her breasts, and her palms felt damp inside her gloves. This was it. This was the chance to fulfill her dream of making a decent life for herself and Jeremy.

Franklin Barnes left the door open for propriety's sake, and Kristy could only hope his booming voice wouldn't carry out of the room. He sat down behind the desk, the chair creaking loudly as he folded his arms over his barrel chest. "Well, now, where were we?" he said. "Ah, yes, the amount of the loan."

Kristy took a deep breath. "I'd like to borrow thirty-five hundred dollars."

He raised his bushy gray eyebrows. "What precisely do you intend to use the money for?"

"To buy cattle and repair the ranch buildings and to meet the payroll temporarily. I have all the expenses worked out, if you'd care to look them over." She reached inside her reticule and pulled out a small black notebook.

Barnes waved it away. "Just a moment, please. Am I correct in presuming that Mr. Donovan is, er, deceased?"

"Yes, my . . . husband died several months ago and

left me the Bar S." She chose not to add that her "husband" had won the ranch in a poker game just a month before his sudden death.

"And why is the ranch in such a sad state of affairs that you must borrow money to make ends meet?"

Kristy clenched the notebook. She'd expected the question and had carefully rehearsed an answer. "We had an unscrupulous foreman who cheated us out of the profits. Needless to say, that man is no longer in my employ. Now, with the help of your bank, I plan to make a fresh start." She leaned forward, determined to convince him. "I assure you, Mr. Barnes, your money will be quite safe. The Bar S has excellent rangeland—in fact, it's one of the finest ranches in the state of Colorado."

He tapped his pudgy fingers on the marble top of the desk. "And what could such a lovely young lady know about ranching?"

"I can keep the books, and I'm capable of directing the branding and roundup. Besides, cattle prices are down because of the drought. Since the Bar S has abundant water, I can buy low now and sell high come spring."

Kristy glossed over her skills with a twinge of guilt. It was best not to mention that she'd been raised in shantytowns along the Mississippi and that until a few short weeks ago, her entire knowledge of ranching had come from an occasional dime novel she'd dug out of a trash can, novels she'd studied in an effort to improve her reading ability.

Though she now knew those books had glorified the harsh reality of the West, her love for ranch life remained undimmed. The wide-open grasslands, the fragrant pine forests of the Rockies, the swift-flowing creeks that coursed through Bar S land—all this and more had made her fall in love with Colorado. And all this she vowed to keep for herself and Jeremy, no matter what the cost.

Franklin Barnes studied her for a moment, then slapped his palms on the desk. "All right, Mrs. Donovan, you've convinced me. You may have your loan."

Her flash of elation was tempered by an inbred caution. Why had he agreed so readily? "Don't you want to see my expense figures?'' she asked, indicating the notebook in her gloved hand.

"That's quite all right. All I need from you is the deed to the Bar S as collateral.''

Her heart lurched. "I was hoping you would accept just a small piece of the acreage,'' she said carefully. "It's good grassland with ample water. I can show you the location on a map I drew up.'' She started to open the notebook, but Barnes made an impatient movement.

"Young lady, a piece of a ranch is of no use to this bank at all. We must have a viable asset, something we can sell should you default. I'm afraid I can accept nothing less than the deed itself.''

Kristy felt a sinking sensation in her stomach. If she were unable to repay the loan, she and Jeremy would lose the Bar S. The very thought made her blood run cold. Without the ranch, where would they go? What would happen to all her dreams for the future?

"Would you accept my proposal if it were for a smaller loan?'' she ventured. "Perhaps I could rework the figures—''

Barnes shook his graying head. "No. You should know as well as I that ranching is a risky business. Without the deed to the entire ranch as collateral, the bank simply cannot lend you any money.''

Kristy felt her throat choke with the bitter taste of failure and resentment. He had her over a barrel and he knew it. She could tell by the greedy gleam in his eyes that he expected her to default and lose the Bar S to his bank. For a moment she was tempted to accept his terms and prove him wrong. But though she was confident, Kristy was no fool. There were too many things over which she had no control—drought, snowstorms, disease—any of which could ruin a rancher. Yet so long as she retained possession of the deed, she and Jeremy would always have a home.

She rose, slipping the black notebook into her reticule. "Then it seems I shall just have to find another bank.''

The complacent expression vanished from his whiskered face. "Mrs. Donovan, be reasonable. Most banks wouldn't even consider lending money to a lady rancher.''

"I'll take my chances on that," she said with icy courtesy. "Thank you for your time." Hiding her battered spirits with rigid dignity, she pivoted and walked out of the office.

Franklin Barnes trotted after her, stopping her just outside his door. "Would you consider selling the Bar S? I might be able to put you in touch with a buyer."

Why was he being so persistent? The swine must be determined to take advantage of her. "No, thank you," she said politely.

"Come now, Mrs. Donovan," he argued with a look of phony fatherly concern. "Ranching is hard work, much too harsh a life for a woman alone. With the money from the sale, you could invest in a business more suitable to a lady—a millinery shop, perhaps."

"I'm not selling, and that's final. Good day, Mr. Barnes."

"But, Mrs. Donovan—"

Ignoring the banker's protest, Kristy started toward the lobby, head held high. Then she caught sight of *him* again. That cowboy still lounged in the chair as if he owned the place, those flinty blue eyes missing nothing of her exchange with Barnes.

She gritted her teeth and fought back the urge to march over and slap the cowboy. Why was she letting his boorish behavior affect her so? He was nothing to her, nothing but another arrogant male. She'd seen enough of those today! Stiffening her back, Kristy swept past him and out of the bank.

The starch left her spine as she emerged onto the wooden-planked sidewalk bordering the bustling thoroughfare filled with fancy carriages and horse-drawn drays. With a despondent sigh she paused out of the way of the passersby. The brick bank building provided shade from the sweltering sun that made the layers of her clothing stick to her skin. From a saloon somewhere nearby came the tinkle of piano music and a gust of boisterous laughter.

Discouragement settled over Kristy like a cloud of dust from the unpaved street. Tears stung her eyes, but she blinked them back. She wouldn't give up—she couldn't! The Bar S was the first real home she and Jeremy had ever known. She'd vowed to make a respectable life for them, and somehow she would find a way to fulfill that dream. She consoled herself with the knowledge that at least they needn't sell the ranch—she still had Parker McClintock's marriage offer as her ace in the hole—but she'd wanted so badly to make it on her own!

Now there was no getting around the cold reality of her dwindling savings. This futile trip to Denver had cost money she and Jeremy couldn't spare. Somehow there must be a way to get the funds they needed. But wouldn't another bank also demand the deed to the ranch? How could she risk losing their only home?

"Mrs. Donovan?"

She straightened the dejected slump of her shoulders and swung around. It was that damned cowboy again! What could he possibly want with her?

He stood towering over her, his hat tilted at a rakish angle on his black hair, his ice blue eyes unreadable in the bright sunlight. Despite the sultry heat Kristy felt a shiver run down her spine. Impatiently she shook off the vague sense of danger.

"Are you addressing me?" she asked in her frostiest tone.

"You're the only Mrs. Donovan I know."

His presumption touched off her temper. That she had to deal with him on top of everything else was too much. "Pardon me, but you're mistaken," she snapped. "You *don't* know me."

Spinning on her heel, she started to stalk off into the crowd, but his deep voice called after her.

"It's about the Bar S."

Nothing else could have induced her to continue the conversation. Swallowing her anger, Kristy swiveled back around, eyeing the stranger cautiously. "What about it?"

He stepped closer, propping a wide shoulder against the brick building. "I take it you didn't get the loan you wanted?"

"That's none of your concern."

"But it could be," he countered. "If you're in the market to make some extra cash, I have a proposition for you."

Fury flared in her again, making her fingers tighten around her reticule. She might have known this disreputable drifter would suggest something crude.

"I've no interest in *your* kind of proposition."

His big hand clamped around her black-sleeved arm before she could walk away. "Hold on a minute, lady. This isn't what you think."

She gave him a look of icy disdain. "Let go of me."

"All right, if you'll calm down and listen before you go flying off the handle."

His fingers loosened their grip on her arm, but he still stood so close she caught a trace of his scent, a pleasing blend of leather and horses. Glaring up at his roughhewn face, Kristy told herself contemptuously that a more genteel man would smell of an aftershaving lotion like bay rum.

Those cool eyes studied her in a way that made her skin tingle with uneasiness. There was something secretive about him that she couldn't quite fathom. She had half a mind to walk away; the other half made her stay put. What harm could there be in hearing him out?

"Well?" she prompted.

"Like I said, I have a proposal you might be interested in—a chance for you to win the money you need."

Kristy tilted her head warily. "Win?"

"By playing poker." When she only stared at him, he added, "Surely you've heard of the game, Mrs. Donovan?"

"Of course," she murmured, too startled to take offense at his mocking tone. What he proposed was gambling, and no gentleman would engage in that sport with a respectable woman.

Unless he saw through her disguise as a lady.

She was swept by the uncanny notion that he knew her most private thoughts. A sense of vulnerability paralyzed Kristy before she managed to get hold of herself. The events of the day had unnerved her, she told herself. The truth of the matter was this cowpoke was too uncouth to be acquainted with the strictures of polite society. After all, this was the rough, uncivilized West, where men like him were unfamiliar with the social graces.

She appraised the rough beauty of his face. Just like the banker, he must view her as an easy mark, a trusting soul who could be fleeced of her small reserve of cash. The idea both infuriated and amused Kristy. He couldn't know her father had been a gambler who'd taught her a few tricks of the trade.

Why not turn the tables on this slick opportunist and beat him at his own game?

Excitement surged inside her. Although she hated the obsessive sickness that had destroyed James Donovan's life, this was different, she told herself. This was a one-time chance to win the money necessary to rebuild the ranch.

"I need quite a large sum," Kristy said cautiously. "Thirty-five hundred dollars, to be exact."

"I can cover that amount."

She stared at him measuringly. Could a mere cowhand possess that much cash? Maybe if he'd recently scored a big win at gambling . . .

"Then why would you want to play with me?" she asked. "I haven't much money to bet."

"You have the Bar S."

Of course. she should have known the ranch was what he was after. Kristy started to say that the Bar S was the one thing in the world she'd never wager, then stopped herself. If she told him that, he'd never play poker with her and she'd never get the chance to win his thirty-five hundred dollars.

"Well, Mrs. Donovan, are you interested?"

His hard expression made her stomach twist. Lydia wouldn't approve of gambling, she thought guiltily, remembering the older woman waiting for her back at the boardinghouse. Kristy pushed aside her misgivings. Anything was worth a try if it meant saving the ranch.

"I don't know what to say," she simpered. Kristy knew she had the wits to outsmart this cardsharp, but it was best to let him believe she was nothing but a brainless female. "This is a most unusual offer, Mr. . . ." She tilted her head, blinking her dark lashes at him in artless confusion. "I'm afraid you have the advantage of me. I don't even know your name."

"Call me Chad."

"Regarding your kind offer, Mr. Chad—"

"Just Chad. No 'Mr.' "

The fact that he withheld his last name only confirmed her suspicions about his unscrupulous nature. For all she knew, he might even be lying about his first name.

"All right . . . Chad." Kristy moistened her lips and was secretly pleased to see his eyes focus on the tip of her tongue. No matter how tough and dangerous he looked, he was still a man, easily distracted by a woman's wiles.

"I do need the money," she admitted shyly, "but I'm afraid I don't know the first thing about playing poker."

"I'll teach you."

"I . . . I'm not sure," she said, frowning up at him in a pretense of indecision. "Is it very complicated?"

"The rules are simple. There's strategy involved, of course, but it's basically a game of chance."

He made it sound so easy, Kristy thought derisively. But she hadn't been born yesterday. What he'd conveniently failed to mention were the skills that made poker a favorite of professional gamblers—the ability to outwit and outguess the other players, to know when to bet and when to fold, to keep one's expression unreadable—all the talents a beginner couldn't possibly master in a few practice hands.

"I could really win some money?" she asked, widening her eyes in childlike innocence.

"If the right cards fall your way. Are you willing or not?"

"It sounds so tempting . . ."

"Make up your mind, Mrs. Donovan."

"All . . . all right, I'll try it."

"Good. We can play at my hotel—it's down the street." Chad took firm hold of her elbow and began to guide her along the crowded boardwalk, past an array of small businesses and office buildings.

Kristy had to step quickly to keep up with his long strides. Her mind was in a whirl as she considered his last words. Would they be closeted alone in a hotel room, just the two of them? The very thought made her blanch. Her hesitation was more than mere propriety—she knew from her father's experience that a prudent gambler always had a quick exit route, just in case.

A barking dog raced past, followed by a ragged urchin who brushed by so close he would have knocked Kristy into another pedestrian had she not clutched Chad's arm for balance. The feel of the taut muscles beneath his stretched shirt gave her an inexplicable thrill, and she yanked her fingers away.

"Must you walk so fast?" she asked testily.

Her breathlessness was no ploy. The afternoon sun made the air shimmer with heat. Wisps of burnished brown hair clung to her damp neck. Her corset cut into her ribcage, and she could feel new rivulets of sweat trickle between her breasts.

"You shouldn't be wearing black on such a hot day," Chad commented, slanting a glance down at her as he slowed his pace somewhat.

His implied criticism stung her already frayed nerves; only good manners kept her voice smooth. "I'm in mourning."

"You're a widow?"

"Yes."

She was relieved when he asked no more questions. The falsehood didn't come any more easily than it had with Franklin Barnes. She'd dreamed of making a new start out West, of living a clean, honest life where she and Jeremy would be respected instead of scorned. But somehow in trying to achieve that noble goal she'd gotten herself tangled up in this lie about being a widow.

She had no alternative, Kristy assured herself. And anyway, what was wrong with deceiving this scoundrel who intended to swindle a naive widow out of her savings, not to mention her home?

She stole a sidelong glance up at Chad. He was looking straight ahead, a frown creasing his tanned forehead. He was probably planning the best way to beat her, Kristy thought disparagingly.

Anticipation swelled inside her. Yes indeed, she decided, she would enjoy outwitting this cocky gambler!

Chapter 2

"Here we are," Chad said abruptly.

He steered her through the ornate entryway of the hotel. The relative coolness inside restored her senses, and she was surprised to see the lobby was more opulent than she'd expected. To the left was a reservations desk of polished oak, manned by two nattily dressed clerks, while to the right she caught a glimpse of an elegant dining room, deserted in midafternoon. A magnificent chandelier hung from the arched ceiling.

Chad must have had a streak of luck at the cards to afford a place like this, she thought contemptuously. Like her father, he probably lived high on the hog for a few days until he'd squandered his entire winnings, then would go back to his usual hand-to-mouth existence.

The sound of their footsteps was absorbed by the plush carpet as Chad guided her toward a staircase that curved gracefully to the second floor. Remembering their destination, Kristy stopped, her heart skipping a beat.

"Surely . . . you aren't taking me to your room?" she asked, with an air of outraged innocence that wasn't entirely an act. The thought of being cloistered alone with this unprincipled stranger frightened her more than she would admit.

"Having second thoughts, Mrs. Donovan?" he asked mockingly.

Kristy knew she couldn't back out, not now when she so desperately needed money. But at the same time, she wanted the deck stacked in her favor. She tossed her chin up and met his flinty blue eyes.

"No, but it wouldn't be proper for you to entertain me

14

in your room without a chaperone. I must insist we conduct this game in a more public place.''

He studied her for a moment, then shrugged. ''Have it your way, ma'am. I suppose we can play in here.''

With a sweep of his hand, he indicated a door to the right of the stairway. Kristy walked through it to find a parlor for the hotel guests, with forest green draperies and rosewood furniture. At least the room was deserted, she noted thankfully, sinking into an armchair as she attempted to hide her nervousness.

''I'll get the cards from my room,'' Chad said. ''I trust you'll still be here when I return?''

His sardonic question rankled her. ''Of course,'' she managed to say calmly.

Kristy watched him walk out of the parlor, his spurs jingling faintly. She was aware of a latent power in him that brought to mind a coiled spring. Her heart knocked against her rib cage at the memory of his low-slung guns. He didn't strike her as a man who liked to lose. What sort of retribution would he take if he discovered she was duping him?

Drawing a deep breath, she reminded herself he was only an ignorant cowpoke and no match for her wits. She would just have to keep one step ahead of him, that was all.

Peeling off her damp gloves, Kristy wished propriety allowed her to unbutton the high neckline that stuck to her perspiring skin. Quickly she repaired her falling chignon and adjusted her black straw hat, then fanned her hot face with her reticule.

A man in the uniform of a hotel employee brought in a glass on a silver tray, which he presented to her. ''For you, ma'am.''

''You must be mistaken,'' Kristy said, eyeing the lemonade wistfully. ''I didn't order anything.''

''The—uh—gentleman said to bring it to you.''

''Oh. Well, in that case, thank you.''

Taken aback by Chad's unexpected thoughtfulness, she accepted the crystal glass. Once the servant was gone, she abandoned her ladylike sips and drank deeply. The cool, tart lemonade bathed her parched throat like the finest nectar as she reveled in the sensuous pleasure of satisfying her thirst.

"I'm glad to see you're enjoying the drink."

The sound of that low voice made Kristy nearly choke on a swallow of liquid. Color warmed her cheeks. How long had Chad been standing there in the doorway, watching her guzzle the lemonade with all the finesse of a street woman?

Hastily she set the empty glass on a nearby marble-topped table. "Oh . . . I didn't realize you'd come back."

"I apologize if I startled you. Guess I walk a little quieter when I take off my spurs."

As Chad strolled into the parlor, she found herself staring. Along with his spurs he'd also shed his Stetson, though the rest of his appearance remained unchanged, right down to the guns belted low on his hips. He looked so arrestingly handsome in his white shirt and form-fitting pants that she had to take a deep breath to calm the flustered beating of her heart.

"Thank you for the lemonade," she said graciously. "It was kind of you to send it in to me."

"Kindness wasn't my purpose. I just don't want you swooning on me in the middle of our game."

Kristy bit back an acid retort. Swooning! Why, she'd never fainted in her life!

"Whatever your reasons," she said with forced sweetness, "it was quite gentlemanly of you to consider my comfort."

"Let's get one thing straight, Mrs. Donovan—I'm no gentleman. I'd advise you to remember that."

His eyes looked almost angry as he picked up a small rosewood table and placed it in front of her, then pulled over a chair and sat down opposite her. She watched in stony silence as he slapped a pack of cards onto the table.

Her fingers gripped the green velvet arms of her chair. His rudeness was annoying. She had the feeling he was deliberately trying to provoke her . . . as if he scorned her for some unknown reason. Staring at his strong, impassive features, she had the sudden impression he was playing a role as much as she was.

Kristy shook off the fanciful notion. There was nothing

secretive about what he was doing; his objective was plain—to bilk her out of her ranch!

Chad drew a cigar out of his shirt pocket and glanced at her. "Mind if I smoke?"

The question was perfunctory, for he was already lighting the cigar when she shook her head. Apparently part of his plan was to distract her with his ill-mannered behavior. Little did he know she was on to his tricks.

He set his cigar in a small porcelain bowl and picked up the deck, his long, lean fingers shuffling the cards with deft precision. "I trust you're at least familiar with a deck of cards?" he asked.

"Yes, I am."

"Good. The first thing you need to know is that each player is dealt five cards. The player with the best combination of cards wins. I'll make a list of all the possible hands in order of their value." Reaching into his back pocket, Chad drew forth a slip of paper and a pencil stub. He started to write, then paused to look at her. "You can read, can't you?"

The hint of condescension in his voice made Kristy bristle despite her better intentions. How brainless did he think she was? She was hard pressed to keep her expression unruffled. "Of course I can read."

"Good." He resumed writing, and for a moment the only sound was the scratching of his pencil. Abruptly he asked, "Do you have a first name, Mrs. Donovan?"

"Do you have a last name, Chad?" she countered.

He shot her a bluntly appraising look. "Point taken, Mrs. Donovan. The less we know about each other, the better. After all, we're hardly a lady and a gentleman attending a social function."

The color drained from her cheeks. Was this yet another hint that he saw evidence of her less-than-sterling roots? Or was guilt at her deception making her imagination run wild?

"Here you go," Chad said, handing her a slip of paper. "As you can see, you can win with anything from a straight flush—that's five consecutive cards in the same suit—to a simple high card. I suggest you take a few minutes and study that paper before we play some practice hands.''

Picking up his cigar, he crossed his long legs. He blew out a curl of blue smoke and leaned back in the chair as if he hadn't a care in the world. Kristy looked down at what he'd written. His handwriting was surprisingly neat, his spelling accurate. Sometime in his past he must have attended school.

Glancing at him through the dark screen of her lashes, she found herself wondering about him. He seemed a loner. Did he have friends? Or a family somewhere? She could picture him returning home after a long absence, kissing his wife, hugging his son, a little boy who looked like a miniature version of him, with black hair and stunning blue eyes . . .

Kristy flushed. Now, where had that absurd vision come from? He was too hardened a man to have such a storybook home life. As the daughter of a gambler, she should know, she reflected bitterly. Hadn't her own childhood been spent in rundown shacks furnished with broken dreams?

''I'm ready,'' she announced.

Indolently Chad straightened and put down his cigar. ''All right, let's get on with the game.'' He dealt out the cards. ''We'll play five-card draw. Go ahead and look at your hand, Mrs. Donovan.''

Obediently she picked up her cards and examined them with a pretense of concentration before returning her gaze to Chad. ''Now what?'' she asked innocently.

''Normally we'd place our bets, but since this is just a practice game, we'll skip that part. Now you have a chance to discard any cards you don't want. I'll show you what I mean.''

Chad came over to crouch beside her and study her cards. His nearness made Kristy's heart pound. All too aware of the hard muscles of the forearm touching hers, she had to force herself to listen to what he was saying.

''You have a pair of jacks,'' he explained, ''so you'd want to keep those. The others are worthless, so you'd throw them out and ask for three new cards in hopes of getting another jack.''

"Ohhh, *I* see," she murmured, as if that were a startling revelation. Deliberately she laid the rejected cards face up on the table.

Chad turned them over. "Don't let your opponent see what you're discarding—you'd give him an advantage."

"Goodness sakes . . . I didn't realize."

He returned to his chair. "Here are your three new cards," he said, handing them to her. "You didn't get another jack, but you've picked up a pair of fours."

"Is that good?"

"Two pairs are better than one, but of course it all depends on what your opponent is holding. Or how well he can bluff you into believing he has a better hand than yours."

"Bluff?" she said with a frown. "This is more difficult than I'd thought."

"Giving up already, Mrs. Donovan?"

His derisive tone grated on her nerves. "I didn't say that."

"Good. Once we play a few practice hands, I promise you'll feel more confident."

He sat back casually, smoke curling from the cigar in his hand. Kristy knew he thought he was manipulating her, and she could scarcely control the urge to wipe that arrogant expression from his devilishly handsome face. He wouldn't be so smug once she'd won all his money!

They played several more trial games, and Chad coached her on the strategies of when to bet and when to pass, taking into account the probabilities of drawing the desired cards. Kristy had to give him credit for honesty. Apparently he was so confident of his ability to win that he didn't see a need to mislead her.

He looked at her across the table. His eyes were unreadable, yet she fancied some secret hidden in those cold blue depths. "Ready for a serious game, Mrs. Donovan?"

"I . . . I think so," she stammered, keeping up her pretense of being an indecisive female.

"We'll set no betting limits. Any objection?"

"I . . . no."

"Good. You can deal first."

Kristy shuffled the deck ineptly. "I'm not very good at

this,'' she apologized, artfully letting a few cards spill onto the table. She reshuffled, then let Chad cut the cards before she began to deal them out, deliberately tilting up the deck.

"I can see the bottom card," he pointed out.

"Oh, my!" Kristy exclaimed, widening her eyes as she hastily lowered the pack. "Does that mean I have to start all over?"

"Yes, Mrs. Donovan."

The dry note in his voice again gave her the uncanny impression he knew exactly what she was up to. Gritting her teeth, she subdued the feeling. Those flinty eyes of his were making her nervous, that was all. She'd feel better once she'd won his thirty-five hundred dollars.

Kristy dealt again, this time without error. Pretending to study her cards, she watched Chad surreptitiously, observing his mannerisms, searching his rugged face for any clue that might indicate what sort of hand he had. But his expression was blank as he leaned forward to tap the ash from his cigar into the porcelain bowl.

He reached into his back pocket and drew forth a thick wad of currency. "I'll open with twenty dollars," he said, casually peeling off a bill and tossing it into the middle of the table.

Kristy blanched, thinking of the sixty-two dollars and seventeen cents tucked inside one of her high-buttoned shoes. "Twenty dollars?" she said faintly. "Isn't that rather steep for an opening bet?"

Chad shot her a look of cool amusement. "Did you think we were playing for pennies, Mrs. Donovan?"

"No, but I thought a dollar or two to start—"

"With stakes that low, we'd be playing until next week. Now, are you backing out or staying in?"

Kristy swallowed to ease the dryness in her throat. Her cash reserves wouldn't buy more than a few scrawny head of cattle. She might as well go for broke.

Pretending intense concentration, she stared down at the pair of deuces in her hand. Could she bluff Chad? "All right," she said after a long moment. "I'll bet twenty dollars too. I . . . I think I'd also like to raise you ten."

He cocked a dark eyebrow. "You think?"

Why did she have the feeling he was laughing at her? His face was bland, his gaze inscrutable. "I will," she said firmly.

"Then let's see the color of your money."

Kristy discreetly lifted her black skirt to unbutton her high-topped walking shoe. In the process of retrieving the appallingly thin purse, something made her glance up at Chad. He was leaning back in his chair, watching her as he puffed lazily on his cigar. A blush heated her cheeks. Hastily she looked away, flustered for a reason she couldn't quite fathom. Why was her heart racing? All he could see was a glimpse of her modest black stocking.

She looked at him haughtily. "I'd thank you not to stare."

"Don't fret, Mrs. Donovan," he drawled. "I've seen a woman's legs before."

"I'm sure you have," Kristy muttered.

By the time she had rebuttoned her shoe and sat up, her ladylike demeanor was back in place. She put thirty dollars on the table and after the next round of betting had the pleasure of winning the pot.

A couple of hours later, Kristy was so flushed with elation that the discomfort of the late afternoon heat scarcely affected her. The pile of currency in front of her had grown until now it topped nine hundred dollars. The few hands she'd lost were far outweighed by the ones she'd won. Chad had been remarkably easy to bluff, so easy she couldn't help wondering if he were letting her win. But that was absurd. What streetwise gambler would set out to deliberately lose his money?

"Not bad for a novice," Chad said, sounding a trifle disgruntled as she raked in yet another win.

Her cheeks dimpled modestly. "I'm sure it's only beginner's luck."

He began to shuffle the cards. "Or perhaps the lady is cleverer than she appears to be?"

Even his implied slur couldn't dampen her spirits. "Never underestimate a woman," she said blithely.

"Never trust a woman is a better way to put it."

Kristy hid a smile at the trace of dissatisfaction in his

voice. She couldn't resist throwing his own words back at him. "Giving up already, Chad?"

"I never give up, Mrs. Donovan."

The ice in his eyes chilled her despite the late afternoon heat. Something ruthless and secretive lay beneath his words, something that hinted at a host of dark emotions rolling just below his surface calm. The intensity of the impression paralyzed her for an instant. Then she gave herself a mental shake. So he didn't like losing, did he? Well, that was his problem, not hers.

Kristy watched in silence as he dealt out the cards. She had to admire his honesty. Not once had her sharp eyes caught him employing the most common method of cheating, dealing from the bottom of the deck. As far as she could tell, the cards weren't marked. Of course, he could have another deck hidden somewhere, but he'd rolled up his shirtsleeves to his elbows, eliminating the most obvious place to conceal spare cards. No, he wasn't cheating, not even now, when he'd lost a bundle of cash.

Kristy picked up her cards. Her heart jumped, though she was careful to hide her excitement. Three aces! Her nerves were beginning to fray from the hours of tension, and she decided the moment had come for more aggressive play.

"I'll open with two hundred," she said, pushing the bills into the center of the table.

Chad's eyes narrowed as he counted out several notes of currency and shoved them forward. "I'll cover you and raise you three hundred."

Kristy concealed her surprise at the high bet. "I'll call," she said, making a sizable dent in her winnings by adding her own three hundred dollars to the pot.

Chad glanced at his cards and tossed a pair of them down on the table. "Dealer takes two."

Perspiration dewed her forehead as she watched him take the new cards. Might he also have three of a kind? Or was he bluffing? His expressionless face told her nothing, but her pulse raced with the knowledge that her aces were high.

"I'd like two also, please," she said primly, discarding the unwanted cards.

"Polite to the bitter end, eh, Mrs. Donovan?"

Ignoring his words, Kristy picked up her two new cards and hid a surge of elation. The fourth ace! Lady luck was still with her. Chad had to have a straight flush in order to beat this hand. The odds against that were as good as impossible!

"Oh, is this the end?" she inquired, meeting his glacial blue eyes with ladylike innocence.

"Maybe, if the stakes get much higher. Your bet, Mrs. Donovan."

The sardonic way he kept saying her name grated on her nerves. He was only trying to fluster her, she told herself. But his ploy wouldn't work, because she held the winning hand.

Recklessly she thrust some cash into the center of the table. "I believe in taking risks. There's four hundred dollars there."

Chad's cool expression didn't change. "I'll cover your four hundred and raise you—oh, how about seventeen hundred?" He tossed out a wad of bills. "You ought to like that, Mrs. Donovan—it'll make the pot worth an even thirty-five hundred dollars."

Stunned, Kristy stared down at the pile of currency between them. Enough cash lay there to fulfill her dreams for the Bar S. The problem was that she couldn't meet Chad's bet with the few dollars left in front of her. She'd banked on him folding, but instead he'd jumped into the game with both feet. Either the cowboy was a complete idiot or he held a strong hand, a full house perhaps.

But even a full house couldn't beat her four aces.

"Your bet, Mrs. Donovan."

She moistened her dry lips. "I'm almost out of cash. You'll have to accept my marker."

"No IOUs. Not while you have the Bar S."

His voice was heartless, implacable. He'd told her the ranch was what he was after. And now she had to meet his bet or fold.

Kristy cursed herself in silence. If she folded now, she would lose all but a few measly dollars, despite the four aces in her hand. Yet how could she put the deed to the Bar S on the table and take even the slightest chance of losing her and Jeremy's home? How could she risk ruining their future?

Her damp fingers tightly clutched the cards. The thirty-five hundred dollars in the pot tempted her. She might never again have the opportunity to get the money they needed, free and clear.

But she couldn't do it. If as dedicated a gambler as James Donovan had loved his children enough not to gamble away the ranch once he won it, then neither would she.

She met Chad's icy eyes. "I won't wager the Bar S," she said slowly.

For an instant he only stared at her with that relentless blue gaze. Then his dark eyebrows descended, a clear sign of the onset of fury, and he flung down his cigar with a savage flick of his wrist.

"The hell you say," he growled in a voice so menacing it almost made her tremble. "You agreed from the start that the Bar S would be part of the stakes."

Her heart was pounding, but she refused to show any fear. "I never said any such thing."

"Then you damn well led me to believe you were agreeable—didn't you, Mrs. Donovan?"

Kristy shrugged, shifting uneasily in her chair. So what if she'd misled him? She didn't owe this shady gambler any honesty, not when he was trying to trick her out of her home! Looking at his angry expression across the small rosewood table, she felt her alarm intensify. Never in the short time since she'd met him had she been more keenly aware of Chad's size and obvious strength. The parlor might be open to the other hotel guests, but for the moment they were alone.

And Chad looked furious enough to kill.

Longingly she thought of her derringer, which she'd left at the boardinghouse with Lydia. What respectable citizen took a gun to a meeting with a bank president?

Unexpectedly anger swept over her. How dare Chad glower at her like an outraged victim when his soul was as black as the ace of spades! Spurred by a little devil of defiance, Kristy lifted her chin. "I'm sorry if you misunderstood. Next time I'd advise you to get it in writing."

"By God, if you were a man . . ." he said through gritted teeth.

"What would you do then?" she prodded, driven by the horrifying memory of her father's violent death. "Shoot me down in cold blood? Isn't that the way men like you solve all your problems?"

Chad settled back in his chair. Coolness came down over his face, blanking out the terrible fury as if it had never existed.

"And just what do you know about men like me?" he drawled.

Plenty! Kristy clamped her lips shut to stop the flippant retort. Under no circumstances did she want to give this shrewd cowboy even a hint of her past.

"I read the newspapers," she said stiffly. "There've been lots of stories about gunslingers."

"So you're branding me a killer." His tone was dispassionate.

Her gaze dipped involuntarily, though the table hid the ominous sight of his weapons. "You wear guns."

"That doesn't mean I've got notches on them."

"There's always a first time."

"Do I frighten you, Mrs. Donovan?"

She looked him squarely in the eyes and told a bald-faced lie. "No."

Chad regarded her with a veiled expression before glancing down at the cards he still held. "Then perhaps I might interest you in a different set of stakes. You haven't conceded the game yet."

"What other stakes?" Kristy asked warily. Besides the Bar S, what could she have that could possibly be of value to him?

"You, Mrs. Donovan."

For an instant his soft words puzzled her. Then understanding dawned, and the blood drained from her face, leaving her dizzy with shock. The polecat was suggesting she wager her body! Who did he think she was, a floozie? Damn him . . . she was a lady!

"How dare you . . ." she sputtered.

His lips crooked into an insulting smile. "Come now,

Mrs. Donovan, don't act so shocked. You've been married—you're hardly an innocent.''

But she wasn't a widow, Kristy wanted to shout; she was a seventeen-year-old girl whose only knowledge of the secret act between men and women came from peeping in the window of Mrs. Murphy's bawdy house at the age of eleven on the dare of a girlfriend. The glimpse she'd gotten of two intertwined naked bodies had appalled her. The thought of doing *that* with this tall, blatantly masculine stranger made her feel hot and cold all over.

"You insult me," she said angrily.

Chad shrugged. "You can always bet the Bar S instead. Or fold and lose all your money. The choice is yours."

He had her backed into a corner. Kristy fumed. How could she ignore the thirty-five hundred dollars lying so temptingly in the center of the table? She glanced down at the four aces in her hand and excitement spurted inside her again. How could she turn down this incredible opportunity?

But an inbred caution tempered her eagerness to win. Why was Chad offering her this chance when he could force her to fold right now? With the money in the pot, he could hire the services of all the soiled doves in Denver's most elegant whorehouse. Instead he was willing to risk losing everything on the gamble that he could possess her too.

Kristy moistened her lips. "Why are you doing this?"

His narrowed eyes tracked the tip of her tongue. For an instant she was seized by an impression of some dark, vibrant emotion in him. Then he lifted his gaze, aloofness masking his thoughts.

"Because I can't lose, Mrs. Donovan. And rest assured," he murmured, "I expect to get my money's worth."

His arrogance made her color rise. She tossed her chin up, thinking of her four aces.

"You have to win first," she said.

"Are you consenting to the bet then?"

Confidence flowed through her. She knew the chance of him beating her was next to impossible. If this arrogant cowpoke was determined to make a damn fool of himself, who was she to stand in his way?

"All right, I accept." Decisively she laid her cards on the table. "There you go—four aces. Unless I'm mistaken, you must have a straight flush in order to beat that."

Chad glanced at her cards, his face impassive. "Quite a hand, Mrs. Donovan."

Kristy couldn't hold back a victorious smile. "As I said before, it must be beginner's luck."

She reached for her winnings, but his lean hand shot out, grasping her fingers and holding them firm.

"Not so fast." He fanned out his cards on the table. "Sometimes an experienced player can get lucky too."

She glanced at his cards, and the breath froze in her throat. King, queen, jack, ten, nine. All diamonds. A straight flush.

Blood pounded in her ears. She felt hot and weak, incapable of movement. She'd lost. It was impossible. Impossible!

In numb disbelief Kristy lifted her gaze to Chad's face. His smile was both sinful and satisfied.

"Well, well, Mrs. Donovan," he drawled, "it seems I just won me a night in your bed."

Chapter 3

Alarm washed over Kristy. Wide-eyed, she stared at Chad as a vivid image of his large hands exploring her nakedness flashed into her mind. Her heart raced, and her senses swam. How could she give this cold stranger her innocence?

"You cheated," she accused in desperation.

His eyes glittered like ice. "Prove it."

She couldn't. Pressing her lips together, Kristy felt paralyzed with panic as he scooped up the cash from the middle of the table, tucking the bills into his back pocket. Throughout the game, she'd watched him carefully, and he hadn't made a wrong move. Still, he must have cheated. But how?

He rose to his superior height. "Shall we proceed upstairs, Mrs. Donovan?"

A wave of dread assaulted her. "No! I . . . I'm hungry. Couldn't we have dinner first?"

"We'll have something sent up to the room—later." He added the last word in a silken undertone as his gaze wandered over the bodice of her modest black gown.

The blatant desire on his face increased Kristy's trepidation. She had glimpsed that look in men's eyes before, but never had it affected her in this shivery, heart-pounding way. Chad stepped over to her chair and held out his hand. Too rattled to form an escape plan, she gathered up her few dollars and stood up on shaky legs, clutching her reticule. His fingers closed firmly around her elbow as he guided her out of the parlor.

Kristy threw a frantic glance around the lobby, wonder-

ing if she could persuade one of the gentlemen there to
come to her aid.

Chad's hand tightened on her arm. "Don't even think
about it," he warned, his voice a rough whisper in her
ear.

Little did he know she dared not make a scene, Kristy
thought in bitter despair. Even if she were to fling herself
on the mercy of some stranger, the prospect of the expla-
nations she'd have to give and the resulting scandal gave
her pause. She couldn't risk such a disgraceful incident
reaching Parker McClintock's ears. The rancher undoubtedly would withdraw his marriage offer, and now that all
her money was gone, that proposal was her last hope of
saving the Bar S.

She tossed a resentful glance at Chad. "There's no need
to manhandle me."

His grip loosened a fraction. "Then don't get any
chicken-livered notion about backing out of our bet."

She narrowed her eyes in disdain. "I'm not chicken-
livered."

"Good. Because I damn sure don't want a scared little
girl in my bed."

His wicked smile made Kristy's stomach twist into a
knot. Frantically she tried to think of some way out. She
might risk running if it weren't for her long skirts. As for
fighting him off, she was sensible enough to guess the
outcome of pitting her puny strength against the honed
power of his muscles.

Helpless as a lamb being led to slaughter, she let Chad
lead her up the sumptuous staircase to the second floor.
The plush carpeting absorbed the sound of their footsteps
as he steered her down to the end of the long hall. He
stopped in front of a door bearing an ornate brass number.
Releasing her arm, he reached into his pocket and drew
forth a key, inserting it in the lock. With a twist of his
wrist, the door swung open.

"After you, Mrs. Donovan." He gave a curt nod toward the room.

Kristy stared at his white shirtfront, unable to meet his
gaze as both mind and body rebelled against entering the
lion's den. Somehow she had to stall for time.

She dragged her eyes upward, hastily avoiding the black chest hair revealed by the opened top button of his shirt. Tilting her head to the side, she forced her features into an apologetic expression. "Would you mind . . . waiting out here for a moment?" she asked hesitantly.

His eyebrows lowered. "If this is some kind of trick—"

"It's not a trick! I need some time to freshen up."

"You look fine to me," he said, giving her body a blunt look of approval.

"I . . . I need some privacy." Kristy ran a perspiring palm down the side of her skirt. "To use the, uh . . ."

She stuttered to a stop, her embarrassment no pretense. Even for the sake of escape, she couldn't bring herself to make reference to a call of nature in front of this arrogant stranger.

He chuckled. The low sound of amusement turned her cheeks a deeper fiery red.

"All right. I'll grant you a few minutes to yourself." The humor vanished from his face. "Just don't make me cool my heels too long."

He reached out and boldly cupped her breast in his hand. The unexpected caress shook Kristy to the core of her being. Despite the layers of her gown and corset, she felt the warmth of his palm searing her flesh.

Outrage boiled inside her. Obviously he regarded her as his possession, a trinket to be used in any manner he pleased.

Yet the naked contempt in his eyes held her paralyzed with confusion. She wanted to slap his fingers away, but her hand seemed incapable of movement. She wanted to toss out an indignant rebuke, but her voice seemed to have deserted her.

She was still gaping like a fool when he moved his hand to her shoulder and gave her a little push inside the room. "While you're at it, Mrs. Donovan," he added in a brusque undertone, "you might as well get undressed."

The door shut with a soft click. Kristy leaned against the wall, her knees weak and her mind in a whirl. The crudeness of his parting words nagged at her like an open wound. Why did Chad regard her with such blatant distaste? He had been the one to propose the final bet, not her. The memory of his hand on her breast made her insides feel odd. Why would he want her in his bed if he disliked her so?

Kristy shook off the disturbing enigma. Chad's behavior disgusted her. The way he had touched her was more evidence of his boorish nature. Only a lout would fondle a lady in a public hallway, where anyone could have walked by and seen them.

Well, she darn sure wasn't going to let that saddle tramp put his crude paws on her ever again! If worse came to worst, she'd steal one of his guns and use it on the stinking polecat!

Hands on her hips, she spun around and surveyed the hotel room. It was large and ornate, with a big brass bed against one wall and a dressing table against the other. Chad's Stetson lay on a chair beside the opened window, where the floral drapes fluttered in a wisp of wind.

Her heartbeat surged. *The window.*

Kristy darted across the carpeting, grasping the sill as she poked her head outside. The room was situated at the back corner of the hotel, facing the blank brick wall of a neighboring building.

She looked down at a smelly, trash-strewn alley. Abruptly her head spun, and Kristy tightened her grip on the windowsill. Closing her eyes to control the dizziness, she lifted her face to the cool breeze of dusk. You're only one floor up, she scolded herself. One floor between you and freedom.

Gritting her teeth, she forced her gaze downward again. The ground might well have been as far away as St. Louis. How was she to get all the way down there without breaking her neck?

Then she spotted a drainpipe at the corner of the hotel, just a few yards away. The metal cylinder looked rickety and not altogether safe. Dare she trust it to support her weight?

Kristy stood in an agony of indecision, her fingers damp and tense on the windowsill. No other means of escape came to mind. She thought of Chad waiting outside the hotel room door. Waiting to violate her virgin body with his cold, contemptuous hands.

A shudder ran through her. Quickly she hiked up her skirt and then clambered out onto the impossibly narrow ledge. As she stood up, her foot slipped. Swaying, Kristy grabbed the window frame, her heart fluttering like the wings of a caged bird.

Only the memory of Chad's icy blue eyes could induce her to go on. She took a deep breath to steady her nerves. Not daring to look down, she inched her way along the ledge, heedless of the rough brick that scraped the tender skin of her fingers. An eternity seemed to pass as she traveled the few yards to the drainpipe, but at last she was there.

Reaching out with a trembling hand, Kristy tested the pipe. It gave a metallic rattle, but at least it remained sturdily fixed to the brick.

She wiped her perspiring palms on her skirt. Then her fingers curled tightly around the cool metal. Closing her eyes, she uttered a brief, fervent prayer.

And stepped off the ledge.

Chad paced the corridor outside his hotel room, hands jammed into his back pockets. A frown creased his tanned forehead. He stared down, seeing not the rich burgundy carpeting but a pair of lovely green eyes. Eyes as fresh and untainted as a new aspen leaf in springtime.

"God damn it," he muttered. Mrs. James Donovan had shot his plans to hell. He had expected a worn-out slut, her face wrinkled and pasty with makeup, her body coarse and sagging with age.

Instead she was a slip of a girl with luminous green eyes and a headful of shiny brown hair. No, not brown, exactly. Mahogany, maybe. Mahogany with a glint of fiery red. Her face was heart shaped, her complexion creamy, with a few freckles dusted across the dainty bridge of her nose.

Freckles, for Christ's sake!

Chad raked a hand through his hair. She looked wholesome, not jaded. A couple of times, when she'd leaned close, he'd even caught a homey aroma of peaches that made him want to put his mouth to her skin to see if she tasted as good as she smelled.

The memory of her guileless eyes made his throat tighten. For a moment something soft stirred inside him, a yearning that he hadn't let himself feel since that terrible day so many years ago when he'd shed his boyish fancies to face the bitter realities of life. A long-forgotten dream haunted him . . . the dream of a happy home life with a woman to fill his empty arms with her love, and children to make the house ring with laughter . . .

Scowling, he crushed the memory. Dreams were for fools. Anyway, no connection could exist between that childish fantasy and a slut like Mrs. James Donovan.

Hadn't he been around enough women of easy morals to know one when he saw one? Look at the way she had teased him and taunted him during their poker game. Yes, hot blood coursed through her veins despite that regal, touch-me-not act of hers.

Besides, hadn't she married herself off to an aging gambler? That fact alone proved she wasn't the prim and proper lady she pretended to be.

The thought of her in bed with Donovan sickened Chad. What sickened him even more was the hot desire throbbing in his own loins. He hadn't counted on her looking so soft and young and vulnerable. He hadn't counted on this longing to feel her breasts against his body, to hear her voice crying out his name in ecstasy.

Chad despised himself for wanting the leavings of a cheat. And he resented her for looking like an angel when he knew she must have the heart of a whore. God only knew how many other men she'd bedded, if she'd leeched off an old coot like James Donovan!

Pacing the hall, Chad glowered at his hotel room door. Damn the bitch for refusing to wager the Bar S! Who would have thought she'd hang onto the deed like a puncher clinging to a bucking bronc? The ranch couldn't mean diddly-squat to someone who'd only lived there a few short weeks, let alone a tenderfoot like her.

Obviously she could use some cash money, judging by the shabby elegance of her clothing. Mrs. James Donovan must be putting on an act so she could demand a higher price for the Bar S, Chad concluded. Nothing else could explain her behavior.

By God, if he couldn't have the ranch, he'd at least have her. The memory of her slender curves and expressive green eyes haunted him with galling intensity. He damn well intended to get his money's worth out of her.

Chad shot another glare at the door. What the hell was taking her so long? A corner of his mouth lifted as he recalled her embarrassment in expressing the need to relieve herself.

Then his amusement withered, and he stopped dead in sudden suspicion. If she'd tricked him again . . .

Three long strides took him to the door. He flung it open without bothering to knock. A swift glance around told him she was gone.

"Son of a bitch!" he muttered.

Stalking to the window, he thrust his head out. A flash of movement in the alley caught his eye. She was hurrying around the corner of the hotel, heading toward the street, her slim, black-gowned form silhouetted against the silver shadows of dusk.

His fist slammed down on the windowsill. That double-crossing hussy! She'd conned him a second time!

Realizing she must have shinnied down the drainpipe, he couldn't deny a grudging admiration for her spirit. At least the woman had spunk, if no other redeeming character traits.

His lips curling into a hard smile, Chad checked the impulse to run after her. She may have beaten him, but only for the moment. He knew where to find the Bar S . . . and Mrs. James Donovan. Whether she liked it or not, he would claim that night in her bed.

But this was the last time he would ever underestimate her.

Chapter 4

"That rascal oughta be tarred and feathered for swindlin' a lady." Lydia Staggs punched the bread dough so hard Kristy had to grab her breakfast plate to keep it from sliding off the kitchen table and onto the plank floor. "Was I to get my hands on him, why I'd shake him till his teeth rattled."

Kristy smothered a smile at the image of Lydia reprimanding a big man like Chad as if he were a naughty schoolboy. Lydia was short, but no one could call her small; her sturdy build strained the seams of her faded calico dress. She had once worked in a bawdy house but had moved in with James Donovan after his lawful wife had abandoned him and their two children, unable to tolerate her husband's gambling anymore.

Though Lydia had never married Kristy's father, she had become more of a real mother than Kristy had ever known. Lydia was both friend and confidante, yet during their return to the Bar S yesterday, Kristy had hidden the truth. She had related only an abbreviated version of the poker game, omitting any mention of herself being part of the stakes. She alone knew how close her escape from Chad had been. The memory of sliding down that rickety drainpipe made her stomach churn.

"I don't know, Lydia. I wouldn't advise you to tangle with the likes of this man. He looked like he'd had plenty of practice with his six-shooters."

"Horsefeathers," Lydia snorted, giving the dough another overzealous whack. "Ain't a man been born yet that can scare me. If you'd of brought that scoundrel to me,

I'd of set him straight in no time flat and got your money back to boot.''

Kristy's spirits plummeted. The money. Oh, Lord, the money. Her appetite vanished, and she pushed away her plate of flapjacks.

Lydia glanced sharply at her. "You done already?"

"I'm not hungry this morning," Kristy said, standing up. "I'd better go make sure Jeremy's awake—"

"Hold your horses, girl. You ain't goin' nowhere without a good breakfast in your belly."

"But—"

"No buts. You sit your fanny down and finish your food. I'll take care of that brother of yours."

Lydia pointed a floury finger at the chair. Kristy sank down with uncharacteristic meekness and picked up her fork. Nodding in satisfaction, the older woman went to the stairs that led to the three tiny bedrooms on the second floor.

"Yoo-hoo, lazybones!" she called out, hands planted on her wide hips, her graying red-haired head tipped back. "Flapjacks is on the table!"

A muffled protest drifted down from upstairs.

"Don't you sass me, boy. If you ain't down here in three minutes flat, you can durn well wait till noon to fill your belly."

Lydia returned to the table, shaking her head in exasperation. "That Jeremy, he's a good boy, but he's slower'n molasses in January at gettin' outa bed in the mornin'."

"Mmm-hmm," Kristy agreed, lost in her own dark thoughts as she toyed with her half-eaten stack of flapjacks.

"You still frettin' about the money, ain't you, sweetie?"

Lydia's kindly tone only made Kristy feel worse. "Yes, I am," she admitted, raising troubled eyes to Lydia. "Everyone was depending on me—you, Jeremy, even Shake. I really made a mess of things this time."

"Now, now, it ain't the end of the world." Lydia plopped the bread dough into a bowl and covered it with a dish towel, then placed the bowl on the wood stove so the dough could rise. Wiping her hands on her apron, she eased her ample bottom onto a chair. "Things'll work out—we'll manage somehow."

"But how?" Kristy said gloomily. "How can we buy cattle with the four dollars and sixty-two cents I have left? And how can we live without any cattle to sell?"

"The Lord will provide," Lydia said, patting Kristy's hand. "Don't fret, girl. We ain't starvin' yet."

"I could kick myself for gambling away all our money."

"Ain't no use cryin' over spilt milk."

"But gambling!" Kristy let her fork clatter onto her ironstone plate. "After seeing how it ruined Papa's life, I should have known better."

"You should of," Lydia agreed bluntly. "And I hope to goodness you learned your lesson once and for all."

"Believe me, I'll never touch a deck of cards again." Kristy sighed in dejection. "Maybe I'm just not cut out for ranch life. Maybe we should sell the Bar S like Papa intended us to. We could buy a house in Denver with the money."

"Is that what you really want, girl?"

The prospect of trading the beauty and freedom of the ranch for a dirty, crowded city was depressing. "No," she admitted.

"I didn't reckon so." Lydia reached out and gently lifted Kristy's drooping chin. "Perk up, sweetie. Your pa meant for you and Jeremy to find yourselves a real home. And that's exactly what you got here."

"Yes, we do, don't we?"

Kristy felt her spirits rise as she glanced around the kitchen, which was lit by the soft glow of a kerosene lamp, since dawn was but a gray promise on the horizon. Against one roughly plastered wall was a dry sink and a battered wood cookstove, its pipe streaked with rust. The only other furnishings were an old rocking chair, the rickety table, and the chairs in which they sat. A single small window framed the mountains, the cracked pane of glass curtained by a pair of lovingly ironed flour sacks.

It was crude, it was humble, but it was home.

Kristy's heart squeezed with pain and pride. They had

been here only the summer, but already she could feel her roots sinking into this wild, magnificent land.

Resolution stiffened her spine. "We're not going to lose this place," Kristy vowed. "Not while I have a way to save it. The Bar S is Jeremy's future, and I'm going to make it the best ranch in Colorado."

"Just what're you cookin' up now in that pretty head of yours?" Lydia's brown eyes narrowed. "You ain't thinkin' to wed that old coot what's-his-name that was pesterin' you—"

"Parker McClintock wasn't pestering me. He was courting me."

"There's something almighty peculiar 'bout a man chasin' after a girl less'n half his age." Lydia shook a finger at her. "That old man's a snake in the grass, you mark my words. Rich men like him ain't never satisfied with what they got. He aims to steal this ranch away from you and your brother."

"I won't let him do that."

"Hogwash. If he's your lawful husband, how're you gonna stop him from takin' what's yours?"

That was the one thing that still troubled Kristy. Somehow she must find a way to keep the Bar S for Jeremy. "I'll work something out with Mr. McClintock. Besides, his main reason for marrying me is that he wants a son."

"He's got that boy that run off."

Kristy had also heard mention of Parker's black-sheep son from a spiteful spinster in the nearby town of Painted Rock who had learned of Parker's interest in Kristy and was anxious to air the McClintock family's dirty linen. But Kristy had refused to listen to the gossip.

"Mr. McClintock hasn't heard from his son in years," she told Lydia. "He must figure the boy's never coming back—maybe he's even dead."

"So you're gonna let yourself get turned into a brood mare?"

The blunt question made Kristy's determination falter, until she reminded herself that marrying Parker was the best choice she had left. The only choice.

"Mr. McClintock has a perfect right to want a son and heir," she said stiffly.

Lydia pursed her lips in disapproval. "You're well and truly serious about this, ain't you?"

"Yes, I am."

"You don't hardly know the man. Why, I hear he's got a daughter your own age! You oughta be hitchin' yourself to a handsome young cowboy instead of some old geezer!"

From out of nowhere an image of Chad's strong features flashed into Kristy's mind. Irritated, she banished the vision. Chad was nothing but a despicable saddle tramp who'd cheat a widow at cards. By contrast, Parker McClintock was a fine gentleman who knew how to treat a lady. So what if he was a recent widower thirty-five years older than she?

"Mr. McClintock is hardly an old geezer—"

Her argument ended abruptly as Jeremy clattered down the stairs, sleepy eyed and yawning. His sandy hair was tousled, and his shirttail hung out of his wrinkled dungarees.

"We ain't done talkin'," Lydia told Kristy before turning to the ten-year-old and scolding him: "That was the longest three minutes I ever did see. You're lucky you come down when you did, 'cause I was just fixin' to feed your flapjacks to the birds."

Despite the threat, she pushed back her chair and went over to the stove to pile pancakes onto a chipped ironstone plate.

Kristy couldn't help grinning at her brother's face, grumpy yet endearingly sweet, with freckles and big brown eyes. "Good morning, Jeremy."

"Mornin'," he mumbled, digging into his breakfast.

"Anything exciting happen while we were gone to Denver?"

Jeremy shrugged and speared a forkful of flapjacks. "Nothin' much. I gotta finish cleanin' out the barn today." He made a face before adding, "Where's Shake?"

"He ate nigh on half an hour ago," Lydia offered from her position at the stove. She cocked an eyebrow at Jeremy. "While *some* folks was still sleepin'."

"Aw, leave me alone," Jeremy grumbled. "I'm up, ain't I?"

"Aren't I," Kristy said, correcting him and frowning as she carried her plate and coffee cup to the sink. The endless work on the ranch left her little time to see to Jeremy's education, except in the evenings when he was dog tired. That was yet another reason to marry Parker McClintock, to give her brother all the advantages of a gentleman's rearing. So why did she have this uncertainty deep inside her, this feeling she was making an awful mistake?

"Howdy, folks."

The cowboy twang intruded on her thoughts. Shake Jones stood in the doorway, a battered Stetson in his hands. Merry blue eyes gazed at her from a face of wrinkled leather, his forehead white above his hat line. His shoulders were slightly stooped beneath a plaid shirt that had seen many wearings since its last washing.

Kristy thanked her lucky stars for Shake's presence on the ranch. The aging cowboy had shown up on their doorstep the previous month, asking only bed and board in return for work. He'd offered no information about his background, and she hadn't asked any questions. Heaven knew she couldn't afford to lose the foreman. Shake had proven to be an invaluable help in teaching her and Jeremy how to run a ranch.

"If you're lookin' for more vittles, old-timer, you can durn well wait till noon," Lydia said.

Shake snorted. "You reckon I'd be wantin' more of them cow patties you call flapjacks? Just gimme a cup of that there black mud." He gestured toward the coffeepot on the cookstove.

"Any time you want, you can start cookin' for yourself out in the bunkhouse," Lydia retorted, though she poured him a cup.

Shake took the coffee with a good-humored nod of thanks and resumed his station by the door. Despite repeated invitations from Kristy, Shake had refused from the first to share the table with them. "Ain't fittin', ma'am," he'd say stubbornly and go outside to eat his meal sitting on the stoop. Finally Kristy had given up the effort. The only concession the grizzled foreman would make was to sometimes stand just inside the doorway, and that was only when he had some information to relay, as he did now.

"Branded a couple of mavericks while you was gone," Shake told her.

"Are you sure they didn't belong to anybody?" Kristy asked dubiously.

His smile revealed crooked, tobacco-stained teeth. "Well, ma'am, if a critter's a-roamin' your range without no brand, who's gonna say it ain't yours?"

Kristy folded her arms across her white cotton shirt-waist. She still wasn't totally convinced it was honest to claim cattle she hadn't paid for. Yet the practice was common here in the West.

"What do you have planned for today?" she asked the foreman.

Shake took a swig of coffee. "Reckon I'd chase down some tracks I spotted yesterday in a gully northwest of here. Got me a hunch they belong to another stray. If I'm wrong, I'll eat my hat."

"You might have to anyway, old-timer," Lydia said. "Food money might be scarce around here pretty soon."

"I didn't get the loan," Kristy explained. Swallowing a spurt of shame, she gave Shake and Jeremy a brief account of how she'd lost the last of the ranch's money to a crooked gambler.

Her gaze went from Shake's weathered features to Lydia's concerned brown eyes to Jeremy's freckled, uptilted face. How they all depended on her! Controlling a sudden trembling of her lips, she refused to succumb to tears of worry and despair. Everything would be all right once she'd married Parker McClintock.

So why did her heart feel so weighted?

She squared her shoulders. "No one will go hungry," she promised. "Shake, if you can wait just a little while longer, I promise I'll get your pay for you as soon as I can."

"Ma'am, ain't no need to fret yourself. I told you when I come all I need is a place to rest my head at night and some decent vittles." He studied his sweat-stained Stetson, then aimed a devilish look at Lydia. "Anyhow, if times get rough, mebbe this here hat might make as tasty a meal as I been gettin' 'round here.''

Lydia was preparing to bake the bread dough in the Dutch oven. "Watch that flappin' jaw, old-timer," she warned. "Else I really might take a notion to make hat stew for supper."

"Beg pardon, ma'am," Shake said meekly, though his twinkling blue eyes showed scant remorse. "Now, don't you folks fret none. If push comes to shove, I'll hunt us some deer meat."

"Why thank you, Shake," Kristy said, touched by his loyalty.

He ducked his face almost shyly, setting down his coffee cup before clapping the Stetson on his gray-haired head. "You ridin' out with me today?" he asked Kristy.

A deep yearning rose in her to gallop free on the open range after wasting three days on the ill-fated trip to Denver. She could put off going to see Parker McClintock until tomorrow . . .

But she must get Jeremy's future—and hers—settled as soon as possible.

Reluctantly she shook her head. "No, I have something else I must do."

Shake nodded, then addressed Jeremy, who was finishing up his breakfast. "Cut Miz' Lydia some firewood afore you head on out to the barn and shovel the sh—" Glancing at the women, he cleared his throat noisily. "Horse patties," he amended, then scurried outside.

"You goin' somewhere again today?" Jeremy asked his sister as he pushed away his plate.

Kristy hesitated, then sat down at the table. "Yes, I am. How would you like to go live in a fine house and have servants to do all of your chores? Maybe someday you can go away to a fancy Eastern college."

Her brother didn't look impressed. "But we got here just a couple of months ago, and I thought you said we were gonna stay here forever."

"It'll just be a temporary move for you. Someday when you're old enough, you can come back to the Bar S."

His freckled face wore a dubious expression. "I don't understand."

Kristy took a deep breath. "I'm marrying Parker McClintock. That means we'll both go live with him on the Diamond M."

"That old goat?" he said derisively.

A muttered agreement came from Lydia, who was finishing up the dishes at the sink.

Kristy pursed her lips in exasperation. Didn't they realize she was doing this for the good of everyone?

"Jeremy James Donovan, you mind your tongue," she said sharply. "I won't tolerate you speaking of Mr. McClintock in that manner."

Her brother scowled. "I ain't moving nowhere. I'm stayin' here with Shake and Lydia."

"That isn't possible." Kristy stood up abruptly, putting an end to the argument. "I'm going to visit Mr. McClintock this morning. When I return, I'll let you know when we'll be moving."

She pivoted on stiff legs and mounted the stairs to the second floor. In the isolation of her tiny bedroom, she changed clothes mechanically, tossing aside her riding skirt and shirtwaist in favor of her second-best dress of sea green gingham, since the black bombazine she'd worn to Denver was in the wash basket.

Her fingers trembled as she reached around back to fasten the buttons. She couldn't even afford enough black gowns to mourn her father's death. How she missed him! Although James Donovan hadn't been the best provider, he'd made up for his shortcomings with an abundance of love.

Fighting tears, Kristy remembered all the times he'd been there when she'd needed him. She would never forget the night, not long after Jeremy's birth, when he'd told her that her mother had run off. Though his need to be alone with his own grief must have been great, her father had comforted her for hours until she'd exhausted her tears and fallen asleep.

Now she swallowed the lump in her throat as hurt and anger battled inside her. Couldn't Lydia and Jeremy see she didn't like this situation either? But without Parker McClintock's money, they'd be forced to sell the Bar S, and probably for a song. If it were just herself, she'd take a chance and go it on her own. But her brother's future was at stake, and this was the only sensible solution.

She tidied her mahogany brown hair in front of the mirror hanging over the washstand. The mottled glass reflected her pale features in the dim light of dawn. Huge green eyes stared back at her from beneath a frown that marred her forehead.

You're going off to see your future husband, she scolded herself. You should look mature and happy, not young and scared.

Resolutely she perched a green-ribboned straw hat on her head and secured it with a faux emerald pin. Then she headed back downstairs and out to the barn. With Jeremy's grumbling help, she got the team hitched to the buckboard and was on her way.

The wagon jolted and swayed down the rutted dirt road that led northward to the Diamond M. Her leather-gloved hands handled the reins with competence, for she'd had much practice driving the buckboard since moving to the ranch.

Her spirits rose with the sun. It was a glorious morning and still cool enough to be comfortable. Dew kept the dust on the road to a minimum. Meadowlarks twittered in a clump of cottonwoods, pecking the earth for insects. And to her left the jagged peaks of the Rockies thrust upward with a wild spendor that stole her breath away.

Kristy tilted her head back, reveling in the brush of the wind on her face. She loved this untamed land. No price was too high to pay for the right to keep the Bar S!

An hour and a half later, she reined the team to a halt in front of the McClintock ranch headquarters. The sight of the white, two-story house with its elaborate gingerbread fretwork made her courage falter for a moment. Did she, Kristina Margaret Donovan, raised in shantytowns and the daughter of a riverboat gambler, really belong in such a grand mansion?

She squared her shoulders. It was only a house. And she was no longer that unschooled urchin; she was a lady.

She stepped down from the buckboard, accepting the assistance of a cowboy. Brushing the dust from her skirt, she walked toward the steps that led to the porch. Morning glories climbed the white railing. Crowning the double front doors was a fanlight window of expensive leaded glass.

Taking firm hold of the brass knocker, she rapped hard. The curtains at the side window shifted as someone peered out; then the door swung open.

Kristy smiled gently at Parker McClintock's only daughter Honey, who stood hugging the door as if for security. A shy, coltish beauty with corn-silk hair and big blue eyes, she was Kristy's age.

"Good morning, Honey. How are you?"

"Fine, thank you," the girl said timidly. "Won't you come in?"

Kristy stepped into a spacious foyer with a polished wood floor and a wide, curving staircase. Plucking nervously at her mauve skirts, Honey hesitated, then showed Kristy into a sumptuous parlor. "Did you come to see my father?"

"Yes—is he here?"

Honey nodded. "He's in his study. I'll go fetch him." She scurried out the door like a startled fawn.

Kristy gazed thoughtfully after the girl, looking forward to a time when they could become friends. Once she and Parker McClintock were married, she would have an opportunity to get to know Honey better.

She started to sit on a rose-and-silver striped settee, then sprang back up, her insides a jumble of nerves. Panic seized her as she paced the parlor. Why did she always feel so ill at ease in this house? She'd been to dinner three times at Parker's invitation, yet for some reason she could never relax here.

Don't make a mountain out of a molehill, she told herself. You're just not used to the place. After you live here awhile, you'll feel more at home.

To distract herself she walked to the fireplace mantel, where a collection of porcelain figures were arranged next to a ticking clock. How curious that she'd never seen any paintings or photographs of family members anywhere in the house. She would have enjoyed viewing a likeness of Parker McClintock's late wife or maybe even his runaway son.

The sound of heavy footsteps out in the hall drew her attention to the parlor door. She knew that distinctive gait; Parker McClintock walked with a slight limp, the result of some long-ago accident on the ranch.

"Kristina!" The limp was scarcely noticeable as he strode to her. "What an unexpected pleasure."

He bent to kiss the back of her hand, his handlebar moustache tickling her skin. Then he straightened, a vigorous man of average height with the broad and muscular build of a bull. His brown hair bore a distinguished touch of gray at the temples. In his dark trousers and crisp white shirt, he looked the very image of the powerful cattle baron he was.

"Good morning, Mr. McClintock. I hope I'm not intruding."

"Never, my dear. What true man would prefer boring business matters to the company of such a charming young lady?"

Kristy gave a self-conscious laugh, never quite certain how to respond to his effusive compliments.

"Sit down, my dear, and tell me to what I owe this welcome surprise."

Her mouth went dry. Automatically she lowered herself to the settee as the rancher sat down in the armchair opposite her. Last-minute doubts assaulted her. Was she doing the right thing? Could she really marry a man she scarcely knew?

Honey came in with a silver coffee service, saving Kristy from an immediate reply. By the time the girl had scurried back out, closing the door behind her, and Kristy had poured coffee into two porcelain cups, she'd managed to regain her composure.

"The purpose of my visit is to see if your marriage offer is still open."

His mouth broke into a smile beneath the handlebar moustache.

"Of course it is, Kristina. Might I presume to think you've come to a decision?"

"I have."

"In the affirmative, I hope."

Her fingers tightened around the fragile china cup. "Yes, provided we can arrive at a suitable agreement."

He cocked one graying eyebrow in slightly amused tolerance. "Agreement?"

"I want the Bar S to be held in trust for Jeremy. When he comes of age, I want him to have full ownership of the ranch, including my share."

Heart thumping, she tried to gauge Parker McClintock's reaction. His smile was gone; his eyes were dark and hooded. What if she'd pushed him too far?

Hastily she added, "Until such time, you may, of course, use the land as you see fit."

Parker felt a rush of rage choke his throat. How dare this . . . this *female* try to maneuver him! Didn't she realize whom she was dealing with? She might be from some hoity-toity family back East, but out here his word was law for miles around.

He swallowed the urge to tell her in crude terms precisely what she could do with her agreement. Kristina was an essential part of his plans for the future. She was young and healthy enough to give him the son he craved. By marrying her, he would finally gain control of the Bar S, cinching his position as the most influential cattleman in Colorado.

The ranch should have been his anyway, he reflected in anger. If only that lazy lawyer had been able to find a loophole in Mavis's father's will . . .

With an effort he leashed his fury. Jeremy was just a nuisance; the boy wouldn't inherit the Bar S until he was twenty-one, eleven years from now. When the time came, Parker would simply buy Jeremy off. Or use another means of persuasion.

Parker leaned forward to set down his coffee cup, coaxing his lips into an indulgent smile. "All right, my dear. If you want the Bar S for your brother, then so be it."

Kristy looked at him in dazed elation, unable to believe he was giving in so easily. "Do you really mean it?"

"How can I refuse my lovely bride her heart's desire? I'll send word today to my lawyer in Denver so that he can get started on drawing up the appropriate document."

"Thank you, Mr. McClintock."

"Parker," he corrected genially. He came to sit next to her, putting aside her coffee cup and taking her hand in his. "We're going to be married, my dear. Don't you think it's time you started calling me by my Christian name?"

"Of course . . . Parker." Privately Kristy felt awkward addressing him in such a familiar manner. She was conscious of his knee pressing against her thigh and his fingers curling around her hand. Stifling an impulse to move away, she reminded herself that, as her intended husband, he had every right to touch her.

"The sound of my name is music, on your lips."

His smooth words only made her feel more uncomfortable, and his dark scrutiny disturbed her. He was a gentleman and would make a fine husband. Why did she feel a vague uneasiness?

"You're a beautiful woman, Kristina."

Parker drew her close, pressing his lips to hers. Having never been kissed before, Kristy wasn't sure what to do, so she followed his suit, clamping her eyes shut and placing her hands on his shirt. She waited expectantly for the melting warmth inside that Lydia had once described to her.

Parker's mouth moved against hers for what seemed like ages. She was conscious of the clock ticking on the mantel. In the distance she heard a knocking on the front door and felt a shamefaced longing for someone to come and interrupt them. Parker's moustache tickled her nose, and he smelled so strongly of shaving soap that she felt faintly nauseated. When at last he lifted his head, she sat back in guilty relief.

His brown eyes glittered. "My dear Kristina," he murmured, running a finger down her cheek. "You'll produce strong sons for me, I know you will."

She closed her mind to the act required to produce those children. There would be time enough later to resign herself to *that*. "I . . . I've always wanted a family of my own."

"Good. We shall get along quite well, then."

He leaned closer as if to kiss her again, but a sudden

hard rap on the parlor door stopped him. "Who the hell—" he began.

The door flew open and Parker turned, partially blocking Kristy's view of the tall man who strode into the room without awaiting an invitation.

She peered past Parker's shoulder at the newcomer. Her heart lodged in her throat, cutting off a gasp of shock.

It was that cheating gambler, Chad!

Chapter 5

For one wild instant Kristy thought she must be suffering from a delusion. Chad couldn't be here at the Diamond M! It was impossible! But he was as real as the frenzied beating of her heart. She would recognize that big, muscled build anywhere, the broad chest beneath his blue cotton shirt, the long legs covered in denim, the finely tooled gun belt riding low on his hips.

Her mind fumbled frantically for an explanation of his presence. He must have followed her here. Had he somehow learned Parker was courting her—from town gossip, perhaps? God above, did Chad intend to tell her fiancé about that foolish card game as retaliation for running out on their bet?

Dread squeezed her chest. She stared at Chad, waiting for the axe to fall. Then she realized he must not have noticed her sitting behind Parker, because he wasn't even looking at her; his ice blue eyes were focused on the older man.

"Hello, Father," he said.

His low voice bore that faintly mocking bite she recalled so well. The meaning of his words took a moment to sink into her overwrought mind. A second shock wave ripped through her. Father! What game was he playing now?

"You!" Parker leapt to his feet, hands clenched at his sides, his normally ruddy complexion now the color of ash. "How dare you come back here after all these years," he snarled. "Get the hell out of my house right now!"

"Now, is that any way to welcome home the prodigal

son?'' Chad drawled. ''Don't you know you're supposed to kill the fatted calf for me?''

''The only thing I'll kill is you, you bastard!''

''Watch your tongue—you wouldn't want to let something slip in front of your lady friend.''

Kristy felt her blood pound with renewed alarm as Chad looked past Parker at her. She knew the instant Chad recognized her; those glacial blue eyes widened slightly, then narrowed. So he hadn't expected to see her here after all. He had come to confront his father . . . the man she had agreed to marry!

''Aren't you going to introduce me to the . . . *lady?*'' Chad asked.

''You're not fit for the company of a respectable woman,'' Parker retorted. ''On second thought, though, I can take great satisfaction in introducing you to my fiancée, Miss Kristina Donovan. She's going to give me a real son and heir.'' He drew her up from the settee and put an arm around her as if flaunting a prized possession.

Chad merely lifted dark eyebrows. ''It's a pleasure to meet you, *Miss* Donovan.'' With mocking emphasis on the title, he touched the brim of his Stetson to Kristy. ''The name's Chad McClintock.''

The derisive look in those cold blue eyes told her he thought she'd lied to Parker, misrepresenting herself as an innocent girl. Her insides trembled with apprehension. Would he reveal that he'd met her in Denver as *Mrs.* Donovan?

She gazed at Chad in mute appeal, hating the need to throw herself on his mercy but realizing what would happen should Parker learn of her indiscretion. She couldn't risk ruining Jeremy's future for the sake of salving her own pride.

A hard smile crooked the corner of Chad's mouth, and his contemptuous gaze traveled down the length of her. She flushed in anger, knowing he relished watching her squirm.

''You keep your eyes to yourself or I'll wring your rotten neck,'' Parker growled, apparently misreading the look his son gave her. ''You're not fit to shine her shoes.''

Chad swept off his hat in exaggerated contrition. "Pardon me, ma'am, if I've offended you."

"You haven't offended me," Kristy said quickly. So long as Chad hadn't yet mentioned her bet with him, she dared not risk antagonizing him.

"Your presence here is offense enough," Parker told his son. "You're not welcome here. Get out of my house before I throw you out."

"I'll go when I've had my say. We have my mother's death to discuss, don't we?"

"There's nothing to talk about—"

"Don't treat me like a fool, Father." Chad pronounced the title with biting sarcasm. "I'm not a gullible kid anymore."

Parker pressed his lips together, glowering at his son before abruptly turning to Kristy. "Please wait in my study until I can get this settled."

Relieved to escape the volatile atmosphere, she started toward the parlor door, but Chad grabbed her arm. "Hang on a minute, Miss Donovan," he said, his fingers digging into her tender flesh. "This is something I think you'll want to hear too."

Parker's face was ruddy with rage. "Let her go!"

Kristy wrenched her arm free. As she turned to flee the room, Chad's low voice froze her in place.

"It's about how your fiancé murdered his first wife—my mother."

"That's a goddamned lie!" Parker roared.

"Is it, now?" Chad advanced on the older man, spurs jingling.

Kristy shrank back against the door in horror, apparently forgotten by the two men. Murder! What dark motive would drive a son to hurl such a terrible accusation at his own father?

Chad stopped in front of his father. Parker stood his ground, and Kristy suspected it galled him to have to tilt his head up slightly to meet his tall son's gaze.

"Mavis died of consumption last April," Parker said coldly. "Read the coroner's report if you don't believe me."

"Oh, I believe she died of consumption, all right. But

she caught the disease because of physical weakness—a weakness that was entirely your fault.''

"Don't you go blaming me for Mavis's feeble constitution!''

"Old Doc Hardy would,'' Chad countered. "He warned you a long time ago she couldn't go through a pregnancy without endangering her health. But you forced her to endure miscarriage after miscarriage, all because you had some fanatic wish for another son.''

"A wife's purpose is to bear children. It says so in the Scriptures.''

Chad threw back his head and laughed, a harsh sound of bitter humor. "Oh, now that's rich. You—quoting the Bible!''

Parker clenched his fingers into fists; then a shrewd look entered his dark eyes. "Did you ever stop to think it might have been grief over losing her only son that caused Mavis to pine away and die?''

Kristy saw the hardness slip from Chad's face, and suddenly she knew he had loved his mother deeply. The glimpse of his vulnerability was somehow disturbing.

"I wrote to her whenever I could,'' he said bleakly.

"Hah!'' Parker snorted. "She never got a letter from you in her life.''

"The hell you say—'' Chad's gaze narrowed; with the swiftness of a mountain cat, he lunged forward and seized his father by the shirt. "You intercepted my letters, didn't you?''

"Take your filthy hands off me!''

"First you answer my question. You stole all the letters I wrote to her! That's why I never got any back from her, isn't it?''

"What if I did?'' Parker sneered. "I damned sure wasn't going to let you be in touch with anyone on the Diamond M land.''

"You lousy son of a bitch . . .''

Numb with horror, Kristy hugged the door, afraid Chad would murder his own father. Abruptly he flung Parker from him.

"You make me sick,'' he spat out. "You haven't changed a bit in twelve years.''

Brushing off his shirt with a distasteful grimace, Parker walked over to stand beside Kristy. "You've said your piece, so you can leave now."

"I see you're limping now, Father," Chad said, lips tilted in harsh humor. "I wonder what happened to your leg."

Parker's face turned even redder. "Get out!" he snarled, pointing to the door. "And this time, I hope to God I never set eyes on you again."

"Don't count on that," Chad said, as cold as ever. "You killed my mother as surely as if you'd put a gun to her head. I plan to stick around and make damned sure you pay."

Spurs jangling, he stalked out of the parlor, shooting Kristy a look of such icy contempt she felt chilled to the bone. Stunned, she stared after him as the front door slammed.

She laced together her trembling fingers. Never in her life had she encountered such malevolence in anyone, not even in the self-righteous snobs back in St. Louis who had scorned her because of her father's gambling.

"Don't believe a word that bastard said," Parker murmured, putting a supportive arm around her. "He's only trying to get some sort of twisted revenge by discrediting me in front of you."

She gazed at her fiancé, unable to speak, unable to put a name to the emotions churning deep inside her. Why did Chad's hatred for her have such power to hurt?

"You look overwrought, my dear," Parker said soothingly. "Come and sit down." He guided her to the settee and took a seat beside her. "Don't let him frighten you," he said. "He's just a good-for-nothing saddle bum."

Merciful heavens, if Chad were to catch her out on some lonely part of the ranch, he might force her to uphold her end of their bargain! "Do you really think he'll stay in the area?" Kristy asked cautiously.

"I doubt it," Parker said. "He was only trying to ride roughshod over me. If he ever dares to show his face on my ranch again, he'll have cause to regret it."

The hatred in his voice both repulsed and intrigued her. "Why do you and your son dislike each other so?"

"It must be fate." Yet his hearty laugh sounded forced. "We've struck sparks off each other almost since the day he was born."

"Did you really steal those letters?"

Parker was silent a moment, gazing at her with dark, hooded eyes. "Yes, I did," he said heavily. "But you must understand—I had Mavis's best interests at heart. Physically she was frail. I was afraid that hearing from Chad might upset her, make her illness worse."

Kristy wasn't entirely convinced. "Why would hearing from her own son upset her? I should think the opposite would be true."

"Ah, but my dear, you don't know Chad. He was always a wild one, and I knew he was headed for ruin. I thought I was doing Mavis a favor by letting her go on dreaming he'd made a success of himself somewhere. After all, what mother would want to learn her son had grown up to be a no-good drifter?"

"You still had no right to withhold his letters."

Parker averted his gaze as if ashamed. "I know. I realize now it was the wrong thing to do." He turned imploring eyes on her. "Can't you at least try to see my side?"

Kristy felt her heart soften at his pleading look. What he'd done was wrong, but at least he was man enough to admit it. Perhaps he'd learned his lesson.

"Yes, I suppose I can understand." Prudently abandoning the subject of the letters, she asked, "How old was Chad when he ran away?"

"Fourteen . . . fifteen, I don't really remember."

"Why did he go?"

"Oh, it was probably some minor disagreement we had. As I said, he was a wild kid, forever getting into trouble."

"But surely you must recall the specific incident . . . ?"

Parker made an impatient movement. "It was a long time ago; it doesn't matter anymore." Taking her hands in his, he gazed lovingly into her eyes. "I'd rather look to the future, my dear, to the children you and I will have."

Kristy itched to ask more questions but reluctantly decided she'd already overstepped her bounds. Parker had a right to his privacy just as she did. After all, there were plenty of things in her own past that she preferred not to reveal!

Pleading a headache, she declined Parker's lunch invitation and headed the buckboard back to the Bar S. She was grateful for the company of the two cowboys Parker sent to escort her home. With a shiver, she knew Chad would be out there somewhere, waiting to catch her on some isolated stretch of road . . .

A flock of meadowlarks flew up out of the tall, rustling grasses. Kristy jumped, then laughed at herself. She couldn't let every sudden movement spook her. Parker might be right about Chad being gone forever. To be safe, though, she'd stick close to home for a while.

Hurrying the team of horses along the hot, dusty road, she couldn't stop pondering the shocking confrontation between father and son. Chad must have inherited his blue eyes and black hair from his mother, though his temper was straight from his father. Today she'd seen a new side to Parker, a hard forcefulness that disturbed her. What else didn't she know about him? The question troubled Kristy, and she wondered again if she were doing the right thing in marrying him.

You can't expect him to be perfect, she argued with herself. Every woman has to accept certain faults in a husband. Look at the kind of husband your own father was.

Besides, had Parker really treated his first wife as callously as Chad claimed? Somehow Kristy found it hard to swallow that such a gentleman could be so cruel. And why should she accept the word of a scoundrel like Chad McClintock? Parker was right—Chad must be trying to get a twisted revenge by accusing his father of murder. Even if there were a grain of truth to the matter, Chad had been quite young when he'd witnessed the so-called cruelty to Mavis and doubtless had blown the whole thing out of proportion.

Kristy stared through the shimmering heat, paying little heed to the magnificent scenery that had so enthralled her earlier that morning. Now she could better understand Parker's desire for another son. Chad McClintock was a gambler and a cheat, probably even an outlaw with a price on his head. He wasn't the kind of son a man of Parker's stature could be proud of.

Angry indignation swept over her as she realized their meeting in Denver had been no coincidence. She should have trusted her first instincts that had told her something hadn't been quite right. Chad must have planned that poker game in an attempt to cheat her out of the Bar S. But for what purpose? To needle his father by gaining possession of the adjacent ranch?

Kristy gazed over the plains stretching toward the foothills of the Rockies. She was on Bar S land now. Back on Diamond M range she'd passed many grazing cattle, but here she saw only the lush grasses waving in the wind. Her marriage to Parker would bring prosperity back to the Bar S. Soon a herd of stock would roam this fertile range, and someday it would all belong to Jeremy.

She would allow nothing to destroy that dream, Kristy vowed. Chad McClintock would never get his greedy paws on the Bar S deed!

Despite her bravado, she felt a kernel of apprehension buried deep inside her. Where was Chad right now? In this lonely area there must be a thousand places a man could hide. Although for the moment she had the protection of two Diamond M cowboys, there'd be times in the days ahead when she might have to ride out alone.

Could she stop Chad if he tried to claim that night in her bed?

The full moon gleamed in the midnight sky like a queen holding court amid a host of subservient stars. An occasional wisp of cloud drifted by, dimming the silver light that gilded the mountainous terrain below.

Chad McClintock leaned back on his elbows, gazing moodily at the star-strewn heavens. The risk of anyone discovering his campsite was minimal: because he'd chosen the location well, in a gully hidden in the foothills of the Rockies, at the most desolate border of Diamond M range. Even if someone were out scouting him, the sides of the gully hid the small fire he'd built to heat his dinner of coffee, beans, and bacon. The blaze had already died down to glowing embers. His big gray gelding was picketed nearby, half-hidden in the shadows.

Since the night air was chilly, he got up to spread out his bedroll. Stretching out again on the hard ground, he stared at the dark mountains, hands linked behind his head. His chest tightened unexpectedly. How he'd missed this land! Not the ranch house—that held too many unhappy memories. The land was what he'd missed . . . riding out in the coolness of morning, tracking cattle in the foothills, stopping to drink from an icy mountain stream.

He thought suddenly of his sister and wished he'd had the chance to visit her before storming out of the house that morning. The last time he'd seen her, Honey had been a shy girl of five. He wondered what she looked like now, whether she'd survived childhood any better than he had.

From the depths of his mind rose an image of himself as a youngster with tear tracks on his dirty face, shivering beside a campfire on a cold night and fiercely pretending he had two loving parents . . .

Chad shook his head impatiently to rid himself of the disturbing memory. That must have been one of the many times he'd run off after getting a whipping from Parker. Young and foolish, he'd always returned the next morning, full of hopes and dreams. But his naivete had ended forever that day when he was fifteen.

Shifting on the bedroll, Chad flashed a bitter smile at the starry sky. Years had passed since he'd thought of Parker as "father." That title of honor was sacrilege when used in connection with Parker McClintock. Still, Chad found a certain satisfaction in addressing him that way, since he knew how Parker loathed acknowledging their relationship.

Now Parker's plan was to whelp a second dynasty with that Donovan bitch.

Abruptly Chad sat up and rummaged in his saddlebags for the makings of a cigarette. Rolling the tobacco in paper, he lit it with a sulphur match and then leaned back to inhale the pungent smoke. Kristina Donovan. The name made her sound like a queen instead of a down-on-her-luck widow of a gambler.

He might have known she'd sink her claws into the richest man for miles around. Her actions only confirmed his suspicions about her character. She might look innocent, with those big green eyes and that shiny mahogany hair, but she was only an adventuress with an eye out for the main chance.

He chuckled grimly. *Miss* Kristina Donovan, indeed. She was hiding her past from Parker, presenting herself as a lady. He'd gladly give his silver-trimmed saddle to witness Parker's wedding night fury on discovering his bride was no virgin!

Imagining those two in bed made Chad feel like a volcano about to erupt. Damn, but he wanted to fling her shameful secret in Parker's face!

He took a drag on the cigarette, forcing himself to think clearly. Exposing Kristina Donovan would be a satisfying but temporary revenge. After all, Parker might overlook his fiancée's past in his greed to gain possession of the Bar S.

With a savage flick of his wrist, Chad flung the cigarette butt into the embers of the campfire. By God, he couldn't sit back and let Parker have the Bar S. Somehow there had to be a way to make the son of a bitch pay for his sins.

In a bittersweet rush of memories, Chad saw his mother as he would always recall her, blond-haired and frail, lying in bed, clad in a frilly nightdress. Through the acrid smoke of the campfire, he fancied he could smell the sweetness of gardenias that had clung to Mavis McClintock's pale skin the few times she'd felt well enough to hug him. He could recall how seldom, during his childhood, she left the dim sanctuary of her bedroom, for she was always in the family way or recovering from yet another miscarriage.

And now Parker thought he could get away with her murder.

A fierce desire for vengeance gnawed at Chad. Perhaps *Mrs.* Kristina Donovan was the key . . .

His lips crooked into a harsh smile. As part of his revenge he would claim that night she owed him. His loins tightened at the thought of stripping away her clothing, touching her naked skin, burying himself inside the heat of her body.

Chad willed away the erotic image and concentrated on the scheme beginning to take shape in his mind. For a long while he sat staring up at the stars, thinking hard.

Tomorrow, he promised himself as he settled down to sleep. Tomorrow he would set his plan into motion.

Chapter 6

Crouching low over the bay gelding's neck, Kristy urged the horse to a gallop. Exhilaration swelled inside her as she raced headlong across the prairie toward a distant clump of cottonwoods near the foothills. Under the force of the stiff breeze, her bonnet flew back and dangled by its tie around her neck. The thunder of hooves filled her ears. Between her thighs she felt the power of the straining horse carrying her toward the magnificent mountains thrusting against the clear afternoon sky.

Yesterday's rain had cleansed the air of dust, washing away the heat that had gripped the land for many weeks. The cool wind yanked strands of reddish brown hair from the coil at the back of her head. She didn't care that her ladylike appearance was in a shambles. To ride so wild and free felt wonderful after spending the past ten days cooped up close to home.

Nearing the trees, she started to slow the horse when a flash of brown shot through the underbrush. A rabbit. The gelding stumbled; the abrupt sideways jerk caught Kristy by surprise. She slid from the saddle, the reins jerking from her gloved fingers.

Her bottom met the hard ground with a thump that jarred her spine. Stunned, she gasped for breath, her heart pounding, as her horse bolted across the prairie.

The rapid thud of approaching hoofbeats penetrated her daze. Squinting against the bright sunlight, she saw the silhouette of a tall man on horseback rein to a halt a few yards in front of her.

"Well, well, Mrs. Donovan, fancy meeting you out here."

Chad McClintock! Panic jolted through her at his familiar mocking voice. What a fool she'd been to take a chance and get caught miles from the safety of home! Her sole protection was the derringer in her pocket, if only she could get to the weapon without alerting him.

Kristy thrust her chin high, refusing to show her alarm. "What are you doing—following me?"

"Maybe."

He swung down from his gray horse and walked toward her, all swaggering male, spurs jangling with each unhurried step. His flinty blue eyes surveyed her in a way that gave Kristy a peculiar shivery-hot feeling deep inside.

"We do seem to meet under the most unusual of circumstances, don't we, Mrs. Donovan?" Pointedly he stared at her sprawled form.

She realized her legs were splayed out in a most unladylike way, her divided riding skirt hiked up past her boots. Blushing, Kristy scrambled up and straightened her clothes, ignoring the ache in her behind. Swiftly she tidied her disheveled hair and readjusted her bonnet, fixing him with her coldest glare.

"Mr. McClintock, you are trespassing on Bar S land."

"I know."

"Then I'd thank you to leave."

"Save your thanks. I'm not going anywhere until I'm good and ready." His voice dropped to a hard-edged murmur. "Don't you think it's about time I collected on that night you owe me?"

Fear gripped her. "You cheated. I don't owe you anything."

She turned as if to storm off, but slipped a hand into her pocket, her fingers closing around the pearl-handled derringer that had once belonged to her father. Yanking out the small pistol, she swiveled to aim the weapon at Chad's broad chest.

"Perhaps this will convince you to go," she said.

He cocked a dark eyebrow. "I like a woman with spirit. But let me warn you, I can draw and fire my gun faster than you can pull that toy trigger."

His amusement infuriated Kristy. He couldn't know her only experience with the derringer was a little target practice, with Shake as her tutor. She abhorred guns, and only the threat of this man had induced her to carry one.

"Then why don't you come closer?" she asked, challenging him. "At this range I could hardly miss."

"Put the gun away, Kristina."

"No."

He took a step toward her. "Put that damned thing away before someone gets hurt!"

Kristy willed her hand not to shake. "The only one who's going to get hurt is you."

He gave her an assessing look and took another step. Only a few feet separated them. Perspiration dampened her palms. Merciful heavens, could she really kill him in cold blood?

"Stay right where you are or I'll shoot," she warned.

To her immense relief, he obeyed. "Look, I just want to talk to you, but not with a gun staring me in the face."

"Talk?" she said with a scornful laugh. "You don't talk, you bully people until you get your own way."

Chad's tightened lips betrayed his irritation, but when he spoke his voice was even. "Let's put our differences aside for the moment. I want to buy the Bar S from you."

Curiosity made her lower the derringer a fraction. "Why?"

"Don't you mean how much? I'm willing to pay you far more than what the place is worth. You can go to Denver and live like a queen, without having to put up with a bastard like my father."

She ignored his disparaging tone. "Why do you want this ranch so badly? If you hate your father so much, why would you want to live so close to him?"

His ice blue eyes were unreadable in the brilliant sunlight. "You really want to know? All right, then, I'll show you."

Abruptly Chad turned and whistled. His gray horse came galloping up from the nearby stand of cottonwoods. In one lithe movement he swung into the saddle and jerked his head at Kristy.

"Come on. Let's find your mount."

His horse went trotting off, leaving her to follow on

foot. He had the manners of a river rat, she fumed. The least he could have done was to offer her a ride!

Not that she'd have accepted, Kristy assured herself. The last place she wanted to be was sharing a saddle with a rogue like Chad McClintock, where she'd be forced to wind her arms around his lean waist for support, to press her breasts to the muscled broadness of his back, to breathe in his ungentlemanly scent of leather and masculine sweat . . .

Her insides clenched in an oddly pleasurable way. Kristy scowled at his tall form as he rode off. Carrying the derringer, she tramped through the high grass, occasionally splashing in a mudhole left by yesterday's heavy rain. Like a faithful hound trailing after its master, she thought resentfully. If only she weren't miles from home! Besides, the Bar S couldn't afford the loss of a precious horse, and she wasn't certain the bay gelding would find its way back to the barn.

At last she reached Chad in a clump of willows alongside a stream. He was crouched beside her mount, running a hand down one of the bay's long legs. Kristy was struck by the lightness of his touch as he checked the animal for injury. She wondered irrelevantly if he would treat a woman with such gentleness.

"Is he all right?" she asked.

Chad straightened, tall and contemptuous. "I'm surprised you care, considering how damn-fool fast you were riding. Didn't it occur to you that he might step in a hole and break a leg?"

In retrospect Kristy knew the accusation was true, but she still resented his chastising tone. "It's not your horse, so it's no concern of yours," she snapped.

Wheeling around, she marched to the stream. The long walk had left her hot and tired, so she put the derringer on the rocky ground within easy reach and peeled off her gloves, stuffing them into her pocket. Then she bent to scoop up a handful of icy water to quench her thirst.

Over the music of the stream she heard the approaching jingle of his spurs. "What's the matter, Kristina?" he taunted. "Can't admit that you might have been wrong?"

She shot an annoyed look up at him. "Stop calling me

that—my name is Kristy!'' Belatedly she added, ''Miss Donovan to *you.*''

''Kristy,'' he murmured caressingly as he took a step nearer. ''I like the way that sounds. I'd hate to call you some high-and-mighty name like Kristina when we finally share that night.''

Her cheeks burned as she snatched up the derringer. ''Come any closer, and I'll make sure you never bed a woman again.''

Chad held up his hands. ''Don't shoot—I'll keep my distance.'' Lips quirked in amusement, he added, ''For the moment, anyway.''

Eyeing him warily, Kristy rose, her damp fingers tight around the pearl grip of the pistol. ''Let's get on with what you were going to show me. I don't have all day to trade insults with you.''

''Whatever you say, ma'am.''

He strode toward the two horses grazing in the shade of the trees. Kristy pocketed the derringer before leading the bay gelding over to a flat rock, needing the added height to mount. She swung into the saddle, conscious of Chad's watchful gaze. Her bottom still throbbed from the fall, and discreetly she shifted her weight in an attempt to ease the pain. Out of the corner of her eye she saw Chad grin at her discomfort. She gritted her teeth, refusing to grant him the satisfaction of a retort.

Don't let him get to you, Kristy scolded herself as they rode off. He's just a good-for-nothing drifter, a cheating gambler without any notion of how to treat a lady.

She considered making a run for home, but curiosity stopped her. What did Chad mean by ''showing'' her how much he wanted the Bar S? Would she learn something to explain this unnatural hatred between father and son? Kristy touched the reassuring weight of the derringer in her skirt pocket. Much as she despised guns, she was glad for the security of the weapon. If Chad McClintock tried anything, he'd be damned sorry.

They rode over the grassy foothills for what seemed like hours, the mountains looming closer. The horses picked their way over a rocky trail that ascended gradually into a

forest of aspens and firs. Birds chattered in the branches.
The air was cool and filled with the pungent scent of pine.

After awhile, they emerged from the trees to ride onto
a small, grassy bluff overlooking the wooded slope. The
glorious view made Kristy catch her breath. Clumps of
iris and paintbrush and lupine lifted their colorful faces to
the sunshine. A twisting mountain stream tumbled downward. Shading her eyes, she gazed toward the distant sea
of grass that was the prairie.

"It's lovely!" Then she frowned at Chad. "But what
has all this to do with the Bar S?"

"This looks down on the Bar S range," he informed
her. "Come over here."

He turned his gray horse toward the far edge of the
trees. Kristy followed, mystified yet cautious, one hand
ready to draw the derringer. As they drew nearer she saw
a rough wooden fence enclosing a small section of grass.
Inside, lined up in a row, were three tombstones. She shot
Chad a puzzled look, wondering why he'd brought her
here.

He returned her gaze without speaking, then abruptly he
dismounted and walked over to the fence, his broad back
to her. After a moment he swung to face her.

"This is where my mother is buried. And my grandparents."

Kristy shook her head. "I still don't understand what
this has to do with me—"

"My mother's parents were the original owners of the
Bar S. The ranch became mine when my mother died six
months ago. You see, my grandfather knew of Parker's
greed and worded his will in a way that stipulated the Bar
S was to pass to me on her death."

Kristy tried to absorb the incredible implication of his
words. "*You* owned the Bar S? But that means—"

"Yes," he cut in, his voice bitter and angry. "I'm the
one who lost the deed to your dear departed husband."

Too stunned to correct him about her relationship with
James Donovan, she slid off the bay gelding and looped
the reins around the fence before turning to look at Chad.

"So I was right—you *did* plan that poker game in Denver. How did you know I was going to be at the bank that day?''

''Franklin Barnes is a friend of mine. He told me the new owner of the Bar S had made an appointment to see him.''

Kristy recalled the way Chad had eavesdropped on her conversation with Barnes and the odd impression she'd had of a wordless exchange between the two men. Yet why would a bank president associate with this no-good drifter?

''Do you really expect me to believe you know an upstanding citizen like Barnes? More likely, you learned about my appointment by accident and then threatened to shoot Barnes if he didn't agree to refuse me the loan.''

His hard blue eyes glittered in the sunlight. ''I don't give a damn what you think, Mrs. Donovan. The Bar S is my heritage. I want it back before you trade it and your body for Parker's money.''

Fury and shame battled inside her at the crude slap of his words. He dared to say she was selling herself to Parker! Who was this disreputable gambler to condemn *her* actions?

''You might as well get on your horse and ride out, cowboy. I wouldn't sell you the Bar S if you offered me a king's ransom in gold!''

Alarm surged inside her as his face darkened with anger. Belatedly Kristy realized she'd pushed him too far.

He took a menacing step forward. ''You cocky little bitch—''

She scrabbled frantically in her pocket for the derringer, but his large hand caught her forearm before she could draw the weapon.

''Let me go!'' she demanded, twisting vainly against his iron grip. She hated having to tilt her chin to meet his gaze, hated the warm closeness of his body. He was too big, too overwhelmingly masculine.

''Hand over your gun first,'' he said.

''No!''

''Then I'll just have to take it from you.'' Chad reached into her pocket to pry the small pistol from her fingers.

She clung desperately to the weapon. "Better let go, Mrs. Donovan, before you get shot by accident."

"Damn you—"

But his strength exceeded hers, and he forced the derringer from her grasp. In furious dismay Kristy watched him tuck the pistol into his gun belt. Angry at her vulnerability, she snapped, "You big brute! You're just the type to take pleasure in bullying a helpless woman."

Chad felt a smile soften his mouth. Watching her stand up to him was like seeing a kitten challenge a wolf. What a little spitfire she was, with those big green eyes and the sprinkling of freckles across her dainty nose. A sudden rush of desire startled him with its intensity. He wanted to pull off that starched sunbonnet and uncoil her hair, test its silken texture between his fingers. He wanted to peel away those prudish clothes and turn that temper of hers into hot-blooded passion. Yet intermingled with his lust was a gentler emotion that he couldn't quite fathom, a feeling akin to tenderness and the urge to protect.

Chad gritted his teeth in disgust. He was the one who needed protection, not her! Kristy Donovan was a black widow spider who'd leap at the chance to lure him into her deadly web.

"You're about as helpless as a hungry rattler after the spring thaw," he said.

"It's no wonder Parker despises you. You're not the kind of man he'd want for a son."

His insides clenched with bitterness. "I take that as a compliment."

"You would," Kristy said disdainfully. "Good day, Mr. McClintock."

Pivoting on her heel, she marched over to untie the reins of her horse. Chad caught her in three long strides. Grabbing her by the arm, he spun her back around.

"Not so fast, Mrs. Donovan. There's still the matter of that debt you owe me."

Fear leapt into her eyes. Yet he felt a grudging admiration for her grit in tipping her small chin and looking him square in the face.

"I told you before," she snapped, "I don't owe you a thing. Winning doesn't count if you do it by cheating."

"Show me some proof that I cheated."

"Anyone who knows anything about poker would agree with me. The odds are next to impossible for me to draw four aces and you a straight flush, all in the same hand."

"Yet you can't deny there is a chance, no matter how remote."

He watched Kristy moisten her lips uncertainly. The glimpse of her tongue sent a sting of fierce desire to his groin. God, how he wanted to taste that sweet mouth, touch the soft breasts hidden by her prim white blouse. Her arm felt warm under his fingers. He fancied he could detect a pulse throbbing wildly beneath her skin as if she, too, felt the passion lurking below the surface of their mutual animosity.

Abruptly she jerked at his grasp. "Will you kindly remove your filthy hand."

"Such outraged innocence. Another man might have been taken in by those pretty green eyes."

Deliberately he let go of her arm to lift his fingers to her cheek. He had only an instant to revel in the satiny texture of her skin before Kristy retreated two steps, backing up against the bay gelding.

"Why don't you just admit you're a cheat," she said. "You ought to be ashamed of yourself for making a living out of stealing other people's money."

Her haughty tone made his mouth tighten in anger. "You sanctimonious slut. Who are you to give lectures on morality, when you were married to one of the most notorious gamblers on the Mississippi!"

She shot him a strange look. "For your information, James Donovan was my father, not my husband. I only told Barnes that I was a widow so he wouldn't think I was too young to get a loan."

Chad let out a hoot of laughter. "How stupid do you think I am? You'd love to make me believe your lies, wouldn't you, *Mrs*. Donovan. Because you're afraid of what I might let slip to Parker." The flash of alarm in her eyes almost made him regret taunting her. Almost. "Tell me, does your fiancé know he's getting used goods?"

"Parker trusts me. He's not going to believe anything *you* tell him."

"Are you willing to take that risk?" Stepping closer, Chad saw her glance furtively at the derringer tucked in his gun belt. "Go ahead, try it," he jeered. "Let's just see if you can get the gun away from me."

She squared her slender shoulders. "I can't argue the fact that you're stronger than me. If you plan to keep my weapon, I don't suppose I can stop you."

Her air of quiet dignity annoyed him. Why did she persist in this virtuous lady act when they both knew the truth about her tainted background?

Yet something about her drew him; he didn't like feeling so weak-kneed around a woman. Especially Parker's woman.

"Maybe if you fulfill our bargain," he said, goading her, "I'll forget everything I know about your shady past."

"Don't try to blackmail me."

"I'm not surprised you reneged on our bet—James Donovan was a cheat too."

She lunged at him and slapped his face. "You're a damned liar! He never cheated in his life!"

The unexpected blow left his cheek smarting. Furious, Chad caught her arms in a savage grip. "You bitch—"

"Let me go!"

"Not until you explain this—if your husband had a clear conscience, why did you two sneak out in the dead of night? He was long gone the next morning when I came looking for him."

Kristy shook her head warily. "I don't know what you're talking about."

But he could see the guilt sketched all over that lovely, fine-boned face. She knew. Oh, yes, she knew.

His fingers dug into her arms as he thought of the dismal day back in April when he'd learned of his mother's death. Whiskey had numbed his grief and dulled his judgment, and the next morning he'd awakened with a blinding hangover and a dim memory of gambling away his inheritance. With renewed rage, Chad recalled the marked cards and the three saloon employees who'd kept him from wresting the deed to the Bar S out of Donovan's shifty hands.

"Let loose of me."

"Like hell," he growled. "I'll be damned if I'm going to let Donovan's wife cheat me too."

Chad yanked her close to take her mouth with brutal desire. He wanted to punish her, to humiliate her, to teach her that he was not a man to be tricked by innocent eyes and coy words. When she tried to cry out, he forced his tongue into her startled mouth, his hand firmly cupping the back of her head to keep her from jerking away. She tasted faintly of ripe peaches, and he felt his passion mount as her wriggling body stroked against his.

He was too lost in the scent and taste and touch of her to be certain of the moment his kiss changed from hostile fury to hungry yearning. And he wanted her too much to question this sudden, overpowering urge to show her tenderness. His mouth moved rousingly over hers, his hands shaping themselves to her slender curves as he coaxed her to accept the passion firing his blood.

Triumph surged inside him when she quieted in his arms like a gentled mare. Her fingers clutched weakly at his shoulders, and her breath came in soft gasps against his mouth. Against his chest he felt the wild cadence of her heart. He shifted his body to press the fever in his groin to the joining of her legs. When she moaned, he captured the low sound with his lips, immersing himself in the glory of another intoxicating kiss.

Abruptly she tore herself out of his arms. Chad opened his eyes to see the derringer pointed straight at him. Cold fury doused his desire—fury at her for duping him and fury at himself for being fool enough to imagine she'd wanted him.

"I should kill you for touching me like that, you slimy crow bait!"

Kristy hurled every riverfront curse she could recall from her youth, trying to convince herself the shaky feeling deep inside her came from outrage and nothing more. The dizziness she'd felt in his arms was undoubtedly the fault of her tightly laced corset. Horror swept her at the memory of that moment when she'd felt an unreasonable urge to surrender herself to Chad. How could this despicable man arouse such raging emotions within her?

"Such cursing from a lady," he said mockingly, when

she'd run out of scathing gutter descriptions of his character. "Maybe I will have that little talk with Parker and set him straight about his lovely virgin bride."

"Go right ahead."

"I'm glad I have your approval." Chad swung onto his gray horse and touched the brim of his hat in a sardonic salute. "Until we meet again, Kristy. It's been a pleasure."

"Just get out of here and stay off my land."

Despite her brave words, Kristy felt a quiver of fear as she watched the broad-shouldered cowboy disappear down the wooded trail. Was Chad serious about his threat to reveal everything to Parker? She consoled herself with the knowledge that she hadn't actually *lied* to her fiancé; she'd just glossed over a few key facts and let him believe she was from a poor but respectable family back East. Would Parker call off the wedding if he found out the truth about her disreputable upbringing?

Yet all the silver in Colorado couldn't have induced her to beg Chad for his silence.

When she was certain he was gone, Kristy pocketed the derringer and glanced at the tiny cemetery inside the crude wooden fence. Recently someone had cleared away the weeds and left a bouquet of now-wilting wildflowers on each of the three graves. Chad?

No. He was too cold and cruel and uncouth, too self-centered and cynical to perform such a loving gesture.

Yet she remembered the softening in those flinty blue eyes when he'd spoken of his mother. Was there a gentler side to him? Although his kiss had been brutal at first, his hands had touched her with such tenderness . . .

Fingers trembling, Kristy picked up the gelding's reins. As she mounted she thought of Chad's accusations about her father. The cowboy must be wrong; James Donovan hadn't been a cheat.

Yet she remembered how, in her youth, moving had been a way of life. "I've got a hankering for some new scenery," her father would announce. Often they'd pack up and leave town at a moment's notice. Back then Kristy had attributed the sudden departures to her father's restless nature, but now the perspective of time made her wonder.

Had they really been fleeing from some irate greenhorn who'd been gulled out of his money?

Horsefeathers!

Kristy straightened her drooping shoulders and slapped the reins to urge the gelding toward the trees. She wouldn't let a damned liar tarnish the cherished memory of her father.

She'd been wrong to let herself believe Chad had given up on his vengeance and had ridden off for parts unknown. It was a mistake she wouldn't make again.

Chapter 7

Chad McClintock rode through the dusk, heading the gray horse toward the outermost reaches of Diamond M range. A cool wind tore at his leather vest and carried the woodsy tang of cedar and pine. Somewhere in the distance he heard a coyote's plaintive cry.

The lonely locale suited his sour mood. Ever since the encounter with Kristy the previous day, he'd been dogged by a feeling of emptiness he didn't understand. Try as he might, he couldn't erase the memory of holding her soft and womanly body in his arms. He cursed under his breath. Kristy was everything he despised in a female: greedy and manipulative, getting whatever she wanted by using that innocent-as-an-angel beauty of hers. She would yield if the stakes were high enough. Oh, yes, she would.

So if he saw through her tricks, why did he still feel this overpowering lust to possess her?

The answer didn't matter, Chad told himself. Kristy would provide a handy means of fulfilling the desire for revenge that had festered in his gut for years. Now that his mother was dead, he'd make damn certain Parker paid for her suffering. If everything went as planned, he'd also stop the son of a bitch from gaining legal control of the Bar S.

Through the twilight Chad spotted the black mound of a boulder. He rode up to it and dismounted, leaving his horse in a stand of trees a short distance away. Returning to the man-sized rock, he melted into the shadows to wait.

After a time he heard the clip-clop of hooves. The evening had grown steadily darker, yet he remained beside the shelter of the boulder to watch and listen. The shadowy form of a horse and rider appeared through the trees.

The newcomer slowed his approach and appeared to be looking around. A low voice called out, "You there, McClintock?"

Chad took a moment to study the dark silhouette; that deep whisper could belong to any of a score of men. When he was certain of the lean cowboy's identity, he stepped away from the boulder. "Over here."

"Christ Almighty!" the rider exclaimed as he slid off his mount. "I thought you weren't here yet. You about scared the pants off of me!"

"I had to make sure it was you. You weren't followed, were you?"

"Hell, no. I told the boys I was riding into Painted Rock to meet my sweetheart."

Chad grinned. Brett Jordan was a hell-raiser with a fondness for dance-hall girls. Lots of girls. In all the years Chad had known Brett, the handsome cowboy had religiously avoided laying claim to any one woman.

"You'll never live that one down in the bunkhouse."

"Well, I had to give 'em some excuse for riding off alone."

"Any news?"

"Not much. Except there's a big wingding planned for the boss and Miss Donovan."

Chad's interest sharpened. "When?"

"Saturday night. Say, you're not thinking of showing up, are you?"

"Maybe."

"Hell's bells, McClintock! You sure that's smart? You just might stir up a hornet's nest."

"I owe the old man my congratulations on his engagement."

"All the hands got orders to throw you off the ranch if we catch you on Diamond M range."

Chad smiled coolly. "Parker won't make a scene. I can guarantee that."

Brett shook his head. "I don't like this sneaking around one bit."

"It won't be for long, and I appreciate the favor."

"Hell, I reckon I owed you one for that time you busted me out of jail. That horse-faced preacher's wife *forced* me to have carnal knowledge of her."

Chad laughed at his friend's indignant expression. "Thanks all the same."

"You're just damned lucky they were hiring on at the Diamond M. Foreman says your pa's about to get himself another ranch."

A dark bitterness rose in Chad, but he kept his voice calm. "That so?"

Brett shot him a suspicious look. "Say, does that have anything to do with why you asked me to spy on your pa?"

"Might. Then again, might not."

"Okay, pardner. I won't stick my nose into your business."

Chad grinned briefly. "Keep those eyes and ears open— you savvy?"

"Will do."

Chad watched Brett swing onto his horse, the saddle leather creaking. The lanky cowhand raised a hand in farewell, then headed off into the darkness. When the clop of hoofbeats had faded, Chad mounted his gray and began the long, chilly ride back to his solitary campsite in the mountains.

Soon, he promised himself with grim satisfaction. The cards were falling into place, and soon he'd have the pleasure of outdealing Parker. If all went as planned, his form of revenge would be even sweeter than seeing Parker hang for the murder of Mavis McClintock.

Kristy frowned at her profile in the oval mirror, then reached back to adjust the modest bustle of her seafoam green gown. The flowing silk skirt and long, puffed sleeves were trimmed with white satin rosettes, and the bodice was cut fashionably low. Her rich mahogany hair had been twisted into a coil atop her head, with tiny curls feathering her face. Kristy knew she'd never looked lovelier, so why was she feeling so morose?

She gave herself a silent scolding to rid her mind of the moodiness that had nagged her too often lately. Tonight's party was the formal announcement of her engagement to Parker. She should rejoice that she was marrying a gentleman who showered her with expensive gifts, like her glorious gown. Who would have thought when she was growing up in a succession of broken-down shacks that she'd one day be mistress of this fine house?

With an air or resolute cheerfulness, she twirled in front of the mirror before turning to face Lydia, who was sitting in a blue velvet armchair, her stout body bent over as she applied a buttonhook to her sturdy leather shoes.

"It was wonderful of Parker to let us dress here." Kristy waved a hand around the blue and cream bedroom. "Isn't this the prettiest house you've ever seen?"

"Pretty is as pretty does," Lydia said darkly, then muttered under her breath as a button went bouncing across the expensive Aubusson carpet.

"You should have taken Parker up on his offer to buy you something new to wear tonight," Kristy added.

Lydia stood up. "If you're ashamed of me in front of your fancy friends, I'll just be headin' on back home right now."

Kristy's heart twisted, and she threw her arms around the older woman in a fierce hug. "Don't be silly—of course I'm not ashamed of you. You've been the only real mother I've known."

"Oh, hogwash." But Lydia's plump face was flushed with pleasure. "I reckon your pa would of been proud as a peacock to see his little girl spruced up in such finery. Even if it does mean hitchin' yourself to some old geezer."

For some inexplicable reason, Chad's image came into her head, bringing the breath-stealing memory of his mouth on hers. Impatiently Kristy pushed him out of her mind, determined not to spoil her engagement party with thoughts of that scoundrel.

"It's going to be a wonderful night," she said gaily. "I just know it is."

Yet as they headed out the door Kristy felt a churning in her stomach. This was the first time she would pass herself off as a lady in front of so many people. What if she made a slip that revealed her gutter roots?

At the top of the stairs she dried her damp palms on her skirt and took a deep breath to ease the tightness in her throat. Then she started down the curving staircase along with Lydia, careful to take small, graceful steps.

Parker was waiting for them in the foyer. "Ah, Kristina, you look positively stunning."

He bent to kiss the back of her hand, and she felt the tickling brush of his handlebar moustache.

"You cut a fine figure yourself." Her fiancé was, indeed, distinguished looking in a formal black coat and tie that made him appear taller than his actual height.

"You remember Lydia Staggs," she added, touching the older woman's arm.

"Ah, yes, your chaperone. How do you do?"

"I'm fine," Lydia said, giving him a rude look, although she refrained from further comment, to Kristy's relief.

"I apologize for not being here to greet you when you arrived," Parker told Kristy as he led them into the parlor. "I was out on the range and lost track of time. Tonight I promise to make up for my ill-bred manners."

True to his word, he fetched the women glasses of punch and entertained them with amusing tales about ranch life. The atmosphere was a trifle strained, since Lydia refused to respond to Parker's charming attempts to draw her into the conversation. Kristy was thankful when the first guests began to arrive.

A barbeque was scheduled for sundown, with a dance to follow. The succulent aroma of roasting meat drifted in through the open parlor windows. Outside, under the trees, Kristy glimpsed long tables covered in linen. A bevy of cooks hurried back and forth between there and the kitchen, carting platters heaped with food.

She and Parker stood on the porch to greet the guests. Some of the people Kristy knew from town; other faces were unfamiliar, and her mind was soon dizzy from trying to remember all the names. Honey slipped downstairs, a shy vision in pink silk. Even Jeremy had washed up and donned his best suit, though he stayed near the bunkhouse with the cowboys.

The sun sank slowly toward the mountains as the guests

feasted on smoked beef and ham, corn pudding and apple pie, along with imported delicacies. The early September night grew cool; the ladies donned their shawls, while the musicians brought in from Denver tuned up their instruments.

Parker drew Kristy onto the wooden platform built especially for the night's festivities. An accomplished dancer, he guided her across the floor in a sedate waltz, his limp hardly noticeable. She found her gaze wandering to the other dancers and was amused to see Shake squiring Lydia. Guiltily forcing her attention back to Parker, Kristy told herself for the umpteenth time that he was a fine gentleman. So why was she aware of a vague sense of relief when the tune ended and he let her go?

Politely she took his arm as they walked back to join the crowd. That was when she spotted Chad.

Her heart gave a wild leap. He was standing on the sidelines staring straight at her, his face cold and cynical. He was wearing a white shirt beneath a buckskin vest, his long legs clad in dark, snug-fitting trousers. Unlike the other guests, he wore his guns. In the torchlight his black hair gleamed like anthracite. He looked as handsome as the devil and just as dangerous.

Kristy wasn't surprised he'd returned after his father had ordered him off the ranch. Chad McClintock would dare anything.

Parker's arm tightened beneath her fingers as he spied his son. "That bastard!" he snarled. "I'll kill him for showing up here tonight!"

Kristy felt a flash of panic. She couldn't risk a shouting match between father and son in front of all these people, not when Chad might use the opportunity to reveal her past.

"Please, don't make a scene." She gazed beseechingly into Parker's florid face. "Can't you see that he wants to ruin the party for us? If you act as if nothing's wrong, he won't get what he came here for."

The fury slowly drained from Parker's dark eyes, and he patted Kristy's hand. "You're absolutely right, my dear. I won't give him the satisfaction of wrecking our celebration."

She breathed a silent sigh of relief. "Good. We'll just pretend that it's perfectly normal for him to be here."

They walked into the crowd, stopping every now and then to talk to the guests. Kristy was keenly aware of Chad's presence, though she avoided looking in his direction.

She felt no shock when they turned to find him blocking their path. No matter how much she dreaded a confrontation, she knew it was inevitable.

"Hello, Father," he said with a mocking nod. "Miss Donovan."

Parker glanced around as if to make certain none of the guests were close enough to hear before hissing, "What the hell are you doing here?"

Chad raised his dark eyebrows at the shorter man. "Don't look so nervous, Father. I just stopped by to wish you two the best. Seems I was remiss in doing so the last time we met."

"If you're waiting for me to throw you out, you can keep on waiting. You'll not goad me into losing my temper in front of all my guests."

"The only thing I'm waiting for is a dance with your lovely bride-to-be." His strong fingers closed around Kristy's arm. "Shall we, Miss Donovan?"

Parker took a step toward him, his face reddened with rage. "Take your damned hand off her—"

"It's all right," Kristy broke in, ready to do anything to ward off an explosion. "I don't mind dancing, really I don't."

"You see—the lady's willing." Chad jerked the shawl from her shoulders and tossed it at Parker. "Here, hold this. I can keep her warm."

Before Parker could utter more than an angry oath, Chad drew her onto the dance floor, just as the string quartet struck up another waltz. One of his arms imprisoned her in a hard circle, while his other hand clasped hers. As they whirled off into the crowd of dancers, Kristy felt suddenly alive. The torches took on a new sparkle, and the music seemed to sing to the night sky. The other guests spun by in a giddy mosaic of color. She was conscious of Chad's muscled body, big and warm, his scent enticing her.

"Well, Mrs. Donovan, we're alone at last."

She tossed back her head to view the rugged planes of his face. "We're hardly alone."

"A pity, but at least I'm holding you in my arms again."

His mouth quirked into a rare smile; she felt an inexplicable urge to caress the curve of his lip. "I'm surprised you even know how to dance," she said tartly.

"You'd be amazed at the things I know. Tell me, who's the better kisser, Parker or me?"

Against her will she found herself comparing Parker's staid kiss to the tumult of emotion Chad had aroused in her.

Flustered, she said haughtily, "There's no comparison."

His grin was wicked. "I thought not. You enjoyed kissing me, didn't you?"

His arrogant misreading of her words set Kristy's teeth on edge. "If you're so damned sure of yourself, why do you feel the need to ask?"

"Touché, Mrs. Donovan." He guided her smoothly through a series of dance steps before drawling, "By the way, I haven't yet welcomed you to my loving family. You're about to become my stepmother, you know."

Intrigued by the hardness in his voice, she tilted her head to one side. "Why do you and Parker hate each other so?"

"The Bar S is my heritage—he's trying to steal it away by marrying you."

She shook her head, unconvinced. "No, it's more than that. What happened to make you run away so long ago?"

His eyes iced over. "Why don't you ask your fiancé that?"

"I did. He . . . said he didn't remember."

Chad let out a harsh laugh. "Didn't remember, huh? And you believed that lying jackass?"

Kristy pursed her lips, subduing a shadow of doubt. "Of course I trust his word. He's going to be my husband."

Chad regarded her with distaste as they glided across

the dance floor. "You've got a thing for old men, haven't you? First Donovan and now Parker."

"It's none of your concern."

"What if I told you I had a fortune? Would you dump Parker for me?"

His cynical slur on her character incensed Kristy. "Where would a man like you get a fortune? Unless, of course, you make a habit out of swindling poor widows."

"Ah, so you do admit you're the poor Widow Donovan," Chad jeered. He bent his head closer, his warm breath stirring the wisps of hair framing her forehead. "Just remember, Kristy, if my father can't satisfy you, you're welcome in my bed."

The retort froze on Kristy's lips as he brushed his hips against hers. Color blazed into her cheeks; she felt flushed with a heat she didn't understand. Why did he possess this tumultuous power over her body?

Feeling shamed and confused, she yanked herself out of his arms just as the music stopped. "I'd sooner share a bed with a stinking polecat."

His narrowed eyes looked as cold and hard as sapphires. "Congratulations. Parker's about to fulfill your wish."

"Since he's by far the better man, that must make you a slimy snake."

"You'd best keep a watch out, then. Snakes have a way of gliding in and striking when you least expect it."

Kristy felt a chill scuttle down her spine. Could Chad have some dark plan for revenge on Parker, a revenge that somehow involved her?

"Take a walk with me," Chad said in a low voice, his eyes intent. "I want another taste of what you owe me."

His gaze strayed to her lips, and Kristy knew he meant to kiss her. In defiance of all logic she felt a sharp surge of yearning. "I'd have to be insane to go off alone with you," she snapped. "You have gall to even suggest such a thing."

"Yet you'll come," he said in a steely tone. "You don't want me to create a scene, do you, Mrs. Donovan?"

Fingers firmly clasping her elbow, he steered her through the crowd toward the darkness beyond the torches. Her heart raced in wild panic, yet she could not stop him, not without taking the risk of him exposing her past. Through the shifting guests she saw Parker in conversation with a buxom matron; his eyes restlessly searched the gathering. He must be looking for her! Merciful heavens, what would he think if he saw her stealing away with his son, the man he despised?

"This is absurd," she whispered sharply, so that only Chad could hear. "You have no right to manhandle me."

"I have every right," he said, leading her toward the fringe of the crowd. "You owe me, Mrs. Donovan. A true lady pays her debts."

"You don't know the first thing about ladies."

Yet despite her scathing words, Kristy felt fear form a knot in her stomach. Frantic to find a safe means of escape, she spied her brother talking to Shake near the bunkhouse.

"Jeremy," she called, waving to him. "Come here."

Chad tightened his grip on her arm. "Don't think you're getting away from me," he bit out.

To Kristy's immense relief Jeremy darted up to them. His presence would give her at least a moment's reprieve.

"This is my brother, Jeremy," she said quickly. "Jeremy, this is Parker's son, Chad."

To Kristy's amazement, Chad released her arm to shake the boy's hand. "Pleased to meet you, pardner."

Jeremy's freckled face was agog with interest as he stared at Chad's gun belt. "Say, those are mighty fine Colts you got there. You ever killed a man?"

"Jeremy!" Kristy chided. "That's not a very polite question."

"It's all right," Chad said. "I have, son, but only in self-defense."

"Someday I'm gonna be the best shot in the West," Jeremy boasted. "I ain't gonna take no guff from nobody."

"Just treat folks with respect, the way you'd want them to treat you," Chad advised. "Taking another man's life is a mighty permanent way to resolve a dispute."

"Surprising words coming from a man as ruthless as you," Kristy couldn't help murmuring.

Abruptly Parker shouldered through the crowd and

limped up to them. "What the hell are you still doing here?" he demanded of his son.

Chad's face hardened. "Just meeting your fiancée's brother," he said coolly. "It's a damned shame such a fine boy is going to be raised by the likes of you." He tipped his hat. "If you folks will excuse me."

Kristy felt a sense of deliverance as he went striding off into the darkness beyond the milling throng of guests. Thank heavens he hadn't carried through his threat to reveal her past!

"What did he say to you?"

Parker's demand startled Kristy, and she turned to see that Jeremy had gone, leaving her alone with her fiancé. "What? Oh, Chad didn't say much of anything."

Parker took her hand in his. "Come now, you two must have talked about *something*. You turned so pale as he was leading you off the dance floor. I want to know what he said."

Recalling Chad's veiled threat, Kristy moistened her dry lips. She was aware of a strange reluctance to reveal any part of their conversation. Why was she protecting that unscrupulous cowboy?

"He just made some comment about watching out."

Parker's face contorted with rage. "Are you saying that no-good son of mine threatened you?"

"Of course not," she said hastily, afraid he might go after Chad in front of the guests. "I'm sure he was only trying to frighten me."

"That settles it," Parker said grimly. "You're moving into my house for good as of tonight."

"But we're not getting married until next month—"

"That Staggs woman can chaperone you. And she can pack all your things tomorrow. I'll send a couple of hands over with her to help out."

"But I can't move here," Kristy protested. "There're chores that need doing at the Bar S. The corral fence needs mending, wood has to be cut and stored for winter—"

Parker patted the back of her hand. "My dear, your devotion to duty is admirable, but I'll handle the assigning of the chores from now on. As my wife, you're to do nothing but sit back and look beautiful."

"But I—"

"No more objections," he stated firmly. "From now on you needn't trouble yourself with anything more important than planning the menus for dinner. Is that clear?"

Kristy swallowed hard. Why did she feel this sharp disappointment at the prospect of leaving the Bar S? Hadn't she always longed to live the leisurely life of a lady?

"Yes, Parker."

But somehow in her heart she no longer felt like celebrating.

Brett Jordan was drunk.

Not a hell-raising, shoot-'em-up kind of drunk, he reflected, but the mellow, aching sort that starts a man thinking about how lonesome he is. It was a damnable thing to feel that way in the middle of such a shindig. He'd gotten all spruced up in his Sunday duds—starched white shirt and rawhide vest with brand-spanking-new denims to boot—but instead of joining in the festivities, he was standing with a shoulder propped against the bunkhouse like some damned wallflower.

The grub was good, the whiskey flowed freely, and best of all, the town girls were pretty. So why wasn't he dancing?

Damn-fool question, Brett snorted to himself as he took another burning sip of whiskey.

He gazed across the yard at the cause of his morose mood. Honey McClintock stood on the fringes of the crowd, in the shadow of a spreading cottonwood. She was speaking to her brother. Or, rather, Chad seemed to be doing most of the talking; his dark head was bent attentively as if to catch his sister's rare words.

Brett couldn't stop staring at Honey. Her spun gold hair was piled atop her head, and a pink gown caressed her slim, coltish curves. She looked like a princess out of one of those fairy tales he remembered Ma reading so long ago. Or maybe she was more like a sprite, for she possessed the uncanny ability to vanish whenever he ventured too close.

God, how he longed to touch her, to see if she was real flesh and blood or just the dream of a lonesome cowboy who'd been too long on the trail. He was thirty-five years old with nothing to show for it but his saddle and his horse. His pay had gone to saloon girls and good times, and now he wished he'd saved enough to buy a little spread somewhere, something to offer a woman—a woman like Honey.

Hell's bells, who are you fooling? Brett asked himself. Even if he did have some cash put away, Honey was too fancy a lady for a rough-and-tumble cowpoke like himself. Old man McClintock would feed his carcass to the buzzards for even thinking about wanting her!

Yet he couldn't tear his eyes from the sweet vision of her face. As Brett watched, Chad touched her cheek and then strode away into the night. Honey stood there a moment, half hidden in the shadows as she glanced hesitantly toward the party. Then she glided into the darkness and was gone.

The whiskey glass slipped from Brett's fingers and thunked onto the ground, rolling into the bushes as he started after Honey, driven by a need to fill the aching hole inside him.

Almost running, he strained to see into the blackness beyond the light of the torches. As his eyes adjusted to the night, he saw her up ahead, strolling to a corral. Her pale hair gleamed in the moonlight like silvered gold. He walked rapidly toward her, a little unsteady from drink, his heart pounding like the hooves of a runaway horse.

He stopped a few feet behind her to drink in her beauty. "Ma'am?" he said.

Honey whirled around. "Oh!"

Her blue eyes were huge and round, like those of a fawn flushed out of the underbrush. She started to dart away, but he caught her arm with one gentle hand.

"Please, ma'am, don't run off. I didn't mean to scare you—I guess you didn't hear me coming, what with all the racket." Brett jerked his head toward the sounds of merriment in the distance.

She made no reply; she just kept staring at him with those big eyes. A pulse in her arm throbbed wildly beneath his fingers. He felt his own blood heat and race. She was no figment of his dreams. She was a real woman, warm and soft.

"I just wanted to talk to you," Brett murmured. "You're the prettiest girl I've ever seen."

"I am?" she whispered.

"Yes, ma'am." He stopped, feeling tongue-tied around a female for the first time in his life. Fumbling for something to say, he latched onto the first topic that entered his head.

"I saw you talking to Chad."

Honey looked startled. "You know my brother?"

Her voice was low and musical, and in his half-drunken state Brett thought it was the sweetest sound he'd ever heard.

"We're old trail partners. Shared a lot of good times. And once Chad saved my"—he cleared his throat, remembering she was a lady—"my life."

She gazed at him curiously. "Does my father know you two are friends?"

Belatedly he realized the whiskey had made him forget his dangerous purpose here at the Diamond M. Somehow he sensed he could trust Honey, but still . . .

"Uh, no, he doesn't. You won't tell him, will you?"

She gave a small, bitter laugh. "When would I? My father and I rarely speak."

Releasing her arm, Brett lifted a hand to her fine-boned cheek, aching to wipe away the sadness on her face. A years-old memory flashed into his head . . . Chad washing up at a mountain stream with his shirt off, exposing the crisscross of faded scars on his back, scars he'd grudgingly admitted were from a long-ago beating administered by his father.

Fierce anger surged inside Brett. If old man McClintock had mistreated this delicate woman . . .

"Has your pa ever raised a hand to you?"

She shook her head. "No."

"It's a damn lucky thing for him," Brett muttered, caressing her soft cheek.

Honey felt an odd fluttering inside her at the brush of his calloused fingers on her face. An instinctive sense of caution urged her to run away, yet somehow his touch seemed to have robbed her of strength. Who was this cow-boy that he could make her knees feel so wobbly?

She'd noticed him before—a drifter hired on to replace one of the hands sent over to work the Bar S. His cocky walk and lean build had caught her attention from afar, but never before had she been so close to him. Shyly she admired the burnished brown of his hair and the caring look in his dark eyes.

He smelled faintly of whiskey, and again Honey felt an arrow of alarm. She didn't trust men, and this cowboy was a big man, a strong man. What did she really know of him? They were far enough from the party that if he should try to overpower her, no one might hear her scream . . .

"I must go." Honey turned and stepped quickly toward the safety of the crowd.

The cowboy caught up to her in a couple of strides, circling in front of her to block her path. "Please, ma'am, don't leave. I . . . haven't danced with you yet."

He looked so earnest and anxious in the moonlight that the panic freezing her heart melted away. Still, Honey couldn't bring herself to comply with his request. "I'm sorry," she whispered. "I couldn't dance . . . not in front of all those people."

"Well, how about right here then? The music's kind of far off, but we can still hear it fine enough."

The distant strains of a waltz drifted to Honey's ears. She was torn by equally intense feelings of fear and long-ing. "But . . . I don't even know your name."

"It's Brett. Brett Jordan." He sketched a mock bow. "Shall we, ma'am?"

His teasing brown eyes erased the last of her resistance. For better or for worse, Honey put her small hand into his. Brett swung her around with such skill that she forgot the awkward shyness that had kept her from dancing in public, forgot the coltish long legs that too often betrayed her in a stumble. For once she was floating on air, her dainty kid slippers barely touching the hard-packed dirt.

The moonlit yard took on an unearthly quality, full of secret shadows and soft, lilting music. Honey thrilled to the feel of Brett's strong arms around her, and his nearness filled her insides with a wondrous warmth. A supreme sense of security wrapped itself around her. She could trust Brett; he wasn't like other men. He wouldn't try to force himself on her.

They glided to a stop as the distant tune faded away. Brett made no move to release her, and Honey stared up at him, caught by the dark intensity of his eyes. He was looking at her with such naked longing that she felt a resurgence of alarm. Her heartbeat quickened, and her hands began to tremble. Maybe she'd been wrong to trust him . . .

"Don't—" she whispered.

But Brett didn't seem to hear her half-choked protest.

He bent his head nearer, his mouth taking hers with a tender sensuality that almost stopped the panic racing through her veins. Then all reason fled before the burgeoning terror of his male body, and she fought wildly against his muscled embrace, pummeling his arms and chest, gasping and sobbing against his lips.

"What in hell—" he muttered.

In drunken amazement Brett stared down at the struggling woman in his arms. The gentle filly he'd held a moment ago had turned into a bucking bronc.

He winced as Honey struck upward with her knee, missing her target by a fraction. Instantly he opened his arms to release her. She darted off toward the house, her hair a shimmery silver-gold cloud cascading down her slender back.

He stood stock still long after she'd disappeared into the darkness. Gradually his loins cooled, and he shook his head to clear his brain of the whiskey haze. Christ, what a fool he'd made of himself!

Brett walked over to the corral, welcoming the support of the fence as he forced himself to face the hard facts. What had gotten into his head to think she'd wanted to kiss him? Only graciousness had prompted her to accept that dance with him! Despair took root in his heart. Honey McClintock was a sweet, delicate lady, and he'd treated her like some whore in a hurdy-gurdy joint. She deserved to be courted by a gentleman, not by an aging cowboy with scarcely two bits in his pocket.

You're a damn fool for making calf's eyes at the boss's

daughter, Brett told himself. Forget about her. Forget about that lovely face and that shy blue gaze of hers.

But when he settled into his lonely bunk that night, he was still thinking about her.

Chapter 8

The early morning sun slipped past the lace curtains, bathing the bedroom in rose-gold light. Kristy burrowed her head deeper into the feather pillow in an effort to return to the oblivion of sleep. But a lark was chirping outside of her window, and she could hear the clatter of horses' hooves in the yard.

She sighed and rolled over, raising herself on an elbow to squint at the clock on the fireplace mantel. Just past seven. Back at the Bar S, she'd have been up for hours already, tending to chores, but here at Parker's house there was no need to rise early. In fact, there was so little for her to do that she could lie abed until noon.

The notion sounded so boring that she yawned.

Sternly she reminded herself that a lady was supposed to enjoy lounging in bed, swathed in a luxurious silk nightdress. Kristy leaned back against the pillows and assumed a dutifully indolent posture. For one long minute she studied the blue and cream bed hangings and listened to the clock tick. Then a restless energy made her fling back the covers in disgust.

No matter what a lady was supposed to do, *she* couldn't bear lying idle another instant!

She stepped barefoot across the Aubusson rug to the armoire. Quickly she readied herself for the day, donning a lavender silk gown over her petticoats, tying a deep purple sash around her tiny waist. After tidying her sleep-tousled hair, she descended the staircase to the foyer.

The smell of fresh-baked biscuits lured her into the dining room. Beneath a crystal chandelier was a long, linen-draped table surrounded by ten high-backed chairs. Parker sat at one end of the table, Lydia at the other. Neither looked as though they were enjoying a scintillating conversation.

"Good morning, my dear," Parker said, rising to give Kristy a chaste peck on the cheek. "My, you ladies are up early today."

"Hmmph," snorted Lydia. "This is what *I* call late."

Parker merely raised his eyebrows at the older woman before returning his gaze to Kristy, who was filling a china plate at the sideboard. "How thoughtful of you to get up in time to see me off to Denver this morning."

"Oh . . . yes." The guilty truth of the matter was that Kristy had completely forgotten he was leaving today. She sat down and settled a damask napkin on her lap. "How long did you say you would be gone?"

"Three or four days, depending on how my business goes." He lowered his voice, "But don't fret, my dear, I'll be back in plenty of time for our wedding on Saturday."

The dark promise in his eyes made Kristy's heart lurch. Less than a week remained until she would speak the vows that would bind her to him forever. A vague sense of panic nibbled at her insides, but she quelled the feeling. For Jeremy's sake she must think only of doing what must be done to keep the Bar S.

"Are you seeing your lawyer while you're in the city?" she asked carefully.

Parker stared at her over his coffee cup. "I presume you're referring to the document we discussed regarding your brother's inheritance of the Bar S."

Kristy knew the faint disapproval on his ruddy face reflected his belief that a woman had no right meddling in male affairs of business. But Jeremy's future was at stake, and this once she refused to bow to convention.

"Yes, I am," she said firmly.

"I'll bring the papers back with me. That was one of the reasons for my trip."

"I didn't know. Thank you."

"You're more than welcome." Beneath his sweeping moustache, Parker's mouth tilted into a charming smile.

"Now, is there anything I can bring you ladies from Denver? Any gewgaws or baubles?"

Kristy shook her head, absently toying with her breakfast. "You've already been more than generous in inviting Madame Gerard here to help out with my trousseau."

"It's my pleasure. A beautiful woman like you deserves the finest clothing money can buy."

She never knew quite how to react to his gushing compliments, and fortunately he focused his attention on Lydia.

"How about you, Miss Staggs? Might I purchase something for you while I'm in the city?"

"I don't need no fripperies," Lydia stated. She shoved back her chair and stood up, a sturdily handsome woman in brown calico, her lips set in the sour pucker that lately seemed perpetual. " 'Scuse me, folks. I got work to do."

When she had disappeared out the door, Parker remarked with a hint of distaste, "Where on earth did you find that woman?"

Kristy felt a thunderclap of alarm. "Haven't I told you?" She put down her fork, afraid that her trembling fingers might betray her. "Lydia was a . . . friend of my family. When my father died, I needed a chaperone and she needed a home, so she journeyed west with Jeremy and me."

"She seems rather inappropriate for a lady's companion."

His bland expression gave her no clue as to whether he was suspicious or just making conversation. She chose her words with care. "Lydia came to live with us after Jeremy and I . . . lost our mother. My father felt we needed a woman's touch, but he didn't want to marry again, so Lydia was the answer to his prayers—she was willing to work hard and give us lots of love and attention." Fingers twined tightly in her napkin, Kristy added with a prudent dash of humility, "You won't send her away, I trust? I realize she tends to be abrupt, but she does have a good heart."

Parker leaned back in his chair, smiling. "My dear, if you enjoy her company, that's all that counts."

Suddenly he looked toward the door and frowned. Kristy

followed his gaze in time to catch the flash of an azure skirt out in the hall.

"Honey," he commanded. "Come back here."

Her blue eyes wide and wary, the girl stepped slowly into the doorway. "Yes, Papa?"

Parker waved a hand at the array of food on the sideboard. "Get some breakfast and join us."

"I'm not hungry."

"Then sit down, please. I have an announcement to make that might interest both of you."

"Yes, Papa."

Honey slipped into a chair close to the door, and Kristy gave her an encouraging smile. The past few weeks had given the two of them time to become better acquainted. Timidly the girl returned Kristy's smile.

"I received a letter the other day," said Parker, "an acceptance from the man I've asked to be my witness at the wedding. You should be proud to learn his name—Horace Webb."

Honey's fair complexion paled, becoming as white as the linen tablecloth beneath her clenched fingers. Kristy stared at her, perplexed. Why had the mere mention of that man's name put such panic in the girl's eyes?

Apparently not noticing his daughter's reaction, Parker went on. "Being new to Colorado, Kristina, you might not know that Horace is likely to be chosen a senatorial candidate in next year's election. He's been in Washington lobbying on behalf of the Cattlemen's Association, and I'm honored he could find time in his busy schedule to take part in our wedding."

Parker rose, a distinguished figure in his dark suit and starched white shirt. "My primary purpose in going to Denver is to meet Horace's train tomorrow. Provided he has no urgent business to conduct there, we'll both return here the following day. I'll depend on you, Kristina, to make certain the guest room is properly prepared."

"Of course," she murmured.

He rounded the table and kissed her on the cheek. "I must be going now. I've got a long ride ahead of me."

She felt a peculiar urge to scrub the place where his dry

lips and moustache had touched her cheek. ''Have a safe journey.''

With a nod to his daughter, Parker limped out the door.

Kristy tilted her head at Honey, who was sitting across the table, gazing fixedly at her clasped hands. ''What's wrong?'' she asked gently.

Honey's troubled blue gaze darted to her, then flitted away. ''I don't know what you mean.''

''Don't you? Who is this Horace Webb that the mere mention of his name alarms you?''

''He's nothing to me,'' Honey said, too quickly. ''Just another of my father's business friends. Excuse me; I must go.''

She leapt up, catching her foot on one of the chair legs and stumbling in her haste to depart.

''Honey, wait—''

But the blond-haired girl was already darting out the door. Frowning, Kristy decided not to follow, sensing Honey needed to be alone. After all, the girl had a right to her privacy.

But Kristy was determined not to let the matter die. When Horace Webb showed up here, she would keep a sharp eye out for undercurrents. Senatorial candidate or not, he mustn't be allowed to frighten her friend.

Chad crouched in a tangle of brush overlooking the Diamond M ranch house. The encircling clump of aspens would have provided good cover even if he were standing, yet he took no chance of being seen.

Without moving his gaze from the cluster of buildings in the distance, he shifted position slightly to ease a cramp in his leg. The rising sun dazzled his eyes. The sky overhead was clear, but Chad was aware of a barely discernible line of dark clouds on the northern horizon. Since it was nearly October, he was betting on snow. A storm would cover his tracks and delay or even halt any pursuit.

The night cold lingered in the trees and seeped beneath his coat. But still he waited, unmoving and patient. The aspens sighed in a gust of wind, tossing a shower of glittering leaves to the damp ground. A short distance away, his gelding snorted and shook its gray mane before returning to its quiet grazing.

Finally Chad spotted the purpose of his solitary vigil. In the distance Parker emerged from the house and swung onto a waiting horse. He rode off with a pair of cowhands trailing after him. Guards, Chad guessed cynically. Parker wasn't taking any chances on being dry-gulched on some lonely stretch of road.

The trio of riders headed south toward Denver. Thanks to Brett, Chad knew Parker would be gone for at least three days.

Leaving his bride-to-be at the ranch.

Chad melted back into the trees to mount his horse. A restless anxiety filled him at the prospect of putting his plan into motion at last. Tonight was the night. With a satisfied smile, he glanced at the sky. Even the weather was cooperating.

For days he'd watched and waited, growing familiar with the daily routine at the Diamond M. The long hours had paid off. Every evening after supper Kristy took a walk out to the corral. That was the only consistent time he saw her venture from the security of the house.

Chad rode off to his campsite high in the mountains. He would pack up the necessary supplies and then return near dusk.

To make his move.

"Here's another page of sums," Kristy said, crossing the parlor to put a sheet of paper on the desk in front of Jeremy.

"Another page? I thought I was done!"

The consternation on her brother's endearingly freckled face made it hard for Kristy to maintain a stern expression. "You still have twenty minutes left until your lessons are over."

"Oh, yeah? Well, I ain't doin' no more." Jeremy flung his pencil down in disgust.

"Aren't," Kristy said, correcting him. "And you *are* going to finish your lessons. If you want to run the Bar S someday, you've got to know arithmetic."

"Why?" he asked with a scowl. "Everything I gotta know I can learn from Shake."

"But he can't teach you how to balance the account books, figure out the payroll, and pay taxes. Now get on with it or you'll have to stay late and finish."

Jeremy heaved a dramatic sigh, but he doggedly picked up his pencil and began to work.

Turning away, she saw Parker's shy daughter gazing out a window at the other end of the parlor; the book Honey had been reading just moments before was now clasped to the lace fichu over her bodice. The girl's intent stare intrigued Kristy. She strolled closer and looked outside, but the only activity was across the yard in the corral, where one of the cowhands was attempting to halter a half-wild mare.

"Do you suppose it'll rain?" Kristy asked with a glance up at the fierce gray clouds.

"I don't know . . . maybe."

Honey sounded distracted. Was she still brooding about Horace Webb, or was something else bothering her? Come to think of it, she'd been dreamy eyed and acting rather oddly before Webb's name had even been mentioned— since the night of the engagement party, in fact . . .

In sudden suspicion Kristy glanced out at the corral again, trying to discern the identity of the lean cowboy. "Isn't that Brett Jordan out there?"

Honey darted her a startled look and then jerked away from the window. "I . . . I don't know. Excuse me; I believe I'll go to my room. I have a headache."

"I'll ask Lydia to fix you a powder—"

"Oh, don't bother, please. I'm sure I'll feel better if I just lie down for a while."

Honey ran out the parlor door and up the stairs.

Thoughtfully Kristy looked outside again at the cowboy in the corral, remembering the blush that had stained Honey's ivory cheeks. Was there something between Honey and Brett Jordan? That was yet another mystery to unravel about Parker's daughter. Given time, perhaps Honey would come to trust her more.

Kristy sat down and picked up her needlework, though she made no effort to concentrate on the nightdress she was embroidering for her trousseau. Instead she found herself gazing fondly at the boy bent over the small rosewood desk in a corner of the parlor.

As usual, Jeremy's sandy brown hair was tousled, and his shirttail hung out of his pants. She could hear the faint scratching of his pencil, the ticking of the clock on the mantel, and the soft snap of the fire. Her eyes grew misty as she saw Jeremy frown down at the paper, counting out the sums on pencil-smudged fingers. He was growing up so fast. With an aching heart she remembered how proud her father had been of his only son.

"I'm done," Jeremy announced, swiveling in his spindle-back chair to wave the paper at her.

"My, that was fast. Bring your work here, please."

Her brother obeyed, handing the sheet to her. "Can I go now?"

"*May* I."

He groaned, rolling his brown eyes. "*May* I go now?"

He looked so eager that Kristy relented, though a few minutes remained of his lesson time. "Yes, you may. But fetch your coat on the way out—it's gotten cold today. And mind you come in if it starts to rain."

"Yippee!" Jeremy raced to the entryway, pausing to toss out, " 'Bye, Sis," before his footsteps clattered down the hall. She heard him grab his coat from the hall tree, then slam the back door behind him.

What a scamp her brother was, Kristy reflected with a smile. Fervently she thanked God for giving her the chance to safeguard his future. And her own.

Her smile drooped.

Irritably she coaxed the corners of her mouth upward again. She was glad to be marrying Parker—yes, indeed, she was. While he was in Denver she would devote her time to making certain everything went perfectly at their wedding.

Resolutely Kristy set aside her sewing and marched upstairs to check on Madame Gerard's progress. She found the seamstress in the spare bedroom, surrounded by a rainbow clutter of fabric bolts, tissue-paper patterns, and unfinished gowns. The woman's plump body was bent over a sewing machine, her foot vigorously pumping the pedal.

"Madame?" Kristy said, raising her voice over the thump and whir of the machine.

The dressmaker spun around on the stool, a hand flying to her broad bosom. "Lordy me—er, *mon Dieu!* You startled me, Mademoiselle Donovan."

Amused, Kristy pretended not to notice the seamstress's amended exclamation. She had a suspicion Madame Gerard was posing as a Frenchwoman for the prestige it lent her business. A sobering reflection made Kristy feel a kinship to the dressmaker; she knew well how the struggle for survival could force a person to conceal the past or assume a new identity.

"I'm sorry, I should have knocked," she said. "I just came up to see how you were doing."

"Your wedding gown is nearly finished. Perhaps you could try it on now, *oui?*"

"Of course."

Within moments Kristy was staring at her transformed reflection in the oval looking glass. The ivory silk moiré dress was trimmed with flounces of Brussels lace and had a sweeping train. Its folds whispered when she moved, and the cobweb of silver thread and seed pearls on the bodice shimmered in the glow from the kerosene lantern that Madame Gerard had lit to augment the cloudy afternoon light.

"*C'est magnifique,*" proclaimed the seamstress. "Monsieur McClintock will be most pleased with his beautiful bride."

A sudden wave of anxiety swept over Kristy and dampened her palms. "Will he?" she said dispiritedly.

"But of course—you look like an angel. Now stand still, *s'il vous plaît.* I must pin the hem." Madame Gerard got down on hands and knees to begin the task.

Kristy frowned at herself in the mirror, wondering why her insides were in such turmoil. Hadn't she always wanted to be the bride of a wealthy man, to walk down the aisle in an elegant dress, to be the envy of every woman for miles around?

She should be radiant with happiness.

Instead she felt like a hapless columbine about to be plucked.

Her mind leapt ahead to her wedding night. Half of her shied away from contemplating what would happen between her and Parker; the other half lingered on the subject with lurid fascination. The thought of baring her body to him made Kristy blanch. She couldn't imagine enjoying what would follow, although Lydia had once told her many women did. How could such a base encounter yield any pleasure? Perhaps if they did it in the darkness, under the bedcovers, and got it over with quickly . . .

Woodenly Kristy turned so Madame Gerard could reach the front hem. Every bride was nervous, she told herself. She must remember that submitting to her husband's carnal desires might bless her with the children she'd always longed for.

She let out a slow breath to ease her tension. Perhaps the act wouldn't be unendurable if Parker touched her with the same wildly arousing tenderness Chad had shown her that day on the mountainside when he'd kissed her. From out of nowhere came an image of Chad lying naked in bed with her, caressing her with his big hands, moving his hot mouth over her body . . .

Her cheeks burned. Where had that preposterous vision come from? Chad McClintock was a scoundrel and a drifter, not the type of man any decent woman would want. She would never allow that ruffian to claim a night in her bed!

Madame Gerard stood up, puffing a little from the effort. *"Merci, mademoiselle.* I have just to sew up the hem, and your gown will be ready."

Kristy removed the ornate wedding dress and listened absently to the dressmaker's report on the rest of the trousseau. Leaving the room, Kristy continued to brood about Parker's estranged son. No one had seen Chad in the weeks since he'd appeared uninvited at the engagement party, but Kristy had the eerie feeling he was lurking somewhere nearby. She didn't trust him an inch. Not only did he want the Bar S, but he'd vowed revenge on his father. Would he try to stop the wedding somehow? She wouldn't put it past him to enlist a few desperados to shoot up the church!

She decided to mention the possibility to Parker upon his return. Nothing must be allowed to stop their wedding.

To forget her troubled emotions, she spent the remainder of the day in a flurry of activity, from polishing the silver to double-checking the menu for the wedding reception. But a sense of restlessness lingered. By the time the supper dishes were cleared, she was anxious to escape the confinement of the house. No one would miss her, Kristy knew. Lydia was cleaning up in the kitchen, Honey was upstairs trying on her bridesmaid gown, and Jeremy was out in the bunkhouse with the hired hands.

Wrapping herself in a warm cloak, she put on a pair of leather gloves and slipped out the back door. The air was keen and frosty, and an icy wind whipped at her hair. At the bottom of the porch steps she paused to let her eyes adjust to the gloom. From somewhere in the distance came the howl of a wolf.

A sudden sense of dread made her shiver. Low black clouds scudded over the rising moon, rendering the evening dark and dismal. Perhaps she ought to forego her walk.

A burst of male laughter came from inside the bunkhouse, where kerosene lamps winked in the windows. Kristy scoffed at her fears. What was there to worry about with twenty strong cowboys within earshot? Besides, she had taken the precaution of placing the pearl-handled derringer in her pocket.

She started briskly toward the shadowy silhouette of one of the barns. The wind tore at her cloak and hurried her over the hard-packed dirt yard. The air smelled of a crisp blend of pines and cedars and a hint of rain.

Stopping at the corral beside the barn, she clambered up onto the lower slat and whistled. The slap of hooves sounded as a white horse loomed out of the darkness; it was the half-wild mare Brett Jordan had been working with earlier in the day.

Kristy had visited the mustang for the past several nights. Reaching into her pocket, she drew forth a raw carrot and held it out in her open palm. The mare hung back, sniffing the air cautiously before venturing close enough to snatch the tidbit.

The animal nudged Kristy's hand, searching for another carrot, which she obligingly provided until the supply she'd pilfered from supper was gone. "Sorry," she said. "That's all until tomorrow."

The mare snorted, shaking her silky white mane before charging off into the shadows.

Kristy hooked her arms over the top rail and watched the animal's graceful pacing through the darkness. The mare seemed more skittish than normal tonight, probably because of the threat of stormy weather. Kristy hated to think of such a magnificent animal spending a cold night out in the rain. Perhaps she could ask one of the cowhands to stable the horse in the barn.

Kristy stepped down from the fence. Abruptly a strong arm was clamped around her waist from behind, catching her off balance and slamming her against a hard body.

A scream of terror formed in her throat. Before the sound could leave her lips, a hand covered her mouth and nose with a sickeningly sweet-smelling cloth.

Fighting futilely against her captor's iron grip, she groped for the derringer in her pocket. Even as her fingers were closing around the weapon, Kristy felt a wave of dizziness. With each panicked breath she inhaled more fumes from the foul rag.

Her head swam drunkenly as she sank deeper into a whirling nightmare.

Everything went black.

Chapter 9

Consciousness returned to her in slow stages. Kristy's first feeble awareness was of a swaying sensation that made her stomach churn. Her cheek rested against something soft and warm. Her body felt stiff with cold; her mouth tasted like parched grass. A muffled clopping sound vibrated in her ears.

She opened her eyes and the world spun giddily. Blinking, Kristy lifted her head slightly, realizing she was slumped over the neck of a roan horse. Falling snow mantled the wild terrain of the mountains. She glanced up dizzily at the pines towering above the steep, rocky slopes.

Memory washed over her in a flood. She'd been abducted! But why? And by whom?

By the indigo gloom of the forest she knew it must be dawn. Had so many hours really passed?

Snowflakes pricked her cheeks as she tried to focus her eyes on the trail ahead. A big man rode a gray horse in front of her, the back of his coat and hat dusted with snow, his collar turned up against the bitter cold.

There was something vaguely familiar about him, but her mind was too dazed to figure out the puzzle.

Her stomach lurched with a wave of sickness. Attempting to shift position, Kristy found her hands were tied to the saddle horn. Panic welled up inside her. She twisted and squirmed to no avail and tried to call out to her captor, but the only sound that emerged from her lips was a dry croak.

Bone weary and nauseated, she abandoned the battle and pressed her cold cheek to her mount's silken mane. With every bouncing step of the horse, her corset rubbed painfully against her ribs, and the saddle horn jabbed her abdomen. She shut her eyes in an effort to combat the roiling sensation in her belly.

The next thing she knew, the sky had lightened to a silver gray, though snow still drifted downward in steady silence.

Silence. The horse had come to a halt.

Kristy lifted her head and the world swayed drunkenly, although she felt somewhat better than she had earlier. When her vision cleared and her eyes could focus, she saw a snow-covered glade in the midst of a stand of tall pines. Her abductor was hunkered down in front of a small fire, stirring the contents of a pot. In one lithe movement he rose and walked toward her, his boots crunching the snow and his spurs jingling musically.

Chad McClintock!

Fury chased the ice from her bones. She should have guessed her kidnapper was that odious scoundrel!

Stopping alongside her horse, he gazed up at her with wintry blue eyes. His hat was tipped back, and the gray morning light dramatized the rugged perfection of his face.

"Good morning, Mrs. Donovan," he drawled. "I trust you enjoyed your night's rest."

Her breath came out in a frosty huff. "I demand—" Kristy's voice cracked dryly; she swallowed and tried again. "I demand that you return me to the Diamond M at once."

Chad regarded her with a look of sinister amusement. "Might I point out you're hardly in any position to make demands."

He began to work at the rope securing her wrists to the saddle horn. Fear scuttled over her skin like goose bumps, threatening to rob her of resolution, but she shoved away the weakness. The derringer was in her pocket, Kristy reminded herself. As soon as she could reach the weapon, she'd turn the tables on Chad McClintock.

"You're a damned fool," she said. "Parker's probably right behind us."

"Parker is in Denver."

Dismay flooded her, but she didn't stop to wonder where Chad had gotten his information. The rope dropped from her wrists, and she flexed her stiff fingers inside her gloves as needles of feeling pierced her icy flesh.

"The Diamond M cowhands will come after me," she insisted. "You can't fight off a posse of men single-handed."

"They'll have to find us first. The snow's covered our tracks."

She squared her aching shoulders. "A little snow won't stop Parker or his men. He'll tear the mountains apart until he makes you pay for this."

"Maybe," Chad conceded. "But until then, I've got you all to myself."

"I'll kill you if you dare touch me."

He smiled. "Will you? Let's see."

His big hands circled her waist, and he swung her down from the saddle. Her feet had scarcely touched the snowy ground when he swooped her up into his arms and started toward the fire, spurs jangling with each step.

Her head swirled, and for a moment Kristy was too dazed to lift her face from the warm crook of his neck. Her breasts yielded to the hard wall of his chest. His musky male scent swept her senses, and something shockingly sweet stirred deep inside her.

Mustering the remnants of strength, she tried to jerk out of his strong embrace. "Put me down!"

"Gladly."

Chad dumped her without ceremony onto the frozen ground in front of the fire. Then he crouched down and picked up the coffee pot as if kidnapping a woman were an everyday event for him. Pouring the coffee, he offered her a chipped enameled cup.

Kristy glared at him in mute hatred. Something inside her balked at accepting anything from this man.

"Take it," he said with a touch of impatience. "I don't want you to freeze to death."

"My, aren't you thoughtful."

Begrudgingly she took the cup, reasoning that it would warm her numb fingers and thus enable her to use the derringer. Tiny curls of steam rose from the hot brew. She took a sip, and the strong liquid burned down her throat, easing the nasty dryness in her mouth.

Watching Chad spoon beans onto a battered tin plate, she felt her stomach contract into a knot of apprehension. He was too close for her to make a try for her gun. She must bide her time and wait for a chance to catch him off guard.

Dread thudded heavily in her heart. What were his intentions? Did he plan to merely hold her hostage and prevent the wedding? Or did he have a darker purpose in mind . . . rape, or even murder? Gazing at his hard features, she found it curiously difficult to accept that he could sink to such a diabolical level.

Parker would track her down, Kristy assured herself. She mustn't allow herself even to think about the chance that her fiancé might fail to find her.

Chad pushed a plate of food into her hand. "Here, eat."

Her stomach rebelled at the smell of beans and beef, and she set the plate aside. "I'm not hungry."

"Suit yourself."

Kristy watched him enjoy his own breakfast. The small fire provided meager warmth, and the cold ground numbed her legs. Never had she been more aware of her own vulnerability. Snow sifted steadily from the leaden gray sky. The lonely sough of the wind through the pines made her shiver. How many miles had they come?

"Where are you taking me?" she asked.

"You'll find out soon enough."

"I want to return to the Diamond M."

"Shut up and eat. We've got a hard ride ahead of us."

Angry frustration boiled up inside her, and Kristy slammed down her coffee cup. "I'm not going anywhere with you."

Chad raised his eyebrows in dark mockery. "You'll go wherever the hell I tell you, Mrs. Donovan."

Fear diluted her fury. She was no match for his size and strength. Inside his unbuttoned coat she caught a glimpse of his low-slung guns. He was armed and dangerous, and she was totally at his mercy.

Unless she could reach her own gun.

Kristy coaxed her face into a defeated look. After peeling off her gloves, she picked up her plate and swallowed a spoonful of beans along with her pride. Let Chad think she had given up. Then, when his back was turned, she would draw her weapon.

As she finished eating, she was conscious that her ribs still ached abominably from the pressure of her corset, but otherwise she felt somewhat better. Chad doused the remains of the fire with a handful of snow.

She stood up on legs so cold and cramped her knees nearly buckled. "If you've no objection," she murmured stiffly, "I need a moment's privacy."

He grinned crookedly. "Just don't try to run off like you did in Denver. That trick won't work on me twice."

That, she thought, was precisely why it might work. She started toward the edge of the clearing, careful not to slip on the icy ground. She'd make damned sure Chad McClintock paid well for abducting her!

"By the way, Mrs. Donovan," he called out before she'd gone more than a few steps, "just in case you wonder what happened to that toy gun of yours, it's buried in the snow back down the trail somewhere."

Horror clenched her heart. She whipped back around to see him standing beside the remains of the fire, his thumbs hooked in his gun belt, his arrogant amusement visible through the veil of falling snow.

Disbelievingly she thrust a hand into her pocket. It was empty except for a handkerchief. The derringer was really gone!

Tears of angry despair misted her eyes as her best hope of defeating him crumbled. Still she held her chin high.

"Then I'll just have to find another way to outsmart you," she snapped.

"While you're debating the matter, you'd best make use of the bushes. We're leaving in five minutes."

Embarrassment stained her cheeks and made her reckless. "I'm staying right here."

Chad hunkered down to collect the dishes. "Fine. But we're not stopping in an hour just to suit you."

"I meant, I'm not going anywhere with gutter slime like you."

His eyes narrowed. "You're the one who crawled out of the gutter and called yourself a lady. Now, you've got exactly four minutes until we ride out."

Snowflakes stung her hot face. The mortifying fact of the matter was that she did feel an urgent need for physical relief. She had no doubt Chad would dump her back on the roan horse whether she acted according to stubborn pride or common sense.

"Damn you to hell," she snapped, then spun around and stalked toward the woods.

"Don't venture too far," Chad called. "You wouldn't want a wolf or a mountain lion to get you."

"On the contrary," she tossed over her shoulder, "I'm sure I'll feel much safer in the company of your betters."

Despite her bravado, Kristy found herself looking around the woods warily. City bred, all she knew of the wild mountain animals were the stories Shake had told her. In particular she recalled one tale of a fierce bear carrying off a newborn calf. Were the grizzlies in hibernation yet?

She jumped as some small creature scuffled through the underbrush. Hastily picking her way across the icy terrain, she strayed as far from camp as she dared and then stopped behind a screen of evergreen bushes to fulfill her purpose.

Reckless plans for escape clamored in her mind, but reason prevailed. The wilderness imprisoned her as effectively as an iron-barred cell. How far would she get in this savage land without a horse or provisions? Anyway, the question was academic. If she failed to return promptly, Chad would come after her in a matter of minutes. All he need do was to follow her trail, which was marked clearly in the freshly fallen snow.

Reluctantly Kristy headed back toward camp, pulling up her hood and clutching the edge of her cloak together to ward off the cold. She would not give in to despair, she vowed. Parker would track her down.

Perhaps she could leave some sign for him and his men. A quick search of her pockets yielded only her handkerchief. She changed direction slightly and found the trail left by their horses. The indentations of hooves were already half covered by the falling snow and gusting wind.

Casting a glance at the camp a short distance away, she saw Chad was occupied with repacking the saddle bags. Swiftly she speared her handkerchief on a bush in full view of any approaching rider. The tiny square of white cloth fluttered in the icy breeze, nearly hidden against the backdrop of snow.

A needle in a haystack, Kristy thought despondently, but it was the best she could do.

She trudged back to camp. Chad was waiting by the horses, his coat buttoned, the collar turned up to provide added protection against the cold. All evidence of their fire had been smoothed away.

"Here," he said, tossing over her leather gloves. "Don't forget these."

"You really know how to treat a lady," Kristy jeered, though she pulled on the gloves. She would survive this ordeal and see him punished.

"Get on the horse," he ordered curtly.

"And if I refuse?"

His eyes were a cold and beautiful blue. "Perhaps you'd prefer I use more chloroform to keep you docile."

Her stomach churned at the memory of the foully sweet odor of the cloth he'd put over her mouth the previous night. She had no doubt Chad would employ the same method again if she pushed him too far. She needed full control of her senses on the remote chance an opportunity for escape presented itself.

Flashing him a look of hatred, she put her foot in the stirrup. He gave her a boost up, and she swung into the saddle. As he tied her hands to the horn, she pressed her lips tightly together and stared straight ahead, holding herself with dignity, determined not to give in to the tears of discouragement that pricked her eyes.

Chad mounted his gray gelding and, leading her horse by a length of rope, started off through the trees. Kristy couldn't detect a path, but he seemed to know precisely where they were heading. As the day progressed, they ascended steadily into the mountains. Snow continued to whisper downward; the air was crisp and pure. Under different circumstances she would have admired the grand and savage scenery, the rocky gorges and tall spires of pines, the steep white peaks thrusting toward the gray sky.

But all she could think about was the hope that Parker's men were somewhere behind, close enough to find the trail of hooves before the snow and wind swept the indentations away.

Dusk was beginning to pool in blue shadows beneath the trees when they entered a deep ravine scattered with huge boulders. After crossing an icy stream, they came upon a small cabin half-hidden in a nest of pines and cedars.

Chad stopped in front of the dwelling and picketed his horse. Without a word to Kristy, he opened the door and went inside, ducking his head to avoid the low frame. Time sifted by as slowly as the falling snow. Sounds of activity came from within the cabin. Her shoulders drooped from bone-deep exhaustion. She was conscious of her numb limbs and the painful press of her corset. Even if her hands hadn't been tied, she didn't feel as if she could have moved.

After a short while a thin curl of smoke drifted from the stone chimney, and Chad strode back outside, spurs jangling. His hat was gone, and in the waning light a few flakes of snow glinted against the dense blackness of his hair.

She straightened her spine with effort. "You'll never get away with this."

"But we are away, Mrs. Donovan," he drawled, untying her hands. "You can't do anything about that now."

A rush of fear robbed her of speech. Chad looked lean and hungry, like a wolf in winter. How was she to prevent him from taking whatever he wanted from her?

He hauled her down from the saddle, and her aching legs would have collapsed without the sustaining force of her pride. Jerking away from the pressure of his hand at the small of her back, she held her head high as she entered the cabin.

The log-walled room looked deceptively cozy. A fire fluttered in the stone hearth, and the furnishings were few and simple: a rocking chair, a dry sink, a rough table with two chairs, a quilt-covered bed.

Kristy turned her eyes from the ominous sight of the bed. Dread curled in her stomach, but she willed herself to remain calm. Though sore and fatigued from the long ride, she would not show any weakness. And she mustn't give up. Hope still flickered in her that Chad would listen to reason.

"I know you don't want your father to have the Bar S," she said, "but abducting me won't stop us from marrying. All you're doing is delaying the wedding."

Chad strolled to the hearth and poked the logs with the toe of his boot, sending a shower of sparks up the chimney. He looked at her, his face inscrutable. "It's true, I don't want Parker to get his greedy hands on my mother's ranch. But that's not the real reason I brought you here."

"If it's money you're after, Parker will pay any ransom for my safe return."

He smiled with dark humor. "It won't cost him one red cent to get you back."

She watched him uneasily. "What do you mean?"

"It's simple. You're free to return to Parker as soon as you're pregnant with my child."

Color fled her face, swept away by horror. How could any man despise his own father so much? She had feared deep down that Chad's intent might be rape, but to hear him voice that intention aloud filled her with numbing panic. He didn't mean to make her endure his loathesome touch just once, but time and time again, until his seed had taken root in her womb.

"You can't hold me captive for weeks," she whispered.

"You'll stay here for as long as it takes." His bold blue eyes studied her slight figure as if assessing her fitness to bear a child. "Think about it this way, Mrs. Donovan. If you play your cards right, you might even enjoy the experience."

"I'd die first!"

He laughed in contempt. "Don't play the dime-novel heroine with me. You can cooperate or not; the choice is yours."

Pivoting sharply, he picked up his Stetson from the table and went outside. The door slammed shut behind him.

For an instant Kristy remained frozen in place. Then she darted after him, but just as she reached the door, she heard a bar thumping into place outside. With a sob of disbelief she shook the latch. The door refused to budge.

Suffocating alarm clogged her throat. She whirled

around, seeking frantically for a way out of the cabin. The dancing shadows revealed no window, no other door. The utter hopelessness of the situation weighed down her soul, and she crumpled to the rough wooden floor, huddled within the cocoon of her cloak.

Her gloved hand went to her mouth to stop the desperate cry that threatened to burst forth. Naively she had thought she'd known the limits of Chad's hostility toward Parker. Never had she dreamed the unnatural hatred of son for father could extend to such vile depths.

Somehow, despite the threat of Chad's guns, despite his scornful treatment of her, in her heart she hadn't truly believed him capable of such a vicious act of violence.

Now she knew better.

Seeing him for the villain he really was gave Kristy new strength. She pushed away the poisonous panic and forced herself to think. Chad must have gone to tend to the horses. That meant she had a few precious moments to find a way to defend herself.

Ignoring her sore muscles, she tore off her gloves and scrambled to her feet to begin a methodical search of the cabin. No poker by the fireplace, no knives on the dry sink. She considered the neat stacks of provisions in the corner. The large sacks of flour and sugar were of no use to her, and she was weighing a can of tomatoes in her hand when she spied a cast-iron skillet hanging from a peg.

Quickly she plucked the pan from the log wall and tested its swing. Cold determination surged within her. If she struck Chad on the head just right, she might knock him out. Then she could make her escape. With a horse and some luck she might find her way back to the ranch.

Kristy took up position beside the door. She wiped her damp palms on her skirt. Apprehension gripped her, and the minutes seemed to drag by. The only sounds were the soft sigh of the fire and the lonely wail of the wind around the eaves.

Suddenly she heard the heavy tread of footsteps outside, followed by the rattle of the bar being lifted. Heart pounding, she raised the skillet high, ready to strike.

Chapter 10

Chad felt tired but triumphant as he unbarred the cabin door. He paused to shake the snow off his hat. By God, he'd pulled off his plan to capture Parker's fiancé! Lady Luck had smiled on him; the snow would have already erased their trail, upping the odds against any tracker discovering this remote hideaway.

The snug cabin was outfitted for a long winter's stay; he'd have plenty of time to achieve his purpose here. Chad smiled in satisfaction at the prospect of Parker's rage on having his fiancé returned pregnant, sullied by the man he hated most. At last Parker would pay in spades for all the pain and suffering he'd caused Mavis McClintock.

There was an added benefit to the scheme for revenge, Chad thought, reaching for the latch. He'd finally have the chance to purge himself of an unreasonable lust for that conniving Kristy Donovan. A hot and vivid anticipation hurtled through him as he imagined sinking into her silken depths.

He pushed open the door. Ducking his head to avoid the low doorframe, he stepped into the cabin and shut the door.

A flash of movement caught the corner of his eye. Reacting instantly, he lifted an arm to shield himself, spinning with the reflexes of a wildcat. His hat tumbled to the floor as the blow struck his upper arm with numbing force.

''Son of a bitch!'' he exploded as he made a lunge for the frying pan Kristy was again swinging at his head.

He grabbed the cast iron weapon in midair. She let out a half-choked sob and clung tenaciously to the handle. He yanked hard on the skillet, and the momentum made her stumble, but still she refused to let go.

Pinning her struggling body against the log wall, he peeled her fingers off the handle. Then he flung the skillet away; it clattered and clanged into a corner of the cabin.

Fury surged hard and hot within him. His arm hurt like hell. He fastened his fingers to her slender shoulders, intent on demolishing her defiance.

"You ever try a trick like that again," he said harshly, giving her a shake, "and by God Almighty you'll live to regret it!"

Panting, she tossed her head back and glared at him. "I'll never stop fighting you—you hear me? Never!"

Her eyes were a vivid and turbulent green, her cheeks flushed and satiny smooth. Beneath his fingers her shoulders felt as fragile as hummingbird bones, and her half-tumbled hair caressed the back of his hands. Her cloak hung askew, revealing the rapid rise and fall of her breasts beneath her lavender bodice.

She was the very image of indignant innocence. Anyone would think she had the right to appear so pure.

Anyone but him, Chad thought darkly; he knew better. Kristy Donovan looked no older than his sister, and already she was the widow of a gambler. James Donovan hadn't been cold in the grave before she'd latched onto another old man, this one rich enough to satisfy her greed.

She and Parker deserved each other. Then why, Chad wondered, was he so enraged that she'd go willingly to Parker's bed but not to his?

With a snarl of angry frustration he bent his head and took her lips. She jerked her mouth away, but he caught her face in his hands and forced her to accept the domination of his kiss. When she flailed and fought, he imprisoned her small body against the wall and diligently sought her surrender.

Only pride kept her from yielding, he told himself. She resented his interference in her plans to marry Parker. But when the chips were down, she'd give in—oh, yes, she would.

His tongue probed her lips in a deliberate sensual assault. Ignoring the pain as her fist struck his sore arm, he concentrated on taming her rebellion with all the heat and fury of a man possessed. Blood burned through his veins at the feel of her: the delicacy of her face in his hands, the voluptuous breasts spilling over the top of her corset, the firm thighs struggling against his own.

Gradually she quieted, and he felt the pressure of her fingertips against his coat. Her lips parted to invite the stroking caress of his tongue, but her submission caused none of the gloating satisfaction he'd expected to feel. An unfamiliar tenderness welled inside him, and his grip gentled. Chad felt his self-control slipping as he himself became the captive, a prisoner to her honeyed taste and peachy scent.

No other woman had ever affected him so completely. Kristy Donovan was an opiate in his blood, and he had to cleanse himself of an overwhelming need for her. That he could avenge himself on Parker at the same time would only make this coupling all the sweeter.

"Let's go to bed," he muttered roughly.

As he drew her across the room, he saw her eyes flutter open and widen, as if in surprise and alarm. "No—" she whispered.

Her show of bluff innocence first confused and then angered him. How dare she look so damned scared when he knew she was little better than a whore? Didn't she realize the time had come to cash in her chips and end this loser's game?

"Yes," he stated firmly, and hauled her over to the bed, giving her a push down onto the quilt. Desire seared his senses at the sight of her sprawled womanly form. He tore off his coat and flung it aside.

Kristy scrambled off the end of the bed and backed away. "Don't you touch me."

"I'll touch you whenever I damn well please." Walking to her, he yanked open the tie of her cloak, letting the garment puddle onto the floor.

She made a dash for the door, but Chad caught her easily. Hands clamping around her slim waist, he tossed her onto the bed and covered her body with his own. She bucked as wildly as an unbroken mare. When she tried to claw his face, he captured her wrists and pinned them above her head.

For another moment Kristy continued to defy him, and then the spunk seemed to drain out of her. She gazed up at him, trembling, her hair a rumpled cloud of mahogany, her fine-boned face gilded by firelight.

"Don't do this," she said, her voice low and quavering.

Her quiet plea affected Chad in a stunning way; he found himself wondering for the first time if the desperation in her stormy eyes might be real. That she could spin her web of deceit so thoroughly filled him with self-disgust.

"Why should you object?" he said brutally. "You sold yourself to the highest bidder."

"You know nothing of my reasons for marrying Parker."

Her aura of hurt dignity made Chad feel an annoying urge to caress her cheek in apology. He kept his hand curled into a tight fist beside her face.

"I know Parker wants you to give him a son," he said. "All I propose to do here is to plant one inside you."

"He doesn't want the spawn of the devil," Kristy shot back.

"If I'm the devil, then you're a fallen angel. That makes us a perfect match."

She held his gaze, unflinching. "Believe what you will about me, just let me go."

"I can't."

It was true; Chad felt bound to her by a force as fierce as the driving desire for vengeance that had eaten at his gut for so long. The women in his life had been few, and none had aroused more in him than a passing physical need. There was a lusty widow up in Cheyenne he visited from time to time, but by mutual agreement they made no claims on each other, and when he rode away no willful tears or angry recriminations dogged his heels.

That was the only kind of relationship he wanted with a woman. Only a damned fool dreamed of something more.

So why did Kristy stir up such a tempest of tenderness in his heart?

Keeping both her wrists imprisoned above her head with

one of his hands, Chad deliberately moved his free hand to the top of her breasts. Beneath the lavender silk of her bodice he could feel the sweetly swelling softness above the rigid edge of her corset.

She wriggled with furious, renewed effort. "Don't!"

Her resistance filled him with angry frustration. "Stop playing the virgin with me," he snapped. "After that old geezer you were married to, you ought to be eager to bed a younger man."

"James Donovan was my father, not my husband. Why can't you believe that?"

"Because you'd tell any lie to save your own hide. You're afraid Parker won't marry you after I've had you, and you won't get your greedy claws on his money. Isn't that so, Mrs. Donovan?"

"No!"

But the panic in her eyes told him he'd hit smack at the heart of her fears. The truth angered him, and purposefully he ground the hardness in his loins against her hips. The feel of her fertile curves fanned the blaze of desire he could no longer keep in check. He let go of her hands and twisted her halfway onto her side so he could wrest open the buttons at the back of her gown. Kristy bucked and thrashed against him, and his sore arm throbbed with the effort of pinning her to the bed.

She grabbed for his gun, but the weapon remained firmly wedged in the holster. Chad caught her hands and yanked them behind her.

"Next time you want to shoot me," he drawled, "remember to first untie the rawhide thong that holds the gun in place."

Her eyes were a spirited, spiteful green. "You miserable lowlife. Does it make you feel like a big, strong man to rape me?"

"Rape?" He let out a harsh bite of laughter. "Tell me you didn't enjoy kissing me. You were melting in my arms until you remembered you like to call the shots."

"That's a lie!"

"Is it? Let's just see."

He yanked down her lavender bodice, revealing the ripe half-moons of her breasts above her lace-edged corset. His breathing quickened. She was the most damnable pretty woman he'd ever seen.

Kristy moaned and tried to jerk away, but he easily held her in place. In the firelight the soft swells of her breasts wore a golden glow that tempted him beyond reason. Hot urgency throbbed in his loins. He wanted to see all of her, to feast on her nipples, to slide his palms down the curving woman shape of her, to envelop himself in her moist, welcoming flesh.

Releasing her captive hands, he reached for the hooks that fastened the front of her corset. Instantly she attacked him, a fighting, scratching hellcat.

Chad cursed viciously under his breath as her fingernails clawed his neck. With wrathful strength he subdued her battling form and dipped his head to storm the citadel of her resistance. His mouth caught hers in a hard, grinding kiss meant to subjugate rather than seduce. Though she tried to tear herself away, he kissed her into surrender with an angry intensity of purpose that brooked no mutiny, until she grew tame in his arms, her breasts heaving against his chest.

He meant to preserve her capitulation with cold self-control, but the honeyed taste of her lips, the breath-stealing feel of her body, the provocative peachy scent of her skin all conspired to drain him of fury, leaving only a maddening desire to please her, to woo and entice her into wanting him. Mere mastery of her was no longer enough; Chad wanted her to wrap her arms around him in passion, to lift her breasts to his mouth, to open her legs and invite him inside her.

"Kristy," he said in a gritty undertone.

He lifted his head to see her watching him with those bewitching eyes, her lips parted slightly, her cheeks flushed. So much for her resistance, he thought cynically. She was feisty—but smart enough to see the deck was stacked in his favor.

Succumbing to impulse, he feathered his mouth over her sweetly swollen lips and then the dusting of freckles over the delicate bridge of her nose. His finger strayed downward, over her small chin, to caress the madly beating pulse in her throat.

Her skin was all cream and silk. With unsteady hands Chad unhooked her corset and tugged impatiently at the lacy border of her chemise to free her breasts. They were made as perfectly as the rest of her, the dusky rose nipples and rounded flesh marred only by the ugly red lines left by the whalebone stays. His hand cradled one breast; it fit his palm as if each were made for the other.

Hunger for her warred with anger that Kristy would endure the punishing prison of the corset all for the sake of vanity. She was so dainty and well shaped she had no need of any such artificial beauty aid.

Rolling off her, he pulled her upright and drew the stiff, beribboned garment from her unresisting body. Turning, he flung the corset toward the hearth. His aim was true; the frilly concoction landed on top of the burning logs, sparks flying and flames hissing.

"You ought to thank me that you won't need to wear that damned contraption anymore," he said, watching in satisfaction as the blaze lapped at the satin and lace.

A muted moan made him jerk his gaze back to Kristy. She was staring not at the fire but at him, her eyes wide and wild and awash with tears, her hands shielding her naked breasts with the crumpled bodice of the lavender gown, her lips forming words he had to strain to hear though she was sitting so close their knees were touching.

"You can't do this to me . . . please, you mustn't do this . . ."

She was trembling visibly, but not with passion.

The realization struck him in a blinding flash.

She was truly terrified of him; her resistance was no calculated act.

The knowledge tore into Chad's gut like a flint-tipped arrow. A torrent of conflicting emotions flailed him, chief of which was shame. What sort of man was he to force himself on an unwilling woman?

Impulsively he let his fingertips graze the silk of her cheek. "Kristy . . . it doesn't have to be this way."

"Don't touch me." She recoiled, fear etched over her lovely face.

Self-disgust sent Chad surging to his feet. With a muttered curse he snatched up his coat and hat, then stalked to the door and slammed out of the cabin. He didn't stop until he reached a close clump of pines, barely visible in the darkness. The night was cold and starless, silent with the peculiar hush only a snowfall can bring.

Propping a shoulder against the rough bark of a tree, he tilted his face to the black sky. Snowflakes needled his hot skin. The scents of pine and ice hung heavy in the air, but all he could think about was the fragrance of Kristy's skin.

His mind was a confusing chaos of regret and frustration and anger. He stood there, coatless, until the bitter cold had cooled the rampaging fire in his loins and he could think clearly. Then he put on his coat and hat, hunching his big shoulders against a gust of icy wind.

Once again Kristy Donovan had managed to stampede his carefully laid plans. The possibility of failing to plant his seed in her was something he hadn't considered.

His chest tightened at the memory of her pale, frightened face. The need to punish Parker had so consumed him that he hadn't given much thought to the tool of his revenge. He had regarded Kristy as no more than a wild mare to be broken to the saddle. He'd been certain she would submit once she saw the advantages of doing so.

The look of stark fear in her eyes had proven him dead wrong.

She was a woman of no morals or scruples, Chad reminded himself harshly. So why should he accord her any respect?

Yet the prospect of rape brought the taste of bile to his throat. Much as it galled him to admit it, he couldn't defile Kristy; he wanted her willing and eager. Why the hell was he saddled with this inborn sense of decency?

Self-loathing ate at his insides as he recalled his arrogance in not realizing sooner the true terror behind her resistance. He'd acted like a savage, treating her as if her feelings didn't make one goddamned bit of difference. She might be no better than a whore, but that didn't give him the right to manhandle her.

Absently he massaged his aching arm, wondering why a manipulative woman like Kristy Donovan would cringe from him rather than use her seductive powers to lure him into her web. She had felt passion for him; her melting response to his kisses was proof of her desire. There had to be some reason why she recoiled like a virgin even as his hands and lips had gentled on her.

Maybe the thought of bearing his baby made her sick.

He cursed under his breath. Was that the cause, or was it something else? Perhaps her late husband had abused her. The possibility filled Chad with cold rage. James Donovan had looked like an affable sort, but then, one could never tell. After all, most people regarded Parker McClintock as a gentleman too.

Thinking of Parker, Chad frowned into the darkness, his face set in hard lines of bitterness. For a brief time he'd held in his hands the chance to achieve the ultimate revenge, to see Parker forced to choose between losing the Bar S or having the first-born child of his marriage to Kristy fathered by the man he hated.

Now that plan had been shot to hell by one small, dainty woman who somehow wielded the power to make him treat her with respect. And to make him half-sick with wanting her.

He turned to gaze broodingly at the dark shape of the cabin outlined against pitch-black forest. She was in there, maybe sleeping already. Just thinking about her lying in bed made him feel as hot and hard as a branding iron.

If he didn't make love to Kristy Donovan, then what the hell *was* he going to do with her?

Chapter 11

Kristy sat motionless on the bed as the numbing storm of fear gradually subsided. Then, shuddering with aftershock, she buried her face in her hands and surrendered to the tears she had fought so hard to keep Chad from witnessing. It was bad enough to be so spineless as to feel stirrings of desire for a man bent on rape; to have given him the smug satisfaction of seeing her reduced to a sniveling, sobbing coward would have been too much.

For long moments the sound of her sobs mingled with the snapping of the fire and the crooning of the wind. Kristy felt battered by a blizzard of contrary emotions, unsure whether she was crying because of relief or despair. Chad might have left the cabin without raping her, but she wasn't fool enough to see his absence as any more than a momentary reprieve. She was still a prisoner.

As her tears began to abate, she faced a bitter truth. Even if she managed to escape with her innocence intact, her reputation was already in tatters. She could well imagine the sly whisperings of the townspeople as they speculated on what had gone on between her and Chad.

Disheartened, Kristy let her shoulders slump. Would Parker still marry her in spite of her soiled honor? And if he didn't, what would happen to her dreams for Jeremy's future? She had left St. Louis in search of a better life for them, a place where they would be free of the stigma of their father's notorious reputation. But Chad had swept away all her plans with one act of cruel vengeance. He wouldn't understand her craving for a real home, she thought bitterly. Chad McClintock was a drifter, a man forever restless, forever resistant to sinking roots in one place.

She felt a sudden, wrenching desire for the security of the Bar S. Now her world had narrowed to these four log walls, the fire shadows cavorting in the corners, the rocking chair in front of the hearth, the quilt-covered bunk on which she sat. The room appeared deceptively homey; in reality it was the lair of a wolf.

Apprehension chilled her skin as she noted the shelves above the dry sink. Enough provisions were stacked there to last the winter. This had been no spur-of-the-moment act; Chad must have planned it for weeks. How could a son hate his father so?

Her tired muscles ached in protest as she reached around to rebutton the rumpled lavender dress. She felt half naked and vulnerable without her corset, but nothing could be done about that. All that remained of the undergarment was a pile of charred whalebone slats on the hearth.

She sprang from the bed to pace the cabin anxiously. The fine linen of her chemise grazed her nipples in a stirring echo of Chad's caress, and in some secret, unchaste part of her she found the memory scandalously appealing. How could that no-good low-life have such an effect on her?

Shame curdled her stomach as she recalled her brazen response to his kisses, her wicked longing for him to touch her naked breasts. Deep in her heart Kristy feared the weakness, for under different circumstances she might have given herself to him like a soiled dove. The realization was unnerving. Was she so wanton she could forget his vile purpose in kidnapping her?

Only the panicky memory of his intentions had kept her from committing such an ignominious mistake. Chad might murmur her name with heart-stopping tenderness and touch her with arousing gentleness, but she knew his behavior was an act designed to entice her into lowering her guard. The truth of the matter was that he viewed her only as a vessel for his vengeance.

Kristy wiped away the last of her tears as resolution began to creep back into her soul. She would not be a willing party to his twisted scheme.

Somehow she must find a way to escape.

In her restless circling of the cabin, she noticed a simple wooden chest at the foot of the bed. Hoping to find something to use as a weapon, she lifted the lid and sat back on her heels in shock. The chest contained a rainbow array of feminine apparel, and not the sort worn by a lady.

Anger budded inside her as she picked up garment after garment, the fabrics rustling erotically. Besides a few lewd gowns, there were lemon satin drawers trimmed with cheap black lace, a cherry pink chemise threaded with matching ribbons, and black silk stockings with frilly dance-hall garters. When she held up a petticoat made from a pearly gauze so sheer she could see clear through to the fireplace beyond, Kristy's temper heated to the boiling point.

She flung the offending garment back into the chest and slammed down the lid, her cheeks burning with fury and mortification. Did Chad expect her to parade in front of him clad in nothing but those . . . those vulgar whore's clothes?

A peculiar pain pierced her heart. Yes, he did expect that. She was a slut to him, an object to be used for his nefarious purposes. Why, then, had he stormed out of the cabin so abruptly?

Kristy stood up, a frown knitting her brow. Chad possessed the strength to overpower her easily, yet he had stopped short of rape. Why?

Dare she dream there might be a spark of humanity in his black soul, a glimmering of conscience that made him regret abducting her? If that were the case, then perhaps there was still a feeble chance she might persuade him to let her go.

That crumb of hope sustained her. Almost dizzy with exhaustion, she sank into the rocking chair in front of the hearth. She glanced at the door, struggling for alertness as she wondered uneasily where her kidnapper had gone and when he would return. Chad McClintock was a dangerous man, tough and clever and unpredictable. It would take all her wits to outsmart him. She would try to reason with him tonight, as soon as he came back.

But her intention to stay awake and confront him eroded under a powerful wash of weariness. The warmth of the fire seeped into her bones, coaxing her eyelids downward, luring her tired body into oblivion.

Kristy swam toward the surface of wakefulness, her mind clinging to the fragments of an erotic dream. Something seemed wrong, but her head was too fuzzy to determine what it was. Drowsing in a nest of wonderful warmth, she resisted the tug of reality. Lazily she snuggled closer to the source of the irresistible heat, and her back grazed the hard form stretched out alongside her.

Kristy's eyes snapped open to the darkened cabin. She was in the bed, not in the rocking chair where she'd fallen asleep last night. And that warm body she was nestled against belonged to Chad McClintock!

She tried to sit up and found her hands tied in front of her. Cursing him under her breath, she managed to wriggle onto an elbow only to discover herself wedged between the wall and her abductor. The banked fire shed barely enough light for her to make out the shadowy forms of the furniture. Chad appeared to be asleep, but in the darkness Kristy couldn't be certain.

Cautiously she squirmed out from under the heavy covers and gasped as the icy air chilled her sleep-warm body. Grimly she told herself anything was preferable to spending one more moment lying next to that damned cowboy.

Her tied hands made movement awkward, but Kristy crept as best she could toward the foot of the bed. The mattress rustled, and she froze as Chad muttered in his sleep and rolled onto his back.

For a long moment she remained motionless, listening to the deep, steady sound of his breathing. Then carefully she resumed her slithering progress.

Panting with effort, Kristy managed to twist herself off the end of the bed, avoiding the square chest below and wincing as her bare feet touched the frigid floor. A sense of victory filled her until she looked down at the short length of rope binding her wrists.

Her eyes widened. Her gown and shoes were gone; all that kept her from total nakedness was a thin linen chemise, frilly drawers, and a muslin petticoat.

Anger boiled up inside her, momentarily heating her

chilled body. That low-down river rat had taken off her clothes! Her cheeks flamed as she thought of him touching her unresisting form. It would be just like Chad McClintock to fondle a sleeping woman!

A horrifying possibility occurred to her. She had been so bone weary, so deep in slumber. Could he have done more than caress her . . . could he have done *that* to her?

Kristy felt no sense of violation in her body, but then, she wasn't certain how a woman was supposed to feel after being used by a man. Freezing and furious, she glared at the bed. Her abductor was still asleep; he hadn't moved even a muscle.

Well, she wasn't going to wait around to confront him on the matter when this might be the chance she'd been praying for. The faintest glimmering around the door foretold the approach of dawn; she had little time to make good her escape.

Tiptoeing to the hearth, she crouched down to work at her bonds by the meager light of the banked fire. The rope had a bit of slack; apparently Chad was so overconfident he didn't think she had the gumption to steal away right under his nose.

Using her teeth, she tugged at the knot, trying to work it loose. A sudden scraping noise paralyzed her. Then she realized the muffled sound must have come from one of the horses, probably stabled outside in a lean-to.

After a few minutes she managed to loosen the knot, and from there it was a simple matter to slip off the rope. Sweet freedom!

Kristy surged anxiously to her feet, searching the darkness for her clothing. She found her gown lying crumpled beside the rocking chair, along with her shoes and stockings. In quiet haste she dressed, keeping her eyes fixed on the long, shadowed form on the bed.

Thankfully, Chad showed no sign of awakening. Spying her cloak on a peg beside the door, she donned the garment, tying it at the throat.

Kristy stood in an agony of indecision. Should she try to incapacitate Chad in some way so he couldn't follow her? Somehow the thought of striking him while he slept repulsed her. Why not just bar the door as she left, locking him in the cabin?

But first she must take his guns to protect herself in case he managed to escape and track her down. The Colts would also provide a means of defending herself against any wild animal she might encounter on the trail homeward.

She peered through the darkness at the bed. Undoubtedly Chad would keep the guns close at hand, yet she couldn't make out anything more than the big black shape of him.

He wouldn't wear the weapons while he slept—would he?

Heart clattering against her ribs, Kristy crept toward the bed to take a closer look. Relief spurted through her as she spotted the leather gun belt draped over the bedpost near his head.

She tiptoed nearer, watching his darkened form all the while. A floorboard creaked beneath her feet and she stopped, her palms damp with fear.

But Chad remained still, the sound of his deep breathing unaltered in the quiet, chilly air.

Driven by determination, Kristy dared one step forward and then another until she arrived at her goal. Chad lay on his back, an arm flung over his head, the rugged angles of his face draped in shadows. He was so close she could have touched him.

Instead she reached for the holster and the faint ivory splotch in the darkness that was the butt of the gun. Her fingers were scant inches shy of the weapon, and she could almost feel its weight in her hand—

In one swift motion Chad flung off the covers and jumped to his feet. Kristy leapt backward, a startled cry choking her throat. In the muted light from the banked fire his face was a mask of hard fury. He was naked to the waist, wearing only a pair of denims. Her horrified gaze fastened on the gun in his hand.

A gun that was leveled at her.

"Why, Mrs. Donovan, you're up mighty early this morning."

Moistening her dry lips, Kristy darted a glance at the

ivory butt still visible in his gun belt and recalled with a sinking heart that he had two six-shooters; the holster hidden behind the bedpost must be empty.

Fear flooded every fiber of her. He looked like a desperado contemplating his next murder.

"I . . . I couldn't sleep."

"And I suppose you just wanted to get in a little early-morning target practice," he said, with more than a hint of irony. "Using me as the target."

He took a menacing step closer, and she retreated until her palms met the rough stones of the fireplace. Prudence told her this was no time for brash defiance. "That isn't true," she said in a placating voice. "I wasn't going to shoot you. I swear I wasn't."

Chad let out a snort of disbelief. "Then why the hell were you stealing my guns?"

"Only for protection on the trail. I was going to lock you in the cabin, that's all."

He was silent a moment, his expression unreadable in the dim light. "You know, Mrs. Donovan, you're damned convincing for a liar. It's just too bad for you that I know you so well."

Bitterness saturated her spirit. "You don't know me at all."

"I knew you'd try to escape. I knew, and I was waiting for it."

Kristy narrowed her eyes in suspicion. "Just how long were you awake?"

His smile glinted through the darkness. "Long enough to watch you wriggle your little bottom out of bed. And long enough to notice how pretty you looked prancing around in your underwear."

Her body blazed at the thought of him seeing her half naked. Then fury seethed inside her as she recalled bits and pieces of the erotic dream that had disturbed her sleep. Had that been a figment of her imagination, or had it been based on reality?

"You had no right to remove my clothing last night," she snapped.

"In case you've forgotten, Mrs. Donovan, I have the right to do whatever the hell I please with you."

His cocky manner fed her fear that he must have already violated her. "Only a scoundrel like you would do such indecent things to a sleeping woman."

His eyes glittered in the faint light. "Just what things are you talking about?"

Kristy was grateful for the shadows that hid her flaming cheeks. "You ought to know," she muttered stiffly. "You're the one who did those disgusting things."

"Disgusting?"

"Yes," she snapped. "You acted like the vile vermin you are."

Chad let out a hoot of incredulous laughter. "You think I made love to you last night?"

"Love had nothing to do with it. Rape is all your kind knows."

"I see," he said, sounding amused. "Are you disappointed you slept right through my vile rape of you?"

"Of course not!"

"Well, don't fret, you didn't miss a thing." Coming closer, Chad feathered the barrel of the gun down her cheek. "I don't know about your other men, but believe me, Kristy, when we make love you'll remember the experience."

She recoiled from the cold caress of the gun, her heart fluttering. "Don't touch me with that thing."

"I'll touch you whenever and wherever I please," he taunted, parting her cloak with the gun barrel to lightly trace the curve of her breast. "And I'm giving you fair warning. Next time you try to run off, I won't be so lenient."

Fighting fear, Kristy pressed her spine hard against the stones of the fireplace in an effort to avoid the tingling touch of the gun. "I'm not afraid of a miserable snake like you."

He chuckled softly. "Beware the sleeping rattler . . ."

"Snakes can die too. You'd better keep your eyes open from now on, McClintock."

"You can bet I will. Especially since I have you to look at."

Kristy felt an onslaught of alarm as Chad sauntered away to buckle on his gun belt. A cloud of gloom threatened to engulf her, but she fought for a glimmer of hope. At least he hadn't yet raped her; there was a certain comfort in that. Perhaps she might be able to reason with him . . . in a moment, when she could rid herself of this limp-kneed fear.

To give her quaking hands something to do, Kristy knelt before the hearth and built up the fire, wishing she owned the strength—and the courage—to heft a log smack into Chad McClintock's mocking face. She jabbed the embers with a bit of kindling, and tiny flames began to lick at the logs, radiating warmth throughout the frigid cabin.

With a heavy heart she removed her cloak, standing aside in silence as Chad broke the skin of ice in the cauldron of water beside the hearth. He filled a basin and walked away with it; then she heard the sounds of him washing up.

Holding her cold hands to the blaze, she cast a sidelong glance at Chad. He was bent over the basin at the dry sink, splashing handfuls of water on his face, his bare back to her. A true lady would avert her gaze from a half-nude man, Kristy knew, but she couldn't keep from staring in fascination.

The muscles of his back hunched with each movement of his arms. His shoulders were powerful, his waist lean. Her eyes widened at the big bruise on his upper arm; the ugly mark must have been caused by the strike of the skillet. She hadn't thought she'd actually hurt him with that abortive blow. The realization was scant recompense for his kidnapping of her, but knowing she'd not given in meekly bolstered her confidence.

Again her gaze was drawn to the burnished skin of his back. By the light of the fire, she could detect a faint tracery of scars there. Had someone once beat him? But who? And why?

Reluctant sympathy rose in her at the thought of the pain he must have suffered, a sympathy at odds with her sense of satisfaction at the unsightly bruise she'd inflicted.

On impulse Kristy took a step toward him. "Where did you get those scars?"

He straightened, wiping the water from his eyes with a towel. A few stray droplets trickled down the furred breadth of his chest to soak into the waistband of his denims. Hastily she yanked her gaze from the front of his pants.

"What did you say?" he asked.

Kristy took a breath to calm the wild beating of her heart. "Those scars on your back . . . I just wondered how you got them."

His eyes hardened to ice, and he threw aside the towel. "You're awfully nosy this morning, aren't you?"

The seed of sympathy inside her shriveled and died. "And you, as usual, are the perfect gentleman." Needing an outlet for her irritation, she marched over to the shelves of provisions and reached blindly for a can. Over her shoulder she exclaimed, "Why don't you put some clothes on? You look indecent."

"Pardon me if I offend you, Lady Donovan." He walked to a chair and began to rummage around in the saddlebags lying there. "Or maybe you're just acting again. Tell me the truth, now—does the sight of a half-naked man get you all hot and bothered?"

She shot him a scathing look and thumped the can onto the table. "Don't flatter yourself."

"I'll be glad to scratch your itch right now, over there." He jerked a thumb toward the rumpled bed.

"I'd sooner wallow in a pen of pigs."

Chad drew a long razor from his saddlebag and began sharpening it on a well-worn strop. "My, you're touchy this morning too. Something put a burr under your saddle?"

The rhythmic scraping of the razor on the leather strop grated on Kristy's already frayed nerves. With each long swipe he made, her fingers clenched on the can, then unclenched. She contemplated the consequences of throwing the can at his face, a face still disgustingly handsome despite two days' growth of beard.

"Not some *thing*—you," she snapped. "You can't hold me here against my will."

"Can't I, Mrs. Donovan?" He smiled darkly, studying her with flinty blue eyes. "I believe I've already proven that I can."

The harsh statement of fact robbed her of defiance. In

bleak silence she watched as he tossed the strop back into one of his saddlebag. Lighting a lantern, he put it on the dry sink. With quick, deft strokes he began to shave the dark stubble from his cheeks.

"By the way," he said, shooting her a glance, "just in case you're contemplating slitting my throat, from now on I'll be storing this razor outside, where you can't get to it."

The notion hadn't even occurred to her, but Kristy wasn't about to add to his ridicule of her by telling him so. Dredging up her lost determination, she wondered how to convince him to release her.

"Why don't you give up this absurd plan for revenge?" she urged. "If you let me go unharmed, I'll convince Parker not to prosecute you."

"No." Chad stopped shaving to study himself in the small mirror. "How do you think I'd look with a moustache?"

The unexpected question took her aback. From her vantage point she could see only the side of him, the carpet of dark hair on his cheek, the muscled strength of his arm. Her gaze moved upward to the black stubble above his lips. Her eyes lingered on his hard mouth as she remembered his kiss.

"You'd still be a damned polecat whether you shave off your stripes or not," she muttered.

As if he hadn't heard, Chad said musingly, "I think I will grow one. Just out of curiosity."

Frustrated and angry, Kristy took a step toward him. "Don't try to change the subject. We were talking about my kidnapping."

He tossed the razor down; it landed in the basin with a plunk. "Wrong," he said, shooting her a glance. "*You* were talking about the kidnapping."

She forced herself to speak calmly when she wanted to rant and rave. "You've already ruined my reputation. Isn't that enough for you?"

Picking up the towel, he dried his face, studying her with steely blue eyes. "I don't give a tinker's damn about your precious reputation, Mrs. Donovan. If I did, I could have simply told everyone what an imposter you really are.''

"But why didn't you? It might have made Parker call off the wedding. He wouldn't get the Bar S without me.''

Chad flung the towel onto the table. ''I told you before, the ranch is only part of it. There's one way and one way alone that I'll let you go back to Parker—and that's with my child planted in your belly.''

His brutal words made her blanch in spite of her prior knowledge of his purpose. What could drive a man to such a sordid vengeance on his own father? Kristy could see how a child could resent a parent; she had experienced similar feelings toward her own mother for abandoning her and Jeremy. But to actually seek such vile retribution was beyond her understanding.

With numb fingers she pulled out a chair and sat down at the table. Slowly she raised her eyes to Chad; he was regarding her with a contempt that somehow haunted her heart.

"Why?'' she murmured, with a bewildered shake of her head. "Why are you doing this?''

"Because Parker put my mother through hell. And now I'm going to pay him back for all her suffering.''

"But he's still your father. How can you hate him so much?''

Hands on his hips, Chad stared at her. Kristy had the odd impression that he wasn't seeing her, that he was wrestling with some inner demon. Abruptly his mouth twisted into a travesty of a smile.

"All right, then, since you're so damned nosy, I'll tell you. Parker McClintock is not my real father.''

Chapter 12

His bitter words caught Kristy by surprise. Trying to absorb the shocking revelation, she frowned up at Chad. "But your last name is McClintock."

He lifted a dark eyebrow in derision. "I wouldn't have thought I'd have to educate a woman like you on the laws of nature. Just because a man is married to your mother doesn't necessarily make him your blood father."

For once Kristy ignored his hurtful slur on her character. "But then, why haven't you or Parker told anyone the truth? Since you two hate each other so much, why would you continue with this farce of father and son?"

"Because I won't see my mother's good name dragged through the dirt. And Parker?" Chad uttered a cold laugh. "Parker never gave a goddamn about her. All he cares about is preserving that monumental pride of his—he doesn't want anyone to know a mere woman once made a fool out of him."

"But surely Parker had a right to be upset if his wife were cuckolding him—"

"They weren't married at the time; they were only engaged."

"Engaged, then," she conceded. "But even so, she should have been faithful to him—"

"You don't even know the whole story and already you're siding with Parker." Chad eyed her with a hostile glare. "I don't know why I expected anything different from you."

He strode to the saddlebags draped over the chair and dug through the contents, jerking out a blue flannel shirt and shoving his arms into the sleeves.

Watching his angry actions, Kristy found herself wondering at the strong love that would prompt a son to avenge his mother. She wouldn't have thought Chad capable of holding any woman in such high regard.

Earnestly she leaned forward. "Why don't you tell me the whole story then. You can't expect me to understand your mother's behavior without knowing all the facts."

Chad looked at her, his eyes a bitter and brooding blue. "Is it facts you really want or lies that'll protect your pretty image of Parker?"

"I want the truth, Chad," she said softly. "Nothing more and nothing less."

He studied her for a moment with that stony gaze before abruptly pivoting to hang the coffee pot over the fire. "All right, I'll tell you."

Turning a chair around, he straddled the seat, arms braced across the back as if he wanted a wall between them. "My mother," he said in a hard-edged voice, "was barely sixteen when she and my grandparents came West on a wagon train. Parker was on that same wagon train and managed to sweet-talk my mother into agreeing to marry him as soon as they reached Colorado. But during the long trip she fell in love with another man who was already married. Being young and foolish, she let the swine use her and got herself pregnant with me."

Chad paused; the only sound was the crackling of the fire. Against her will, Kristy felt a stirring of sympathy for him and for his mother. Despite the ice in his voice, his deep respect for Mavis McClintock warmed Kristy's heart.

"Do you know who your real father is?" she asked.

"All I know is his name. He was a miner, one of thousands who came West seeking a fortune. After I left home, I tried to track him down and found out he was long dead, shot down by a sniper in Virginia City." A muscle tightened in his jaw. "I suspect Parker was behind the killing."

Kristy frowned in disbelief. Her fiancé was no murderer! "Do you have proof of that?"

"No, but a bullet in the back is exactly that coward's style."

She wanted to scoff at his unfounded accusation, but something in his expression warned her to hold her tongue. "So Parker still married your mother, knowing she was to bear another man's child?"

"He didn't know. She was scared and confused, afraid to tell anyone she was pregnant. She went ahead with the wedding only so her baby wouldn't be born a bastard. Parker didn't find out until after I was born seven months after the wedding, and then he was too proud to let anyone know he wasn't my father." His eyes hardened. "But he made my mother pay."

"Don't you think he had a right to be angry?" Kristy ventured.

"He didn't have the right to put her through years of misery," Chad lashed out. "My mother made a mistake she deeply regretted. She begged her husband's forgiveness, but Parker refused to absolve her. Instead he demanded she give him a son of his own blood, even though she suffered miscarriage after miscarriage, even when the doctor warned him she was too frail to withstand all those pregnancies."

"Honey was their only surviving child?"

With a curt nod, Chad rose to pour two cups of coffee, silently handing one to Kristy before sitting down again. "My mother spent most of my childhood in bed, either suffering from a hard pregnancy or recovering from yet another miscarriage. On the rare occasions when she did feel strong, she'd visit her parents at the Bar S. I spent a lot of time at the Bar S too—I suppose we both liked a few hours of freedom from Parker."

Kristy studied Chad over the rim of her coffee cup. "So Parker was the reason you ran away from home?"

He nodded. "I was fifteen when I overheard an argument between him and my mother and learned he wasn't my real father. At last I understood why he'd always hated me. I realized what a damned fool I'd been to dream that someday he might change his mind and love me the way a father should love his only son. When he came out of my mother's bedroom that day, I shot him. And then I left for good."

His cold and remorseless recitation sent an arrow of horror through Kristy. "You *shot* Parker?"

"Yes, and it's a goddamned shame I was too angry to aim well. The bullet I intended for his black heart hit his leg instead." Chad's mouth twisted into a smile as wintry as the winds whipping outside the cabin. "The only bright spot about meeting that son of a bitch again after so many years was seeing him walk with a limp. Every step he takes is a reminder of how much I despise him."

Kristy curled her hands around the coffee cup, seeking warmth against the ice of Chad's hatred. She could scarcely believe a gentleman like Parker could be so cruel to his wife and to the boy he had acknowledged to the world as his son. Yet the conviction in Chad's voice told her he believed every word he said. How much was truth and how much was the interpretation of a young, hurting child?

A curious pain lurked in her heart at the thought of Chad as a boy longing for a father's attention. What an unhappy youth he must have had, seeing his mother ill treated and receiving no love from the man he called father.

Was she wrong about Parker? Was he as much the villain as Chad?

A sick sensation assailed her as she realized the true purpose behind this kidnapping. "And now," she said slowly, "you want the ultimate revenge by forcing Parker to accept another bastard child—your child."

"If he wants the Bar S so damned bad, that's exactly what he'll have to do to get it."

His words were like the sting of an ice storm. Chad was driven by a hatred more chilling than she'd feared, and Kristy despaired of ever convincing him to release her. But she had to try.

"Your plan for revenge makes you no better a man than you claim Parker is," she pointed out. "You're quick to condemn him for making Mavis suffer, yet you're doing very much the same thing to me."

Chad felt his nerves stretch taut with bitter irritation. Why did Kristy Donovan have the power to make him feel guilty about his perfectly justifiable plan? She sat there at the table so prim and self-righteous, her mahogany hair charmingly tousled from sleep, her guileless green eyes full of accusation.

An accusation that made him feel like the lowest snake hibernating beneath the winter blanket of snow.

He resented the prick of his conscience. Yes, he was using her, but his cause was worthy. He was acting according to his own stringent code of ethics, meting out justice that couldn't be gained in a court of law. Then why did he suddenly feel ashamed for seeking a retribution that would avenge his mother's suffering?

"You have a way of twisting things around to suit your own selfish wants," he snapped. "For one thing, you already owe me a night in your bed. I aim to collect that debt, plus interest."

"I don't owe anything to a cheat like you."

"For another," he went on as if she hadn't spoken, "you're hardly innocent. You're engaged to one of the most ruthless men in the state. If you want to align yourself with a son of a bitch like Parker, you'll have to accept the consequences."

"That doesn't give you license to rape me."

The quiet statement struck a raw nerve, and Chad slammed his coffee cup onto the table in frustration. If only she had responded like the whore she was, they wouldn't be having this pointless conversation. They'd be in bed right now, and he'd be sating the hunger gnawing at his loins.

He surged to his feet, the chair legs scraping the floor. "You listen to me, Kristy, and listen good. Parker killed my mother as surely as if he'd put a gun to her head, and I'm going to make damned certain he pays."

"Fine. Just don't use me as your means of revenge."

"I wouldn't have thought you'd mind being used," Chad taunted. "You're perfectly willing to let Parker use you to give him a son."

"Parker intends to marry me first."

His lips crooked into a chilling smile. "Then it's the money, isn't it? You don't mind a man using you so long as you have a legal claim to his wealth."

Kristy subdued a twinge of guilt. Yes, she *was* marrying

for money, but she wasn't a fortune hunter as Chad implied.

"Parker is offering Jeremy and me a secure future. As soon as we're married, he's going to turn the Bar S into one of the finest ranches in Colorado. And it'll all be Jeremy's one day."

Chad let out a hoot of derisive laughter. "Don't try to tell me you're naive enough to believe Parker's promises! Your brother's just a convenient front for your own greed."

"I'm not surprised you don't understand the importance of family ties," she said scathingly. "You're just a no-good drifter. You never even found the time to visit your own mother and sister all those years."

His face hardened to stone. "And what do you call a woman who sells herself to the highest bidder? Tell me, Mrs. Donovan, would you surrender your body to me if I paid you for the privilege?"

The insult struck her like a slap in the face. Even as her cheeks paled, she held her head high with dignity, unwilling to let him see how much his words had hurt. "If you could offer me all the money in the world, it wouldn't be enough."

There was an instant of silence. Chad's eyes narrowed to chips of ice, and Kristy feared she might have pushed him too far. What protection did she have against his wrath?

Her heart thudded frantically as he prowled toward her like a mountain lion moving in for the kill. Stopping beside her, he lightly ran his fingertips down her cheek, and despite her animosity, the caress made her feel shivery and warm inside.

"Then it's a good thing your price doesn't matter," he said in a steel-edged undertone, "because I don't intend to pay you one red cent for the use of your sweet little body."

She flinched from his touch, her insides tortured by a curious combination of dread and desire. How could she feel anything but disgust for a man who believed her a slut?

Yet the sensation of his calloused fingers lingered on

her skin, and his subtle scent of leather and horses surrounded her. Her eyes were on a level with the front of his pants and she flushed, jerking her gaze up to the harsh contempt on his face.

"You're digging your own grave," she said in a low voice. "I warn you, Parker will kill you for this."

"Your concern for my welfare is touching."

Pivoting sharply, he strode over to the bed to pull on his boots. He donned his coat and hat and then retrieved the razor from the dry sink before leaving the cabin.

The sound of the bar thudding into place outside brought a rush of bleak discouragement to Kristy's soul. Propping her elbows on the table, she buried her face in her hands. Now what was she to do? She had failed miserably in her attempt to appeal to his sense of decency; Chad McClintock clearly had no scruples.

At least now she understood what was driving him. If she could believe even a portion of his accusations toward Parker, no wonder the two of them despised each other so.

And she was the pawn caught smack in the middle of their hatred. Why did this have to happen when she'd been so close to realizing her dream for the future? Even if she were to escape, she wasn't sure if she could still wed Parker, knowing how he'd treated his first wife.

Pushing aside her doubts, Kristy stared at the frolicking flames of the fire. Somehow she must find a way to flee before Chad raped her. But how? The situation seemed hopeless. Even if she found something to use as a weapon, her success in overcoming him was doubtful; now that she'd tried to flee twice, he would be doubly on guard against further attempts.

A sudden rhythmic chopping sound came from outside the cabin. Chad must be cutting firewood. Her mind filled with an image of him at work: his coat and hat discarded as his body warmed with physical exertion, his big hands easily gripping the axe handle, the strong muscles of his back bunching beneath his shirt with each swing, his face gleaming with a sheen of sweat, the black silk of his hair tousled by the frigid breeze.

Thunk. Thunk.

Each strike of the axe seemed to vibrate through her body. Against her will she found herself recalling the taste of his lips, the touch of his hands. What was this fatal flaw in herself that made her long for a man who would use a woman so vilely?

Kristy sat straight up in the chair. Perhaps a weakness could be turned into a strength . . . perhaps desire could be used as a weapon. Chad believed her to be a woman of easy virtue. What if she convinced him she'd thought things over and decided the most sensible course of action was to submit to him?

Then, while he was distracted by passion, she would make her move.

She drew in a deep, doubting breath. Could she pull off the plan? She knew little of what pleased a man. In her youth she had observed a few riverfront sluts plying their trade. She could sway her hips, flirt a little, flutter her lashes. But would he see past her amateur efforts and guess at her true purpose?

Despite the risk, she had no choice but to grasp at what might well be her last opportunity to escape.

Thunk. Thunk.

Chad wouldn't remain outside cutting wood all day. And while he was gone, she must begin her preparations.

Kristy leapt up and took a quick survey of the larder. All Chad had had that morning was strong coffee, so when he came back inside he'd be hungry and ornery. The first step in mellowing his mood would be to fill his belly.

Then she'd have to satisfy his other hungers.

Her heart fluttered. How would she go about seducing him? Kiss him first. Then what? Pray God he'd take over from there.

Quickly she mixed up a batch of biscuits, sprinkling flour on the table before kneading the dough. After wiping her floury hands on a towel, she ground beans for a fresh pot of coffee. She wanted to fry some salt pork, but there was no knife to cut strips off the slab; that task would have to wait until Chad returned.

Thunk. Thunk.

The sound of the axe splitting wood was a persistent reminder that time was wasting. Glancing up, she caught

a glimpse of herself in the mirror over the dry sink. Her
eyes were big and round, and her hair curled wildly around
the pale oval of her face. Merciful heavens, how was she
to seduce a man when she looked such a fright?

Breakfast preparations were forgotten as she hurried
through her morning ritual of washing up and tidying herself. Assessing the sadly wrinkled state of her lavender
gown, she remembered the chest at the foot of the bed. If
she were to play the slut, why not dress like one?

She opened the lid, staring at the treasure trove of jewel-
toned garments. Disgust knotted her stomach at the notion
of wearing such immodest apparel. What a contrast this
clothing was to the demure wedding dress she was to have
worn in a few days. Only the urgency of her purpose could
induce Kristy to grit her teeth and strip off her gown.

Thunk. Thunk.

The thought of Chad working right outside the cabin
lent speed to her fingers. At random she selected a chemise
of turquoise satin trimmed with a froth of black lace. She
donned matching drawers and petticoats before stepping
into a gown of a periwinkle blue, the most demure of the
three gowns in the chest.

If, she thought darkly, standing on tiptoe to view herself
in the minuscule mirror, "demure" could even be used to
describe a bodice cut so low and tight her breasts seemed
in imminent danger of spilling free of their mooring.

She looked bold and brazen; she felt nervous and naive.

Soon Chad would finish his work and walk back inside
the cabin. Could she play the courtesan convincingly?
Could she make him believe she'd really changed her
mind?

She must.

Taking a deep breath for courage, Kristy busied her
shaky fingers by putting some dried beans to soak for supper. If all went well, she didn't plan to be around long
enough to cook that meal, but the preparation would help
foster the illusion that she was resigned to staying here at
the cabin.

She was standing at the table, pouring a dipperful of
water into the cast-iron pot of beans, when she realized

something was different. Her heart leapt and her palms dampened.

All she could hear was the hiss of the fire; the sound of the axe had ceased.

Chad wiped his brow on his shirtsleeve and balefully surveyed the tidy stack of firewood piled in the snow beside the cabin. All that time to think, and still he'd failed to resolve the problem badgering his brain. He wanted Kristy. She didn't want him. He wanted to pay Parker back by getting her pregnant. She didn't want to be his means of payment.

He leaned on the axe handle and looked up at the ashen sky. Sometime during the night the storm had ended, leaving the stark monoliths of the mountains looming over a frosted forest of trees, branches bowed beneath the snow. The air was keen and pure, and he took in a deep breath, half hoping to cleanse his mind and see an easy solution.

It didn't work; he still felt as confused as ever.

Rape was out of the question. He had never taken a woman by force, and the thought of defiling even that tramp Kristy by violent coercion made him feel ashamed.

So what the hell was he going to do with her?

He hadn't the vaguest notion.

A gust of chill wind ruffled his hair, turning his sweat-dampened shirt to ice. Yet still Chad lingered, reluctant to reenter the charged atmosphere of the cabin, unwilling to face the accusation in Kristy's eyes.

Instead, he thought about how sweet and small she'd looked last night, curled up like a child in the rocking chair, fast asleep. He'd told himself he didn't give a damn if she woke in the morning feeling cramped and stiff. Yet some irresistible impulse made him draw her gently into his arms and carry her to the bed.

Desire quickened his cold body as he recalled the feel of her womanly curves, pliant with slumber, and the way she'd murmured his name and nestled her head against his shoulder. Taking care not to awaken her, he'd removed her gown and shoes and then tucked her beneath the quilt. Only as an afterthought had he loosely tied her wrists together. As it turned out, he was damned lucky to have taken that precaution; otherwise Kristy might have moved quietly enough to succeed in stealing his gun.

Would she have killed him?

She had said no, but Chad doubted her denial. Why should she spare the life of the man who'd abducted her and then threatened to rape her?

His lips curled into a humorless smile. Maybe he should have let her go on thinking he'd made love to her in her sleep last night. Maybe then she would have surrendered the battle.

A blast of arctic wind made him shiver. Chad collected his coat and hat from the ground and brushed off the clinging crystals of snow. After donning the coat and hat, he lifted his face to the leaden sky, cursing the inborn weakness that made him wonder if he were misjudging her.

But Chad couldn't let her go, not yet. He couldn't abandon the violent need for vengeance that ate like acid at his gut.

Somehow he had to find a way to bend her will to his. Perhaps by courting her a bit he could soothe her vanity and salve her pride. Given time, she would come to realize the expediency of joining forces with him. At least he hoped to God she would.

After unbarring the door, Chad picked up an armload of wood and entered the cabin. Kristy was standing at the dry sink, her back to him. She turned to face him, a can of tomatoes in one hand, opener in the other.

"Hello," she said breathlessly, her mouth curving into a tentative half smile. "I'm glad you came back in. Could you please show me how to do this?"

He didn't answer. He couldn't answer. He was too preoccupied with staring at her. The periwinkle blue gown accented her womanly shape to perfection: the curve of her hips, the narrowness of her waist, the fullness of her breasts. His gaze lingered on the lavish display revealed by the low-cut bodice. He'd meant to humble her with clothing fit for a whore, yet somehow Kristy managed to look as pure as a newly blooming columbine.

She shivered, and for an instant he thought she was scared of him, of the lust that must be rampant in his eyes.

Then he realized the door was still open, letting in gusts of frigid air. And there he stood, gaping like a dolt.

"Hang on a minute," he said curtly.

He stomped the snow off his boots and strode across the cabin to dump the split wood beside the fireplace before turning back to close the door. Pivoting sharply, he walked toward her, shedding his coat and hat without taking his hungry gaze from her. God, she looked good. How in holy hell was he supposed to keep his hands off that beautiful body?

"Give me that," he growled, snatching the can and opener from her. Instantly Chad regretted his brusqueness; it was no way to win her over.

"I've never used anything out of a can like this," she said, watching closely as he demonstrated how to operate the gadget.

"Out on the range we call it an airtight."

"An airtight then. I've never had occasion to cook with store-bought tomatoes because I've always canned my own."

He looked at her askance. Why was she chattering as if they were friends? And Kristy Donovan doing her own canning? Somehow he couldn't picture her sweating over a hot stove. Matter of fact, with the way she was leaning over his arm, he couldn't think about anything but the generous mounds of breasts. Breasts that he knew fit his palms to perfection.

Annoyance resurfaced in him. "I thought all ladies did was sit around and gossip."

Kristy tilted her head up, snaring him with her eyes. "But we both know I haven't always been a lady," she said with calm dignity. "I grew up quite poor."

"Oh."

Chad was taken aback by her confession. Of course he'd known all along she'd risen from the gutter, but this was the first time she had ever come right out and admitted it to him. Something inside him softened, and he crushed the weakness.

You goddamned fool, he told himself. She's just trying to get you to feel sorry for her so you'll let her go.

"Here," he said tersely, handing her the opened can.

"Thank you." She began to walk away, then swiveled back around. "Oh, by the way . . . I hope I wasn't being presumptuous in borrowing some of the clothes from the chest over there. I figured you meant them for me."

Almost anxiously she fingered the neckline of her gown, drawing his eyes to the expanse of rounded flesh there. Her breasts were as tempting as ripe peaches waiting to be plucked. Desire consumed him as he wondered which of the provocative undergarments she was wearing beneath the gown.

Was Kristy deliberately trying to entice him? No, that was absurd; instead of using his brain, he was thinking with the stiff rod inside his pants. He hoped to God she couldn't tell how easily she aroused him. A woman could wind a man around her little finger with knowledge like that.

"Of course the clothes are for you. Who the hell else is going to wear them?"

The words came out gruffer than he'd meant. Angry with himself, Chad strode to the hearth and threw another log onto the fire. Sparks showered and the flames leapt higher, greedily consuming the wood. Smoke wafted up the chimney, but in his mind he could smell only the haunting peachy fragrance of her skin.

"Could I trouble you to do something else for me?"

Swinging around, he saw Kristy nervously pleating the folds of her skirt between her fingers. *You scared her again, you stupid ass. Why can't you keep a lid on that temper of yours?*

He forced himself to speak mildly. "What is it?"

"Would you mind cutting some salt pork for our breakfast? I didn't have a knife or I'd have done it myself."

For the first time Chad noticed the meal preparations, the flour smudges on the table, the biscuit dough ready to be rolled, the beans soaking in a cast iron pot. Of course, why else would she ask him to open the tomatoes? He wasn't normally so unobservant . . . He wasn't normally so wracked by unslakeable desire either.

He swallowed a cynical remark about dirtying her ladylike hands in such domestic activity, muttering instead, "Sure."

He found the slab of salt pork in the larder and crouched down to unwrap the burlap surrounding the meat. Drawing the knife from the scabbard strapped to the outside of his boot, he sliced a few strips and trimmed the rind. When he got up, he saw Kristy waiting behind him with the skillet.

Her eyes were alight with mischief. "Don't worry," she teased. "I won't try to hit you with it this time."

The sight of her sweetly smiling mouth sent a curl of warmth through him, and without thinking he smiled back. "A wise move," he said, tossing the salt pork into the skillet. "I get especially mean when I'm hungry."

"Then I'll just have to be extra nice to you, won't I?"

She waltzed away with the frying pan, and Chad stared after her, mesmerized by the sway of her hips. She was actually flirting with him. He could hardly believe it, when just an hour ago she'd been a spitting hellcat. What had brought about the abrupt change in her? Dared he hope she might already have reconsidered her position and decided to submit to him?

Heat flared inside him, but suspicion dampened the blaze. Maybe this was just another of her tricks. Maybe she was planning to catch him off guard.

Washing the grease from his hands, he moodily watched Kristy's graceful movements as she rolled and cut the dough for biscuits and placed them in a round pan. When the pan was full, she put it into the Dutch oven, which she hung from a pothook over the fire. It was an incongruous sight to see her engaged in such a housewifely task while wearing a dress suited to a dance-hall girl.

She emptied the tomatoes into a pot and added some spices. Then she knelt down to turn the skillet around on the trivet beside the burning logs so the pork would brown evenly. The meat sizzled and spat, wafting a succulent aroma throughout the cabin.

She glanced up at him. "Breakfast won't be ready for a little while yet. Would you like some coffee?"

"Thanks. I'd be obliged."

She poured a cup and brought it to him. In handing him the coffee, their fingers touched, and her eyes widened to a deep and jeweled jade. Chad stared at her, his blood pumping hotly. Her cheeks were flushed from the heat of the fire, and her lips were parted slightly. If he leaned forward a little, he could indulge himself in tasting that ripe cherry mouth.

Maybe the time had come to call her bluff.

Chapter 13

Chad set the cup on the table, and his hand swallowed hers, his thumb stroking her delicate wrist. "I can think of a better way to pass the time than drinking coffee."

"What . . . oh." The blush on her face deepened, and for a split second her eyes looked wild, almost panicky. Then her lips formed a smile that managed to be both naughty and naive. "But if I don't tend to breakfast, it'll burn."

"So take it off the fire."

"It'll be ruined for sure then. And I . . . I'm hungry. Aren't you?"

"Starved," he agreed huskily. "However, my most pressing need isn't for food."

She ducked her head shyly and then looked up at him, her mouth still wearing that sultry, saintly smile. "But some things are worth waiting for," she murmured. "Don't you agree?"

Chad told himself he ought to simply toss her onto the bed and relieve the throbbing pressure in his loins. Was she playing a game or not? He wasn't sure, and he hated himself for falling victim to her artful innocence. Grudgingly he relented. "I suppose we can satisfy our other needs later."

"You won't be sorry. I promise you it'll be well worth the wait."

Kristy drew her hand free and scurried back to the fire. Her heart was beating wildly, and she wondered if Chad could sense her tension. She hated acting the harlot.

Angrily she stabbed the cooking meat with a fork, and the fat sputtered. She despised the way he made her feel inside, all shivery and liquid and warm. The caress of his thumb lingered on her wrist like the touch of a phantom. Why couldn't she control her bodily response to him? She was supposed to be seducing him, not vice versa. Damn Chad McClintock to hell for forcing her into this humiliating situation!

Only a sobering thought brought her runaway temper to heel. She would ruin her chance to escape if she let her emotions goad her into revealing her true thoughts. As Lydia always said, you could catch more flies with honey than with vinegar. It was true; already Chad was falling into her trap.

Using an iron gouch hook, Kristy lifted the hot lid from the Dutch oven to find the biscuits brown within. She took the pot off the fire and set to work making gravy in the meat drippings. Chad had seated himself at the table, and she felt his eyes following her every movement. Only by force of willpower could she keep her hands steady and her mind focused on the role she was playing.

When the meal was ready, she heaped two plates with biscuits and gravy, meat, and stewed tomatoes and put them on the table.

"I hope I didn't burn anything," she said, refilling Chad's coffee cup before sitting down opposite him.

"It's fine." He ate a biscuit, eyeing her in curiosity. "There's an art to cooking over an open fire instead of on a stove. Where'd you learn that?"

Kristy hated speaking of her past, reluctant to give Chad more ammunition for ridicule, yet she couldn't be rude when she was supposed to be playing up to him. "As I said, I grew up poor. A lot of the places where we lived didn't have a cookstove, so I learned how to make do with a fire."

"Didn't your mother do any of the cooking?"

"My mother left when I was seven."

He gave her an inscrutable look. "Left?"

Kristy toyed with her stewed tomatoes, her stomach in knots. Why couldn't he just keep quiet and eat? "My mother deserted us not long after Jeremy was born." Unable to stop herself, she added bitterly, "I suppose it satisfies you to know you were right, that my background hardly qualifies me to be a lady.''

''The only satisfaction I care about,'' he said meaningfully, ''is having you in my bed, just as you promised me back in Denver. And I want a woman there with me, not some prim and proper lady.''

In the soft firelight his eyes smoldered with sensual promise. Kristy felt warm color surge to her cheeks at the notion of lying naked with him in bed. Some secret part of her ached to share that experience with Chad, to see if the intimacies between a man and a woman could be as pleasurable as Lydia had told her they were. Why did she feel so drawn to him?

She tried to concentrate on eating her breakfast, but her eyes strayed irresistibly to Chad, who was steadily working his way through the substantial amount of food on his plate. Watching his hand grip the fork, she thought about his fingers touching her breasts. Watching him put a bite of meat into his mouth, she thought about his lips tasting her skin.

Her blush deepened. She wanted to flee from him, yet she also wanted to stay. Why was she having lewd fantasies about a man she despised?

Concentrate on escape, she told herself sternly. Work out all the details of your plan so nothing goes wrong this time.

''Is it still snowing?'' she asked in a conversational tone.

Chad swallowed a bite of biscuit and shook his head. ''It's stopped—for the moment, anyway.''

That was encouraging news; fair weather would make traveling easier. ''Do you think we'll get another blizzard anytime soon?''

He eyed her suspiciously over the rim of his coffee cup. ''Why should you care one way or the other?''

''I just wondered,'' she said hastily. ''You see, I . . . I was thinking how warm and cozy it would be to lie in bed and listen to the sound of the wind outside.'' She lowered her voice to a sultry murmur. ''Wouldn't you like that, Chad?''

''Yes, but we aren't waiting to make love until there's a storm outside.'' Setting down his cup, he pushed back his chair. "Not when we can create our own storm, right here and now."

Sudden panic chilled her blood as he rounded the table, his blue eyes glittering purposefully in the firelight. This was happening too fast; she had intended to be the one in control.

"I haven't finished eating yet," she protested.

"In a few minutes I promise you won't be thinking about food."

"But the dishes—"

"Can wait," he said, drawing her up against his lean length. "I can't."

He bent his head and captured her lips in a burning kiss that buried her alarm beneath an avalanche of longing. Her fingers clutched tightly at his shirt, and her heart gave a wild leap. She loved the feel of his arms around her, the pressure of his hard chest against her breasts, the stroking of his hands over the bare skin of her shoulders. And, oh, his mouth. He tasted of coffee and heat, and she melted beneath the insistent seduction of his tongue, parting her lips, urging her to invite him inside. The stubble of his moustache deliciously abraded her skin.

In a daze of desire Kristy wondered why she'd protested. This was what she'd planned, to ensnare him with passion so he would forget all caution. Then when he let down his guard she would make her move. All she had to do was keep her wits about her and control the aberrant fire glowing deep within her belly. A tiny cauldron of anger simmered inside her. She could douse the flames of passion at any time with the mere thought of his callous purpose of revenge.

With cool deliberation she slid her palms over the firm contours of his shoulders and up the strong column of his neck, threading her fingers into the thickness of his hair. She would do whatever was necessary to convince him she was his willing bedmate. With instinct as her guide, she touched her tongue to his and was rewarded by a growl deep in his throat. Her heart surged with a sense of power. The pressure of his mouth increased, setting her blood ablaze despite her better intentions.

His fingers followed her feminine shape down to her

bottom, fusing their hips together in a slow, erotic rhythm that spread heat throughout her body. One hand moved back up to work at the buttons of her gown. All too soon he uttered a sound of impatience against her lips and yanked the gown from her shoulders. The tissue-thin silk ripped softly, leaving only her chemise to shield her upper body from nakedness.

His hand came between them to cradle one tender, yielding breast. When his thumb stroked across the tip, she felt a sweet tightening inside her that scorched downward to the place between her legs, destroying her ability to think. His mouth left hers to kiss a path down to her throat, slipping lower still to ensnare the peak of her breast in moist, arousing heat.

She heard a gasp and then realized the soft, shaken sound had emerged from her own lips. Her hands clung to the breadth of his shoulders for support as he suckled her breast through the filmsy silk of her chemise. All of her seemed focused on that one pleasure-filled place, and she thought nothing in the world could ever feel better—until he jerked down the lace-edged chemise and applied his mouth to her bare nipple.

She arched her back to offer more of herself. His lips were hot and devouring on her willing flesh. Then in one abrupt motion he straightened and swung her up into his arms.

Her head swam dizzily, and Kristy opened her eyes to find him carrying her across the cabin. She struggled for sanity and found a fast-budding alarm. "What are you doing?"

Chad looked down at her, his eyes glowing a deep, dark blue. "I'm taking you to bed. I don't want to make love standing up . . . at least not this first time."

She wanted to tell him he could do whatever he wanted to her wherever he wanted. But the bitter reality of his purpose came crashing back to her. No love existed in what he meant to do; she was only a receptacle for his vengeful lust.

"Wait," she protested as he was lowering her to the bed.

His dark brows descended in a dangerous frown. "If this is another of your tricks—"

"Why would I trick you?" Hastily she stood, forcing a flirtatious smile onto her lips. "I just want to undress you before we lie down. Surely you wouldn't object to my touching you . . . ?"

"Hell, no," he breathed. "Do whatever you want."

Chad felt a rush of heat as she reached for the buttons of his shirt. God, she excited him. He couldn't remember ever wanting a woman with such violent desire. His heart drummed hard and fast with the knowledge that Kristy wanted him too. He felt her fingers trembling as she undid his shirt, watched her bare breasts rise and fall with each quickened breath, saw her nipples pucker like tiny rosebuds. Her passion, at least, was no lie.

His fingers kneaded the smooth, naked shoulders beneath the luxuriant tumble of her hair. The freckles strewn across the bridge of her nose gave her the appearance of innocence. His attention returned to the voluptuous glory of her breasts. The black lace edging of her turquoise chemise was tucked beneath the generous swells of flesh. In his wildest dreams he hadn't thought a woman could appear so pure, yet so erotic. Even in whore's clothing she managed to look like an angel.

A fallen angel, he reminded himself, tightening his hands on her fragile skin. He would enjoy her until he'd accomplished his mission of getting her pregnant, and then he would take great satisfaction in sending her back to Parker. Those two were well matched: a bitch and a son of a bitch.

Yet somehow the derogatory description of Kristy no longer rang true, and Chad found himself yearning to believe she was no liar, that only bitter circumstances had forced her into Parker's arms.

Then all rational thought fled his mind as Kristy put her hand inside his opened shirt to caress his bare skin. She glanced up at him almost hesitantly, her eyes large and expressive in the fireglow. She leaned forward to press her lips to his chest.

The simple gesture set him on fire, the blaze stoked by the feel of her fingers tracing the leanness of his waist.

God Almighty, when would she reach for the hot, hard center of his passion? Any other woman would have had his pants unbuttoned by now. Instead Kristy continued to tease without mercy, provoking his passion with butterfly caresses that were somehow both carnal and chaste.

With a tortured groan he kissed her again, a deeply intimate kiss, making love to her with his mouth. The urge was fierce in him to toss her down on the bed and take her without further love play, but that impulse was overruled by a stronger need to linger and ensure her pleasure. For the moment he settled for stroking his aching loins against the ripe curve of her hips.

He felt her small body tremble in response. A storm of powerful emotion swept over him, and he was too lost in the taste and touch and scent of her to put a name to those unfamiliar feelings. All he knew was a need to make himself one with this woman, a need so great it was fast becoming a physical pain.

Tenderly he cupped her head, moving his mouth over the fragile curve of her cheek. Closing his eyes, he savored the peachy fragrance of her skin. He found the fullness of her breast with his hand, his thumb plying the taut nipple until she moaned into his throat, her breath coming fast and hot. Ah, yes, she was ripe for him. As ripe and ready as he was. In just a few more moments he could sink into her sleek, silken warmth—

Abruptly she wrenched herself from his embrace. Chad's eyes snapped open to see the barrel of his Colt aimed at his heart.

For an instant he could only stare in disbelief at her heaving naked breasts and beautifully tumbled hair. Then rage flamed inside him, as hot as the passion still knotting his loins, a fury directed as much at himself as at her. How in holy hell had she drawn the gun from the holster without him noticing? What a prize fool he was to fall for another of Kristy Donovan's tricks!

Blinded by wrath, he made a menacing move toward her. "What the hell do you think—"

"Hold it right there, cowboy!"

Chad froze at the audible click of the hammer being cocked.

"You make one wrong move," she said in a tight, tremulous tone, "and I swear before God and the devil I'll kill you."

Though the gun shook slightly in Kristy's hands, the wild look in her eyes told him she meant every word. A return of cool reason reduced the heat of his anger to a banked fire. Nothing was more dangerous than a greenhorn with a loaded gun.

"Easy, now," he said, keeping his voice low and soothing, his palms open to her. "I'm not going to try anything."

"Damned right you're not. I want you to drop your other gun to the floor. Use two fingers only, please. And don't move too fast or I just might get nervous and pull the trigger."

"Whatever you say."

Chad reached slowly for the holstered Colt, his eyes trained on Kristy's lovely flushed face. He was confident he could draw and fire before she'd even realize what was happening, yet the thought of spilling her blood sickened him.

He gritted his teeth and dropped the gun; it thudded onto the rough-planked floor.

"Now kick it under the bed," she ordered.

He complied, hating himself for being so weak, hating her for looking so damnably desirable. Even now, he couldn't stop his eyes from straying to the beauty of her naked breasts, to the rumpled allure of mahogany brown hair cascading over her shoulders, to the shapely curve of hips half-hidden by her torn gown. He looked back at her delicate face. Murder blazed in those gorgeous eyes, and he cursed his carelessness in falling into her trap.

"I want you to walk over to the table and sit down," she said. "Nice and slow."

As he seated himself in the chair she'd indicated with a wave of the gun barrel, Chad clenched his fingers into fists, keeping his fury under firm control. "Your wish is obviously my command, Mrs. Donovan."

She backed toward the larder, keeping the gun trained on him. Finding a length of rope, she tossed it to him, the same rope he'd used to bind her hands to the saddle. "Tie your ankles together."

"My, this is getting interesting," he drawled with dark humor. "If you're so anxious to have your way with me, there's no need to tie me up to get me to cooperate."

She blinked at him as if confused, then the rosiness of her cheeks deepened. "Just keep quiet and do as I say."

Her show of naiveté spurred his anger. Why did Kristy persist in that virginal charade when she already had the upper hand?

"Pardon me for not knowing the proper way to act," he snapped, bending forward to loop the rope around his ankles. "This is the first time a half-naked woman has ever pulled a gun on me."

He darted her a glance just in time to see the Colt waver in her hands as she looked down at herself. Blushing furiously, she removed a hand from the weapon to yank her chemise back into place. She tried to pull up the gown too, but the ripped bodice wouldn't stay put.

"Look your fill, you slimy crow bait," she spat. "In another five minutes I'll be out the door. And all you'll have to keep you company are your crude manners."

He *was* guilty of staring. Her full breasts pressed against the filmy chemise of black lace and turquoise silk. In spite of his fury, Chad felt himself throb with renewed desire.

"You sure as hell didn't think I was crude a few minutes ago," he taunted, jerking the rope into a loose knot. "You were ready to give me whatever I wanted."

"That's a lie!"

"Is it, now? If you hadn't stolen my gun, I would have used you like the whore you are. And you would have loved every minute of it."

Kristy felt the color fade from her face as the insult struck home. Hurt and shaken, she remembered all too well her passionate response to him. Only the thought of his foul plan for revenge had given her the willpower to put an end to the seduction. Even now the unsettling sight of his bare chest threatened to make her forget her resolve.

Though the Colt was far heavier than her lost derringer, she managed to hold the weapon steady. "But I did get the gun, didn't I?" she said coolly. "Which proves I must not have enjoyed your lovemaking as much as you'd like to think. All that talk about forgetting everything but you was just bragging.''

His eyes glittered like blue ice. ''You lying bitch. You and Parker are a better match than I thought.''

''That's good, because he's going to be my husband—not that your opinion matters in the least.''

''You hope. Do you think he'll still marry you after I tell him I had you first?''

She lifted her chin scornfully. ''And you have the nerve to call *me* a liar? Anyway, you won't be telling Parker a thing, since you'll be stuck here in this cabin.''

Despite her bravado, her heart squeezed painfully tight. What would happen to her and Jeremy if Parker did, indeed, call off the wedding? Unless she could come up with the money to run the Bar S, they'd be forced to sell their first real home.

Burying her emotional turmoil beneath thoughts of escape, Kristy backed toward the larder, keeping the gun trained on Chad. His ankles might be secured, but she didn't trust him an inch. She felt behind a pile of cans for the cord she'd hidden earlier; the string had bound the neck of a sack of beans.

''Put your hands behind the chair,'' she commanded.

When he obeyed, she crouched behind him, cord in hand. To enable her to secure his wrists, she eased down the hammer of the Colt and set the gun on the floor.

Abruptly Chad twisted, making a lunge for the weapon. The chair crashed to the floor between them, on top of the Colt. With a choked cry Kristy grabbed for the gun, her hand colliding with Chad's.

Somehow her fingers managed to close around the ivory butt. Acting on instinct, she hurled the gun across the floor to the hearth, out of his reach. She flung herself after the weapon and got there first, since his tied ankles impeded his movements.

Snatching up the Colt, she spun around, cocking the hammer. Chad was reaching beneath his pant leg for the knife secured to his boot. The knife she'd completely forgotten about.

"Drop it," she gasped out, and squeezed off a wild shot that smashed into the log wall behind him.

He dropped the knife with a clatter. "For Christ's sake, be careful with that gun!"

"Don't tell me what to do, you bastard! Now get back in that chair!"

His eyes gleamed with murder as he righted the chair and sat down. Kristy approached him cautiously, her heart still pitching furiously against her ribs. This time she crouched down and laid the gun on her knees, poking the barrel through the slats of the chair and into his back while she quickly wound the cord around his wrists.

His hands were big and rough with callouses, and she couldn't help remembering how wonderful they'd felt on her skin. Angry at herself, she yanked a knot in the cord, leaving it loose so that he might eventually work himself free. Chad McClintock deserved to die, but somehow she couldn't bear the thought of killing him herself.

Satisfied he was secure for the moment, Kristy walked over to the dry sink and put down the Colt while she swiftly gathered a small sack of food.

"You're really going to leave me here to freeze to death?" Chad said.

She turned and gave him a scathing look. "You won't freeze. You're too cold-blooded."

His jaw tightened. "Damn it, Kristy, this is no time to play games. It'll be cold as hell in here when the fire dies down."

"Then a devil like you should feel right at home." Kristy fought back a surge of concern; he was only trying to make her feel sorry for him so she'd let him go. "However, I suppose I could put another log on the fire."

"Don't strain yourself on my behalf."

"It's the least I can do. Unlike you, I do have a heart." Depositing her supplies by the door, she went to the hearth and built up the blaze. The flames shot up, heating the small cabin. "There," she said, "that should warm your miserable hide for a while."

"Thanks," he muttered sardonically. "I don't suppose I could trouble you to button my shirt too."

Her gaze dipped to the dark pelt of hair on his chest, and her heart skipped a beat. The last thing she wanted was to touch Chad again. Yet how could she leave him exposed to the wintry weather?

Slowly she walked toward him, Colt in hand. Laying the gun on the table within easy reach, beside the cold remains of their breakfast, she extended her hands to the buttons of his blue flannel shirt. Starting near the collar, she matched a button and a hole. The task required her to lean close . . . too close. His scent beckoned her with a blend of leather and horses and honest sweat. She could almost taste the salty tang of his skin, feel the carved strength of his muscles beneath her fingers.

Her hands brushed against the springy silk of his chest hair; the contact startled her, and she glanced up at his face. That was a mistake. His eyes glinted with a dark desire that made the breath catch in her throat.

"It's not too late," he murmured. "You can still untie me, and I'll forget this ever happened."

"Don't be absurd." She felt an unreasonable urge to run a finger over the black stubble above his lips, to press her mouth to his and taste his kiss one last time. Jerking her gaze back to his shirt, she tried to concentrate as the next button refused to fit through its opening.

"You're a spirited woman, Kristy. I want to make love to you."

Her fingers fumbled with another button as his low, gritty voice spread warmth throughout her body. Her eyes strayed to the network of black hair that disappeared into the waistband of his denims. She swallowed hard, forcing herself to finish fastening the shirt.

"Love," she said sharply, "has nothing whatsoever to do with what you want from me."

"Would it make a difference if it did?"

She straightened, ignoring the peculiar ache inside her. "No. Even if it did, you don't know the first thing about love."

He arched his black eyebrows. "And you do? You, the woman who's marrying Parker for his money?"

Kristy flushed angrily. She'd had enough of that mocking tone of his. How had she let herself get involved in this ridiculous conversation anyway?

"What makes you so sure I don't love Parker?"

Chad's face hardened. "If you're so devoted to that snake, then get the hell out of here and go to him."

"Fine. I will."

She snatched up the Colt, then went to retrieve the second gun from beneath the bed. Both fit awkwardly into her pocket. After donning her cloak and gloves with irate jerks, she picked up her sack of food and shot one last glare at Chad. "I hope to God I never set eyes on you again."

"You may very well get your wish, since you're leaving me here to die."

She laughed in contempt. "You're like a bad penny, Chad McClintock. I'm sure you'll turn up again. But by then it won't make any difference, since I'll be married to Parker."

He was only trying to make her feel guilty, Kristy told herself as she slammed the cabin door behind her and set the bar in place. But she'd had to tie him up to buy herself time to get away. Once she got home, she would send one of the cowhands to make certain Chad had freed himself. That was more than that rotten polecat deserved.

Then why did she feel this nagging concern about his welfare?

Following the path tramped in the snow, she found the lean-to behind the cabin, where the horses were stabled. She put down her small sack and set to work saddling the roan gelding. The task seemed to take forever. No doubt Chad was already working on undoing his bonds. Heart racing, she glanced toward the log wall separating the cabin from the lean-to. What if he somehow managed to free himself more quickly than she'd anticipated?

Desperate determination gave her the strength to heft the heavy saddle into place. She tightened the cinch and fastened her supplies behind the cantle, using the leather ties provided for that purpose. As a precaution she took Chad's gray also, securing the gelding's reins to her saddle. Leading both horses out of the lean-to, she stepped up on a small boulder to mount, fighting for balance on the icy rock.

Her breath condensed in the frosty air as Kristy swiveled in the saddle to take one last look at the cabin. Smoke curled lazily from the chimney, vanishing into the snow-bowed branches of the pines. The place looked snug and inviting, nestled within the bower of trees. More inviting than the bitterly cold journey ahead of her.

Resolutely she adjusted the hood of her cloak and turned her eyes away, in the direction of the Bar S. She slapped the reins, and the gelding began plodding through the deep snow. There was no trail, only a parting of the trees, a space winding through the scattering of huge boulders.

The silence was profound. Except for the muffled footfalls of the horse, the snowy forest was as hushed as a cathedral. The tall pines rose like spires against the brooding face of the mountains. An occasional clump of aspens still glinted autumn bright through the frosting of snow, reminding her it was not yet winter, despite the frigid weather.

Worriedly Kristy glanced up at the gray, gloomy sky as a few flakes of snow drifted downward to melt on her face. By her reckoning it was no later than midmorning, though the clouds rendered the woods dim and dismal. Was she even heading in the right direction? The Bar S lay to the east of the mountains, but which way was east?

Her apprehension increased as the snowfall thickened. Her only comfort lay in the knowledge that she was steadily descending the forested, rocky slope. The gelding's hooves slipped on an occasional ice patch, and Kristy breathed a sigh of relief each time the horse caught its balance.

Straining to see landmarks through the veil of snow, she spotted a lightning-struck pine towering against the leaden sky. Hadn't she noticed that tree on the journey to the cabin? Or were her eyes playing tricks on her?

She prayed she would find her way home through the forbidding, frozen wilderness. Tiny clouds of breath formed before her face. The flimsy gown and woolen cloak provided inadequate protection against the keen bite of the wind. Her skirt was hiked up because she was riding astride, and the arctic air numbed her legs.

A wolf howled in the distance. Kristy clutched the reins tightly in her cold, gloved hands and found herself half wishing she were back in the warmth and security of the cabin.

But Chad McClintock was a greater menace than any wild animal, she reminded herself. She touched her guns, thankful for the heavy weight of the Colts against her thigh. Out here she at least had weapons for protection and a fighting chance to return home.

As the gelding continued to trudge through the snow, Kristy was tormented by worried thoughts about Chad. Was he still tied up in the chair or had he managed to work himself free? What if she'd miscalculated and knotted the cord too tightly? And if he did manage to release himself, would he be able to get out of the cabin with the door barred?

Then again, perhaps he was already on her trail.

Foreboding clutched at her like icy fingers. He'd really be furious this time. But he didn't have a horse, she reminded herself. Still, the sense of danger lingered. She dug her heels into the horse's flanks to urge him to a faster pace.

The gelding snorted and broke into a trot. And promptly stumbled on some icy debris beneath the snow.

Even as Kristy grabbed wildly for the horn, the horse's momentum jolted her from the saddle, jerking the reins from her numb fingers.

She heard herself scream, saw a blurred image of dark branches against the gray sky.

Then a hard impact jarred her body, and the world went black.

Chapter 14

"You incompetent fools!"

Parker glared at the circle of men gathered in the opulent parlor. The cowhands looked exhausted and bedraggled, and the smell of sweat and snow-dampened denim mingled with the smoky scent of the hearth fire. But Parker didn't give a damn for their comfort; he was too furious. He'd returned from Denver just moments ago to discover his fiancée had disappeared.

Of all the goddamned luck, this had to happen right in front of Horace Webb, the politician with whom he was hoping to curry favor. Horace was to be his best man, but unless the bride was found there'd be no wedding.

Conscious of the dapper statesman lounging in the wing chair by the fireplace, Parker clenched his fingers and fought the urge to vent his rage by smashing his fist into one of the tired faces gazing at him. He focused his irate attention on his foreman, Jeeter Rhoades, a husky, middle-aged man who shifted nervously under his boss's scrutiny.

"How the hell can you tell me there's no sign of Kristina?" he ranted. "You had how many men out there looking? Twenty?" His voice rose. "Twenty men and no one could find even a trace of her?"

Rhoades turned his hat in his big hands. " 'Fraid not, boss," he admitted. "We went lookin' all day yesterday and today, and there just ain't hide nor hair of Miz' Donovan nowhere. There ain't no horses missin', so she must have gone for a walk, night before the storm hit. Nobody even knowed she was gone till yesterday mornin', and by then the snow'd covered her tracks."

"Well, she didn't vanish into thin air, you goddamned

idiot!'' Parker snapped. ''Why wasn't I notified immediately that she was missing?''

Rhoades scratched his balding pate. ''You didn't get my telegraph? I sent a man into town right off.''

In a frenzy of fury Parker rushed forward and grabbed the brawny foreman by his shirt. ''Don't you lie to me! I ought to nail your blundering hide to the wall for not keeping a closer watch on her!''

A weather-beaten cowboy stepped forward. ''Now jist hold yer horses there,'' he said. ''Mebbe the snow knocked out some o' the telegraph wires.''

''Who the hell are you?'' Parker demanded, releasing Rhoades's shirt and shifting his murderous scowl to the interloper.

The grizzled cowhand stared back without flinching. ''Shake Jones, foreman over to the Bar S.''

The Bar S. Parker felt another stab of impotent anger. If they failed to locate Kristina, he'd be cheated for the second time out of getting control of the neighboring ranch. Damn his lawyers to hell for failing to find a loophole in Mavis's father's will! The Bar S should have gone to him, instead of to that no-good bastard Chad. He'd been elated to learn that Chad had gambled the deed away and the new owner was a young and vulnerable girl who needed money. The ranch had been almost within his grasp; now he felt it slipping away again.

Shake cleared his throat. ''I jist wanna say we all been doin' the best we can. We wanna find Miz' Donovan as much as you do.''

''I rather doubt that,'' Parker said, sneering. ''All an old goat like you can worry about is not losing your job. I've got a good mind to fire you . . . all of you lousy excuses for men—''

Jeremy pushed his way out of the group of cowhands, his dirty freckled face full of belligerence. ''You leave him alone, you hear? You can't fire Shake, 'cause he works for me!''

''Why, you little . . .'' Swept by a desire to beat some respect into the boy, Parker balled his fingers into fists. That Jeremy spoke the truth only made Parker angrier. But an audience of cowhands was watching, and he dared not explode into violence. Once Kristina was found and the boy was under his legal control, he'd teach that whelp who was boss.

" 'Scuse me, folks. I brung some coffee."

Lydia stood in the parlor door, carrying a tray with a battered enameled pot and a pile of cups. The aroma of hot, strong coffee wafted across the room.

Parker looked at her in annoyance. "I didn't order any coffee."

"That's fine, 'cause it ain't for you," Lydia said, lifting her sturdy chin in lofty disdain.

Parker gritted his teeth. Why did everyone connected with Kristina treat him with such insolence? By God, the sooner he controlled the Bar S, the sooner he could rid himself of these insubordinate fools.

"Get the hell out of here—the whole goddamned lot of you," he snarled. "You hands can drink your coffee in the bunkhouse where you belong." As the weary men began to shuffle out of the parlor, he called out. "You, Rhoades."

The broad foreman turned back. "Yes, boss?"

"Who's the best tracker you know?"

Rhoades scratched his head. "Prob'ly Injun Charlie. Met him once when I was workin' an outfit up Laramie way. That Injun could trail a feather over a mile o' bare rock."

"Find him and bring him back here."

"That was more'n ten years ago. Got no idea where he's at now—"

"Find him, I said!" Parker growled. "Unless you're ready to go looking for a new place to hang your hat."

"Okay, boss," Rhoades said hastily. "I'll get on it first thing tomorrow."

"No, you head out right now. You've wasted enough time already."

Rhoades darted a dubious glance out at the lavender twilight. "Sure, boss, whatever you say."

"And before you go, you make damned certain the men know they're to ride out at dawn," Parker added. "I'll be going with them this time. Maybe someone with brains can succeed where you've failed."

Rhoades tightened his lips, but he made no comment, merely nodding his head before striding out of the parlor. Parker was almost sorry the foreman hadn't responded to the insult. Damn that fool for failing to track down Kristina! Two days had passed, and now the trail was cold, buried beneath a foot of snow.

Angrily Parker paced across the spacious room, trying to work the stiffness out of his game leg. The old wound ached after the long trip back from Denver, and he cursed under his breath, brooding on the man who'd caused the troublesome physical weakness.

A man who hated him enough to abduct Kristina.

Unlike everyone else, Parker didn't believe for an instant she'd wandered off into a snowstorm. It was no coincidence his plans had been smashed at the same time Mavis's bastard was hanging around the area.

"Chad." He spat the hated name like an oath. "By God, I know that son of a bitch is behind this."

The man lounging in the wing chair by the hearth shifted slightly, drawing Parker's startled gaze. He'd been so wrapped in furious thought he'd forgotten the politician's presence.

"Chad?" Horace Webb repeated, a spark of interest in his pale blue eyes. "Isn't he your son, the one who ran off years ago?"

Parker felt bile rise in his throat. "Yes."

"And you're suggesting he has something to do with Miss Donovan's disappearance?"

Parker saw the gleam of avid interest beneath Webb's bland expression, like that of a busybody woman absorbing a juicy bit of gossip. God damn it, this humiliating situation was all Chad's fault. "It's a possibility I intend to look into," he ground out.

Horace Webb stroked his muttonchop whiskers. "Well, well. There must be some awfully bad blood between you two for a son to abduct his father's bride."

Buying time to think, Parker walked to the sideboard, consciously controlling his limp. He picked up a crystal decanter and looked at Webb. "Whiskey?"

The politician inclined his sleek, graying head. "Thank you."

Pouring two generous glassfuls of amber liquor, Parker handed one to his guest. Horace Webb was too astute to swallow any lies. Better to tell a version of the truth and enlist Webb's sympathy. Much as he hated plowing the family dirt in front of such an influential man, he'd do whatever was necessary to turn this disgraceful situation into an advantage.

Lowering himself to the settee, Parker took a gulp of whiskey. "Chad's held a grudge against me ever since he was a youngster," he said, injecting the proper hint of regret into his voice. "Claims I mistreated his mother, though Lord knows Mavis had everything a woman could ever want. But Chad thought she was too weak to bear any more children—matter of fact, I wouldn't put it past Mavis to have planted the notion in his head herself. You know the ways a woman can use to weasel out of performing her wifely duty."

"Indeed so," Webb commiserated, taking a small sip from his glass. "My dear, departed Clara claimed to suffer from headaches. Not, of course, that I ever let that stop me. A man must hold the reins of control in his own household."

"Damned right. Anyway," Parker went on sadly, "Mavis passed on back in the spring, and Chad showed up a few weeks ago, blaming me for her death and making some vague threats about paying me back. I tried to reason with him, but he wouldn't listen. I had no choice but to throw him off the ranch. I never imagined he'd do this to me."

"So he kidnapped your bride—to soil her, no doubt. Who'd have thought a son could hate his father so?"

Parker was too embroiled in his own dark thoughts to take offense at Webb's almost gleeful question. The thought of Chad raping Kristina, taking what should have been his, rekindled Parker's rage. He drained the rest of his whiskey in one furious gulp. Only the knowledge that Webb was watching kept him from smashing the empty glass on the marble hearth.

"I don't know where I went wrong in raising that boy," he said, forcing a look of fatherly sorrow onto his face. "After all the advantages I gave Chad, who'd have thought he'd turn out to be a worthless drifter? Or that he'd take all the kindnesses I showed him and turn against me?" Disregarding the stiffness in his leg, he got up to pour himself another drink from the decanter. "This situation with Kristina is my own damned fault for not taking Chad seriously enough. I guess I just didn't want to believe the depths he'd sunk to."

"Your distress is understandable." Webb uncrossed his legs and straightened the already perfect cease of his dove gray trousers. "This current predicament is quite a shame. If your boy had had a less . . . notorious reputation, I might have considered him as a husband for my daughter, Ethel, as a way of uniting our families. With your money and my political influence, we both could have benefited."

Parker's hand tightened around the whiskey glass as he walked back to sit down. Before Kristina's untimely disappearance, he'd planned to broach a similar alliance. Maybe there was still hope for his scheme.

"There is another way to join our families," he suggested. "You could marry my daughter, Honey—once this scandal over Kristina's disappearance dies down, of course. I can assure you, Honey is not at all like Chad."

The politician savored a sip of whiskey. "An intriguing suggestion. I hadn't considered remarrying, but then Honey's quite the demure little beauty."

Parker recognized the ill-concealed lust in Horace Webb's pale blue eyes. Excellent, he thought in satisfaction. If the politician desired Honey, the battle was already half won.

"When you're elected senator, you'll need a proper hostess," he commented. "Especially since it sounds as though your daughter will probably be married off by then."

"That's true. However, Honey struck me as rather timid the time we met last spring," Webb countered. "I need a wife who can use her feminine charms on my political opponents."

"All she requires is the firm guidance of a husband. I have great confidence in your ability to shape her into the sort of wife who'd be an asset to you."

"You do have a point there," Webb mused, smoothing

one of his muttonchop sideburns. "I'll be sure to give your proposal some serious consideration."

"While you're thinking about it, I might add that as my daughter's husband, you could anticipate a sizeable contribution from me to your senatorial campaign."

Horace Webb's face lit up with inelegant greed. "Perhaps we can come to some agreement during my stay here."

"I was hoping you'd say that. We'll discuss this further then, as soon as my problem with Kristina is resolved."

"Of course." Horace rose gracefully, adjusting his impeccable gray jacket. "If you'll excuse me now, I'd like to change out of these dusty traveling garments."

"My daughter can show you to your room." Parker went out into the hall to the wide, curving staircase. "Honey," he bellowed. "Are you up there?"

The golden-haired girl appeared at the top of the steps, hands worrying the dusky pink folds of her skirt. "Yes, Father?"

"Come down here at once."

Obediently she descended the stairs. Parker frowned in annoyance at the almost fearful way his daughter clutched the mahogany balustrade. She cowered as if he intended to strike her, something he'd never done. Yet despite his irritation with her shy nature, he took pride in her beauty.

At the bottom of the stairs she lifted anxious blue eyes to him. "Has Kristy been found?"

"No. I want you to escort our guest up to his room."

Her gaze darted to Horace Webb, and she seemed to shrink back, more timid than ever.

"Well, go on," Parker urged. "Don't keep him waiting."

"Of . . . of course, Father."

Slowly she stepped forward to take Webb's proffered arm. As the pair started up the stairs, Parker congratulated himself. The dapper, middle-aged politician would make a valuable son-in-law. Just as he'd hoped, Webb had leapt at the bait of a campaign contribution. Now only the size of the dowry remained to be negotiated. The match would be good for Honey too. Webb would give her sons, and perhaps the social life in Washington would draw her out of her shell.

As Honey turned at the top of the stairs, the cameo perfection of her profile brought a stinging reminder of the past to Parker. Mavis had possessed that same ethereal blond beauty.

For a moment he stood with one hand gripping the carved newel post as bittersweet memories rushed over him. How well he could recall the first time he'd seen Mavis on the wagon train. The years rolled away, and he was again that besotted young man, certain he'd found the right woman to share his dream of building a prosperous life. She'd paid him little heed in the beginning, and he remembered his burning jealousy at watching her sigh over a married man traveling to the gold fields without his wife. Parker had used all his persuasive powers to convince Mavis to wed him. How proud he'd been to stand before the preacher and take her as his wife.

How proud and how beef brained.

Parker clenched the newel post, the grinding pain of that long-ago betrayal eating at his insides. The first disillusionment had come on their wedding night with the discovery that his lovely bride was no virgin. And the deathblow to his love for her had come seven months later with the birth of that gold-miner's bastard. Only pride had kept him from renouncing the baby. How could he admit to the world that a mere woman had played him for a fool?

Pivoting on his booted heel, Parker limped into the library to pour another glass of whiskey. All those years and Mavis had failed to produce another son. Each pregnancy brought a renewed surge of hope that this time he would have a true namesake and heir. And each miscarriage had deepened his bitter resentment of Chad.

Frowning fiercely into the fire, Parker took a swallow of whiskey. Now Chad had stolen the woman who would have produced a dynasty of sons. By God, he'd track down that son of a bitch and kill him for taking Kristina! Since the day of his birth, Chad had represented the ruin of so many dreams and schemes.

But no longer, Parker thought grimly. The time had

come to make sure that bastard never again got the upper hand.

Honey walked quickly down the dim hallway, all too conscious of the elegant older man beside her. She felt a panicky urge to run, and only the thought of incurring her father's wrath induced her to stay put. Webb's smell of bay rum made her stomach roil, as did the feel of his smooth sleeve beneath her fingers. The instant they reached the door to the guest bedroom, she snatched back her hand in relief.

"Here's your room, Mr. Webb. I . . . I'll see you at dinner."

"Hold on there, pretty girl." He caught her arm before Honey could make her escape. "A good hostess would come in for a moment and make sure nothing's amiss."

Her heart leapt in alarm at the lascivious look in those pale blue eyes. Although Horace Webb was the polished image of a gentleman, his sharp features reminded her of a weasel. And she knew all too well how depraved he could be.

"The housekeeper can help you. I'll call her—"

"I don't want the housekeeper. I want you."

His fingers dug like claws into the tender flesh of her arm as he abruptly yanked her inside. The room was dim and shadowed, lit by a twin-globed kerosene lamp on the bedside table.

Webb released her, and Honey stumbled backward, retreating until her legs met the firm edge of a dressing table. She swallowed past the dry lump of fear in her throat, fighting to keep her terror at bay. At least he hadn't closed the door. Someone would hear her if she screamed.

"Your father would like us to get to know each other better." He came closer and ran a finger down her cheek. "I rather fancy the notion, don't you?"

Honey recoiled from his loathsome touch. "Leave me alone," she choked out. "Please."

"Ah, but I can't," he murmured. "Since I held you in my arms last spring, I haven't been able to put you out of my mind."

She felt sick as the repressed memory of their first and

fateful meeting came flooding back. On the morning of her mother's funeral Webb had found Honey weeping in her bedroom. Under the guise of comforting her, he'd drawn her close. And had her half-undressed before her grief-stricken mind had comprehended his vile purpose. He'd shoved a handkerchief into her mouth and subdued her struggles with his wiry strength. When the shameful act was over and he'd gone, she'd felt filthy and defiled, too ashamed to confess the incident to anyone. Who had there been to tell anyway? she thought bitterly. Her father certainly wouldn't have believed such a tale about an up-standing citizen like Webb.

"You felt so good the last time we were together," he said.

His smile brought to mind an image of some nasty thing that had crawled out from beneath a rock. "Stay away or I'll scream," she warned, her voice trembling.

"Go right ahead—no one will care," Webb said with a cultured laugh. "Your father means us to marry, and I doubt he'll object if I dip into the honeypot a bit early."

Marry him! The horrifying prospect squeezed the breath from her lungs. Numb with disbelief, she stared at Webb's leering face, at the pale blue eyes glittering in the lamp-light.

"I look forward to the day I can call you wife," he murmured. "But until then . . ."

Before Honey realized his intent, he touched the side of her breast with his loathsome fingers. Terror surged inside her. She struck out blindly, thrusting him aside with all her might.

He stumbled and cursed, and she seized the momentary advantage to run from the room, panic dogging her heels. She fled down the stairs and caught a glimpse of her father in the parlor. He was facing the fire, and she managed to steal past unnoticed, scurrying along the darkened hall and out the back door.

The evening air was cold and crystalline against her fevered cheeks. Black scudding clouds veiled the sliver of moon. Despite her lack of a shawl, Honey plunged down the porch steps and into the snow. Her thin shoes slid on the icy path. With no conscious destination in mind, she found herself heading toward the murky shape of the barn.

The hinges gave a mournful squeak as she opened one of the double doors and slipped inside. A kerosene lamp hung from a rafter toward the end of the corridor of stalls, though the place where she stood was draped in shadows. Somewhere a horse snorted and stamped a hoof.

Shivering more from aftershock than cold, Honey closed her eyes and rested her brow against the rough wood of the doorframe. Her heart was racing, her head spinning. It couldn't be true, it just couldn't be. Her father wouldn't make her marry such a demon.

But her father didn't know what a villain Webb was.

Or maybe, she amended miserably, he did know and didn't care.

"Miss McClintock?"

The low male voice made her spin around in a flurry of panic. Then the icy alarm thawed beneath a warm surge of blood as she recognized the rakishly handsome features of Brett Jordan.

He wore faded denims, and his heavy rawhide coat hung open to reveal a dark flannel shirt and leather vest. This was the first time she'd been alone with him since the party, and the sight of his lean body roused a curious fluttery feeling inside her.

"Sorry if I scared you, ma'am. I just heard a noise down here and came to check it out."

Wary and watchful, she wrapped her arms tightly around herself. "I . . . I didn't realize anyone was in here."

The tall cowboy took a step closer, frowning as he held the lantern aloft so that its hazy glow illuminated her face. "Why, ma'am, you're shivering. Here, take my coat."

Before she could protest, he set down the lamp and shrugged off the coat, draping the heavy garment around her slender shoulders. The warmth of his body lingered on the lining, along with the scents of leather and man. Honey felt a strange, quivery sensation inside her at his kindness. She burrowed into the coat, feeling as if she were wrapped within the security of his embrace.

But that was crazy. A man's touch meant terror, not safety.

"Thank you," she murmured. "Won't you get cold though?"

"I kind of doubt it, ma'am."

She tilted her head in bewilderment and saw a dull flush creep over his sun-burnished cheeks. Or did the flickering light of the lantern deceive her?

"What I mean to say," Brett went on, "is that I'm more used to being outdoors than a delicate lady like you. Why did you come out without a coat?"

Her blood froze. She couldn't speak of that appalling scene with Webb. Brett would look on her with disgust if he were ever to learn of her lost innocence. Somehow she couldn't bear the thought of him viewing her with revulsion.

Honey moistened her lips, loath to lie, yet even more reluctant to tell the truth. "I, um, suppose I was just so worried about Kristy that I forgot."

"I see." A wealth of understanding lit Brett's face. "We've all been worried about Miss Donovan. Me and the boys been out looking for her since yesterday morning."

For the first time Honey noticed the tired lines around his mouth, and she felt an absurd urge to reach up and soothe away those marks of weariness. "Have you found any sign of her yet?"

"No, ma'am. If there were any tracks, the snow covered 'em."

Honey's anxiety over Webb vanished beneath a deeper dread. She took a step toward Brett, clutching his coat tightly around her. "Kristy's been missing for two days already. Do you suppose there's any chance she might still be alive somewhere?"

Brett looked down at fearful, fine-boned face and knew in his gut he couldn't let her go on thinking Kristy Donovan was dead. Yet how could he reveal the damnable deed her brother had committed? Or his own unwitting part in the plot?

"There's something I've got to tell you," he said roughly, picking up the lantern and gesturing to her to follow. "Come over here and sit down."

He saw her glance fearfully around the shadowy darkness of the barn. "I . . . I shouldn't. You're tired, and I mustn't keep you from whatever you were doing."

She made a move as if to dart out the door, but he stopped her with a gentle hand on her shoulder. "Don't go, please."

Those big blue eyes stared up at him, and he thought for a moment she would run away despite his plea. He was intensely aware of the fragility of her shoulder beneath the thick coat that swallowed her slim, coltish figure. A tendril of silver-gold hair touched the back of his hand, and he resisted an urge to rub the corn-silk strand between his fingers. More than a month had passed since the party . . . more than a month since he'd held her in his arms and kissed her.

He jerked back his hand. He'd made a jackass of himself over a woman who was as far out of his reach as the stars. He wouldn't push himself on her again.

"What I have to say is important. It's about Miss Donovan."

Her ivory complexion turned a shade paler in the lamplight. "What is it?" she asked anxiously. "You didn't find some proof that she's . . . she's dead, did you?"

"No, of course not," Brett said quickly. "Matter of fact, I think she's alive."

"You know what happened to her?" she asked in a breathless whisper.

Her eyes were wide with hope, and he wondered gloomily if she'd still look at him with such sweet eagerness when he told her the truth and admitted his own role in the criminal deed. "I have a pretty good notion," he said heavily. "You'd best sit down while I tell you about it."

This time she showed no reluctance at accompanying him deeper into the barn. He found an empty stall and motioned her over to sit on a bale of hay while he hung the lantern from a hook and then propped a shoulder against the rough wood partition. She looked like a child huddled within the folds of his coat, her face tilted expectantly up at him.

"I think your brother kidnapped Miss Donovan."

Her brow wrinkled. "Chad? But why . . . ?"

"He and your pa never got along," Brett said. "I reckon Chad wanted to get back at him."

Understanding dimmed the light in her eyes. "I should have guessed," Honey said, her voice soft and sad. She took a deep breath and sat up straight. "Where do you suppose he took her?"

Brett shrugged, shaking his head. "I wish I knew. Chad never was one to confide in anybody."

"Does anyone else know about this?"

"No, ma'am, just you." He paused, then forced himself to add, "Miss Honey, I reckon you should know Chad asked me to pay him back a favor by taking a job here at the Diamond M. For the past couple of months I been keeping him posted on all the goings-on."

Honey didn't recoil in horror; she just kept gazing at him with those beautiful blue eyes. "So you knew he meant to abduct Kristy?"

He shook his head. "I figured he was planning something, but I swear to God I never guessed it was this."

Brett could see her hesitation as she looked away, biting her lip. Please, Lord, don't let her hate me for this. He stood rigidly, a shoulder propped against the partition, waiting for some sign of her thoughts. From down the long corridor of stalls a horse blew gently, and then the barn was so silent he could hear the pounding of his blood in his ears.

Her shy gaze lifted to him again. "Can I trust you with a secret?" she said. "Chad isn't my father's son."

The statement was so far from what Brett had expected that he could only say stupidly, "What?"

"It's true," Honey said gravely. "Nobody ever told me for sure, but I figured it out from bits and pieces of arguments I overheard between my parents."

Suddenly everything was clear to Brett. "And Chad knew too. That's why he hated the boss enough to kidnap Miss Donovan."

Honey nodded and glanced away, and Brett saw her fingers tremble visibly in her lap. She seemed to shrink back as she looked at him again, her eyes full of a fear he didn't understand.

"You don't think Chad will do something awful to her . . . I mean . . . He won't hurt her, will her?"

Brett felt a fierce urge to take Honey into his arms and shield her from whatever was frightening her. Instead he shoved his hands into the pockets of his pants. "No, he won't. Chad's a decent man. He'd respect a lady."

He hoped to God he hadn't misjudged his old friend. But what the hell else could he tell Honey when she looked so scared? He knew he'd done right when the quivering of her hands quieted.

"I'm glad to hear that," she whispered. "I'd hate to think my own brother could be so . . ." Her voice trailed off, and she buried her face in her hands.

Concern shot through Brett. Before he realized what he was doing, he was kneeling on the hard earthen floor in front of her, reverently stroking the moonbeam softness of her hair.

"Hey, you're not crying, are you?" Gently he tilted her face up and saw tears misting her eyes. His insides twisted, and he felt helpless and awkward, unsure of how to comfort her. "Chad won't hurt Miss Donovan," he repeated. "I'm sure he'll bring her back soon. He just wants to give the boss a scare."

"I know. Forgive me . . . for acting like a baby. It's just . . . everything that's happened . . ."

Brett reached into the pocket of the coat she wore and pulled out his bandana, using the red cloth to dry her cheeks. He fumbled for a way to stop her weeping, but the only thing he could think of was to keep on talking.

"I want you to know I'm mighty sorry I got myself tangled up in all this." He cupped her small hands inside his. "But you know what, Honey? I'm glad I took this job here, because otherwise I wouldn't have met you."

She gazed at him mutely, her eyes big and blue and moist, like a mountain lake in summertime.

"I never had a chance to tell you," he went on, his voice low and rough. "I'm real sorry for the way I kissed you that night at the party. I was half-drunk, but that's still no excuse for treating you like less than the lady you are. You have my word I'll never do that to you again."

Honey felt his apology envelop her, as warm as the coat

wrapping her body, as firm as the fingers gripping her hands. Still, she couldn't dismiss a sense of dismay. Why did she feel this peculiar urge to lean forward and press her lips to his?

"I know it's asking a lot," he said, "but do you suppose we could be friends, you and me?"

The wistfulness in his dark brown eyes, so at odds with his cocky good looks, arrowed straight to her heart. Somehow Brett made her feel safe and protected. Maybe he really wasn't like other men.

"I'd like that," she murmured shyly.

"Good."

His lips tilted into a smile so appealing Honey couldn't help but smile back. His hands tightened around hers, and his eyes strayed to her mouth. She caught her breath, feeling a shiver oddly akin to excitement at the thought of him kissing her again.

Abruptly his smile withered, and he stood up. "I'd best walk you back now, ma'am."

Brett's sudden change in mood confused Honey, and she felt her own spirits droop as she accepted his helping hand and rose from the bale of hay. The last place she wanted to go was back to the house, but how could she show any fear without revealing her shameful secret to Brett?

At the porch step she slipped off his coat. "Thank you," she said, awkwardly holding out the garment and wishing she could think of something clever to say, something to prolong the moment.

His expression was shadowed as he took the coat. " 'Night, ma'am." Turning, he strode away, flinging the coat carelessly over one wide shoulder.

Honey watched him go, absently rubbing her sleeves against the invading cold. The night air was crisp and frosty, and she drew in a deep breath, trying to fathom her feeling of disappointment. She should be glad he was gone; she didn't like being alone with any man.

Then why did she want to believe Brett was different?

Chapter 15

Kristy was adrift in a sea of darkness.

Her first faint sensations were of warmth and softness, of muted sound and dimmed light. Bit by bit her awareness grew, and the bliss of oblivion slowly gave way to relentless reality. A dull ache in her head blossomed into talons of torment, and she moaned, twisting in an attempt to retreat into painless sleep.

A voice floated to her from afar, its deep and gritty tone somehow familiar to her. The sound mesmerized her, lulling her battered body, luring her to the surface of consciousness.

The words became distinct and intelligible. "Kristy, can you hear me? Kristy?"

The voice made her feel warm and protected, giving her the strength to open her eyes. For a moment the world was a blur of light and shadow. A hand gently stroked her brow. Blinking, she tried to focus on the dark shape bending over her. With a jolt she identified the lean, handsome face of Chad McClintock.

Memory returned in a rush, and she tried to sit up. The sudden effort brought dizzying stabs of pain to her head and her ankle. She sank back down, her eyes squeezed tightly shut against the throbbing agony.

"For God's sake, lie still," he commanded. "Don't you ever stop fighting?"

Concern laced the harshly spoken words. Too weak to respond, Kristy lay in a daze as something cold and clammy was draped across her forehead. Gradually the awful ache there ebbed, and she lifted a trembling hand to her brow to touch a smooth, wet cloth. Her head felt better, though pangs of pain still plagued her right ankle.

Ever so slowly she opened her eyes again. This time she noted the offensive familiarity of her surroundings: the rough ceiling, the windowless log walls, the stone chimney. The softness beneath her was a bed, the warmth enveloping her a quilt. She caught a whiff of something cooking, something delicious.

Despair gripped her as tautly as the physical distress she suffered. Dear God, she was imprisoned in the cabin again.

Tilting her head slightly, she sought out her jailer. Chad sat in a chair beside the bed, his eyes a deep, inscrutable blue. His moustache appeared to have grown thicker overnight, lending a rakish air to his ruthless good looks. A crimson flannel shirt covered his broad chest; his hands rested on the thighs of his long, denim-clad legs. Though his posture was casual, she sensed a watchfulness about him that ignited a spark of anger in the vast gloom of her soul. Had he been waiting for her to awaken just so he could make her suffer his vengeful rape?

"What—"

The word came out a dry croak. Chad sprang to his feet and fetched a tin cup, removing the cloth from her forehead before slipping an arm beneath her shoulders to lift her slightly. "Drink, Kristy." He pressed the cup to her lips, and she felt the welcome coolness of water trickling down her parched throat.

When her thirst was quenched, he lowered her to the pillow again. His kindness confused Kristy, and her flicker of fury faded into uncertainty.

"What are you going to do to me now?" Somehow the words sounded small and meek.

Chad regarded her with eyes gone darkly blue and brooding. "I suppose I'll play doctor until you've recovered. How do you feel?"

"Like I've been trampled by a herd of cattle," she admitted. Her entire body felt stiff and bruised, with the worst of the pain centered in two places—her aching ankle and throbbing head. Lifting a hand, she found a large, tender lump nestled within the tangle of her hair.

"That was some fall you took," he said. "You're

damned lucky I was able to track you down before you
froze to death.''

"I'm surprised you bothered.'' She averted her eyes,
feeling a wave of bitter wretchedness at her predicament.
"But I suppose you just couldn't give up your precious
plan for vengeance on Parker, could you?''

"Would you rather I'd left you there to die?'' he asked
curtly.

The resentment drained from her. "How did you get
out of the cabin?'' she said in a more subdued tone.

"You didn't tie me up very tightly,'' he said, turning
to set down the cup. "As for the door, all it took was
brute force. A man can do a lot when he's furious
enough.''

Looking at the door, she noticed several newly hewn
planks of a lighter shade than the rest of the seasoned
wood. Her insides churned with dismay as she imagined
Chad's rage at being locked in. What would he do to her
in retribution?

"How did you find me without a horse?'' she asked,
striving to keep her voice calm.

"The horses had the sense to come straight back here.''

Chad spoke tersely, remembering his alarm when he'd
found both animals waiting outside the cabin, the rope that
had bound them together hanging loose from the roan's
saddle. With a sickening rush of fear, he'd known something must have happened to Kristy.

Urgently he'd saddled his gray gelding and followed the
faint impressions of hooves, which were all but obliterated
by a fresh fall of snow. Several times he lost the trail and
was forced to backtrack. The afternoon light was waning
when he finally came upon Kristy sprawled in a drift, her
fragile form covered by a sifting of snow, her face as pale
as death.

He could still feel the heart-pounding dread he'd experienced as he'd knelt beside her, as well as the surge of
relief at finding the thread of a pulse in her throat. Swiftly
he'd ridden back to the cabin with her nestled against him
like some rare treasure.

Now, viewing her wan and weary face, her tumbled
red-brown hair and shadowed green eyes, he felt a storm

of longing so intense it startled him. Why did this one small woman wield such power over him?

"You have to eat," he said abruptly. "Can you sit up for a few minutes?"

"I think so."

Gently Chad assisted her up against the pillows. Once he heard a swift intake of breath, though she uttered no complaint. He went to an iron pot hanging over the fire and ladled some broth into a bowl. Returning to the bed, he sat down on the edge.

"This'll help you get your strength back," he said, lifting the spoon to her lips.

Too weary to protest, Kristy automatically swallowed the hot soup he put into her mouth. She was mystified by his considerate treatment of her. Why would Chad McClintock care about her comfort? Was there a crumb of goodness somewhere in the barren void of his heart?

No, she reminded herself, his only concern was to keep her healthy so she'd be fit to bear his bastard. The stinging thought gave her the energy to reach for the spoon. "I can feed myself, thank you."

He shrugged. "Suit yourself. You always do anyway."

As she took the utensil, her fingers brushed his, and something inside her leapt. Her eyes darted to Chad's, but the expression on that darkly handsome face was indecipherable. She was conscious of how close he was, seated on the bed beside her, only the quilt separating her hip from his.

Silently he held out the bowl to her, and she dipped the spoon into the broth. The simple task required all her concentration; her throbbing head and stiff body made her as clumsy as a child.

Kristy was carefully lifting the spoon to her mouth when she noticed the patterned green flannel covering her arm, the long sleeve folded back above her wrist. Startled, she glanced down at herself, and the abrupt movement made her momentarily dizzy. The spoon dropped from her fingers, splattering her shirt with broth. Her shirt? Heat surged into her cheeks. She was swathed in one of Chad's shirts . . . and she felt decidedly naked beneath.

Chad set down the bowl and fetched a cloth. When he

started to wipe at the damp spot on her shirt, she snatched the rag to angrily do the task herself. "You undressed me," she said accusingly.

He arched his black eyebrows. "So? You were wet from the snow. Would you rather I'd left you lying in damp clothing for two days?"

"Two days?" Surprise diluted her embarrassment. No wonder his moustache looked so much thicker, she thought irrelevantly. "I've been unconscious for that long?"

Chad nodded. "You took quite a blow to your skull, not to mention twisting your ankle. Speaking of which . . ."

He threw back the quilt, and Kristy felt her blush deepen. The shirt ended at midthigh, and her legs were bare. "Just what do you think you're doing?" she gasped.

"Checking your ankle." Chad seemed oblivious of her half-naked state as he bent to examine the cloth strips binding several splints to her ankle. "Swelling's gone down some," he said. "It's looking much better."

Kristy found that hard to believe. Her stomach clenched as she noted the puffy black-and-blue bruising above the edge of the bandage. As she tried to shift position, shards of pain shot through her injured leg. "Is it broken?" she asked.

"To be honest, I'm not sure. It could be just a bad sprain. Only time will tell."

Absently she massaged her aching head. If two days had passed, that meant tomorrow would have been her wedding day, she reflected miserably. The longer she was gone, the less chance there was that Parker would still be willing to marry her. Now it looked as if she might be stuck here for weeks, plenty of time for Chad to accomplish his depraved goal.

"You've got to get me to a doctor," she said in the dim hope he'd agree.

"Nonsense. All you need is bed rest." Chad ran light fingers up her injured leg. "You can count on me to take good care of these pretty legs."

His touch ignited a warm pulsebeat deep within her belly. Mortified, she leaned forward to snatch the quilt up to her chin. The action cost her dearly as waves of pulsating pain gripped her head. She sank against the pillows, and when the dizziness had subsided, she snapped bitterly, "I'll bet you're thrilled to play doctor. You've got me trapped but good now, so why don't you just rape me and get it over with?"

He stared down at her, his eyes narrowed. "Would it really be rape, Kristy? Seems to me you liked the way I touched you."

"You flatter yourself," she lied. "You don't know the first thing about what pleases a woman."

"That sounds like a challenge."

She resented the gleam in his eyes . . . and the illogical yearning his words aroused. "That's just the sort of remark I'd expect from a worthless drifter," she jeered. "Only a sneaky varmint like you would be low enough to force himself on an injured woman."

Anger hardened his face. "For Christ's sake, don't you know when to quit?" he demanded. "Maybe I should have left you lying out in the snow—at least then I wouldn't have to put up with your vinegary tongue."

Spinning around, he snatched his coat from a peg on the wall and stalked out of the cabin, slamming the door shut behind him. Kristy closed her eyes tiredly and tilted her aching head back against the pillow. Chad had looked almost hurt. Why did she feel vaguely ashamed of taunting him?

The only feelings Chad McClintock understands are vengeance and lust.

He was a cold-hearted man, incapable of any gentle emotions, she told herself. He didn't deserve any sympathy from her.

But he saved your life.

She could not flee that fact. No one had forced Chad to search for her and carry her back to the cabin. No one had forced him to splint her injured ankle and sit beside the bed waiting for her to wake up. She blushed at the thought of him stripping off her damp clothing, caring for her most intimate needs, yet he'd done nothing that wasn't necessary.

The only reason Chad rescued you was to use you.

His sole purpose was to avenge himself on Parker by

getting her pregnant. And once he'd accomplished his goal, he would cast her aside. He wouldn't care if Parker refused to wed her and her baby was born a bastard. For that matter, he wouldn't care if Parker *did* marry her and then treated her baby with the same disdain he'd shown Chad.

But does his motive matter in a choice between life and death?

She had no wish to die. Perhaps a true lady would choose to perish rather than endure rape, but Kristy knew she could not and would not, even if it meant the demise of her dream to save the Bar S. Somehow she and Jeremy would survive. Somewhere they would make another home.

Wearily she tried to summon hatred for Chad but found only confusion. He had shown her many small kindnesses—making broth for her, caring for her while she was unconscious, splinting her injured ankle. She remembered the gentleness of his hand on her brow when she'd first awakened, the thread of concern in his voice. Would a man who was totally wicked act that way?

Yet her only thanks had been to lash out at him.

Belatedly she regretted her attack on Chad. Like it or not, she was stuck here with him for the next few weeks, and her stay would be far easier if she encouraged his compassion with a more tractable temperament.

She eased into a more comfortable position beneath the quilt. The small effort drained her of strength and renewed the rhythmic hurting in her head. Closing her burning eyes, she slid into an exhausted sleep.

When she next awoke, the cabin was cloaked in shadows. Cautiously she pushed herself up on an elbow, afraid to invite a return of that awful pounding pain. But only a dull twinge assaulted the side of her skull, though her ankle still throbbed when she tried to move her leg.

A muffled crash drew her attention to the hearth. Chad was crouched there on one knee, the handsome angles of his face gilded by the light from the growing fire. He tossed another split log onto the blaze and the flames hissed and snapped at the wood.

After a moment he rose and turned to look at her. "Good morning," he said in the deep, rough tone that never failed to kindle a spark inside her. "How are you feeling today?"

"Better," she murmured. Noticing the blankets spread out in front of the hearth, she felt a twinge of guilt. "I didn't mean to steal your bed."

"Contrary to what you believe of me, Kristy, I wouldn't make an injured woman sleep on the floor. Even a worthless drifter like me can show a little decency."

His sarcasm spurred her sense of shame. Still, the words of apology almost stuck in her throat. "I'm sorry for the things I said to you," she forced out. "You saved my life, but I didn't show you much gratitude."

He cocked a black eyebrow. "What's this—the lady would deign to thank a sneaky varmint like me?"

Kristy flushed to hear the names she'd called him thrown back at her. "I really am indebted to you, Chad," she said stiffly. "I just wanted to let you know."

"I'll just add it to your account then. Don't forget, you still owe me a night in that bed—plus interest."

"I do not," she snapped, abandoning her brief softening as she pushed herself into a sitting position, heedless of the pain in her ankle. "You cheated in that card game, and you know it!"

A smile flirted with the corners of his mouth. "Did I? You've never given me any proof of that."

His look was innocent . . . too innocent. "I don't need proof," she shot back. "Anyone who knows beans about poker would agree that it's next to impossible for me to draw four aces and you a straight flush, all in the same hand."

His grin became blatant. "Watch out, Kristy, your immoral background is showing. No true lady would know the odds so well."

"Don't talk to me about immorality. If there were a contest for wickedness, you'd win first prize."

"I know," Chad murmured. "I won you."

The lusty look in his eyes quickened her heartbeat. Breathlessly she protested, "You didn't win me. You stole me."

His gaze traveled down to her breasts. "Or maybe," he said softly, "the outcome of the game is yet to be determined."

Turning, he began to grind coffee beans, using the grinder nailed to the wall near the dry sink. Moodily Kristy watched his deft movements, unable to deny the undisciplined longing he aroused in her. His words were a promise that he still meant to seduce her. Could she fight him off despite her injured ankle?

Did she want to? Perhaps that was more the question . . . a question too troubling to answer.

In reluctant fascination she gazed at Chad as he went to the table to mix flour and tinned milk together. His face reminded her, not of the prissy perfection of Apollo, but of the dark beauty of Lucifer. She longed to touch the black growth of his moustache and test its softness. Her mind filled with the memory of how hard and strong his muscled chest had felt to her fingertips. And how good his groin had felt pressed against the cradle of her hips. Irresistibly her gaze dipped to the front of his denims, then darted away. Warm color rose to her cheeks. Ladies weren't supposed to think about that part of a man's anatomy. That knock on her head must have addled her brain.

Abruptly Chad picked up an enameled bowl and left the cabin without a word of explanation. A moment later, a gust of frigid air accompanied him back inside. The bowl he carried was filled with clean snow. From her perch in bed, Kristy watched in surprise as he began adding the snow to the batter.

"What are you doing?" she asked.

"Making snow pancakes," he said, glancing briefly at her. "It's an old ranch recipe."

"You can really cook?"

"As well as any cowhand who's spent the winter by himself in a line shack. You either learn fast or starve."

She could see Chad fitting into that job well, a loner, preferring his own company. Yet she couldn't imagine anyone—not even Chad—failing to miss the comfort of human companionship.

"Did you ever get lonesome there?" she asked.

Stirring the batter, he shot her another enigmatic look.

"Not much time to be lonely. You spend all day in the saddle, so come nightfall you're too damned tired to talk to anyone anyhow."

He hunkered down before the hearth, dropping several spoonfuls of batter into the skillet. The fat he'd added earlier sizzled and spat, wafting a lovely scent that mingled with the rich aroma of brewing coffee.

Watching his harshly handsome profile, Kristy found herself asking, "Have you ever thought about settling down in one place?"

His mouth twisted into a flippant smile. "And give up my footloose ways? I thought you had me pegged as a no-good drifter."

"I mean it, Chad," she persisted, curious, for some unfathomable reason. "Haven't you ever thought about getting married and raising a family?"

The grin faded. "No, thanks," he said. "I'll leave the dynasty building to Parker and his kind. I've had enough of family for one lifetime."

Something in his jaded words burrowed into Kristy's heart. Was he really as cold as he made himself out to be? Or was there a core of gentleness inside him, a hidden place the right woman might discover and nurture?

Pensively she watched Chad turn the flapjacks and wished she could see into his soul. At one time his character had seemed as black as the ace of spades to her, yet now, somehow, she was seeing shades of gray. Yes, he'd kidnapped her with the vilest of intentions, but days had passed and still he hadn't raped her. Didn't that prove he wasn't as villainous as she'd once thought?

Chad walked toward her. "Here's your breakfast," he said curtly, placing a plate of food and a cup of coffee on the chair beside the bed.

"Thank you," she murmured.

He started to turn, then paused as Kristy attempted to find a comfortable position against the pillows. "Need some help?" he asked.

Her insides clenched at the prospect of his hands on her body. "I . . . no, thank you. I believe I can manage."

He sat down at the table and focused his attention on his breakfast. Kristy picked up her plate, and the sight of the rich brown flapjacks made her aware of a gnawing hunger. She began to eat, but despite the delicious, airy taste of the pancakes, she was able to consume barely half her portion.

When Chad came to fetch her dish, she tilted up an apologetic look at him. "The pancakes were wonderful, truly they were. But for some reason I'm too full to finish."

"Stomach's shrunk," he diagnosed. "You've gone several days without eating." He turned to set her plate aside. "Now, if you don't mind, I'd like to take another look at that ankle of yours."

Without waiting for her permission, Chad drew back the quilt. Kristy discreetly adjusted the flannel shirt hem over her thighs. Somehow this morning it didn't seem quite so mortifying to sit here in bed with her bare legs vulnerable to his view.

He bent over her, examining the injured limb before glancing up at her. "I'm going to unwrap it so I can get a better look."

With one big hand supporting her calf, he began to carefully unwind the cloth bandage. An occasional needle of pain pricked her ankle, but she bit her lip, determined not to cry out. To distract herself, she studied the contours of the muscles in his broad shoulders, the black hair brushing the back of the collar of his dark crimson shirt, the strong arms that had felt so good around her, the long, calloused fingers that could ignite such wonderful warmth inside her.

"Am I hurting you?" he asked, shooting her a look.

Concern softened the rugged lines of his face. She felt the sudden urge to run her fingers over his features, to savor that gentle expression and hoard the sight and feel of it inside her heart.

Instead she pressed her fingers into the mattress on either side of her. "I'm fine."

Chad returned his attention to her ankle. His hands were competent and sure as he finished unwinding the bandage and removing the splints. "Swelling's almost gone," he said, studying the injured limb. "It looks a lot better."

"It does?" Kristy asked doubtfully, staring down the

slim length of her leg to the mottled network of black-and-blue bruises on her ankle.

"We'll have you dancing again in no time flat." He winked at her and grinned, the moustache adding a rakish quality to his rugged good looks. "And the doctor claims the right to the first dance."

Flustered and warm at the thought of him holding her close, she glanced away. A vivid memory came into her mind of the time they'd danced at her engagement party. Why did he have to be so diabolically attractive? "We can't dance without music."

"Then we'll make our own." His voice dropped to a sensual undertone, and he bent nearer to let his calloused hand caress her calf. "We could be good together, don't you agree, Kristy?"

A slow, heavy pulsebeat began deep within her. God help her, she wanted to give in to him, to follow the lure of his hands and mouth, to discover where all these warm and wonderful feelings inside her might lead.

But his purpose loomed before her like an insurmountable wall.

"There's nothing good in what you want from me, Chad," she said stiffly. "That's what makes it so wrong."

He started to scowl, then unexpectedly his lips twitched into a shadow of a smile. "Spoiling for another fight, Kristy? You'd like that, wouldn't you?"

"What are you talking about?"

"You want to goad me into kissing you." His hand slid higher, tracing the sensitive skin behind her knee. "Then you won't have to take responsibility for your actions. You can let yourself be swept away by passion and blame it all on me—the no-good scoundrel who took advantage of you."

She jerked her leg away, disregarding the stab of pain in her ankle. "That," she sputtered, "is the most absurd reasoning I've ever heard!"

Chad sat down on the edge of the bed, a wicked glint in his eyes. "Is it? Maybe we ought to test my theory and find out the truth."

His fingers feathered up the length of her bare legs. Her heartbeat accelerated as he paused at midthigh to toy with the edge of her shirt. "Such soft legs," he murmured. "I wonder if you're just as soft underneath this shirt."

"Get away from me," she said stiffly.

"You don't really mean that, do you, Kristy?"

She couldn't reply, for his hand continued its breath-stealing journey upward, over the garment. His fingers began a slow massage of her hips, and a bud of longing swelled within her. He bent closer, so close she felt the warmth of his breath on her lips. So close she smelled the subtle and unsettling scent of him. So close she was tempted to indulge her urge to investigate the dark new growth of his moustache. His devastating eyes held her mesmerized. She curled her fingers into fists as forbidden passion bloomed inside her.

"Chad, don't do this." She pressed her fists against his chest but made no move to push him away.

"Still fighting?" he chided. "Why is it so difficult for you to admit you want me?"

The lazy stroking of his hands seduced her senses. Her mind told her this was wrong; her body told her it was right. How could she crave his touch when he meant only to use her?

Kristy shook her head in confused denial. "All I want," she said in a choked whisper, "is for you to leave me alone."

"Give in, Kristy," he urged softly. His hands slid upward, shaping themselves to her narrow waist and then to her ribcage. "Give in and find out what you're denying yourself."

"No."

Yet she didn't move away when his thumbs began to torment the undersides of her breasts. A wonderful warmth grew within her. She desperately wanted him to kiss her and desperately wanted him to stop. Unclenching her fists, she hesitantly touched his shirt, absorbing the pleasing strength of his muscles. Oh, why didn't he just stop teasing and cradle her breasts in his hands, kiss her and caress her until she forgot all her scruples—

Abruptly Chad drew back, running a hand through the dark thatch of his hair. "God damn it," he muttered.

Kristy's hands fell to her lap, and she frowned at him,

feeling bereft and abandoned . . . and absurdly hurt. He must not want her very much if he could pull away like that.

"Forgive me, Kristy," he said, his tone subdued. "Guess I almost got carried away there." His gaze raked her from head to toe. "I didn't mean to force myself on an injured woman."

Was that a twinkle in the blasé blue of his eyes? The desire withered inside her, a victim of suspicion. She didn't know if her inner agitation was due to anger or to disappointment.

"Chad McClintock acting noble?" she scoffed unsteadily. "I don't know what game you're playing, but I don't like it."

He lifted his dark eyebrows. "You don't? Are you saying you want me to get into bed with you?"

She pursed her lips and glared at his too-mild expression. "Of course not," she said huffily.

"Then why are you so angry?"

"I'm not angry!" Hearing her own wrathful tone, she avoided his gaze, adding hastily, "I'm in a foul mood because my ankle hurts."

He jumped up from the bed to examine her injured limb. "God, I'm sorry," he said, with what sounded like genuine regret. "I didn't realize you were in pain. Why didn't you say something?"

His concern mollified her—but only somewhat. "What, and hear you mock me for complaining too much?"

"For God's sake, Kristy, I wouldn't have done that." Chad sounded annoyed as he carefully began to rewrap the bandage. After a moment's silence, he added in a gentler tone, "What do you say we call a truce, you and I? Like it or not, we're stuck here for a while, and it won't be very pleasant if we're at each other's throats the whole time."

His proposal caught Kristy by surprise. Watching him deftly rebandage her ankle, she directed a dubious frown at his rugged profile. Chad McClintock tendering a peace pact? What heinous scheme did he have up his sleeve this time?

"I'll agree on one condition," she said slowly. "You have to promise to keep your hands off me."

Chad tied a neat knot in the bandage and straightened up. "All right, I promise." The teasing glint was back in his eyes, and he looked pointedly at her breasts. "Unless, of course, you invite me to touch you."

She whipped the quilt back up to her chin. "Don't hold your breath about that, cowboy."

He made no reply, though his lips were tilted into a smug half-smile Kristy found most irritating. If his plan was to seduce her slowly, he was in for the longest siege of his life. They'd be here until the turn of a new century before she'd even consider giving herself to a scoundrel like him!

Yet Chad wasn't as corrupt a man as she'd first thought. Watching him build up the fire, she admitted to a grudging respect for his character. His hatred for Parker may have spurred him to kidnap her, but he possessed a strict code of honor which kept him from raping her. His self-control was all the more admirable, considering how she'd tied him up and stolen his horses.

She couldn't fault his compassionate treatment of her either. Being confined to bed with the injured ankle made certain needs difficult to accomplish, and Chad was the soul of discretion as he silently handed her a basin and then left the cabin.

She was sitting up against the pillows when he came back inside, accompanied by a gust of frigid air. Keenly aware of how gritty and dirty she felt after several days without washing, she said, "If you don't mind, I'd like to take a bath, please."

"Mind?" His gleaming eyes dipped to her breasts. "I'm at your service, ma'am."

She found herself flushing and clutched the quilt to her chin. "I don't mean I want you to bathe me," she said haughtily. "I can do it well enough myself, thank you."

"And get the sheets all wet?"

Kristy assumed a scathing look. "Just help me into a chair, please. I can prop my foot up on the bed." In a more temperate tone she added, "Some warm water would be greatly appreciated."

Chad grinned. "Your politeness sounds a little forced this morning," he said, stripping off his coat before hanging a cauldron of snow to melt over the fire. "Does it bother you to be civil to the stinking polecat who saved your life?"

The reprimand struck home, though pride kept her chin high. "I like to think every person is deserving of common courtesy."

"A lesson from Kristina Donovan's school of etiquette?"

His mockery stiffened her spine. "I wouldn't expect you to appreciate the finer aspects of what a lady is like."

"Ah, but when I look at you, Kristy, I don't see a lady." His gaze dipped to her breasts. "I see a woman."

His soft words kindled heat inside her despite the stern admonitions of her mind. Irritably she watched Chad move about the cabin, cleaning up the breakfast dishes and making preparations for the noon meal. When the bath water was warm, he swung her up into his arms and deposited her impersonally in a chair, gently propping her injured foot on the mattress. She felt almost disappointed when he made no improper advances; he merely placed a basin on a chair beside her and then left the cabin.

Washing her face, she was struck by the realization that today was to have been her wedding day. Instead of being trapped in this crude cabin, she should be clad in exquisite white silk, ready to walk down the aisle and speak her vows to one of the wealthiest ranchers in Colorado . . . the man who was to have saved the Bar S in return for the gift of her innocence.

So why did she feel a vague sense of relief, as if she'd been spared some abhorrent fate? Why did Chad arouse a passion in her that she'd tried so hard to feel for Parker?

Slowly Kristy unbuttoned her shirt and recalled how Chad's hands had felt on her naked flesh; the vividness of the memory made her nipples pucker. Angry at herself, she ran a cake of soap over her breasts, then scrubbed her skin with the wet cloth. But no matter how furiously she tried, she could not wash away the need for him throbbing within her body.

As the days went by, desire continued to nag at her like

a persistent toothache. She felt almost let down when Chad acted the perfect gentleman, fixing her meals, fetching a book for her from his saddlebags, entertaining her with amusing tales about his experiences as a cowhand. From time to time he teased her, but not once did he try to seduce her, a fact she somehow found more irritating than pleasing. He seemed to relish a serious discussion of cattle ranching as much as he did trading barbs with her. He was alternately hot and cold, mellow and mocking, until she was no longer certain which man was the true Chad Mc-Clintock: the caring doctor or the vengeful scoundrel.

Each little bit of information he revealed about himself made her hungry for more. And each little kindness he showed her chipped away at the wall around her heart.

Five days passed before he pronounced her injury a bad sprain, and, with his help, she was able to stand up.

Leaning against him, Kristy felt more at ease than she had in days. Her hand clutched his waist for support; his arm supported her shoulders. Chad had declared today washday, and she'd relinquished the big flannel shirt in favor of a cherry satin gown from the risqué hoard of garments in the chest. The indecent décolletage was trimmed in black lace with tiny jet beads that shimmered when she moved. Still, her spirits were high; though the gown was rather lewd, she felt wonderful to be dressed like a woman again.

"May I sit at the table for a while?" she asked, tilting an entreating look upward to find Chad staring down at her.

"Sure." The word sounded yanked from his lips. His mood seemed to have soured as much as hers had soared. Doing the laundry must have put him into a grouchy humor, she decided.

Unceremoniously he settled her into a chair by the table, propping her foot up on the seat of the other chair. Then he strode over to the hearth and stirred the clothes boiling in an iron pot of soapy water.

Kristy suppressed a smile at the incongruous sight of Chad McClintock doing women's work. Served him right for kidnapping her! Picking up a wooden paddle, he plucked a shirt out of the iron pot and put it to rinse in a bucket.

"Are you sure you boiled that long enough?" she asked with teasing helpfulness.

He grunted a rude reply that she decided to ignore. The scent of lye soap hung in the air. Resting her arms on the table, she watched him swirl the shirt around in the clean water, then rinse it again in a second bucket before wringing it and hanging it to dry on a rope stretched across a corner of the cabin.

"You really ought to rinse that three times if you want to be sure to get all the soap out," she offered.

Snaring another shirt from the boiling water, he darted her a disgruntled look. "Don't you have anything better to do than criticize?"

"I'm sorry," she said, hiding a smile. "Actually, you're doing a fine job there. I'm beginning to see why you don't need a wife. You can do laundry, you can cook, you can wash dishes, you can—"

"Work a hell of a lot better when it's quiet," he growled.

"There's no need to saddle yourself with a woman when you can do everything yourself," she reiterated.

With a loud splash, Chad flung the washed shirt into the rinse bucket. "I can think of one good use I could put a woman to," he muttered.

Kristy saw his ill-humored gaze linger on her breasts, and the precise origin of his bad mood dawned on her. Why, he did still want her after all! His hands-off attitude over the past few days must have arisen out of respect for her, rather than from a lack of desire. The knowledge made her glow inside.

On impulse she leaned forward so the mounds of her bosom nearly escaped the froth of black lace and cherry silk. "And what use might that be, Chad?" she asked in her most naive tone. "To iron?"

He slammed the shirt into the second bucket, and water sloshed onto the rough plank floor. "Keep flaunting yourself in front of me," he growled, "and I might just show you what I mean."

"I'm not flaunting myself. It's not my fault the only

clothes you bought for me are more suited to a soiled dove.''

Chad narrowed his eyes. "That must be why the dress looks so perfect on you.''

Kristy slumped back against the chair, her sense of humor evaporating as the insult knifed into her heart. So he still thought her a whore, did he? His opinion of her shouldn't matter, she told herself, yet somehow it did.

"You're wrong about me,'' she said quietly. "I'm not the sort of woman you think I am. Since I can't prove that to you, all I can ask is that you accept my word on it.''

"Your word?'' With one angry twist Chad wrung out the shirt and stalked over to hang it up. "You expect me to accept your word when you were married to the gambler who cheated me out of the Bar S?'' He shot her a dark, meaningful glance. "You know what they say about birds of a feather.''

Kristy swallowed hard against the hurting lump in her throat. "I've told you before, James Donovan was my father, not my husband.''

"So we're back to that lie again, are we? How about this, then: you want me to accept the word of the woman who's engaged to marry one of the most ruthless men in Colorado?''

"Parker has always been the perfect gentleman around me,'' she pointed out. "How do I know you're not telling me lies about his supposedly cruel nature? All I have is *your* word to go by.''

"Oh, so you want proof? All right, I'll give it to you.'' He jerked open the buttons of his shirt and flung the garment to the floor. Pivoting sharply, he pointed to the scars crisscrossing the broad width of his back. "You see these?'' he bit out. "Parker put them there. Every time my mother had a miscarriage he got rid of his frustrations by beating me.''

Horror swelled inside Kristy. Her hand went to her mouth as she stared in sickening shock at the faint ridges marring the muscled beauty of his shoulders. How could Parker have done such a vicious, spiteful deed? Yet it would explain so much. Now she could understand why Chad had hated Parker enough to shoot him.

And why he despised her so much for being Parker's fiancée.

She bit down hard on her lip. Dear God, she'd almost married that vile man! With bitter clarity she saw the truth. She had been so eager for Parker's money, she'd let herself get taken in by his smooth manners rather than following the instincts that had warned her she was making a mistake.

No wonder she was so much more drawn to Chad. He had his faults, but behind his tough exterior he was a man of integrity and compassion. Her heart wrenched at the thought of the pain he must have suffered as a child, emotional as well as physical. Suddenly it struck her how much she'd grown to care for the moody, unpredictable man standing before her so full of belligerence. She longed to put her arms around him, to help heal the old scars of bitterness inside him, to soothe away his hostility.

But her injured ankle kept her frustratingly seated. "Oh, Chad, I'm so sorry . . ."

He snatched up his shirt. "I don't want your phony sympathy, Mrs. Donovan. I was only proving a point."

A sense of hopelessness washed over her as she watched him don his shirt with angry tugs. When was the last time he'd called her Mrs. Donovan in that disparaging tone? She couldn't remember when. The soft drip-drip of the laundry hanging in the corner echoed her dispirited mood. Just when she'd begun to hope their relationship was improving, they were back at the beginning. How could she ever escape this mire of misconceptions?

She held out her hands in supplication. "I've made some mistakes in my life, Chad, but I'm not the sort of woman you think I am. I only wish there were some way to make you believe that—"

"The only thing I'd believe would be blood on the bedsheets after the first time I make love to you." He let out a bark of ill-humored laughter. "But there's not a hell of a lot of chance of that, is there?"

Kristy's heart lurched. Lydia had told her there was pain the first time, but not blood. Or had she just blocked the details from her mind, believing she was to endure that base experience with Parker? But now she no longer viewed such an intimate encounter as sordid as long as she shared the experience with Chad. She confronted the daring thought lurking at the back of her mind. Here was the ultimate proof she could offer him of her innocence.

Yet yielding would mean being a willing party to his scheme for vengeance. Worse, could she risk bearing a baby out of wedlock? Chad would never marry her. And she could not do what Mavis McClintock had done, marry another man simply to protect her good name.

Torn by indecision, she watched Chad go to the door and toss out a bucket of rinse water. A gust of wintry wind swirled into the cabin, but the icy air failed to douse the glowing fire inside her. How many hours had she spent over the past few days observing Chad like this, savoring the sight of his lean, powerful body as he performed mundane daily chores? She thought about him putting his tongue inside her mouth, his hands on her breasts, and delicious anticipation curled deep within her.

Face it, Kristy told herself. What you really want is to find out what it's like to make love with this intriguing man.

Once wasn't too risky, was it? Just once and she could satisfy her longing and prove her innocence. Chad would be man enough to admit his mistake and return her to the Bar S. Beyond that she would not let herself think.

Kristy watched him lift the iron washpot from the fire. "Chad, may I ask you something?" she asked cautiously.

He turned, impatience drawing down the corners of his mouth. "What?"

She ran her tongue over her dry lips. "Is there always blood the first time? I mean, is that all it would take to convince you the woman was innocent?"

"Probably." His face bore a hint of contempt as he dried his hands on a towel. "Or did you lose your virginity so long ago you've forgotten?"

His harsh words stung. It was high time he discovered just how wrong he was about her. Lifting her chin, Kristy met his scornful blue eyes.

"I want to prove to you I'm not the woman you think I am," she said decisively. "I want you to make love to me."

Chapter 16

Chad stared at her lovely face, unable to believe his ears. Kristy Donovan was offering herself to him? After all the days of denial, the protests of innocence, the pretenses of virtue, this had to be some sort of trick.

"You're no more a virgin than I am," he scoffed.

"I can prove you wrong, Chad."

Not a hint of guile lurked in the pure green of her eyes. Something in her steady gaze crept past the hard shell of his cynicism to the soft core hidden beneath. What if she were telling the truth? What if she really were untouched?

Angry annoyance rose in him, and he cursed his own gullibility. Of course she was lying. Hadn't she lied to Parker about her background? Deliberately he moved his eyes to the beauty of her breasts. With every breath she took, the tiny jet beads on her bodice shimmered and danced in the firelight. She was, he reminded himself, no more than a greedy opportunist who intended to marry Parker for money.

Then how did she manage to look the essence of innocence even in that gaudy gown? God, how he longed to breathe in her faint peachy scent, to bury his hands in the lustrous mahogany silk of her hair, to sheathe himself inside the heat of her body, and relieve the pent-up passion he'd kept in check for so many days.

But first he had to figure out her game. Kristy couldn't be planning another escape attempt, not with her ankle still too weak to support her weight and with him on his guard. Maybe she was bluffing, putting all her chips on the reckless bet that he'd fold and let her go. What kind of damned fool did she take him for?

"All right," he said in a hard-edged voice. "Shall we muss those sheets now, or will you force me to wait until later?"

"There's no need to wait," she murmured. "Unless you're afraid of finding out the truth."

Her fingers moved to the bodice of her cherry-hued gown, and slowly she began to pluck at the jet buttons, undoing them. Desire ran rampant through Chad even as he fought a sense of exultant disbelief. She was actually going through with this farce.

Maybe it was her monthly time, and she planned to trick him with a little blood.

Then again, maybe she really *was* innocent.

But that was absurd; she'd be losing her virginity to prove her virginity. No, she must have something else planned, but her scheme eluded him.

Then a surge of heat burned away all rational thought as Kristy leaned forward to slide the flashy gown down to her waist, leaving her slim upper body clad in a chemise of black lace so sheer he could detect the twin dusky circles of the nipples beneath. Reaching up, she began to draw out the pins securing her hair. Chad watched, transfixed by desire, as she shook her head and the heavy mass of mahogany hair tumbled past her bare shoulders, curling down to her hips.

She placed the pins in a neat pile on the table and looked up at him, almost hesitantly, as if unsure of what to do next. "Will you help me into bed, please?" she asked.

The artless invitation was like a feast offered to a starving man. Chad started toward her, heart hammering inside his chest, then caught himself. "Hang on a minute," he said, unbuckling his gun belt. "I hope you're not planning on grabbing one of my guns. Believe me, I won't fall for that trick again."

Her green eyes gazed gravely into his. "This is no trick, Chad."

When she looked at him like that he could almost believe she was what she claimed to be. Almost. Gritting his teeth, he hung the gun belt from a peg on the wall. She was just a whore, and he intended to use her as such.

Yet somehow he found himself turning to ask with gentle gruffness, "Are you sure that ankle of yours isn't hurting?"

"I feel fine." Kristy paused, a corner of her mouth curved into a beguiling half-smile. "My mind is made up, Chad. I'm tired of fighting you."

Chad walked toward her and bent to swing her up into his arms. She felt soft and small and sweet, like a child. As she laced her hands around his neck, he could feel the pliancy of her breasts yielding to the hardness of his chest. The blood coursing to his loins blazed and left him reeling. Her eyes were tender and inviting; her lips were moist and willing. How many days had he yearned for her to look at him that way, ready for his touch, honest in her desire?

"By God Almighty," he muttered as he carried her to the bed, "nothing is going to stop me from taking you this time."

"No, nothing," she softly agreed, tilting her face to kiss his throat.

The simple gesture inflamed him. He lay down atop the quilt, molding chest to breasts, hip to hip, thigh to thigh. Then he joined his mouth to hers, drinking in her provocative peachy flavor with an urgency that left him half-dazed. He must be dreaming, he told himself. No mortal woman could taste and feel so damned good.

Lifting his head slightly, he saw reflected in the drowsy depths of her eyes a passion to match his own. Her lips were parted and reddened from his kiss; her hair fanned out on the pillow in a wealth of wild red-brown silk. With an index finger he traced the freckles dusted across the dainty bridge of her nose. Something soft stirred inside him, something that made his throat tighten and his heart melt. He wanted this moment to last forever. He couldn't stand the thought of her giving herself to any other man.

But she already had and no doubt would again, Chad reminded himself bitterly. And why should he care anyway? All he wanted was to enjoy her beautiful body and then send her back to Parker, pregnant. What happened to her after that didn't matter.

Determined to drown his misgivings, he took her mouth with all the fierce frustration eating at his gut. Damn her for lying so convincingly. Damn her for trying to worm her way into his heart with her feisty spirit and artless charm. He plunged his tongue past her parted lips in a dominating kiss meant to prove once and for all that he felt nothing more for her than a passing physical need. A need that had grown a hundredfold since they'd been cooped up in this cabin. She tasted sweeter than honey and peaches, and he would feast himself on her body until he filled the gnawing emptiness inside him.

He stroked his hard loins against her hips. The movement brought only a fleeting satisfaction.

Sitting, he drew down the skimpy black chemise to expose the fullness of her breasts; in the firelight the soft, womanly swells were the color of gilded cream. Chad reached for the gown bunched at her waist.

"I want everything you have to give," he muttered.

"And I want to give you everything," Kristy said softly.

She lifted her hips in willing compliance, allowing him space to strip the rustling folds of cherry satin down over her hips and legs. The tawdry dress slipped from his fingers to the floor. He had seen her naked before, when she'd been unconscious from the fall from the horse, but that hadn't prepared him for viewing her body flushed with desire.

Her breasts were full and beautifully shaped, the undersides hugged by the sheer black chemise. The dusky brown tips were as tight as tiny rosebuds. His gaze roamed downward, and a new surge of hot blood flowed to his loins. Her underdrawers were a mere wisp of black lace, the shadow of her womanhood plainly visible through the delicate fabric.

Kristy was dressed like the whore she was. Why was he still so bedeviled by doubts? Why was his desire for her laced with such a nagging need to cherish and protect her? He hardened his heart against the woman in his arms. No matter how sweetly vulnerable the expression in her eyes, no matter how pure and fine boned her face, no matter how fresh and young her body, he couldn't let himself believe in her innocence. He couldn't because that would make his intentions toward her so unspeakably vile he could not live with himself.

Unable to take his eyes from Kristy, he sat down on the edge of the bed and yanked off his boots, dropping each to the floor with a thud. Then he moved to kneel above her, straddling her slim bare thighs between his denim-clad legs. He smoothed his trembling hands over her hips and waist, bending to kiss her through the diaphanous barrier of lace. His fingers slid to her breasts, kneading and stroking the fullness of flesh as he kissed a trail upward to the madly beating pulse in her throat.

She moaned his name, moving sinuously beneath him. His spirit soared with the realization of her passion. Her hands caressed him over his shirt, tracing the broad shape of his shoulders, the hard muscles of his chest. Her eyes were a deep, dazed jade. A powerful wash of tenderness blended with the heat of his blood. God Almighty, how could he resist a woman who looked at him as if he were fulfilling her dearest dream?

"Undress me," Chad muttered, pushing himself upright.

Her tongue wet her lips in a way that was both artless and seductive before Kristy obediently reached for his shirt. She met his gaze with a shy half-smile, her fingers working on the buttons. When the task was complete, she reached inside and moved her hands over his bare chest in unsure, exploratory strokes. Heat shot through him, and he shrugged his wide shoulders out of the shirt, flinging it aside.

"Keep going," he urged in a low, hoarse voice. "You're not through yet."

He saw Kristy dart a glance at the fly of his trousers, her eyes growing wide and uncertain. With a sudden sour jolt he remembered her pretense. So she was still playing the virgin, was she? Again those awful misgivings plunged past his defenses, creating a turmoil of confusion he didn't want to feel.

"Well, go on," he goaded, taking her small hand and guiding it to the buttons. "Don't act as though you've never done this before."

Kristy opened her mouth as if to speak. Then she lowered her gaze and set her fingers to work, her white teeth worrying her lower lip. Anticipation made his lungs labor to draw in air; only iron willpower kept Chad from giving in to the frantic urge to finish the task himself. When she was done, her hands fluttered to the tops of his thighs, and she looked hesitantly at his opened pants, where his swollen manhood was still half-hidden inside the denim.

"For God's sake, touch me, Kristy," he said, his voice rough with frustration. "Can't you see how much I want you?"

She glanced up at his face before slowly reaching inside. The first tentative touch of her fingertips made him suck in a searing breath. Then her hand curled around his hot, hard shaft, and he almost died from delight. In a delirium he wondered if this was her plan . . . to kill him with pure pleasure. He grasped her waist as her fingers moved more boldly, exploring the length of him, driving him wild, but it was the look of wonder on her lovely face that almost sent him over the edge.

With an agonized groan, he jerked himself from the temptation of her touch and rolled onto his back, breathing hard as he tried to regain a measure of control.

Kristy rose on an elbow, her flushed features full of anxiety. "Did I do something wrong? I . . . I didn't hurt you, did I?"

The naiveté in her voice was at odds with the eroticism of her appearance. An alluring tumble of hair framed her face, cascading downward over the voluptuous thrust of her breasts. The sheer black lace of her undergarments did little to conceal her feminine curves.

Chad cradled the fragility of her cheeks in his palms, unable to stop himself from reassuring her. "God, no," he breathed. "I love what you do to me."

"Then why did you turn away?"

Her perplexed frown stirred up the simmering cauldron of doubts buried deep inside him. Curtly he said, "Because when I spill my seed I intend for it to fall on fertile ground . . . inside you."

Kristy blanched at the blunt reminder of his intention. How could she have forgotten his vengeful plan to get her pregnant? The scent and sight and feel of him had so enraptured her that she'd thought of nothing else but the passion building in her body, a passion that felt so pure and right she had let herself succumb to the fantasy that he wanted to make love to her for no other reason than to satisfy their mutual needs.

He shoved down his pants and kicked them aside. Hurt wrenched her heart as she saw the grim intensity of purpose on his face. She ought not let him use her, but the sight of his powerful naked body burned her scruples to cinders. In the firelight he was all hard-honed muscle and burnished skin, beautifully masculine and so very different from herself. Gazing at his rigid male part, she felt a fever burn in her breasts and belly, aching unbearably in the place between her legs.

Chad sat up to peel away her chemise and drawers, rendering her naked. The feel of his hands and the scrutiny of his dark blue eyes sent a shiver through her, yet she felt no shame; she gloried in the raw hunger on his face.

"Why the hell do you have to look so damned pure?" His gritty voice sounded half-angry, half-agonized.

His fingers played with the peak of her breast, and she drew in a breath, feeling her nipple tighten with fiery feeling. But his harsh expression of mistrust slashed into her soul. Though she knew it would be useless to argue her innocence, she couldn't bear to have Chad touch her with such cold deliberation.

Placing her hand over his, she held his fingers still against her breast. "Please, Chad, don't be angry," she begged in a husky whisper. "Not now . . . not while we're sharing this."

On impulse she drew his hand to her mouth and planted an imploring kiss on his big, calloused palm.

Chad felt an irresistible tide of tenderness wash over him. God, how did she do this to him? How could she smash his shield of resentment with just a few entreating words? He'd expected another coy protestation of her virginity. But Kristy was so unlike other women that he was no longer sure what to think, what to believe. He knew only that he wanted her with a need more powerful than anything he'd ever felt before.

Yet the driving force of his desire was intermingled with a maddening urge to give her pleasure. She might have had other lovers, but he would be the one she remembered on cold, lonely nights.

He matched his palm to her smaller one, lacing his fingers with hers, marveling at the differences in size and texture. She felt so slight and delicate against his solid, work-roughened hand. The contrast was echoed elsewhere in their bodies: where she was fragile, he was strong; where she was soft, he was hard.

He made one last failing effort to summon the barrier of animosity but found he no longer gave a damn about her past. All that mattered was the here and now, the fulfillment of the passion that had been surging between them for so many days.

"God, Kristy," he said, his tone low and despairing. "I don't understand what you do to me."

Her smile was rueful. "And I don't understand what you do to me." ·

Careful to avoid her injured ankle, he shifted to cover her completely, feeling her breasts yielding to the wall of his chest, her hips cushioning his hard and throbbing shaft. Christ, she felt sweet . . . perfect. He nuzzled her throat, letting his lips graze her skin down to the swell of her breast. He heard her gasp as he took the nipple into his mouth, and the soft sound set him ablaze. When he suckled her, brushing his moustache over her skin, he felt her move convulsively beneath him, her fingers first clenching his shoulders and then sliding delicately across the scars on his back.

Always before he had wanted to hide those thin ridges of flesh from the women he'd known, but now he felt a stirring of some intensely pleasurable emotion deep within his heart. Too taken with the blistering magic of her body to examine the feeling, he let his hand glide down the silken curve of her side, impatient to discover the mystery of her womanhood.

He eased a gentle finger into the lush nest of curls, and she stiffened beneath him, clutching at his arms. She felt hot and slick to his touch, wet with a willing passion that excited him beyond anything he had ever known. Keeping a tight rein on his own savage need, he began caressing her until she was quivering and moaning, her thighs opening in the sweetest of invitations.

He positioned himself above her, his breath heavy and rasping as the tip of his spearhead probed her silken portal. Half out of his mind with wanting her, Chad thrust into the sweetly snug passage . . . and partway inside he met a barrier of resistance.

He was so awash with the incredible tight warmth of her he almost failed to comprehend the evidence of her innocence. Then the realization ripped through him like a bullet. He groaned a curse, knowing he should stop and knowing he couldn't stop. Had Kristy shown the slightest sign of fear or unwillingness, he might have found the strength to withdraw. But her eyes were drowsy with passion, her cheeks flushed, her lips parted.

Carefully he pressed against the membrane until it gave way. She uttered a sharp cry and arched off the mattress as he buried himself deep within her virginal channel. When she had accepted all of him, he went still, sucking in great gulps of air, reveling in the awesome sensation of possessing her at last.

Mingling with the vastness of his pleasure was bitter remorse. Hands trembling, he cupped her face in his palms, not knowing how to make amends for the immense wrong he had done her, but certain he should try. "I'm sorry, Kristy," he muttered against her lips. "Christ, I'm sorry."

Her eyes were soft, soulful, sensuous. "Don't be," she murmured, touching his cheek. "I wanted to make love with you."

Her honesty only made him feel worse. But even regret couldn't dilute the breath-stealing feel of her womanly sheath fitting him like a tight glove. God, she felt good. Like a fantasy come true. He felt his control slipping and knew the only thing that could make this coupling more perfect was to share the pleasure with her.

"We'll go slowly until you're ready," he murmured in her ear.

She looked puzzled. "Ready for what?"

He chuckled at her innocence. "You'll see."

Bending his head, he fused their mouths with tender

urgency, mating his tongue with hers, giving as much as he took. He began to move his hips, slowly at first and then faster as his need for release intensified. Yet still he strove for control, seeking her surrender before his, determined to hear her moan with the ultimate pleasure.

"Oh, Chad . . ." Her breathless gasps of delight filled him with fiery exultation. Heart hammering against his ribs, he thrust into her deeper and harder until she was writhing beneath him, clutching tightly at his shoulders, her face rapt with dreamy arousal.

"Yes, Kristy, yes," he groaned. Never before had a woman felt so exciting, so impossibly good. Never. It was like the first time for him too. They were one flesh, one body moving instinctively in rhythm. And when at last he felt her quiver and cry out in ecstasy, he plunged with her over the edge, holding her close as his own tumultuous release spun him away into paradise.

Long moments passed, moments in which Chad lazed in the perfect peace of sated passion, his face nestled in the sweetly scented crook of her neck, his heartbeat slowing and the sweat drying on his body. Slowly he grew aware of the soft snap of the fire, the quiet plop-plop of the drying laundry, the lonely sough of the wind around the eaves of the cabin.

Kristy sighed and stirred beneath him. Cold, cruel reality ruptured his contentment. Good Christ, he had kidnapped and defiled an innocent girl. The very thought made him feel sick. Without the slightest qualm he would have killed another man for treating Kristy as he'd just done. She hadn't lied to him . . . she really was Donovan's daughter. All along she had been honest about her past, but he'd been so hell-bent on vengeance he'd refused to believe a word she'd said.

Self-disgust spurred Chad to wrest himself from the warm cradle of her body. He swung his legs over the edge of the bed and sat up, burying his face in his hands. A fathomless regret seized him as he remembered every taunting word he'd ever spoken to her, every arrogant touch he'd ever forced on her.

The fact that she'd offered herself to him was scant consolation; she'd done so only out of a desperate desire to

convince him she was telling the truth. Of course, Chad
thought cynically, what had driven her to such a reckless
act was her burning need to get back to Parker before he
changed his mind about marrying her.

And what about her story of wanting Parker's money
only to save the Bar S for Jeremy's sake? Chad doubted
the nobility of her cause. She probably saw Parker's wealth
as her ticket out of a life of poverty, a chance for her to
become a respectable lady. Yet even her motive failed to
lessen Chad's sense of remorse, for whatever else she
might be, she was no common whore. Even though he'd
done his best to make her one.

Kristy propped herself up on an elbow and stared in
dismay at Chad's broad back. Did a man and a woman
always part so quickly after making love? She longed to
linger in the sweet aftermath, to draw Chad back down
beside her and feel his strong arms around her again, but
unsureness held her back.

Why was he sitting there with his head in his hands,
looking so grim, so unapproachable? Perhaps she had done
something wrong . . . displeased him in some way. Perhaps she had been too wanton, too wild in her responses.

A blush crept over her as she gazed at his unclothed
body and recalled the intimacy of his caresses. From where
she lay, she could see just a glimpse of his furred, muscular chest and flat abdomen. She glanced lower, staring
in half-guilty fascination at the male part of him, now
relaxed against a nest of black, curling hair. The memory
of how he'd felt inside her deepened her blush. His touch
had unveiled the shamefully wicked woman deep within
her, destroying the ladylike demeanor she had struggled
so hard to affect.

Still, she felt not the slightest regret for what they had
done. Their lovemaking had answered needs in her she
hadn't known existed. How could she feel such a wanton
attraction to the man who sought only to use her for revenge?

Gazing at his fierce, forbidding expression, Kristy was
at a loss. She'd had a hazy expectation of taunting him
about her virginity afterward, but now she wanted only to
feel his embrace again. I'm sorry, he'd said in that heart-

stopping moment before he'd possessed her completely. Did he regret only causing her that brief moment of physical pain? Or did he truly regret all he'd said and done?

She edged over to him and laid a hand on his warm, bare shoulder. "Chad?"

He jerked his head toward her, lowering his arms. "What?"

His bad-tempered expression was daunting. "Is something wrong?" she asked hesitantly. "You look so angry."

Chad felt her fingers trace the scars on his back, and the gentleness of her touch began to melt the lump of ice in his gut. "Nothing's wrong," he said tersely. Nothing but the fact that you're too damned beautiful, he added to himself.

A rumpled mass of red-brown hair framed the fragile face still aglow from their lovemaking. Arousal leapt within him at the sight of her lovely, full-curved body. Her bare breasts were a scant inch away from his arm, so close he could reach out and capture that voluptuous softness in the palm of his hand.

He dug his fingers into the sheets. How could he even think such self-centered thoughts when he could see a trace of virginal blood smeared on her thigh?

"Are you in any pain?" he asked abruptly.

Frowning a little, she shook her head in denial. "I told you before, my ankle feels a lot better."

"That's not what I mean." Sheepishly he added, "To tell you the truth, I'd forgotten all about your ankle."

To Kristy's surprise he shot to his feet and shoved his long legs into his pants. Not bothering with his shirt or boots, he headed across the cabin, rebuttoning his trousers as he went. She couldn't keep from staring at the magnificence of his body. Chad was all taut muscle, burnished skin, and uncompromising masculinity. His shoulders were broad, his waist narrow, his buttocks and thighs firm from years in the saddle. She remembered how the rough texture of his skin had deliciously abraded her tender flesh, how his moustache had tickled her breasts.

Returning to the bed with a basin, he dipped a square of cloth into the water. "Lie back," he said curtly.

More than a little puzzled, she complied, and he began to wipe away the splotches of blood on her inner thighs. Her confusion cleared, and a blush warmed her skin. But Chad appeared neither to notice nor to care that she was naked. He cleansed her with impersonal strokes, rewetting the cloth several times, his dark head bent over her so she could not see his expression.

The black silk of his hair seemed to beckon to her fingers. Wanton longing washed over her in an incredible, heavy wave. She wanted to run her hands over every part of him, to see if the magic they'd shared could happen again. How naive she'd been to think that one time with Chad would be enough.

Apparently once had been enough for him though. His touch was gentle but dispassionate. Painful uncertainty wrenched her insides as she again recalled her unbridled response to his lovemaking. Maybe a man didn't like that in a woman. Maybe she was supposed to lie there sedately and let him take his pleasure. A woman could enjoy the act too, Lydia had told her. But how much? Kristy wondered. Had she been wrong to reveal her desire so openly? Bleakly she remembered Chad's contemptuous treatment of her when he'd believed her to be a whore. Now she'd acted like one, instead of like a modest virgin.

Chad tossed the cloth into the basin. "About what happened—" he began.

"You don't have to say anything," she broke in, before his word could spoil the exquisite memory of their lovemaking. Pushing herself up against the pillows, she folded her arms over her bare breasts, focusing her eyes on the gun belt hanging by the door. In a low, trembling voice, she added, "It's over now. There's no need to dwell on what happened."

Chad felt her words hit him like a fist in his gut. God, how she must regret squandering the precious gift of her virginity on the man who'd kidnapped and abused her.

He snatched up his shirt and jerked it on. "I just wanted to tell you I'm sorry for not believing you," he said gruffly. He concentrated on buttoning his shirt before he forced the words out. "And I'm taking you back to the Bar S."

He saw Kristy dart a wide-eyed glance at him. "You are?" she said, before lowering her thick dark lashes, the curtain of her hair half-hiding her face so he couldn't read her expression.

"Yes. We'll head out in a couple of days, as soon as your ankle is fully healed."

"All right."

He cleared his throat, trying not to gape at her shapely body. At least she hadn't insisted on leaving instantly. "Just tell me when you feel well enough to travel."

"I will, Chad."

Why didn't she say something more? Taunt him with I-told-you-sos? Flay him with accusations? Venomous spite he could understand. Her silence confused him; he felt as if he were walking blindfolded through unknown territory. He didn't like the feeling. Not one bit.

He picked up his boots and sat down on a chair to yank them on. Then he stood up to drink in one last look at her loveliness, all tousled mahogany hair and pale, creamy skin. "I'd better go check on the horses," he said, reluctantly turning away to fetch his coat.

"All right," she said again.

Kristy watched Chad clap his Stetson over his black hair before he strode out the door. Weakly she leaned back against the pillows. He was going to take her home to the Bar S. Why didn't the knowledge thrill her?

Because somehow she felt more at home in Chad McClintock's arms than she ever had anywhere else. A piece of land couldn't compete with the flesh-and-blood warmth of his embrace. She was afraid to examine the source of these new and awesome emotions inside her.

Now that he knew she hadn't lied about her virginity, his code of honor dictated that he let her go. Chad McClintock was not the man she'd thought he was. She could understand that now. Yet an absurd pain gnawed at her heart. If he'd felt any desire at all for her, his passion would surely have overridden his scruples.

But, of course, he was disgusted by her. She'd behaved precisely like the sluts he so scorned.

And how could she bear it if he never again touched her?

Chapter 17

Chad came back inside the cabin to find Kristy dressed again, propped up against the pillow. The tawdry gown of black lace and cherry satin framed her breasts; her hair flowed in sultry splendor around her shoulders and down to her hips. Desire stabbed his loins in spite of his resolve to resist her. She was the image of lost innocence, a perfect blend of purity and eroticism. He wished to God he'd bought her something more decent to wear.

Pivoting sharply, he hung up his coat and hat. How could he stand spending a few more days alone with her, knowing how sweet her skin had tasted yet not being able to feast himself on her, knowing how wonderfully wild her responses had been yet not being able to feel her move beneath him?

"Chad?"

The soft sound of her voice made him spin back around. Half-guiltily he prayed she wouldn't notice the hard bulge inside his pants. "What?"

"Could you hand me my hairpins, please? I left them over there on the table."

"Sure."

Chad went to the table and scooped up the pins, then walked to the bed. Her serious gaze observed his approach, and he wished to hell he knew what she was thinking. Undoubtedly she was glad to be going back home. Did she regret the price she'd paid to convince him of her innocence? Did she wish she'd saved herself for Parker?

A knot of bitter rage tightened his chest at the thought of her submitting to that son of a bitch.

Chad dumped the hairpins into her open palm. "Here."

"Thank you," she murmured.

Without looking at her face, he strode away to busy himself with supper preparations. He couldn't help stealing glances at Kristy as he worked. She sat up straight in bed, her hands graceful and deft as she tamed her unruly tresses into a prim coil at the back of her head. A few tendrils resisted her efforts, fringing her fine-boned face. He wanted to plunge his fingers into her prudish bun and restore her to that sweetly tousled look of a woman recently pleasured.

Angry at himself, he slammed a slab of bacon onto the table and sliced off a couple of strips, putting them to fry in the skillet; the meat sizzled and spat. Maybe he shouldn't feel so damned guilty. After all, Kristy Donovan was the daughter of a cheat. Just because she'd been crafty enough to hold onto her virginity didn't automatically make her a saint.

Yet his principles kept him from taking advantage of her again. He'd intended to get her pregnant, but now he knew how dishonorable that goal was.

Unless she had conceived already.

God! His heart leapt, and he flashed a stunned look at Kristy, imagining her heavy with child. His child. A tempest of tender and troubling emotions stirred within him. He went cold with sweat and slammed the door on those feelings. No need to worry about such an unlikely event as pregnancy, he told himself. Surely his seed wouldn't have taken root so swiftly.

Steadfastly Chad refused to look at Kristy again until the meal was ready. When he finally turned to her, she was sitting on the bed watching him, her eyes solemn and secretive, her hands folded in ladylike fashion in her lap. Again he felt a flash of fierce desire . . . a desire she'd undoubtedly scorn. She'd proven her virginity and that was all she'd wanted to do.

"Would you like to eat at the table?" he asked gruffly.

"Yes, thank you—if you don't mind helping me."

"I don't mind."

But he did mind. Because he didn't possess the right to touch her as a lover. Drawing her into a standing position, he slanted a steadying arm across her back and wrapped his fingers around her slim waist, assisting her across the cabin. She was small and fragile, the top of her sweetly scented hair on a level with his mouth. If he turned her in his arms, he could gratify the passion burning inside him.

He yanked out a chair, the legs scraping harshly on the wood floor. After sitting her down at the table, he filled their plates and then took a seat opposite her.

"This looks good," Kristy said brightly. "I don't know why I'm so famished."

Seeing Chad raise his dark brows, she belatedly recalled the activity that had given her such an appetite. Blushing, she stared down at her food, her hunger vanishing. Chad was acting so cold, so forbidding. He'd slipped back into that doctor-patient relationship as though nothing between them had changed.

Maybe he was right, she reflected miserably. Maybe nothing *had* changed . . . for him. Though he'd agreed to escort her home, he'd achieved a measure of revenge on Parker by making love to her first.

Morosely she picked at her meal with a fork, watching Chad from beneath the veil of her lashes. A delicious ache nestled heavily within her belly, leaving little room for food. How often did a man and a woman make love? Once a day? Twice a week? Was there something wrong with her that she could want him again so soon?

Bitter loneliness crept into her heart. Chad had put her aside easily enough. Not only had she behaved like a hussy, she was also still officially the fiancé of the man Chad hated. She had given him the means for his precious revenge. Now he could simply forget her.

Absurdly, though, she didn't regret their lovemaking, because by initiating her into womanhood, Chad had gifted her with a marvelous memory. A shiver ran through her as she again recalled the finesse of his hands and the coaxing of his mouth. Although she lacked the experience to make comparisons, she knew his skill was expert and must have been acquired somewhere. How many other women had felt the heat of his desire?

Watching him now, so cold and aloof across the table as he ate, she would never have thought he could have been so warm and giving in bed. Had he always been such a loner? So remote and self-possessed? She knew so precious little about him.

Kristy set down her fork. "Tell me about yourself, Chad. What did you do after you left home?"

He looked up from his plate, his eyes narrowed. "Why do you want to know?"

Ignoring his suspicious stare, she said, "I'm just curious. Where does a fifteen-year-old boy go when he runs away from home?"

Moments ticked by as Chad traced the tines of his fork through the remains of his food. "I went to Texas," he said, abruptly putting down his fork. "Spent a few years there punching cattle."

"And then?"

"I came back to Colorado and dabbled in mining, drifted around some." He arched his dark eyebrows. "That is what you wanted to hear, isn't it? That I really am a no-good drifter?"

Kristy took no offense at his mockery; she longed only to learn more about this fascinating man. "I just want you to be honest with me," she said gently. "Anyway, I can't fault you for being a drifter. I suppose I've been one myself."

"Why do you say that?"

"Because when I was growing up, we—my father, Jeremy and I, and Lydia—never stayed in one place very long. I never had much chance to put down roots anywhere. That's why I want so badly to keep the Bar S."

Chad picked up his coffee cup and studied her over the rim. The soft crackle of the fire filled the silence. She stared back at him, bracing herself for an argument.

"Who's Lydia?"

The mild question was not what Kristy expected, not when she'd mentioned the volatile topic of the ranch. "She was my father's . . . companion. She came to live with us after my mother deserted us. When my father died last June, Lydia came West with Jeremy and me."

"Why didn't Donovan marry her?"

Kristy shook her head. "He couldn't. He didn't know whether or not my mother was still alive." She lifted her chin in pride. "He *did* have scruples, no matter what you believe of him."

Chad gazed at her, brushing a finger over his moustache. "How did your father die?"

Grief tightened her insides. "He was shot," she said in a low voice. "In a tavern near St. Louis. All I know is that the man he was playing cards with made some unjust accusations and then pulled a gun . . . " She swallowed hard. "According to witnesses, my father never had a chance to defend himself."

Fighting tears, Kristy held her head high, waiting for him to utter some disparaging comment about James Donovan's honesty, but his expression remained inscrutable.

"I'm sorry," he said. "No man should die that way."

Though his words were brusque, she detected a sincere note of sympathy that warmed her heart. Somehow she couldn't have borne it if Chad had again accused her father of cheating.

"That's enough about me," she said, striving for a lighter tone. "I want to hear more about you."

"Such as?"

Kristy shifted on the hard chair, unsure of how to phrase the question nagging at her. She decided she had nothing to lose by being forthright. "Have you known many women?"

He glanced at her breasts, his blue eyes gleaming. "A few. Why do you ask?"

She lifted a casual shoulder. "Curiosity, I guess. I just wondered if somewhere . . . sometime . . . you might have had a sweetheart, a girl you thought about marrying—"

"I've told you before how I feel about marriage," he cut in, slamming down his cup. "Or are you hinting that you think I ought to offer *you* a proposal? Are you afraid Parker won't want you anymore when he finds out I took your virginity?"

She stiffened. "Of course that's not what I meant. I was just making conversation."

A corner of his hard mouth tilted with faint amusement. "There are some things a man doesn't talk about," he drawled. "I don't kiss and tell."

His smug attitude annoyed Kristy. "Excuse me for prying," she said, miffed, "but I don't understand why you're so reluctant to tell me anything about yourself."

He stood up, plate and cup in hand, more than a hint of irony in the midnight blue of his eyes. "Maybe I don't understand why you're so interested in a stinking polecat like me."

She blew out an exasperated sigh. "I thought we were beyond name-calling. My God, Chad, we just made love." Her voice lowered to a husky murmur. "We were together in the closest way a man and a woman can be. Doesn't that make any difference to you?"

"It doesn't mean I have to spill my guts to you," he said curtly, walking off to clean up the supper dishes.

Kristy pursed her lips. Why did he always erect a wall whenever she brought up his past? From time to time he would reveal some fascinating tidbit about himself, but Lord help her if she started digging. The moment she got a little closer to him, he clammed up. Sometimes she thought he *wanted* her to continue disliking him.

Little did he know she didn't dislike him anymore. No longer did she think of him as crude and cruel. He could exasperate her with his reticence as much as he wished, but he couldn't quite hide the compassionate and caring man behind the harsh mask he wore. The fact that he respected her enough to take her back to the Bar S only confirmed her assessment of his character.

Yet perversely she wished his code of honor weren't quite so stringent. Didn't he even want to keep her here at the cabin with him? Of course, Kristy reminded herself bitterly, she was too forward for his tastes. He didn't desire a woman who responded like a strumpet.

Heartsore, she watched Chad scrub out the skillet and hang it to dry from a peg on the log wall. When he moved, the muscles of his arms and back strained against his shirt. The impossibly perfect feel of his body was imprinted on her memory in minute detail, the strength of his arms drawing her close, the pressure of his chest against her yielding breasts, the brush of his moustache over her skin.

She shouldn't feel this absurd longing to make love with him again, Kristy told herself. The risk was far too great.

If she were to get pregnant, Chad would never marry her. He was a loner, too cynical about love and family to settle down with one woman.

And now she knew she would not, could not, marry Parker simply to spare herself the scandal of unwed motherhood, as Mavis McClintock had done. The cruel nature behind Parker's gentlemanly facade was only a small part of Kristy's decision. Something inside her recoiled at the notion of giving herself to anyone other than the terse, testy, yet infinitely tempting man who had introduced her to the wonders of womanhood.

"Will you help me into the rocking chair, please?" she asked. "I'd like to sit by the fire for a while."

"Of course."

Chad dried his hands on a towel before striding over to her, his darkly handsome face devoid of emotion. His touch was impersonal as he lifted her into a standing position. As they started toward the hearth, Kristy sagged against him for more support than her almost-healed ankle required. She loved the closeness of his arm around her. She tilted her head up to better catch his scent; he smelled good. Focusing her eyes on his mouth, she felt her insides turn to warm liquid at the memory of the exquisite sensations those lips could arouse in her.

"Your moustache is getting thicker," she murmured.

Without thinking, she stroked a finger over the half-grown thatch of black hair outlining his upper lip; the moustache was downy and smooth to her touch, unlike the bristly whiskers that had sprouted on his cheeks in the hours since he'd shaved early that morning.

Chad seized her wrist, his fingers fierce around her tender flesh. "What the hell do you think you're doing?" he snapped.

His obvious distaste tore at her heart; belatedly she remembered he didn't like her to be so brazen. "N-nothing," she stammered. "I just wanted to . . ." She stopped, swallowing her foolhardy words. Why embarrass both of them with a confession of her wanton desire? "I'm sorry," she said huskily, studying the top button of his shirt. "I didn't mean to make you angry."

"Angry!" The word was forced out through gritted teeth. "For God's sake, look at me, Kristy."

Something in that gutteral command made her obey. Slowly she lifted her chin, and his gaze caught her as firmly as his hand. His eyes were as dark as the evening sky. Trapped in a trancelike fascination, she felt unable to move even if her ankle were capable of supporting her weight. His heart drummed heavily against her breasts; the hiss of the fire mingled with the rasp of his breathing.

"What was it you wanted?" he demanded hoarsely. "What was it you stopped yourself from saying?"

She couldn't answer, couldn't speak. She could only gaze helplessly at him, afraid to open herself to his ridicule and disgust, afraid to say she desperately craved the man who had kidnapped her for the sake of vengeance.

"Was it this?" he asked roughly.

He brought her captured hand to his lips, taking her fingertip into his mouth, subjecting her tender skin to the gentle torment of his teeth and tongue.

Kristy drew in a sharp breath. How could such a simple act ignite such fiery feelings inside her? One by one he kissed her fingertips, awarding each the same wildly arousing treatment. Delicious lassitude poured through her limbs and left her pliant and weak-kneed, though she was careful not to reveal her response.

Chad let loose of her hand. "Was that it, Kristy?" he said in a gritty undertone. "Or was this what you wanted?"

He touched his mouth to hers in a whisper of a caress. His moustache feathered across her lips, then his tongue traced the outline of her mouth. She parted her lips, and he deepened the kiss, his hot and hungry mouth bringing her body to vibrant life. Clinging to his muscular shoulders, she fought the urge to unbutton his shirt and run her hands over his strong chest. The scent of him was like a heady wine; the taste and feel of him were all the more tormenting now that she knew where this kiss might lead. Was he merely exerting his masculine power over her or did he feel the same beautiful urgency rising inside him?

Chad reared back, breathing hard as he ran a hand

through his hair. "Christ," he muttered. "We're not supposed to be doing this."

Kristy felt bereft, dizzy, confused. "Why not?"

"Because . . ." He paused, moodily staring down at her for a moment. Then he let out a short, humorless laugh. "I guess because I didn't want to take advantage of you again. But you do want me, don't you, Kristy?"

The thread of uncertainty in his voice wrapped itself around her heart. She must be mistaken. Such a confident man surely wouldn't feel vulnerable. Lowering her eyes, she reminded herself not to repel Chad with a display of wanton impatience. He didn't want a shameless hussy in his bed.

He seized her chin and lifted it. "Answer me."

His eyes stripped her of defenses. "Yes," she whispered, "I do want you."

He groaned a curse which she only half-heard, for his mouth came down on hers and swept away her slight hesitation. Kristy closed her eyes, reveling in the glorious pressure of his lips. When his hands coasted down her back and cupped her bottom, molding her to his rigid arousal, her soul soared with the knowledge that his passion was as great as hers. Emboldened, she indulged herself in the pleasure of twining her fingers in his hair.

His palm found her breast and cradled the soft fullness. She melted within his supportive embrace, her heart leaping crazily. Without removing his ravenous mouth from hers, he slipped a hand between their bodies to open the buttons of her bodice. Then he reached inside to stroke his thumb across the pebbly peak of her breast.

Kristy bit back a moan of deep delight, clinging to the notion that she mustn't diminish Chad's pleasure by behaving like the brazen woman within her, who longed to respond with wild abandon. Dear God, it was difficult to hold back the urges clamoring inside her when his mouth moved so arousingly over hers, when his caresses fed the fiery tension throbbing deep within her belly. She ached to glide her fingers over the sweat-sheened muscles of his back, to feel his hard nakedness against her soft skin.

Chad's big hands framed her cheeks, and Kristy opened

her eyes to find him staring down at her, looking vaguely baffled. "Are you feeling all right?" he asked.

I feel enchanted, glorious, wonderful, she thought. "I'm fine," she said.

"Are you sure?" he persisted. "You're not hurting, are you?"

Only with pleasure, she thought, touched by his concern for her well-being. "No, of course not."

He drew in a deep breath. "Good . . . because I want to take you back to bed—just one more time."

His hands went to her hair, withdrawing the pins to send her long tresses tumbling to her waist. Bending forward, he plunged his fingers into her loosened hair and kissed her deeply. She felt her insides turn to hot liquid that pooled in the place between her legs. Then he drew back to slide her gown down over her hips. Bracing her hands on his muscular arms, Kristy stepped out of the puddle of cheap cherry satin, feeling shy but unashamed as his gaze raked the curves beneath her sheer black undergarments. The hungry look darkening his eyes sent a quiver of intense yearning through her. She needed him to fill the emptiness inside her, to hold her close and share the awesome ecstasy only he could arouse in her.

Swiftly he stripped off the rest of her clothing and carried her across the cabin. Her arms wound naturally around his neck, her breasts yielding to the firmness of his chest, her cheek nestling against his hard shoulder as she breathed in his exciting scent. She could take pleasure in him, she rationalized, so long as she didn't make a spectacle of herself.

He lowered her to the bed, but she barely felt the coolness of the sheets. All she could think about was the loss of his heat as he sat down on the edge of the mattress, yanking off his boots and dropping each to the floor with a thud. He stood up to divest himself of the remainder of his clothing, and she pretended not to stare at his gloriously naked body, the muscled, hair-strewn chest, the narrow waist and lean hips, the fully aroused maleness.

Then he came down on her, his mouth seeking her bare breast. The rasp of his tongue and moustache provoking her nipple, the stubble of his beard abrading the sensitive skin of her breast, were almost her undoing. She subdued the urge to part her thighs with all the eagerness of a common street woman, contenting herself with pressing her palms to his muscular shoulders.

He spoke her name in a guttural whisper, angling off her to give his hand space to slide down over her flat belly. His fingers brushed her mound for one long, tantalizing moment, then slipped inside the petals of her womanhood to caress her pleasure point. Kristy bit down hard on her lip, barely able to restrain the whimpers of ecstasy clogging her throat. Her entire body felt rigid with the effort of suppressing a scandalous desire to arch against his arousing hand, to pant and moan and move her hips with the wild abandon of a whore. All that kept her from succumbing to the insistent urges leaping inside her was the half-coherent thought that she could not bear the idea of Chad regarding her with icy disdain, not again.

Abruptly he withdrew his hand and pushed himself up on an elbow, his face as dark as the devil's. "What the hell's wrong with you?" he bit out.

She blinked in bewilderment. "Wrong? What do you mean—"

"You know damned well," he cut in. "First you tell me you want this, and then you lie there like some goddamned dried-up spinster. What kind of game are you playing now?"

A needle of anger pierced her passion, and she sat straight up in bed, folding her arms over her naked breasts. "Don't you curse at me, Chad McClintock. For your information I was only trying to please you."

"Please me?" he said with a disbelieving laugh. "How? By impersonating a stick of wood?"

A fiery blush hastened to her cheeks. Was she wrong to think he preferred her to lie there sedately? "But you treated me with contempt when you thought I was a loose woman," she said in confusion. "Then after I responded . . . immodestly when we made love the first time, you were cold and angry, and I thought . . . Well, I didn't want to act like the sort of woman you despise." She stopped, embarrassed.

The grim mask slipped from his harshly handsome face,

and a crooked smile began to bloom in its place. Suddenly Chad rolled onto his back and burst into hoots of laughter, unbridled amusement convulsing his splendid, naked body. Kristy pursed her lips and glared at him, too disconcerted to see any humor.

"What's so funny?" she demanded.

His laughter faded to a wide grin. "Oh, Kristy love, you're priceless," he said, his eyes still glowing with amusement as he turned to skim his hand over her slim thigh. "Where'd you come up with such a crazy notion?"

She tried to ignore the warm feel of his hand, the teasing affection in his voice. "Well, don't blame me," she said, lifting her chin disdainfully. "Since you won't talk to me, how do you expect me to know what you're thinking?"

His eyes gleamed in the instant before he seized her waist, lifting her and depositing her in a sitting position on top of him before she could so much as squeak in protest. Not that she had any objections. She could think of little else save the wonderfully erotic feel of his rigid maleness underneath her.

"Get this straight, Kristy," he said, his tone rough and unsteady. "When it comes to you, I'm hot. Every moment, day or night, I'm burning for you. Is that clear?"

"Yes," she breathed, bending to touch her breasts to the black thatch that covered his chest, her long hair streaming around them.

He sucked in his breath. "I want you to do whatever pleases you," he added gruffly.

"You mean like this?"

Surrendering to wicked impulse, she rubbed her bottom over his hard shaft, feeling a surge of feminine satisfaction when he groaned, his hands clutching in reflex at her hips.

"Yes, by God, yes," he muttered.

Reaching up, he cradled the back of her head with one hand, drawing her down to meet his kiss. His lips were fierce with need, his tongue plunging deep inside her mouth. His hands moved to her breasts, caressing her with such expertise that she felt herself go liquid in his arms, melting against his hard, strong body, ready and willing and eager.

No longer was there a need to resist the passion burgeoning within her. She reached down between them and took the hot length of him in her hand, driven by a desperate desire to give him as much pleasure as he was giving her. The breath left his lips in a sharp hiss. His head was tilted back on the pillow, his utterly handsome face taut with emotion. In that instant Kristy knew the power she wielded over this tough, moody man, for she sensed their lovemaking was as extraordinary to him as it was to her.

The knowledge left her awestruck and aching, and she moaned softly, her trembling fingers bringing the tip of his shaft to her wet warmth. He needed no further invitation; he grasped her hips and thrust upward, and the feel of him sliding into her body wrested a whimper of delight from her lips.

When he had buried himself to his full length, he lifted his head and put his mouth to her breast, his tongue flicking her nipple. Pleasure rose in her, wanton and wild and wonderful. The lovely sensation flowed through her veins like heated honey, and she moved her hips, the better to feel him inside her.

"Ah . . . Kristy." Her name sounded wrenched from deep within his chest. In one swift motion he rolled her onto her back and pressed into her, withdrawing almost to her entrance only to thrust inside her again, repeating the rhythm until she cried out. She was lost in the salt tang of his skin, she was awash with the musky scent of his body, she was delirious with the incredible throbbing heat of his possession. Her fingers clutched frantically at his muscled, sweat-sheened shoulders as she felt the rushing waves of fulfillment break over her. Even as she sank into ecstasy, she felt him stiffen above her, shuddering from the impact of his own release.

Afterward, Kristy lay exhausted in his arms, her heartbeat slowing as she drifted in blissful contentment. Chad's face was nuzzled in her hair, his breath warm against her ear. His body covered hers completely, and the solid weight of him made her absurdly happy.

He sighed and shifted slightly, rubbing his stubble-roughened cheek against hers. "So," he said, his voice sounding sleepy with satisfaction, "do you still think making love with me is worse than wallowing in a pen of pigs?''

She couldn't subdue the half-guilty giggle that rose in her throat. ''Did I really say that to you?''

''Umm-hmm.'' He raised himself on an elbow and gazed down at her, his mouth crooked into a smile. He ran a finger down the bridge of her nose. ''It was that morning you snuck out of bed and tried to steal my gun.''

Kristy felt like laughing. ''Oh, yes,'' she said demurely. ''I remember now.''

''That was also the time you thought I'd done all those disgusting things to you while you were fast asleep.''

She blushed, dipping her head from the teasing glint in his eyes. ''You're a scoundrel to remind me of that.''

His fingers grasped her chin and gently brought her face back up; the dark blue intensity of his eyes ensnared her. ''Do you still think you could sleep through my lovemaking?'' he asked in a husky murmur.

''You know the answer to that.'' Kristy spoke lightly, concentrating solely on the physical sensations she had experienced, afraid to examine the new and wondrous emotions warming her heart. ''I love what you do to me, Chad,'' she whispered, lifting a caressing hand to his cheek. ''I never knew that what happened between a man and a woman could be so good.''

''I take it you didn't feel that way when Parker kissed you, hmm?''

At first she thought the sharp edge to his voice was due only to his hatred of Parker; then, with a shock of gladness, she realized Chad was jealous. Maybe he did care for her, just a little bit.

''I don't kiss and tell either,'' she couldn't resist saying, teasing him.

A muscle in his jaw tightened. ''No?'' he murmured, his voice like silken steel. His fingers began to drift over her belly, tantalizing her tender flesh. ''Then maybe I ought to keep you here and make damned certain you never forget your first lover.''

A quivery thrill ran through her. Yet Kristy couldn't help but feel a twinge of pain. After all they'd shared, did he still intend to use her for vengeance?

"Is that the real reason you want to keep me here?" she asked, trying to hide the distress in her voice. "Or do you still mean to get me pregnant before you send me back to Parker?"

His big hand went motionless on her belly, and for the space of a heartbeat she fancied he was imagining her swollen with his child. But his face remained expressionless.

"I'll take you back to the Bar S right now if you're so hell-bent on selling yourself to that son of a bitch."

His harshness hurt. So he still thought her greedy and selfish. Kristy wanted to tell him she no longer had any intention of marrying Parker, but couldn't force the words past the aching lump in her throat.

Abruptly Chad got out of bed and studied her with chilly blue eyes. "We'll leave here whenever you say the word. The decision is yours."

Pivoting, he strode to the hearth. Kristy shivered at the loss of his body heat and drew the quilt over herself. She felt torn and confused inside, reluctant to make the agonizing decision Chad had put before her. Could she willingly agree to be his tool of revenge?

She watched him crouch down to build up the dying fire. The flames illuminated the rugged angles of his cheeks, glowed on his sun-darkened skin. There was something supremely savage about his naked body, something that dissolved her scruples and made him impossible to resist. She ought to go back to the Bar S, Kristy told herself. She ought to, yet she couldn't, not yet. She could only hope the force of her fascination for him would begin to subside over the next few days.

But it didn't.

Each time they made love she felt the same exhilarating excitement. She learned there were many ways a man and a woman could take pleasure in each other. She told herself the enchantment couldn't last, that Chad would get on her nerves, sharing such close quarters in the cabin.

But he didn't.

They idled the time away talking and laughing and playing cards. Chad taught her a few tricks at poker, though he steadfastly insisted he had never cheated. When her ankle was healed, he took her outside for long walks in the snow. At any time she could have gotten on her horse and ridden away.

But she didn't.

Some three weeks had passed when two discoveries shattered her cocoon of contentment, two discoveries that thrilled and frightened and worried and elated her all at the same time.

The first was that she had fallen in love with Chad.

The second was that she was pregnant.

Chapter 18

Brett Jordan peered past the campfire into the dusk-darkened forest. One of the horses picketed nearby stirred restlessly, ears pricked, a hoof pawing the snow. Brett set down his coffee cup and rose onto cold-numbed feet, his fingers reaching in automatic reflex for the six-shooter beneath his heavy rawhide coat. Shake Jones and the other two cowboys who'd been relaxing around the campfire also came alert, guns in hand.

"Somebody's coming," Brett said, though no sound of a rider's approach could yet be discerned.

"Yep," agreed Shake from across the campfire.

After a few moments the crunch of horses hooves on snow could be heard over the snap of the fire. A pair of riders emerged from the murky woods.

"It's just Rhoades," Brett said, as he holstered his gun.

Feeling half-frozen and bone weary from another exhausting day in the saddle, he walked toward the approaching men. For a month now they'd been scouting the wilderness for a sign of the boss's fiancée, and the fruitless search was wearing on everyone's nerves. Sometimes they holed up for the night in an abandoned cabin, other times, like tonight, they were forced to shiver under the stars. Everyone was anxious to get back to the comforts of a warm bunkhouse and decent grub. But more than that, Brett added silently, he longed to see Honey again.

Rhoades unwrapped the scarf protecting his face. "Hey, boys, we found somethin'," he said as he swung down from the saddle. Tossing the reins to one of the cowhands, he strode toward the campfire, spurs jangling. "Lookie here," the brawny foreman added, digging into his coat pocket and proudly pulling forth a bedraggled square of embroidered white cloth.

"What's that?" asked Brett, frowning.

"Miz' Donovan's handkerchief," Rhoades said. "At least Injun Charlie reckons it's hers. We're gettin' closer, boys. We're gonna find Miz' Donovan yet."

"Maybe . . . maybe not." The quiet comment came from the diminutive man who'd dismounted after the foreman. Injun Charlie, his steps silent as a wildcat's, his eyes black and sharp, walked toward the group gathered around the fire. Brett knew that for all his smallness, Injun Charlie was not a man to get on the wrong side of, because he could track you down anywhere.

" 'Course we're gonna find her," Rhoades exclaimed confidently. "An' we're gonna whup that Chad McClintock's ass when we do. Any man that'd shanghai his own daddy's bride deserves to be strung up from the nearest tree."

Watching Rhoades pour himself a cup of coffee, Brett felt a familiar anger at Chad mixing with a fear for his friend's life. Parker McClintock had finally told the cowhands that Miss Donovan had been kidnapped by Chad, although apparently no one but Brett knew that Chad was not Parker's true son.

"Maybe that's not even Miss Donovan's handkerchief," Brett said cautiously, crouching down before the campfire alongside the husky foreman. "Maybe Chad took her to Cheyenne or Denver or someplace like that."

Rhoades made an impatient move of his hand. "Hell, no. They're out there somewhere. An' Charlie here's the man to find 'em. Why, he was the one who spied her handkerchief caught on a bush after I rode right on by. Ain't you the best damned tracker there is, Charlie?"

The scout's dark, wizened face showed no emotion. He stood aloof as usual, sipping a cup of steaming coffee a short distance from the campfire. "I do what I can," he said, "but I make no promises."

"There be a thousand places a man can hole up out there," Shake commented. "The trail's covered by a couple o' foot o' snow."

"Yeah," put in a cowboy named Slim, spitting a stream

of tobacco juice. "I reckon wolves got 'em anyhow. We oughta just give up afore we all get frostbit."

Rhoades straightened up. "We'll keep searchin' until our tails freeze off," he retorted. "The boss said to find Miz' Donovan an' I aim to do just that. Any of you boys wanna go lookin' for another job, you can head on out right now."

Pointedly he glared at each one of the men in turn. Slim scowled but didn't speak. Brett knew Jeeter Rhoades spoke harshly out of worry over keeping his own job; the foreman had a wife and a passel of young 'uns to feed. Secretly, though, Brett had doubts as to whether even a crack scout like Injun Charlie could follow a month-old trail through the dead of winter.

"Ain't none of us gonna quit on you," Brett said. "We want to find Miss Donovan as much as you do."

"Good," said Rhoades, his face relaxing. "Now I promised the boss I'd send word if we found anythin'. Jordan, tomorrow mornin' I want you to take this here hankie back to the ranch an' make double sure it belongs to Miz' Donovan." He handed the square of embroidered cloth to Brett. "The rest of us'll keep on lookin'."

Brett pocketed the handkerchief, clamping his lips tight to stifle a whoop of elation. Honey, he thought. He was going back to the Diamond M, and maybe he'd catch a glimpse of her. Though he knew she could never be his, something inside him ached for the sight of her gentle beauty.

That night he didn't even mind sleeping on the frozen ground, his only shelter a bower of pines, his pillow an inverted saddle. Long after the other men were snoring around him, he lay staring into the red flames of the campfire, listening to the far-off howl of wolves and dreaming of a woman with moonbeam hair.

When the first faint blush of dawn tinted the eastern sky, Brett was already riding toward the Diamond M. Gradually the sky lightened to a deep azure through the lacework of barren tree branches and needled evergreens. He drew in an icy, pine-scented breath. The frosty air was still, the only sound the crunch of snow under his horse's hooves. The mountainside swept downward, gashed by deep canyons, buried beneath a shroud of snow. Brett let the horse pick a path through the rocky landscape. They passed a glittering frozen lake, an icy creek, clumps of spruce and pine and aspen. His gloved hands grew numb around the reins, and the bitter cold penetrated even his scarf and hat and coat. But all he could think about was Honey . . . Honey with her sweetly shy smile and beautiful blue eyes.

The afternoon sun hung low over the mountains as he crossed the foothills onto Diamond M range. The last few miles seemed to stretch into forever. He urged his tired horse onward until at last the ranch house grew from a speck on the horizon to a fancy two-story home with a wraparound porch decorated by gingerbread fretwork. Smoke rose from the chimney. After spending so many cold days in the saddle and even colder nights on the frozen ground, he thought civilization had never looked more warm and friendly.

Brett handed his horse over to one of the other cowboys and strode toward the house. He tried to tell himself he was hurrying to get the news about the search to the boss. But that didn't explain why his guts felt as twisted as barbed wire.

His knock on the back door yielded no answer. After a long moment spent pacing the porch impatiently, he stomped the snow from his boots and removed his spurs. Opening the door, Brett saw the hall was dim and silent. He felt a stab of disappointment. Well, what the hell had he expected? That Honey would be there to greet him?

A tiny clink drifted from somewhere down the hall. He peeled off his gloves and shoved them into a pocket, then hung his coat on a hook beside the door, along with his hat. Running cold fingers through his hair, Brett started toward the source of the sound, aiming to find somebody who could tell him where the boss was. His feet made no sound on the floral rug that ran the length of the shining wood floor. The clean scent of beeswax polish scented the air. He felt ill at ease in such a fine house and wondered belatedly if he should have removed his boots.

The clinking noise emanated from the first room to his right. Brett stepped inside and stopped, his heart surging. Honey stood at a sideboard in the dining room, her delicate hands full of the silverware she was lifting piece by piece from an open drawer. The last rays of afternoon sunlight burnished her silver-gilt hair and dramatized her ethereal beauty. He could see only her fine-boned profile . . . the face that had haunted his dreams for so long. She was frowning, her teeth worrying her lower lip, and he felt a powerful yearning to see her smile.

Quietly he walked up to her and put a hand on the mauve silk covering her slim shoulder. "Miss Honey?"

With a gasp she recoiled from his touch. The silver clattered back into the drawer as she whirled toward him, her blue eyes huge with alarm. Then the fright faded from her face, and her shoulders slumped. "Oh . . . Brett . . . it's you."

"I'm sorry, I didn't mean to scare you," he said, baffled by her tremendous show of fear. "Who did you think I was?"

Her eyes widened with a peculiar panic. Abruptly she turned back to the sideboard, picking up a piece of spilled silver. "No one . . . I mean, I guess I wasn't expecting anyone."

"You didn't hear me knock at the back door?"

She darted a glance at him over her shoulder, eyes big and blue. "No. I . . . I suppose I was lost in thought."

Brett still had the uneasy feeling something was wrong. He ached to pull her into his arms and protect her from whatever was making her so nervous. "Honey, what's the matter?" he asked gently. "What are you so scared of?"

"I don't know what you mean."

When she didn't look at him, he had a suspicion she was lying. "Something's got you as jumpy as a kitten being stalked by a wolf." A sudden thought sparked rage inside him. "Your pa hasn't been mistreating you, has he?"

She swiveled around, skirts swishing, her fingers gripping a silver fork. "No! That's not it at all—"

"Then what is it?"

She bit her lip, her lovely face drawn in anxiety. "I . . . I can't tell you, Brett. I just can't."

Bitter despair trickled through him. He'd been a damned fool to dream such a lady could trust a weatherbeaten cowhand with scarcely two bits to his name. "Then I reckon it must be me you object to," he said stiffly. "Well, don't fret, ma'am. I won't bother you anymore."

Honey felt a burst of distress as he pivoted sharply and strode toward the door. Dear Lord, she hadn't seen Brett in weeks, and now he was leaving! Leaving because he thought he was the cause of the gnawing fear inside her!

The silver fork dropped from her fingers and clattered onto the floor as she rushed after him, driven by the urgent need to correct his misconception. "Brett, wait!"

She caught his arm just as he reached the door. He looked down at her, his dashingly handsome face wary and watchful. "What is it, ma'am?"

She couldn't bear to have him regard her with such hurt in his brown eyes. The muscles of his arm felt hard and strong beneath his red flannel shirt, and she was swamped by a sudden desperate longing to fling herself into his secure embrace.

"Please, you mustn't go," she said, her voice low. "You've gotten this all wrong. You weren't bothering me—I'm glad to see you." Feeling suddenly shy, she bowed her head. "I'm not afraid of you, Brett."

"How do you expect me to believe that when you won't tell me what is wrong?"

Honey withdrew her hand. Surely Brett would view her with revulsion if she told him the truth. Yet how could she let this kind, compassionate man go on thinking she feared him?

"All right," she said despairingly. "I'll tell you."

Feet dragging, she went to the dining room door and closed it. Her father mustn't catch her and Brett alone together. Dread squeezed her heart. And Brett mustn't know that the man who had abused her was right down the hall in her father's study . . . that was why she was so on edge. Horace Webb had recently returned from visiting several other ranchers in the area, trying to drum up support for his senatorial campaign. Thus far she'd been able to thwart his advances, wedging a chair under the knob of her bedroom door at night, making sure someone was always nearby during the day. Today for a moment she'd been alone, and Brett had walked in to scare her out of her wits.

She gazed at his stern, sun-burnished features and felt a quivery warmth inside her. Then tears stung her eyes, for she knew he was waiting for her to speak.

"I *was* a little afraid of you at first," she said slowly, "but I'm not anymore. I know now you won't hurt me like . . . " Her voice dropped to a whisper. "Like that other man did."

Brett closed the distance between them in two long strides, his hands coming down on her shoulders. "What man?" he asked fiercely. "What did he do to you?"

She ducked her head, staring at his shirt through blurring eyes as the awful memory flashed through her head. "He caught me alone. He . . . he took advantage of me, forced himself on me . . . "

Brett stared in shock as tears began to course down her ivory cheeks. "Christ!" he muttered and drew her into his arms, the need to comfort her overpowering even his rage. He buried his face in her cornsilk hair, breathing in her sweet scent, giddy with the awe of holding her close again. He should have guessed by her shrinking shyness that she'd been abused. But hell, what did he know of real ladies? Honey was like a fragile flower . . . a flower to be cherished, not used and discarded.

Violent fury surged inside him. Brett angled back slightly, tipping her chin up to gaze into her tear-drenched eyes. "Tell me who did this to you," he demanded.

She shook her head. "His name doesn't matter—"

"It does to me. I swear to God I'm goin' to kill the son of a—" He caught himself, remembering she was a lady. Savagely he added, "No man's gonna get away with treating my woman that way."

Her eyes widened in wonderment. "You mean . . . you're not disgusted with me then?"

"Disgusted?" Baffled, he stroked a gentle finger over the moist softness of her cheek. "Why would I be disgusted?"

The happiness slid from her face, and she lowered her gaze. "Because I'm not . . . pure."

His gut twisted. "You're ashamed?" he asked, incredulous. When she gave a wretched nod, he added, "Why, for God's sake? What happened wasn't your fault!"

Reverently he pressed his lips to her hair, and at the same time she tilted her face up, her eyes a deep and dreamy blue. Before Brett realized what he was doing, he was kissing her with all the tender passion inside him. Her body felt soft and sweet to his starving senses. He groaned, desperately wanting her, yet fearful of frightening her. She was a lady, he reminded himself. A lady who'd been subjected once before to a man's rough touch. With an iron effort he reined in his hot urges, instead brushing a loving hand over the gilt of her hair.

"You're a fine woman," he murmured unsteadily. "Don't you ever think otherwise. Not ever!"

Shyly she looked away. "I'll try."

"You do more than try," he said, giving her shoulders a gentle shake. "And while you're at it, tell me the name of that low-down snake in the grass who took liberties with you."

"I told you, his name doesn't matter."

"Honey," he growled in frustration, "I won't let the man get away with treating you like some saloon girl."

"And I won't see you jailed for murder."

Her concern made him feel warm inside. He'd known a lot of women, but not the kind who cared whether he lived or died. "Please, sweetheart," he cajoled. "You've got to tell me."

Her obstinate expression softened, but she shook her head stubbornly. "No."

Brett gritted his teeth, realizing he'd get nowhere with her. Apparently Honey could be just as bullheaded as her brother.

Chad. Brett froze, the purpose of his visit flooding back. "Hell's bells . . . excuse me, ma'am . . . but I almost forgot why I came back here to the ranch." He pulled the handkerchief out of his shirt pocket. "Injun Charlie found this up in the mountains. Do you know if it's Miss Donovan's?"

Honey examined the bedraggled square of embroidered linen. "I'm not sure." She looked at Brett, her eyes shining. "But if it is Kristy's, then maybe you're close to finding her."

"We sure hope so," he said, and hoped to God she was right. "Now, where's your pa?"

"In his study. I'll take you to him."

Honey led the way down the hall and through the foyer to a room opposite the parlor. Knocking, she waited for an answer before hesitantly opening the door and preceding him inside.

Parker McClintock was sitting beside a massive oak rolltop desk, a half-smoked cigar in his hand. Lounging in a crimson velvet armchair by the fire was McClintock's natty politician friend, Horace Webb.

"Excuse me, Father. Mr. Jordan has come to see you."

Parker threw down his cigar and sprang to his feet. "Have you fools found my fiancée yet?" he barked.

Brett controlled his annoyance. "No," he said, holding out the handkerchief. "But we did find this."

Parker snatched up the small white cloth. "Are you trying to tell me this belongs to Kristina?"

Brett shrugged. "Rhoades thought you might know."

"Hell, I don't keep account of every blasted handkerchief she owns!" He turned to his daughter, irritation on his face. "Honey, do you recognize it?"

When she shook her head, he leaned his head out the door and shouted, "Lydia? Get in here at once!" Parker paced, his limp pronounced. "Where in tarnation is that fool woman?" he muttered. "Lydia!" he bellowed again. Then, "Jeremy!"

"Jeremy is probably outside somewhere—" Honey began.

"Still sulking because I forbade him to go gallivanting after his sister," Parker snapped. "That boy could do with a good whupping."

"I'll go find Lydia—" Honey said, edging toward the door.

" 'Scuse me, folks—somebody holler for me?" The haughty-faced woman stood in the doorway of the study.

"Is this Kristina's?" Parker asked, thrusting the handkerchief at Lydia.

She examined the tattered cloth closely. "Sure as shootin' is. Where'd you come by it?"

"Tracker found it, ma'am," Brett said. "Up in the mountains."

"And Jordan and I'll be heading up there first thing in the morning," Parker said grimly. He turned to Horace Webb, who sat like an elegant statue by the fire. "Sorry to run out on you like this, Horace, but I want to be there when Kristina's found."

"I understand," Webb said, stroking his neat mutton-chop whiskers. "I'm due to visit the Carmichaels in a few days, but in the meantime, might I stay on here in your absence?"

"Of course," Parker said affably. "Stay as long as you like. My daughter'll take care of you, won't you, Honey?"

Brett saw an unmistakable flash of fear in Honey's eyes before she lowered her gaze and said, "Yes, Father."

Brett turned his eyes to Webb's debonair features and saw the politician watching Honey closely. Christ, was he the son of a bitch who'd raped her? A red-hot rage burned inside Brett. He clenched his fingers into fists, controlling his murderous impulse with effort. He didn't know anything for sure, he told himself. Honey was afraid of all men. And she'd be horrified and disgusted if he jumped the gun on the wrong man.

Fury and frustration battled within him. He couldn't watch over Honey because tomorrow he had to escort the boss back to camp. If he objected to doing so, he'd lose his job and never see her again. So how the hell was he to make certain of her safety?

At McClintock's curt dismissal, Brett followed the women out of the study, closing the door behind them. Honey accorded him only a brief smile before scurrying back to the dining room. The fierce urge to protect her twisted his insides. If anything ever happened to her—

"You're sweet on the gal, ain't you?"

Lydia's voice intruded on his thoughts. He turned to see a smile on her sturdily handsome face, a smile that told him he could trust her. "Reckon so, ma'am," Brett admitted. "I just wish to God Almighty I didn't have to go off and leave her alone."

"If you're worried about Webb, I'll see to it that shifty-eyed snake never gets near the gal."

Brett clutched at her words like a rider hanging onto the reins of a bucking mustang. "I'd be in your debt, ma'am. But how can you watch over her every minute?"

"Don't you fret about nothin'," Lydia said, patting his arm. "Who do you reckon's been lookin' after her all this time?"

Brett prayed the woman could keep Honey from harm. By God, he swore savagely, if he ever learned Webb had touched a single golden hair on Honey's head, that smooth-talking politician could kiss the world good-bye!

Chapter 19

Bending over the basin, Kristy prayed Chad wouldn't come back into the cabin until the miserable wave of sickness passed. Each morning she awoke feeling fine. And each morning her sense of well-being ceased the moment she sat up in bed. She'd gotten into the habit of pretending sleep until Chad left to feed the horses.

Cold sweat beaded her brow as another wretched spasm clutched her stomach. He mustn't guess about the baby, Kristy swore silently, for deep within her heart she was afraid he'd send her straight back to Parker. She couldn't bear to find out Chad still intended to go through with his vile scheme for revenge. It was far sweeter to let the days drift by, to abandon herself to the rapture of his touch, to revel in the new-found magic of her love. Eventually she would have to tell him the truth, but not yet . . . not yet.

Meanwhile she had formed a plan to make sure he didn't guess she was pregnant, a plan she intended to set in motion this morning.

Kristy straightened carefully. The roiling inside her had quieted to a faint queasiness. She managed to wash and dress and was cautiously sipping a cup of coffee by the time footsteps sounded outside and the door opened.

An icy swoosh of air accompanied Chad inside the cabin. Her breath caught, as it always did whenever she saw him; his dazzling, dark handsomeness never failed to make her blood flow faster. He closed the door and hung up his hat. Then his eyes met hers and he smiled, a slow, rakish tilt of his lips that promised pleasure.

"I see you finally dragged yourself out of bed, lazybones.'' Unbuttoning his coat, he walked toward her, all lean masculinity and swaggering virility.

"I wouldn't have to sleep late if you didn't tire me out so at night,'' she teased, returning his smile.

He drew her into his arms and nuzzled her ear, his moustache tickling her tender skin. "Can you think of a better way to pass the time?'' he asked, his voice low and husky.

Her hands crept inside his coat to touch his chest. "We could always play cards.''

His mouth meandered to her cheek. "Only if I run out of disgusting things to do to you.''

"I thought we'd already done everything.''

He let out a low chuckle. "I'm far from done with you, Kristy Donovan. Just tell me if you get bored. A scoundrel like me can surely dream up something new to hold your interest.''

"Such as?''

"You could tie me up like you did before.'' His eyes gleamed wickedly. "But this time, instead of running off, you could have your way with me.''

She pretended shock. "Oh, I could, could I?''

Nodding, he sought her breast. His fingers were cold and she squealed. "You're freezing,'' she cried, playfully attempting to wrest herself from his strong embrace.

"So warm me up, pretty lady.''

His lips met hers in a deep, hungry kiss, and she melted against him as lovely sensations swirled through her body. The clean scent of the outdoors clung to him, along with his unique essence of leather and man. His touch always ignited the blaze of passion in her. She had given up hoping her need for him would burn out in time, for each day her love for him flared brighter than ever.

"I want you,'' he muttered, his warm breath feathering her lips. "Right now.''

Kristy longed with all her heart to succumb to the magic of his lovemaking. But when he began to unbutton her gown, she remembered what she must do. Reluctantly she put her hands on his solid chest to push him away.

"Please, Chad, we can't,'' she forced out.

His dark brows lifted. "Can't?" he asked with a disbelieving laugh. "Why not?"

She ducked her head to stare at his shirt. "I don't want to stop, but . . . well, we can't make love for a few days. You see . . . I've started my monthly time."

He was silent, his hands tight on her shoulders. Did he guess she was lying? Driven by guilt and fear, she lifted her gaze to his face, but his closed expression told her nothing.

His fingers tracked seductively along the décolletage of her gown. "That doesn't have to stop us, you know," he murmured, his voice low and silken.

Her pulse leapt as much from panic as from passion. Was he calling her bluff? Did he know she was hiding her pregnancy from him?

"Please," she said hastily, "I . . . I'd really rather not. I don't feel quite well this morning."

That, at least, was the truth. Kristy fought the urge to avert her eyes from his penetrating gaze. He mustn't learn about the baby. He mustn't send her away just when he'd come to mean so much to her.

Chad touched her cheek. "I'm sorry you're not feeling well," he said gruffly. "You go sit down and I'll fix breakfast today."

Relief poured through her. Merciful heavens, he believed her. "I'm perfectly capable of helping you—"

"No." He looked at her suspiciously. "Unless it's my cooking that's making you sick."

"Of course not."

"Good, then don't argue. Just sit."

"I'll do the dishes," she promised.

"It's a deal." He propelled her to a chair by the table and gently pressed her down onto the hard seat. Bending close, he captured her lips in a swift but sweetly tender kiss. Then he walked away to start breakfast.

Kristy's heart swelled with love as she watched him work. Chad tried to hide his true self behind a brusque mask, but each day she was more keenly aware of the goodness within him. She'd been wrong to agree to marry Parker; all the money in the world couldn't buy the fulfillment she found in Chad's arms. Parker regarded her as a lady, a porcelain doll with no brains; Chad treated her like a woman, someone capable of working at his side.

Parker was Chad's one blind spot. His loathing for the man he called father ran deep and dark, a wound that had festered for so many years she doubted despairingly that the damage would ever heal. Hatred so clouded Chad's judgment that Kristy dared not let him know he'd accomplished what he'd set out to do. She moved a protective hand over her belly. Never would she let her child be used for the sake of vengeance!

A wave of pure joy rushed over her as she pictured herself rocking a baby with downy black hair and sweet blue eyes. Yet her happiness died in a stab of wretched misery. Chad wouldn't be there to share in the birth of their child. She was foolish to dream she could change him. He was a loner at heart, and once he left, she would never see him again. He was not the sort of man to entangle himself in any permanent relationship.

Gazing at his lean, strong body, the body she knew now as well as her own, Kristy experienced a pang of yearning so intense she felt faint, and she had to grip the seat of the chair for support. How much longer did she have here with him before he guessed her secret? A few weeks? A month? She vowed to guard what time they had left, hoarding memories for the lonely years to come, telling whatever lies were necessary to buy a few more blissful moments in the arms of the man she loved.

Over the next few days Kristy made certain Chad had no cause to doubt her deception. She washed out some clean rags and discreetly hung them to dry in the corner. She buried the contents of her chamber pot beneath the snow. She uttered no protest when at night Chad stretched out on a pallet before the fire instead of joining her in bed. Hurt tore at her heart. The message was painfully clear: he saw no need to hold her close unless they were making love. All he felt for her was lust.

Still, her body ached for his touch. She missed sleeping beside him, curling into his virile heat. She missed his nearness, his kisses, his caresses. But most of all she missed the warm friendship that had bloomed between them. Now during the day he was moody and withdrawn, conversing little. Twice he was gone hunting and didn't return until dusk. He left the door unbarred, apparently so confident of her desire for him that he saw no need to hold her prisoner.

Pride urged her to escape while she had the chance; love made her stay. She missed Jeremy and Lydia and the Bar S, but her passion for Chad overrode all else. Impatient to feel his arms around her again, Kristy forced herself to wait an appropriate amount of time before putting an end to her deceit.

On the afternoon of the fifth day, she dug through the chest of indecent clothing, trying to decide what to wear, for tonight she would tell Chad her monthly flow was over. She felt as nervously excited as a bride preparing for her wedding night. Critically she held up a frothy pink chemise with matching satin ribbons. Or should she wear something more erotic, that sheer black silk Chad liked, perhaps?

The cabin door opened abruptly. She spun around, clutching the dainty chemise to her bosom. Chad strode inside, and a trembly excitement stirred within her. Much to her disappointment, he barely glanced at her, muttering a greeting as he set down the rifle he used for hunting and hung up his coat and hat. Then he headed to the hearth and poured himself a cup of coffee.

"I didn't expect you back so early," Kristy ventured, admiring his lean profile. "Did you have any luck hunting?"

Chad swiveled toward her, running a hand through his dark hair. "What? No. Took a shot at a good-sized buck, but my aim must have been off." He sounded distracted.

"Well, that's all right," she said soothingly. "We've got plenty to eat here. In fact, I made a pie this morning with some of those dried apples."

"Oh."

The negligent way Chad was sipping his coffee told her he'd scarcely heard her. Her gaze was riveted on the long fingers circling the cup . . . fingers that felt so good on her body, fingers she ached to have touch her again. Why wait until tonight?

"I was just trying to decide what to wear," she murmured. "Which do you like better? This?" She held up the pink chemise. "Or this?" Picking up the sheer black chemise, she held it against her body.

To her delight his eyes sharpened, following the slide of her hand as she smoothed the lacy fabric against her breasts and waist. He stared for a moment as if mesmerized, then looked away, muttering, "Either one's fine."

Kristy pursed her lips in frustration. Was that all he could say? Maybe he didn't realize what she meant.

Tossing aside the chemise, she boldly walked toward him, hips swaying, a saucy smile on her lips. Those incredibly blue eyes stared at her without revealing a hint of his thoughts. She took his coffee cup from him and set it down. Then she wound her arms around his neck, her fingers threading into his hair.

"Maybe you'd rather I wear nothing at all," she murmured.

But when she tried to kiss him, he sucked in a sharp breath and pulled back, hands on her arms. "Don't, Kristy." His tone was hard, his face serious.

She looked at him in bewilderment. How blatant need she be? "It's all right, Chad. What I'm trying to tell you is there's no longer any need for us to sleep apart."

"I know what you're saying." His voice sounded strained.

Uneasiness swept over her. Had he guessed about her pregnancy after all? "Then what's the matter?" she asked cautiously. "Why are you acting so moody?"

Chad gazed at her intently before walking away. Propping a shoulder against the stone mantel, he said, his voice low and heavy, "I've been doing some thinking these past few days. I've decided it's time I took you home."

Her heart jolted with shock and hurt. Had he tired of her already? "I thought you were leaving that decision to me," she said numbly.

"I was." He paused, and his eyes seemed to be focused on a point somewhere over her head. "However, you've just gotten your first taste of physical pleasure. You aren't thinking of much else."

Anger engulfed her pain. "Oh, so I'm the victim of unbridled lust, am I?"

His gaze shot back to hers. "I suppose that's one way of putting it. You're so aware of your body right now, you're not thinking straight."

"I see," she said bitingly. "And since this is hardly the first time for you, you're so much more in control than I am."

His jaw tightened, and he avoided her eyes. "As a matter of fact, yes. I'm concerned because you could get pregnant."

"I thought that was what you intended all along, Chad."

He raked an impatient hand through his hair. "I've changed my mind—it's unfair of me to saddle you with a bastard."

Hurt, Kristy folded her arms over her breasts. Why didn't he come right out and say he'd never marry her? "How noble of you," she said bitterly. "But my child wouldn't have to be a bastard. Don't forget, I can always marry Parker."

"Of course," Chad snapped, his hands clenching into fists. "So you ought to be thrilled that I'm taking you back to him—now you can still get your greedy hands on his money."

A bleak storm of pain drenched the heat of her anger. Would Chad never stop viewing her as selfish and grasping? Why did she bother arguing with him anyway? He was too cynical, too aloof to ever form any emotional attachment to her . . . or to the baby they had created together. Kristy knew she must accept that. And since their relationship held no future, she would not squander the precious present. She loved him, and nothing else mattered.

On legs as weak as water, she walked toward Chad, stopping just inches away. "I'm not leaving," she said in a firm, clear voice.

"The hell you won't—"

"I mean it, Chad. If you're so anxious to get rid of me, you'll have to haul me back the way you brought me here—tied to a saddle."

He stared at her, his body stiff, his jaw tight and hard. "You don't know what you're saying."

"Yes, I do." Her voice shook as tears sprang to her eyes. "I want you, Chad. I'm not ashamed to admit that."

Her body quaked with emotion, but she forced herself to stand straight, meeting his gaze with all the pride and love inside her. He closed his eyes, and she knew he was fighting a battle against her. He wanted to shut her out of his life. He wanted to do what his stringent code of honor told him was the right thing.

Then he looked at her again, and she knew by the softening of his gaze that she'd won. Her heart gave a wild leap as his arm shot out to pull her close, and he buried his face in the curve of her throat. "God," he groaned, "how can I resist you, Kristy?"

"Don't," she whispered, stroking his hair. "Just make love to me . . . please."

He did. Slowly undressing her, he caressed every part of her body with reverent intensity until she was aching and moaning with need. Passion leapt between them like a fire storm. When at last he entered her, she felt awed and full of wonder, as if this were the very first time. Ecstasy came in a shower of stars, and when the last of the brilliance was over, she clung to Chad, loath to return to the real world.

He slept beside her that night, as if he, too, felt an aching need for closeness. But when she awoke the next morning, he was gone, with only the depression of his head on the pillow beside her marking where he'd lain. He must have left to feed the horses.

Feeling bereft, Kristy sat up in bed. The familiar, awful nausea wrenched her insides. She barely reached the chamber pot before losing the contents of her stomach. When her mind cleared a little, she was thankful Chad hadn't been there to witness the evidence of her deceit. After what they'd shared the night before, she couldn't bear to give him cause to take her home.

Swiftly she splashed some icy water on her face to revive herself, then dressed. She was buttoning up the back of her gown when a shot exploded outside. Her fingers froze, then relaxed. Chad must have killed a rabbit or some other small game that had ventured by.

Then came the muffled shout of a man's voice. A voice

that didn't belong to Chad. Dread curled inside her already trembly stomach. Dear God, the gunshot! What if Chad lay dead or dying?

Driven by a flurry of fear, Kristy darted to the door and wrenched it open, stepping out into the cold. The morning sun dazzled her eyes; then she saw Chad standing near a corner of the cabin. Her fleeting relief dissolved into horror. Half a dozen men on horseback ringed the clearing. Her widened eyes focused on the man in the center, the man who was aiming a rifle at Chad.

It was Parker.

Chapter 20

Chad stared at Kristy, who stood outside the door, her face pale, one slim hand clutching her low-cut bodice. The icy wind tore at her neatly coiled hair. She looked shocked and scared and infinitely adorable. The urge to protect her clawed at his gut.

"Get back inside, Kristy!" he snapped.

"No, Chad, I'm not leaving you." Her huge eyes were trained on Parker, watching as the bull-like older man dismounted and limped toward her, his boots crunching the snow. He carried a rifle negligently in one hand. Chad stared at the armed posse behind Parker. Brett Jordan would be an ally, but the rest of the men Chad didn't recognize. The unknown factor alarmed him. God! If one of those fools were trigger-happy . . .

"Kristy," Chad growled again, "for Christ's sake, I told you to get back in the cabin!"

She flashed him a defiant look. "No," she repeated, crossing her arms over her bosom. "This is my battle too."

An indefinable emotion tormented Chad. Was she glad her fiancée had come at last? Would she forget the weeks of bliss and share Parker's bed with all the womanly passion that had been awakened within her?

"You okay there, Miz' Kristy?" called out a grizzled old cowboy at the edge of the posse.

"I'm fine, Shake," she replied, gazing wide-eyed as Parker limped to her side.

"You're all right now that I'm here," he said, sliding a possessive arm around her slender shoulders. "This rotten bastard can't hurt you anymore."

251

Kristy made a move as if to pull away. "But he hasn't—"

Ferocious fury exploded inside Chad. "Get your filthy hands off her!" He surged forward, but Parker let go of Kristy to jack the lever of the rifle.

"Hold it right there, boy," he snarled.

"Don't shoot!" Kristy gasped out.

Chad froze, leashing his savage rage. He couldn't risk any shots being fired, now when Kristy might be hurt in the crossfire.

"This is between you and me," he told Parker. "Don't involve her in our quarrel."

"You were the scum who involved her, not me. Thank God one of my men heard a rifle shot yesterday that led us right to your little hideaway here."

Silently Chad cursed his carelessness in firing the rifle. He'd been so blinded by his obsession with Kristy that he'd lowered his guard. The mistake might well cost him his life.

Glancing at the posse, Parker ordered, "You, Slim, get over here and take this bastard's guns."

"Sure, boss." A lanky cowhand spat out a stream of tobacco juice before he dismounted, saddle leather creaking. He sauntered over to jerk both guns from the holsters inside Chad's unbuttoned coat.

"Now tie him up," Parker bit out.

Slim fetched a length of rope from his saddle and yanked Chad's hands behind his back. As the rough twine dug into his wrists, Chad felt a rush of helpless fury. God, if only Kristy weren't nearby, he would have tried to shoot his way out.

Frowning, she took a step toward Parker. "Is all this necessary? Chad can't escape you—he's outnumbered."

A sneer twisted the lips below Parker's handlebar moustache. "I'm only treating him like the animal he is."

"Like father, like son," Chad drawled.

The look of smug satisfaction vanished from Parker's ruddy face. "You goddamned cocky bastard," he snarled. "You'll die for what you did—by God, you will!" Turning to the posse, he yelled, "Rhoades, get a rope and string him up!"

Stunned silence reigned for a moment; the only sound was the crooning of the wind through the pines. Saddle leather groaned as Parker's hired men shifted uneasily.

"Come on, boss," Brett Jordan spoke up. "You can't mean to hang your own son."

"What kind of man would I be if I let him off easy?" Parker snapped. "Look at this innocent woman. See how he treated her."

"I ain't so sure about this neither," said the leathery old cowboy named Shake. "I thought we was gonna take him back to town to stand trial before the judge."

"We don't need some fancy judge!" Parker spat. "God Almighty, we're talking about a low-down bastard who kidnapped and raped a decent woman!"

"The boss is right," said a husky, middle-aged man, his voice heavy. "Ain't no man got any call to treat a woman so bad. We gotta see justice done here."

He dismounted and took a loop of rope from his saddle, then walked to a nearby pine.

Kristy let out a strangled gasp that yanked Chad's attention to her. She stood alone with the wind whipping her skirts, one hand frozen to her mouth, her eyes wide with horror as she stared at the man tossing the rope over a branch.

Turning her gaze to Parker, she choked out, "You can't do this."

"He's only getting exactly what he deserves," Parker growled.

"But . . . it isn't legal—"

Parker patted her hand. "If it upsets you, my dear, why don't you run along into the cabin and wait until this is over?"

She stayed rooted to the icy patch of snow, gazing wide-eyed at the noose Rhoades was tying in the rope. "No, I'm staying."

"All right then," Parker said with a shrug. "I don't blame you for wanting to see justice served."

Seeing Kristy's pale face, Chad felt emotion twist his gut. He knew with burning clarity that he wasn't ready to die, not now when the need for her warmth and sweetness still blazed inside him, when he'd finally found some meaning in his life.

But Christ! How was he to escape Parker's code of justice?

One of the horses snorted and danced, iron-shod hooves pawing the snow. Chad glanced at Brett Jordan just as his friend put a hand to his holstered gun. Catching Brett's eye, Chad jerked a glance toward Kristy and shook his head warningly. Brett tightened his lips, his face dark with anger as he lifted his hand from the six-shooter.

Parker looked at Chad. "I've been waiting a long time for this, boy," he said in a low voice.

Hatred seared Chad's soul; pain shadowed his heart. He remembered the defenseless youngster he'd once been, craving a father's love and getting the lash instead.

"It's too damned bad you can't get rid of that limp so easily," he taunted. "You'll think of me with every step you take for the rest of your life."

"Why, you lousy—" Parker's brown eyes flashed with fury, and he spun around to shout, "What the hell are you waiting for, Rhoades? Let's hang the bastard and get this over with!"

Rhoades drew a horse over to the makeshift gallows, then came toward Chad, misgiving reflected on his rough-hewn face. "You want a blindfold, McClintock?"

"Or will you die like a man?" Parker jeered.

Chad felt icicles of fear slide down his spine. God! He was really going to die. He flashed a look at Kristy; she was staring at him, her beloved face drained of color, her emerald eyes glazed with horror. He felt a violent longing to take her into his arms one last time, to comfort her and draw courage from her warmth, but he knew he must not. Better to let Parker think she'd been raped rather than learn she'd given herself willingly.

"No," he told Rhoades, "I don't need a blindfold."

Slowly the big man came forward and took him by the arm. Chad felt the jaws of hopelessness clamp tightly around his chest. He shot Kristy one last glance; her lips formed his name, though no sound could be discerned. He felt his heart wrench, and in that instant he knew how precious she was to him.

Numbly he pulled away from Rhoades and walked alone to the noose swaying in the breeze. Sunlight glittered on the snow-bowed branches above. His steps were heavy with fear, a fear he refused to display. If Kristy was to witness this, then at least she would see him die like a man.

He removed his hat and tossed it aside. Avoiding his eyes, Rhoades settled the noose around Chad's neck; the rope was a cold, coarse weight against his skin. The two cowboys hoisted him up onto the waiting horse. As Rhoades pulled the rope taut, Chad battled a storm of panic. His eyes swept the posse, met Brett's tormented gaze, then looked away in steely determination.

"No." The word was a mere wisp of sound that jerked his gaze across the clearing to Kristy. *"No!"* she said again, louder and more vehemently.

She ran to Parker, wildly clutching at the sleeve of his coat. "You can't kill him, you can't!"

Parker frowned. "Hush up, gal," he said, patting her hand. "He's only getting what he deserves."

She shook her head violently. "But Chad didn't do anything! He didn't commit any crime!"

"You're overwrought, my dear. Go on inside and leave this to the men."

He tried to lead her toward the cabin, but Kristy shook off his hand and backed away. "No, I won't," she said, her voice impassioned. "I won't let you murder an innocent man. Chad didn't kidnap me—I ran off with him of my own free will!"

Chad felt his insides twist with shock. Why would Kristy lie to save his life after all he'd done to her? Why would she throw away her chance to marry Parker and become a rich woman?

Parker's face had gone ashen. He looked at his men, who were moving restlessly and glancing at each other. "You don't know what you're saying, Kristina—"

"Yes, I do, and it's the truth."

"Then how come you didn't speak up the minute we got here?" Parker demanded. "You're lying, gal, and you know it!"

"What makes you so sure of that?" Kristy lifted her

chin and looked challengingly at the posse. "If you or any of your men don't believe me, I'll be more than glad to swear to it before a judge and jury."

"We gotta let him go then," Brett spoke out. "It ain't no hanging offense for a man and a woman to run off together."

The other hired hands muttered their agreement. Rhoades untied Chad's hands, his dark eyes showing relief. "Climb on down, boy."

Still half-stunned, Chad lifted the noose from his neck and dismounted to the hard-packed snow. An overwhelming feeling of relief at his deliverance swamped him. Slowly he picked up his hat, brushing off the snow and willing his heart to stop pounding.

His gaze sought Kristy. She was watching him, but the moment he caught her eye, she looked away. Fierce feelings burned inside him, tenderness and longing and other emotions too unfamiliar to identify. God! Why had she sacrificed all her plans just to save his neck?

Parker started toward his horse, then turned to Kristy. "I should have known you were his whore," he spat out, his gaze raking her low décolletage. "You're certainly dressed for the part."

Kristy hugged her arms over her bosom. "I'm not a whore."

Furious, Chad stepped toward Parker. "Keep your filthy remarks to yourself, or by God I'll shove them down your spiteful throat."

"Come on, boy," Parker taunted, shaking his rifle. "Give me an excuse to shoot your worthless hide."

Shake spurred his horse, coming between the two men. "Ain't gonna be no shootin' here. We're done, so let's git on out."

"Amen," said Brett.

Parker looked as if he wanted to argue; then he uttered an explosive curse and limped to his horse, vaulting into the saddle. When he turned to glower at Chad, his ruddy face was convulsed by rage. Chad could well understand the violent emotions that must be raging inside Parker; pride ruled his life, and he'd just been badly humiliated in front of his men. He must be itching to order Chad murdered, but none of the hired hands would cotton to harming an innocent man. Especially, Chad thought cynically, when that man was supposed to be the boss's own son.

Parker shifted his glare to include Kristy. "You two haven't heard the last from me," he stated.

Wheeling his horse around, he rode off into the tangle of snowy trees, his men following.

Shake hung back to address Kristy. "Don't you fret none about Jeremy and Lydia. I'll be takin' 'em back to the Bar S."

"Thank you," she murmured.

The leathery-faced cowhand shot a scowl at Chad. "Mebbe you oughta ride on back now—with me, ma'am."

Kristy straightened her spine. "No—I'm staying."

Shake looked suspicious. "You sure?"

"Yes. Please tell Lydia and Jeremy I'm fine."

Even from a short distance away, Chad could tell her smile was forced. But it appeared to reassure Shake, for he merely frowned and tipped his hat to her. "Okay, ma'am." Aiming another dark look at Chad, the older man rode away.

The crunch of hoofbeats faded, and the wind wailed a lonely lament. Kristy stood with her arms folded over her breasts, gazing toward the path Parker and his men had taken. Chad felt a rush of fierce emotion. By God, he'd protect her from whatever revenge Parker planned! Her slender body was convulsed by a shiver, and for the first time Chad realized she wore no cloak.

"Let's go inside, Kristy," he said gruffly. "You must be freezing."

Without even a glance at him, she turned and walked into the cabin. He followed, hanging up his coat as Kristy went to the fire and held her hands toward the blaze.

"I'll get you some coffee," Chad said, pouring her a cup from the pot that had been left to warm on the hearth.

Her icy fingers brushed his as she accepted the cup. "Thank you," she murmured.

Leaning a shoulder against the stone mantel, he watched her sip the coffee. Her skin shone pale and translucent in the firelight. Wisps of wind-blown hair framed her face. She kept her lashes downcast, as if mesmerized by the dancing flames. His eyes strayed to her breasts, full and ripe above the low décolletage of her gown. He ached to make slow, sweet love to her, but he couldn't take her to bed, not before he got some answers. He forced himself to be patient until a trace of color had returned to her cheeks.

"Why did you lie to Parker?" he asked.

Kristy set down the coffee cup. "It was the decent thing to do. Anyone would have done the same."

"No, I don't buy that. My God, Kristy, you ruined your reputation by saying you ran off with me."

She lifted her face to him, her eyes unfathomable pools of green. "My reputation was ruined already. I'd never have lived down the gossip about what we'd done for so many weeks alone."

"But Parker would still have married you," Chad said flatly. "He wants the Bar S—and a son—too damned badly to care what a few busybodies might say."

Kristy conceded the point with a shrug. Chad sensed she was hiding something and felt a burning need to root out the truth.

"You wanted Parker's money," he added roughly. "Why'd you throw it all away? Why would you save my life after everything I've done to you?"

A tumult of emotion passed over her exquisite face. Sadness? Regret? He wasn't sure. Then she straightened her shoulders and raised her dainty chin. Looking him square in the eyes, she said, "I did it because I'm pregnant, Chad. I couldn't stand by and watch my baby's father murdered."

Her soft voice hit him like a fist. Pregnant? She must be mistaken. He shook his head in bewildered denial. "You can't know that so soon. You just had your monthly time."

"No, I didn't."

Chad stared. God Almighty . . . she'd lied! His gaze slid down her slim figure, searching for some physical sign to give testimony to her words. How soon did a woman's belly begin to swell? He tried to recall from his mother's pregnancies, but hell, he'd only been a kid back then. He hadn't paid attention to details like that.

"Are you absolutely certain about this?" he asked hoarsely.

"Yes, I am."

Kristy was going to have a baby. His baby.

Pride and panic surged inside him. He was thrilled at the thought of her bearing his child, yet dismayed too. What if Kristy suffered a miscarriage? How well he remembered the pain his mother had gone through, confined to bed for weeks at a time.

His palms broke out in a cold sweat. What if she carried the baby full term? She was such a small-boned woman, and birthing was dangerous. Good God, why hadn't he considered the misery Kristy would endure when he'd thought up his idiotic plan to get back at Parker?

"Why did you lie to me?" he asked, his voice harsh with fear.

Slowly she walked away and sat down at the table. "Maybe I wasn't anxious to see you gloat over how quickly you'd achieved your goal of vengeance."

Remorse rushed through Chad. God, he deserved that. That and more. What she didn't know was that he felt no glory in his dubious victory over Parker.

"When did you intend to let me know about it?" he asked in a more subdued tone.

"My baby is not an 'it,' " Kristy said angrily, putting a hand over her belly. "And I would have told you about him when I damn well pleased."

"I deserved to know the truth right away."

Her eyes flashed with fury. "You don't deserve anything, Chad McClintock. You were ready to use your own child for the purpose of vengeance. You were ready to give an innocent baby to a man who probably would have beaten him the same way you were beaten!"

The bald statement of truth tore into him like talons. No longer able to meet her accusing gaze, Chad pivoted to stare at the rough stone of the fireplace. Kristy was right. What he'd done was reprehensible, dishonorable, depraved. He'd been so hell-bent on revenge that he truly hadn't considered the fate of the child.

Until now. Now he knew he could never allow another man to raise his child. Especially a man like Parker.

He heard Kristy get up and begin to move about the kitchen area. Turning, he watched her shapely form with all the guilty longing of a condemned man. Even now, knowing the condition he'd forced on her, he felt himself go hard with desire. He could not, would not, give in to his hot, aching need for her; respect was the least he could offer to atone for his sins.

Shame swelled inside him, leaving a sick sensation in the pit of his stomach. Kristy had been a willing bed partner, but that was scant consolation. He'd brought her here against her wishes. He'd kept after her until he'd worn down her defenses. He'd had many opportunities to take her home, but each time his weakness for her had eroded his resolve.

And now she faced the stigma of unwed motherhood; her baby would be branded a bastard.

No, not *her* baby. *Their* baby.

Abruptly he realized Kristy was gathering food into a burlap sack. "What are you doing?" he asked.

"Packing." She gave him a cool glance before beginning to cut a pie into wedges. "I'd like to go home, if you don't mind."

His insides twisted at the thought of leaving this cabin where they'd shared such sweet loving. "Are you sure you feel well enough to travel?"

"I'll have to, won't I?" she said with chilly sarcasm. "I'm certainly not staying here until the baby comes."

"Of course not—I didn't mean that."

"We can still make half a day's travel if we start out soon. I can be back at the Bar S within a couple of days."

"No, you can't."

Her hands froze on the pie; her eyes flared like green fire. "Are you going to stop me?"

"No, but I'm not taking you straight back to the ranch. We're making a detour on the way. To Denver."

"Denver! Why would I want to go there?"

Nervously Chad clenched and unclenched his hands. Could he really go through with the idea taking shape in his head? Yes, he was doing the right thing; it was the only possible solution.

He cleared his throat. "We're getting married there."

Chapter 21

Kristy was so stunned she could only gape at his fiercely handsome face. Married! The gruff announcement was the last thing she'd expected from a loner like Chad McClintock!

All her anger and hurt vanished beneath a rushing river of joy. Chad wasn't going to use her and discard her. She didn't have to say good-bye; she could spend the rest of her life with him. He loved their baby as much as she did.

Or did he?

His fists were clenched as if he'd had to force himself to make the offer. Her happiness dimmed beneath a storm of suspicion. Why *did* he want to marry her? Out of pity or guilt? Had his sleeping conscience suddenly been awakened?

Her lower lip trembled, but pride subdued the impulse to cry. "Did it ever occur to you to ask me instead of tell me?" she snapped. "Maybe I don't want to marry you."

"Kristy," he said softly, "be reasonable. You can't run the Bar S all by yourself and take care of a baby too."

"I won't be alone. I have Lydia and Jeremy. And Shake's my foreman—he'll help out too."

"Can he defend you if Parker tries to run you off the land? You made yourself a powerful enemy today, Kristy. Parker's not going to sit back and let you win."

A premonition sent icy fingers of dread scurrying over her skin. That Parker might seek revenge was something she hadn't considered.

Kristy lifted her chin. "I won't marry you just to protect myself."

"Stop being stubborn." Impatiently Chad raked a hand through his black hair. "You're city bred, for God's sake. You don't know the first damned thing about ranching."

"Shake will teach me whatever I need to know. So you see, I don't need you, and you don't have to feel guilty. You can go on being a drifter and a gambler, just as you've always been."

His eyes narrowed. "Maybe it's time I settled down. And what better place than the Bar S? Don't forget, the ranch used to be mine."

The truth struck her with sudden clarity. How could she have been so stupid? Chad hadn't given up his scheme for vengeance. By marrying her, he'd gain control of the Bar S . . . the ranch Parker coveted. Rage and hurt warred inside her. Dear God, why couldn't Chad just love her for herself? Why did his hatred for Parker always come between them?

Tears gathered in her eyes. Furious at him and herself, she shoved the wrapped pie into the sack of provisions.

"Well, the Bar S belongs to me and Jeremy now," she asserted coldly. "And I'm not marrying you."

Chad uttered a curse under his breath. "My God, Kristy, you're going to have my baby! Do you think I can just walk away and never look back?"

"That was what you planned all along, wasn't it?"

Chad straightened to his full height, jabbing a finger angrily at her. "You listen to me, Kristy Donovan, and listen good. We're getting married if I have to hog-tie you and haul you off to the preacher kicking and screaming. My kid is not growing up without the love and guidance of a father. That happened to me, and I'm not letting my own child get the same rotten start in life."

"You should have thought of that earlier."

Guilt flashed over his handsome face. "Maybe I should have," he conceded. Abruptly he slammed his palm onto the table. "But what's done is done, and by God I'm not giving up my child."

His domineering tone ought to have made her angrier, but instead Kristy found her resistance melting like a spring thaw. Her heart contracted with tenderness. Chad really did care about this baby. Somehow the fact that he hadn't professed any love for her no longer mattered so much.

"All right then," she said softly.

He looked startled. "You'll marry me?"

"Yes."

"You're not going to back out at the last minute?"

"No."

The stiffness left his wide shoulders. "Good," he said gruffly. "It's settled then. I'll go saddle the horses."

They were ready to leave within the hour. From her perch on the roan gelding, Kristy turned to take one last look at the snug cabin nestled within the lodgepole pines. Her breath came out in a frosty sigh. Already the place appeared deserted and forlorn.

As desolate as her own heart.

Her thoughts churned as she followed Chad down the trail, the midmorning sun making the snow glitter and gleam. Was she right to agree to this marriage? Holding the reins tightly in her gloved hands, she studied Chad's broad back. His collar was turned up against the cold, his hat tilted at a rakish angle. He was far too quick tempered, too overbearing, too taciturn for her taste. She sighed again. Yet despite his faults she adored him. He was kind and considerate, gentle and generous. Her body went liquid at the thought of what he could do to her in bed . . . and out. He was the only man in the world she wanted as her husband. Then why did she feel so miserable? Because he didn't love her.

His background had hardened him against love, Kristy reminded herself. Marrying Chad McClintock could mean a lifetime of pain for her. And yet, maybe there was a chance for them. Maybe once the baby arrived and they were a family, he would let down the guard around his heart. If he could care for the child, maybe someday he could learn to care for her too.

Kristy put a hand beneath her cloak to touch her abdomen, thrilled and awed at the thought that her body sheltered a baby. Chad's baby. Together they had created the wonder of a new life, a miraculous result of their lovemaking.

She would make their marriage work, she vowed. She would be agreeable and docile, the perfect wife.

They had ridden only a couple of hours through the wild, snow-swept mountains when Chad reined to a halt in a wooded glade. "We'll stop here for a while," he said. "You need to rest."

Kristy was anxious to please him. "Oh, but I'm not tired yet, truly I'm not. Please don't stop on my account."

"Don't argue," he said curtly. "I'll not see you miscarry out here in the middle of the wilderness."

Her heart lurched. Even when she tried not to, she made him angry. "Yes, Chad."

As they ate a cold lunch, Kristy endeavored to draw him into conversation. But Chad seemed disinclined to talk, muttering one-word replies until she lapsed into frustrated silence. Was he having second thoughts about giving up his footloose ways?

Well, she was not about to release him from their agreement. The more she thought about it, the more she wanted this marriage. Perhaps their desire for each other would bring them closer together, she reflected. In bed he might let down his defenses.

But when they made camp that evening beside a sheer wall of rock that provided protection from the icy wind, and Kristy had settled down in a nest of bearskins and blankets, Chad put his bedroll on the other side of the fire. Forgetting her resolve to be submissive, she blurted out, "Aren't you going to sleep over here with me, Chad?"

He stared at her for a long moment, his eyes dark and distant. "No. You get some rest. We've got miles of hard traveling ahead of us."

"But I feel fine, really I do." With a seductive smile she let her cloak fall open to reveal her low-cut gown.

He barely glanced at the lush display of her bosom. "For God's sake, Kristy, just go to sleep." Turning his back to her, he lay down and yanked a blanket over himself.

His harsh rejection hurt. Kristy felt the heat of desire seep from her body, leaving her cold and lonely. Drearily she huddled beneath the warm bearskins, propping her head on the inverted saddle that was her pillow. She gazed up through the pines at the winking white stars, aching to share the beauty of the moonlit night with the man she loved.

Any hope she had of breaking through his aloofness dwindled over the next few days. They rode for several hours at a time, stopping to rest at intervals before pressing onward through deep, snowy gorges strewn with boulders and fallen trees. The weather remained fair, the sky as blue as columbines. The air was crisply cold and carried the spicy scent of the pines.

Kristy could not fault Chad's considerate treatment of her. He was courteous and kind, especially when the nausea struck her each morning. Without complaint, he would hold her until the wretched spasms quieted. Yet the detached quality of his manner tore at her heart. He wasn't acting out of any particular regard for her, Kristy decided gloomily. He would have treated any ill person with the same consideration.

The final day of their journey was spent crossing the rocky slopes of the foothills. With the evening sky blazing crimson and gold over the purple peaks of the mountains behind them, they rode toward the sprawling city of Denver.

Darkness had nearly fallen by the time they entered the muddy streets. Streetlamps lit the night as the peace of the wilderness gave way to tinny piano music from saloons, hoots of revelers, and the rattle of horse-drawn trucks. The odors of sewage and manure upset Kristy's stomach. Curbing a rush of dizziness, she clung to the reins and followed Chad into a quiet residential area, where stately homes lined a wide thoroughfare.

At last he led the way up a paved drive swept clean of snow. He dismounted before a large brick house, the elegant entryway lighted by twin gas lamps. Grasping Kristy by the waist, he swung her down from her horse. Her weary legs threatened to fold, and she clung to his arm for support.

Concern softened Chad's face. "You must be dead on your feet." Drawing her up the steps to the porch, he grasped the brass knocker and rapped hard.

"Whose house is this?" she asked.

"A friend's," was all he said before the door swung open to reveal a somber-faced woman dressed in the severe black of a servant.

"Good evening, Mr. McClintock," she said, as if seeing him on the doorstep were an everyday event. "Are you expected tonight?"

"No. Is Frank in?"

The woman inclined her head in a formal nod. "If you'll wait in the parlor, I'll fetch him."

The housekeeper led them into a rather gloomy room decorated in maroon velvet and heavy Gothic furnishings. Kristy gave up her cloak, uncomfortably conscious of the indecent gown she wore beneath it. Feeling weary and bedraggled, she headed for the glazed tile stove to warm her numb hands and feet.

Chad poured himself a drink from a decanter on a marble-topped table as if he felt completely at home. Kristy was about to inquire again about his friend when the tread of footsteps drew her attention to the massive double doors of the parlor. A portly man with graying, muttonchop whiskers hastened into the room.

"Chad McClintock! Why, this is a surprise! Haven't seen hide nor hair of you in months."

Kristy stared, startled. The man was Franklin Barnes, the banker who'd turned down her request for a loan! She'd known Chad was acquainted with Barnes, but not well enough, she'd have thought, to be received so warmly.

"Hello, Frank." Chad downed his drink in one gulp and set aside the glass to shake the banker's hand. "Do you remember Miss Donovan?"

Barnes raised bushy gray brows. "Well, of course. I wouldn't forget such a lovely face, but . . . wasn't it *Mrs.* Donovan?"

"You're mistaken," Chad said coolly, without offering any explanation.

The banker shot Chad a perplexed look, though he bowed graciously to Kristy. "Pleased to make your acquaintance again, Miss Donovan." If he had heard gossip of her engagement to Parker and her kidnapping, Barnes hid it admirably.

"It's a pleasure to see you again too," she said courteously.

"Well. You two must have just gotten into town." Barnes eyed their travel-stained clothing. When his glance passed swiftly over Kristy's immodest gown, she felt gawky and gauche. "Might I offer you a place to stay during your visit?"

Chad grinned. "You're a mind reader, Frank. Kristy and I are getting married in a few days, and I was hoping Emmie wouldn't mind helping out with all the arrangements."

The banker's brows lifted in surprise; then his pudgy face beamed a smile. "Married! Well, well, what do you know? Never thought you'd take the plunge, Chad! Guess it just took the right woman to hook you. Wait till Emmie hears—she's been plotting for years to get you married off."

Trotting to the door, he called, "Em? Are you there, hon?"

A moment later, an elegant, middle-aged woman glided into the parlor. Emmie Barnes was as tiny as her husband was portly. Her garnet silk gown was stylishly grand, her gray hair perfectly coiffed in a pompadour. Beside her, Kristy felt awkward and anxious. What must these people think, meeting the fiancée of a man they clearly considered a friend and seeing her dressed like a cheap saloon girl?

Once the introductions and congratulations were over, Emmie Barnes took control of the situation like a general directing his troops. "What's Chad put you through?" she asked Kristy. "You look done in, dear." She ushered Kristy up a magnificent winding staircase and into a bedroom done in regal golds and blues. Within moments servants were bustling everywhere, lighting a fire in the nickle-plated stove, filling a copper tub with steaming bathwater, laying out a light supper on a rosewood side table.

For all her appearance of high-handed hauteur, Emmie Barnes was the soul of kindness. Apparently noting Kristy's lack of luggage, she provided her guest with a frilly nightgown and robe, then discreetly left Kristy alone. Kristy was so exhausted she could scarcely find any pleasure in the luxury of a hot bath and a tasty dinner. She fell asleep the instant her head touched the soft feather pillow, not awakening until late the next morning.

She sorely needed the rest, for the following few days were a tempest of activity. Emmie Barnes escorted her to what seemed like every millinery and dressmaker's shop in Denver, spending an alarming amount of money on a complete new wardrobe.

When Kristy protested, the banker's wife waved a gracefully dismissing hand. "Don't fret, dear," she said. "Chad can afford a proper trousseau for you. Isn't he the most fascinating man?"

As Mrs. Barnes chattered on, Kristy gathered that Chad spent a few months each year in the city, though he refused to participate in Denver society, adamantly insistent on keeping his loner image. Nothing the woman said, however, gave Kristy a clue as to where Chad had acquired his apparent wealth. With numbing dismay, she could only conclude the money must have been won through his gambling. Yet why would people of the Barnes's stature associate with a man who'd gained his fortune by so shoddy a means?

Kristy burned to discover the truth. Several days passed before she could wrangle a moment alone with Chad; she had the distinct impression he was avoiding her. Though painfully aware he didn't care for her company, she rose early one morning and paced the foyer, waiting for him to come down to breakfast.

When at last she saw his tall form at the top of the stairs, her heart fluttered as erratically as the gas jets hissing gently on the walls. Only the barest pause in his stride revealed the moment when he caught sight of her. He descended the curving staircase, watching her with guarded eyes. The greeting died in Kristy's throat. He looked large and imposing in a crisp white shirt and dark trousers. But his face was what snared her attention.

"What happened to your moustache?" she asked, staring at the shorn spot over his lips.

"I shaved it off."

"Just now?"

"Of course. I still had it last night at dinner, didn't I?"

Kristy was too awash with memories of how good his moustache had felt against her skin to take offense at his sardonic tone. "Why did you do that?" she asked in a voice gone breathless. "I liked it."

"I didn't."

"I see," Kristy said woodenly, cut by his curtness. She understood all too well. Her opinion didn't matter to him because he didn't love her; he was only marrying her for the sake of the baby. Drawing in a breath past the lump in her throat, she asked, "May I speak to you in private for a moment?"

His black brows lifted, his inscrutable eyes flicking over her. "Sure."

With a swirl of her topaz skirt, Kristy turned and led the way into the parlor. Chad went to a window draped in maroon velvet hangings and glanced out at the frosty morning. She couldn't keep from staring at the broadness of his back, the leanness of his waist and hips. Her blood warmed and throbbed at the memory of his strong body on hers. Dear God, why couldn't she forget her desire as easily as Chad seemed to have lost his?

Abruptly he turned. "Well, then, what's on your mind?"

You, she wanted to say. Why can't you love me the way I love you? She clasped her hands, unsure of how to start. "I wanted to thank you for the clothes."

His face tightened. "I couldn't very well let you go on dressing like a whore."

Silence stretched. Kristy stared at him, wondering how to phrase her objection to his profession of gambling.

He made an impatient move. "If that's all you have to say—"

"No, I . . ." She swallowed hard. "Why didn't you tell me you had so much money?"

Hands shoved into his pockets, he paced over to the glazed tile stove. "It isn't something I go around announcing to the world."

"Franklin Barnes knew."

"Of course. My money's in his bank."

Frustrated, she took a step toward him. "It's embarrassing that the Barneses know more about you than I do. For heaven's sake, Chad, I'm going to be your wife."

"That doesn't mean I have to tell you everything."

His aloofness hurt. Still she pressed on. "You made your money by gambling, didn't you?"

"Does it matter? I thought all you cared about was living like a lady. You want a house like this one?" He waved his hand around the opulent parlor. "I'll buy you one."

Furious tears filled her eyes. So he still saw her as greedy. "You think you know everything, don't you, Chad McClintock? Well, you can keep your filthy money—I don't want it!"

Half-blinded by tears, she stormed toward the door. She hadn't gone more than a few steps into the foyer when his hands gripped her shoulders and swung her back around.

"Are you ashamed of me, Kristy?" he demanded, his face dark with anger. "Doesn't a low-down gambler fit into your plan to be a lady? Maybe you'd prefer to marry a pillar of the community like Parker."

"Can't you ever forget about Parker?" She dashed the moisture from her eyes and glared up at Chad. "I just don't want my baby's father to end up like my own father, shot to death in some seedy saloon!"

Abruptly the harsh lines of his face gentled. He let go of her shoulders and ran a hand through his black hair. "I'm sorry. I forgot all about your father." He paused, then said heavily, "The money didn't come from gambling, Kristy. I earned it mining a silver claim in Leadville, through my own sweat and a hell of a lot of luck."

Relief spread through her, followed by bitter despair. "Why am I always the last to know anything about you, Chad?" she said softly. "Can't you trust me at all?"

"I told you I'd been a miner for a while. You never asked how successful I'd been."

"I shouldn't have to ask."

He gazed at her with moody blue eyes. "It's the way I am, Kristy. You'll just have to accept that."

The sound of footsteps ended their conversation as Franklin Barnes descended the stairway and greeted them cheerfully. Chad's reticence was the least of what she had to accept, Kristy reflected miserably as she went in to breakfast. His lack of desire for her was far more heart wrenching. Even in anger, the feel of his hands on her shoulders had stirred up hot longings inside her, longings that still burned and ached without mercy. No passion, no love. What kind of marriage did that promise?

Yet even such disquieting thoughts could not induce her to break the engagement. She had to consider the baby. And her heart still harbored the hope that someday Chad might learn to love her.

That hope sustained her on the afternoon of the wedding, when she stood before the oval mirror in her bedroom, a maid fussing over the stiff gown of tulle and satin. The perfect coil of her hair bore a spray of white hothouse rosebuds. Her eyes stared back at her, woeful but willing.

"Thank you, Celeste," said Emmie Barnes, motioning the maid away before gazing admiringly at Kristy. "You look positively lovely, my dear. I can see why Chad fell in love with you."

Kristy forced a smile. If only Mrs. Barnes knew the truth!

Moments later the banker's wife escorted Kristy down the magnificent staircase. The soft strains of organ music floated from the parlor. Since the wedding was small, Kristy had opted to hold the ceremony at the Barneses' home. Emmie Barnes had outdone herself in making all the necessary arrangements in so short a time. The heavy maroon draperies of the parlor had been drawn back to let in the watery winter sunlight. Clusters of roses with trailing satin ribbons rendered the usually somber room festive and cheery.

From her position near the great double doors, Kristy could see the guests already in place. Her heart contracted as she caught sight of the sandy-haired boy and sturdy older woman sitting on a medallion-backed sofa. Jeremy and Lydia! Chad must have sent for them, Kristy realized with a rush of gladness.

Then her pleasure vanished in a swamping tide of nervousness as Franklin Barnes led her toward the tall man standing silently by the minister. Chad looked dashing and noble in a formal coat and matching dark trousers, his appearance as different from the rough cowboy who'd kidnapped her as coal from a diamond. His gravely handsome face gave no clue to his thoughts.

Panic liquified her legs and nearly made her stumble. Tightly clenching her nosegay of roses and ribbons, Kristy took her place at his side. The minister began droning words, but nothing seemed real save the solid, brooding presence of the man standing next to her. His deep, gritty voice spoke the vows with unwavering certainty. Her own voice came out soft and shaky.

Then he was slipping a cold gold band onto her quaking finger and tilting her face up for his kiss. The warm familiarity of his lips was fleeting, but it brought her back to joyful reality. For better or for worse, she was wed to the man she loved.

With a lighter heart she tucked her hand into the crook of Chad's arm and turned with him toward the guests. Lydia hurried forward, her stoutly handsome face wreathed in a smile, Jeremy tagging along after her.

Tears of happiness misted Kristy's eyes as she welcomed Lydia's embrace. "Oh, Lydia, I'm so glad to see you again!" She turned to her brother. "And you, too, Jeremy."

"Aw, don't get so mushy," he grumbled, though he didn't pull away when she gave him a hug.

"How I've missed you both. When did you get into Denver?"

"Last night," said Lydia, beaming at Chad, who stood beside Kristy. "We was pleased as punch when Mr. Chad here sent for us. Now that I can see him with my own eyes, I know why you two run off like that. I would of done the same with such a handsome cowboy."

Lydia's obvious admiration gave Kristy a glow of pleasure. With a smile she turned to her husband and took hold of his arm, gazing up into his enigmatic eyes. "Well, you can't have him—he's all mine."

"Now, that's what I like to see," Lydia said in satisfaction. "Two young folks as happy as church mice at a picnic. Ain't that right, Jeremy?"

"Speak for yourself," Jeremy muttered, glowering at Chad.

"Shush, boy," Lydia chided. "Ain't you gonna wish your sister happy?"

Kristy had but an instant to worry about her brother's contrary manner before the other wedding guests crowded around to offer their congratulations. Most were friends and neighbors of the Barneses, and Kristy had a time keeping the names and faces straight. She clung to Chad's arm in a haze of bliss that lasted through the wedding supper and beyond. Her husband was courteous toward the guests and treated her with such courtly attentiveness that she dared dream he'd fallen in love with her at last. She wouldn't let herself think he was merely putting on a show for propriety's sake.

They were to stay the night with the Barneses before leaving the next morning for the ranch. As the hour grew late, Chad turned to her and gently touched her cheek. "You should go on to bed, Kristy. We've got a long day ahead of us tomorrow."

Anticipation welled inside her. "Are you coming to bed too?"

His eyes went dark as he looked away, taking a drink of whiskey before answering. "In a little while."

She refused to let his sudden moodiness mar her joy. Not caring who was watching, she rose on tiptoes to give him a lingering kiss ripe with sensual promise. "Don't tarry too long," she murmured.

Hugging her hopes close to her heart, she went willingly to their marriage bed. Once in her arms, she assured herself, Chad would let down the wall around his heart. How could he not, on their wedding night?

In a flurry of quivery excitement, she donned a nightdress of cambric and lace. Quickly she brushed out her long hair and applied a dab of perfume between her breasts. Then she climbed into the big bed to await her husband. The fire had died to glowing coals by the time she accepted the bitter, awful truth.

She would sleep alone tonight; Chad wasn't joining her.

Chapter 22

With the bitter slap of the wind on his face, Chad rode north toward the Bar S. Behind him, the runners of the sleigh scraped on the ice-encrusted snow. Frank and Emmie Barnes had insisted on lending them the sled so Kristy and Lydia could ride in comfort. Hot rocks covered with hay warmed their feet; blankets and buffalo robes kept the rest of their bodies snug, with only their faces peeking out.

But for all the discomfort of the raw November afternoon, Chad preferred the saddle. He felt more at ease with the reins in his hands and the familiar bunching muscles of the gray gelding between his thighs. And today he sorely needed the icy air to revive him, for his head throbbed and his belly churned.

Last night he'd gotten stone drunk. Drunker than he'd ever been in his life. So drunk he'd passed out in a chair in the parlor long after the wedding guests had departed and had awakened at dawn with a stiff neck and a sour stomach.

And with unslaked desire for Kristy still blistering his loins.

Kristy. His wife. Chad felt his insides contract at the awesome thought. She wore his ring on her finger, bore his baby within her womb. She was his now by the laws of God and man. The knowledge stirred a fierce storm of gladness in his heart.

A gladness he didn't deserve.

Remorse settled over him like a shroud. When he'd tucked Kristy into the sleigh that morning, she'd acted cool and distant and hurt. He couldn't blame her. What woman wanted to spend her wedding night alone?

That Kristy had been willing to give herself to him last night was all too obvious. But, sweet Christ, how could he go to her bed and gratify his own selfish needs when guilt weighed so heavily on his soul? He'd ruined her dream of becoming a lady through marrying Parker. He'd thrust motherhood on her without a thought about how a baby would change her life.

She might even die giving birth.

The notion was too horrifying to contemplate.

Clenching his teeth against the sick fear rising in his throat, Chad gazed grimly at the sun-sparkled expanse of snow stretching out before him. He couldn't turn back time. But he could try to rectify his sins.

He could prove to Kristy that she was more to him than an object of lust and a means to gain vengeance. He could prove it by keeping his hands off her and treating her like the lady she was. He didn't know how the hell he was going to eat meals at the same table with her, sleep in the same house with her, without ever assuaging his passion, but he was damned determined to try.

No longer did he view her as greedy and conniving. Finally he could accept the truth—she had agreed to marry Parker to protect her brother's inheritance. In restitution, Chad vowed, he would fulfill her dream for the Bar S.

Chad glanced back over his shoulder at the boy riding silently beside the sleigh. Sullen and grumpy, Jeremy had adamantly refused Kristy's invitation to ride in the sled with the women. Chad felt a brief flash of amused sympathy. That was a typical reaction for a boy of ten; no doubt Jeremy thought only a sissy would sit with the ladies.

Yet the boy's attitude seemed to be more than mere moodiness. He had responded with hostility the few times Chad had tried to draw him into conversation. Something was bothering the boy, and Chad had the distinct impression the antagonism was directed at him. Maybe Jeremy was still angry about the kidnapping of his sister. Chad shrugged to himself. There was nothing he could do about that. Jeremy would work out his anger in time.

Through the waning winter sunlight, familiar landmarks began to loom ahead. The ice-crusted remains of a fallen cottonwood. The serpentine twist of a frozen stream. A pock-marked boulder frosted with white. To the left the mountains marched along the horizon like silent sentinels. The crimson sun dipped low, painting the peaks with fire.

Impatient excitement surged inside Chad as he rode up a gentle, snowswept knoll. At the top he reined his horse to a halt and gazed out over the frigid land. The ache vanished from his head as he exulted in the welcome sight before him. How he loved this country! The wind had blown the snow into drifts, exposing the dried grasses beneath. Come spring this rich range would be dotted with a grazing herd.

The sleigh, with Jeremy alongside, drew up beside Chad. "Why are we stopping here?" Kristy called out.

Chad swiveled in the saddle to glance at her and nearly laughed; she was bundled up in blankets, with only her rosy face visible. "We're nearing Bar S land," he said with pride. "Can you see the ranch house 'way out there?"

Kristy looked toward the dark speck he pointed at, and the miracle of her smile melted his insides. "Oh, my!" she said excitedly. "I'll be so glad to get home."

"So will I," he said in a low, intense voice.

Their eyes caught and held. Her smile turned tremulous, yet didn't die. The sudden flaring of Chad's blood burned the numbing cold from his body. He felt a savage urge sweep over him to kiss that ripe cherry mouth, to reach beneath those blankets and find her warm, womanly curves. By God, he wanted to tumble his wife right there in the sleigh, to celebrate their homecoming in the most primal way possible.

Abruptly Kristy looked away, biting her lip. Chad felt chilled and empty again, starved of sustenance. The dull throb returned to his head. She was the only woman he'd ever longed to share his most private thoughts with. He didn't deserve a woman like her. Yet perversely he vowed to prove to her that he did.

Lydia cleared her throat. "We ain't gonna get nowhere by sittin' here like bumps on logs," the woman observed from her perch beside Kristy.

Reluctantly Chad pulled his gaze from the pink perfection of Kristy's face. Abysmal regret ached inside him as he started down the gentle slope toward the Bar S. He reminded himself that all he could do to rectify the immense wrong he'd done her was to demonstrate how much he respected her. That meant curbing his hot passion, no matter what the cost to his sanity.

Night was spreading amethyst shadows over the land by the time they drew up before the ranch house. The stoop-shouldered old cowhand called Shake emerged from the ramshackle barn and hallooed a greeting to them. Shake helped Lydia down from the sleigh while Chad went to the other side to offer his hand to Kristy. With barely a glance at him, she accepted his assistance, but the instant her feet touched the snowy ground, she jerked her gloved fingers from his. Her coolness hurt Chad, even though he knew her attitude couldn't be remedied. Yet.

The women went into the house while the men and Jeremy tended to the horses. The barn was dismal and dark, and Shake lit a couple of kerosene lamps. A musty scent underscored the smells of grain and hay and horses. The place sorely needed repair, Chad thought, seeing a gaping hole in the wall and a stall door hanging crookedly from rusty hinges. He couldn't blame the grizzled foreman for the sad state of the building. As the sole employee, Shake must have had his hands full helping the few head of cattle weather the winter.

As they curried and fed the horses, he queried the foreman about conditions at the ranch. Shake was good-natured about answering the questions, although he seemed to be measuring Chad's worth as much as Chad was assessing his. Chad decided he liked the merry-eyed old man; the foreman appeared to know cattle ranching, and most important, he spoke respectfully of Kristy.

"Gal's got spunk," Shake said stoutly, giving Chad a blunt once-over as if he expected an argument. "I ain't gonna beat around the bush, McClintock. You're the new boss and you're bigger'n me to boot, but if you don't treat Miss Kristy right, you'll be answerin' to me."

Secretly Chad was pleased at the foreman's loyalty. "I

hear you," he said coolly. "But you haven't any cause for worry."

"Good," Shake said, his leathery face showing satisfaction.

Chad became aware of Jeremy rubbing down his horse in a stall across the way. The boy was listening to their conversation, and more than once he aimed a scowl at Chad.

"That's a fine-looking horse you have there," Chad commented in an attempt to breach the rift between them.

"Belonged to my pa," Jeremy spat. "So don't get no notions about takin' him for yourself."

"I was only admiring him," Chad said mildly.

The boy's attitude failed to improve over supper. Lydia insisted that everyone eat together at the rough wooden table in the kitchen. A kerosene lamp hung overhead, shedding a hazy glow over the gathering. Shake looked uncomfortable, Jeremy was sullen, and Kristy was quiet, which left Chad as the recipient of Lydia's animated conversation. The moment the meal was over, Shake headed for the bunkhouse, and Jeremy leapt to his feet to follow.

"Don't stay up late," Kristy told her brother. "I want you in bed in an hour."

Jeremy's freckled face showed resentment. "I ain't tired. I'll go to bed when I durn well please."

Chad had had enough of the boy's ill humor. Setting down his coffee cup, he rose. "You heard your sister. You'll do as she says."

"Don't you tell me what to do, you damned kidnapper!" Jeremy snapped. "You can't come in here and start bossin' everybody around like you own the place. The Bar S belongs to me and Kristy, not you!"

"Jeremy James Donovan, you mind your tongue. As my husband, Chad does have a right to my half of the property." Kristy flashed Chad a veiled look before returning her eyes to Jeremy. "I want you to apologize to him right now."

"I won't," her brother asserted belligerently. " 'Cause I ain't said nothin' I'm sorry for." Wheeling around, he grabbed his coat and darted outside, slamming the door behind him.

"Jeremy!"

Kristy sprang up from her chair as if to run after him, but Chad caught her arm. "Let the boy go."

She jerked herself free. "He's upset—I've got to go to him."

"He needs to work things out in his own mind," Chad said gently. "You won't be helping matters any by coddling him."

Her eyes narrowed. "Coddling! All I mean to do is talk to him!"

"Don't go after him as if he's a baby. He's old enough to start figuring things out for himself."

"Chad's right," Lydia said, still seated calmly at the table. "Anyhow, there ain't nothin' you can say while the boy's so hot under the collar with that Donovan pride. Might as well set down and finish your supper."

Eyes flashing anger, Kristy looked from Lydia to Chad. "I *am* finished," she said coldly. "Good night." Pivoting, she marched up the stairs, her trim hips swaying indignantly.

Feeling like a heel, Chad sighed in frustration. Kristy was pregnant, and he ought to be pampering her, not upsetting her. "Christ," he muttered, running a hand through his hair, "I shouldn't have interfered."

"You only done what was best," Lydia said in a kindly tone. "Jeremy'll come around. Jest give him time." The stout woman rose and began to collect the white ironstone dishes.

Coffee cup in hand, Chad wandered to the window to stare out into the darkness. With the reflection of the lantern on the cracked pane of glass he could discern little outside, but he was too lost in thought to care.

A couple of months ago, when he was plotting his revenge, he'd never imagined he'd end up here at the Bar S married to Kristy. Back then, he'd never aimed to get married at all. He'd always ridden alone, content to keep his own company, leaving romantic notions to fools who still knew how to dream.

Now, Chad reflected in sour humor, he'd become one of those fools. Nothing had turned out the way he'd planned. He was besotted by the very woman who was to have been his means of retribution. And not for all the revenge in the world would he give up the child she'd conceived.

He was fiercely proud to have Kristy as his wife. Proud for reasons that had nothing to do with foiling Parker's schemes. Proud for reasons that had nothing to do with regaining the ranch that had belonged first to his grandparents and then to his mother.

Absently he sipped at his coffee, tasting not the strong black brew but the peachy essence of Kristy's skin. She was a fine woman, a woman with grit. Despite the ever-present desire aching in his loins, Chad was aware of a sense of well-being, a vast comfort and ease the likes of which he had never felt as a loner riding a solitary trail.

He only hoped Kristy wasn't too sorry to be married to him.

Fighting the familiar nausea, Kristy glanced out her bedroom window as she dressed. The snowy peaks of the Rockies gleamed like opals in the rosy sunrise. Straining to reach the buttons at the back of her gown, she chided herself for lying abed so long this morning. Ever since they'd returned to the ranch a month ago, a bone-deep lethargy seemed to have invaded her body. Lydia said a sense of weariness was normal for the first three months of pregnancy. But privately Kristy suspected her fatigue resulted from lying awake at night in her lonesome bed, longing for her husband, who slept in the spare room down the hall.

Leaving the small rag rug before the washstand, she winced as her bare feet touched the icy plank floor. She sat down on a hard-seated chair to pull on her stockings and shoes. To her surprise the chair no longer wobbled, and she looked down to see the broken rung had been fixed. Chad's doing, no doubt. Her heart warmed as she reflected on all the small, thoughtful ways he had made life easier. The kitchen pump now worked smoothly, without groaning and squawking. The fireplace in the parlor no longer belched smoke back into the room. The broken pane of glass in the kitchen window had been replaced.

Chad had done much outside too. The past few days

he'd been repairing the dilapidated barn. Despite the pain over his lack of desire for her, Kristy admired his tireless efforts, for he labored long and hard from dawn until dusk. In the evenings he sometimes sat with her and Lydia in the parlor, mending tack. Her own fingers were engaged in sewing baby clothes as she watched him through the veil of her lashes, loving the sight of his strong and competent hands working the leather.

Even now, in the chilly air of her bedroom, her body warmed beneath an avalanche of memories. Chad's hands caressing her hair. Chad's mouth kissing her breasts. Those days back in the cabin seemed like a wistful, wonderful dream. Sometimes she could hardly believe they were married and she was going to have his baby. But the dreadful nausea was a daily reminder.

As she went down the narrow stairs to the empty kitchen, the fragrant odor of baking sourdough biscuits threatened the delicate balance of her stomach. She poured a cup of coffee from the pot on the woodstove, sipping some to ease the queasiness.

Lydia came in from outside, all bundled up and carrying a basket of eggs. "Land sakes, it's right nippy out there today," she said, taking the scarf from her graying red hair and hanging up her coat.

"I'm sorry," Kristy exclaimed. "It was my turn to collect the eggs this morning, wasn't it?"

"Don't fret, girl. You and that baby need your rest. Now, if you want to help, you go on and set the table."

Obediently Kristy fetched the plates from one of the shelves by the sink while Lydia put some bacon on to fry.

"Saw that husband of yours workin' outside in the cold," Lydia remarked.

"Did you?"

With an air of nonchalance, Kristy peeked out into the pearly dawn to see Chad across the yard, hunkered down before the broken hinge on the corral gate. She set her hands to work plucking knives and forks from a drawer, though her gaze remained riveted on Chad. His dark coat emphasized the breadth of his shoulders. Beneath his hat, she could see his black hair touching the back of his collar. Although more than a month had passed since they'd last made love, the rough, silken texture of that hair remained vivid in her mind—as vivid as the feel of him buried deep inside her. The place between her thighs ached at the memory.

She swallowed to ease the knot in her throat. How could she want a man who scorned her? But God help her, she did. No matter how much she tried, she couldn't stop herself from recalling what he looked like beneath that coat and shirt and pants . . . the magnificent muscles of his chest, the coppery skin brushed with black hair, the narrow waist and long, firm legs. Wrapped in his arms she felt so safe, so protected.

"Way you two stare at each other," Lydia observed sagely from her stance by the stove, "a body'd reckon you'd be sharin' a bed."

Blushing crimson, Kristy spun around and began to place the forks and knives on the checkered tablecloth. "Well, we don't," she said, though she avoided Lydia's eyes.

"It's almighty peculiar for two young married folk to sleep apart," Lydia said, turning the sizzling bacon. "If you two had a fallin' out, it's long past time to bury the hatchet."

"It's not that."

"Then what's frettin' you, sweetie? You ain't afraid of hurtin' the little one, are you?"

"No . . . no, of course not." Kristy hesitated, her insides gnarled with pain. She preferred not to talk about the situation, yet Lydia was like a mother to her and deserved an honest answer. "Chad just isn't interested."

"Hogwash," Lydia snorted. "How'd you get in the state you're in if he don't feel nothin' for you?"

"Whatever Chad felt for me is gone."

"Huh." The oven door creaked as the older woman pulled out the biscuits. "Then why can't the man keep his eyes off you?"

Kristy's heart jolted, yet she wouldn't allow herself to build up false hopes. "He's probably just wishing I hadn't gotten pregnant. Then he wouldn't have had to marry me."

Lydia shook her graying red hair doubtfully. "I don't know 'bout that. Seems to me any man'd reckon himself lucky to marry a pretty gal like you."

"Thanks, Lydia," Kristy said affectionately. "Just don't worry about Chad and me. We'll work things out somehow."

"I sure hope so. Smiles have been scarce as hen's teeth around here between you mopin' an' Jeremy sulkin'. A body'd think we was gettin' ready to hold a wake."

Kristy forced her face into a cheerier expression. "There, you see, I can still smile, so you've nothing to worry about. If you'll excuse me, I'll go fetch the butter for the biscuits."

Before the forgery of her smile could be caught by Lydia, Kristy slipped out of the kitchen. She headed through the parlor to the front door, where a sadly tattered lace curtain veiled the tiny square of window. The front entryway was seldom used, and a box outside on the stoop held their perishable foods, kept fresh by the cold, since the kitchen icebox Chad had ordered from Denver had not yet arrived.

Intending to be outside for only a moment, Kristy didn't bother with a shawl. The hinges groaned as she swung open the door. She must remember to ask Chad to oil those hinges. Funny how she'd come to depend on him for so many little things—

Halfway out the door she froze. Her heart lurched; her eyes widened in horror. Directly in front of her, dangling from the eave of the small porch and swaying gently in a gust of wind, was a rope knotted into a hangman's loop.

Her mind exploded with the memory of Chad with a noose around his neck. A scream tore from her throat. She backed up, clutching the doorjamb.

Chad came dashing around the corner of the house. His eyes met the noose, and he paused for a split second. Then he vaulted up onto the porch and pulled her roughly against him. "Are you all right?" he demanded.

Kristy gave a weak nod, her voice paralyzed with shock. Clinging to the solid security of him, she burrowed her cheek against the front of his coat, drawing strength from the familiar feel and scent.

Lydia scurried out from inside. "What's goin' on here? That holler could of raised the dead!" She stopped, her brown eyes focusing on the noose. "Mercy me! Where'd that come from?"

"I can make one hell of a good guess," Chad said darkly.

Kristy felt the awful panic begin to clear from her mind. "You mean Parker?" she asked, tilting her face up to his harshly drawn features.

"Who else?" he bit out.

Shake came loping around to the porch, Jeremy trotting along after him. "What's the trouble?" the foreman called. "We heard you 'way inside the barn."

"What're you doing to my sister?" Jeremy broke in. "You take your dirty hands off her!"

The boy leapt onto the porch and launched himself at Chad, pummeling and kicking.

Chad let go of Kristy and grabbed hold of Jeremy's flailing arms, thrusting the boy away. "Stop it, for Christ's sake!"

Shake hurried up the steps to pull Jeremy back. "Cain't you see what's in front of your eyes, boy? Lookee here," he said, pointing to the dangling noose. "That's what's got your sister in such a dither."

"Who put that there?" Jeremy asked.

"Parker McClintock, more'n likely," Shake observed, with a piercing glance at Chad.

Jeremy turned belligerent brown eyes from the noose back to Chad. "Even your own pa hates you," he sneered. "You got no right pawing my sister. She don't like it, and neither do I!"

Chad's face hardened with anger. "I've had enough of your snide remarks, boy. Kristy's my wife, and it's no damned business of yours if I choose to touch her."

Kristy shivered, more from distress than from cold; the antagonism between her brother and her husband wrenched her heart. "Please, stop." She took a step forward, her legs wobbly. "Jeremy, Chad was only trying to help me, not hurt me. I . . . I'd had a shock and I'm grateful he came to my aid so quickly."

Chad regarded her keenly. "And you still look like a feather could knock you over. You should go sit down."

He slid a supporting arm around her back, his fingers

curling around her waist. She leaned thankfully against his strong body.

Jeremy glowered at them, but Lydia spoke before he could start another argument. "Breakfast's about ready, so go on and wash up, boy. An' that includes you, old-timer," she told Shake sternly. "I ain't havin' no stink of cattle in my kitchen."

Shake shook a gloved finger at her. "Now don't go blamin' no stink on me. It's them burnt stones you call biscuits you must of been smellin'."

"You watch that flappin' jaw, old man. 'Less you reckon you can do better cookin' for yourself out in the bunkhouse."

"Beg pardon, ma'am," Shake said meekly, though his faded blue eyes twinkled merrily beneath his sweat-stained Stetson. "Come on, boy. I'm hungrier than a woodpecker with a headache."

The gathering broke up, with Shake and Jeremy heading for the pump and Lydia returning to the kitchen.

"Come inside," Chad told Kristy, gently drawing her toward the open door.

"Aren't you going to take that down?" With a grimace she nodded toward the noose swaying in the icy breeze.

"Later. First you have to sit down." His arm still sheltering her, he propelled her inside and shut the door.

"I'm fine, really I am," Kristy protested, though her heart soared at his protective manner. Maybe Chad did care for her. Maybe there was hope for their marriage—

"Don't argue," he said crisply. "It isn't good for you to get so frightened when you're pregnant. You might lose the baby."

Her heart plummeted like a stone. So his concern was only for the child she carried, not for her. Bitterly she reminded herself he had married her out of guilt and the desire to safeguard his baby. The passion he'd felt for her back in the cabin had withered once he'd achieved his revenge. Now he must resent being tied down when he was used to being a drifter. But oh, dear God, how could he feel nothing for her when her own senses were alive with the sight and smell and touch of him?

She was too dejected to protest as he escorted her into

the warm kitchen and pressed her down onto a chair near the stove. Lydia was busy setting platters of food on the checkered tablecloth, paying no heed as Chad fetched a glass of water from the pump.

"Drink, Kristy," he said, crouching down to hold the glass to her lips until she took a swallow of icy water. "Maybe you ought to go lie down," he added. "You look tired."

"I'm all right."

"Are you sure?" He set aside the glass and turned to look at Lydia. "Aren't pregnant women supposed to get a lot of sleep?"

"That's what I keep tellin' her," the older woman said. "Maybe she'll mind her husband better'n me."

Chad rose, gazing at Kristy in concern. "I want you to go upstairs right now," he said, giving her hand a tug.

Kristy no longer found joy in his attentive behavior; she was too miserably aware that he cared only for the baby, not for her. She yanked her hand free. "Oh, stop it. I'm perfectly fine."

"Don't be stubborn, Kristy."

He reached for her arm, but again she shook him off. "Leave me alone," she snapped. "You're upsetting me more than the sight of that noose did!"

His mouth tightened, and his eyes iced over. "Pardon me," he ground out. "I won't bother you again."

Pivoting, he strode out of the kitchen, the stiff set of his shoulders apparent despite the thickness of his coat. Lydia clucked her tongue and shook her head in disapproval, though she voiced no comment.

It was a good thing too, for had the woman spoken even a word of reproach, Kristy knew the tears stinging her eyes would have turned into a deluge.

Chapter 23

"Brett?"

The melodic voice penetrated Brett's gloomy thoughts, yanking his attention to the door of the tack room. Honey stood there, half-swallowed by shadows, a vision with moonbeam hair and coltish curves.

Brett's hand froze on the polishing rag. He stayed hunkered down before his saddle, which was slung over a bench beneath a kerosene lamp. He told himself she was only a dream conjured up by a lonesome man. Then she took a few steps inside the tack room, and he knew Honey was no apparition but a real woman, the one woman in the world he yearned for.

The one woman in the world he couldn't have.

"I'm so glad I found you here," she said quietly. "You've been so busy working these past few weeks I've scarcely even seen you."

Her shy smile could have softened the most hardened of hearts. To Brett, whose insides already felt like mush when she was near, the guileless glow of her face brought an almost painful pleasure.

He looked down at his saddle. What would she say if he admitted he'd been deliberately avoiding her? That he wanted her so damned bad he didn't trust himself around her?

He forced his hand to resume polishing with the rag and saddle soap. "You shouldn't have come here," he said heavily. "What if somebody catches us together?"

"I don't care if everyone on the whole ranch sees us," Honey said with uncharacteristic defiance. "Anyhow, I had to find you. Christmas is only three days off, and I didn't know if I'd have another chance to give you this in private.'' From beneath her shawl, she drew forth a package and held it out to him.

Brett stared mutely at the gaily wrapped box. When was the last time someone had cared enough about him to give him a Christmas gift? Probably not since Ma had died, back when he'd been just a kid still longing for his first pair of real boots.

Numbly he stood up and walked to Honey to take the parcel. The ribbon felt smooth and slippery to his work-roughened hands; the paper rustled as he removed it. Then he was opening the box to find a belt with a fancy silver buckle. A blend of gratitude and regret assaulted him as he fingered the finely tooled leather. How could he afford to give Honey something so fancy in return?

''Do you like it?'' Honey asked.

Her anxious query drew his eyes to her. ''Of course I like it. Thanks,'' he hesitated to reassure her. ''But you shouldn't have gotten me anything.''

''I wanted to.'' She ducked her head timidly. ''Isn't that what Christmas is about, giving gifts to the people you care for?''

The lantern light dramatized the innocence of her face. Suddenly Brett felt old and jaded. Yet he couldn't stop looking at her . . . looking and yearning. You're a fool to fall in love with the boss's daughter, he told himself for the hundredth time. What do you have to offer a lady like Honey?

Carefully he set aside the box and cleared his throat. ''Honey, I've been thinking,'' he said, his words weighted like stones. ''Maybe it's best we don't see each other anymore.''

The light in her eyes dimmed. ''What do you mean?''

''You need to forget about me,'' he forced out. ''There can't ever be anything between us.''

She shook her head in disbelief, her fingers twisting into the rose fabric of her skirt. ''I don't understand,'' she murmured. ''That day you brought Kristy's handkerchief down from the mountains, you called me your woman.''

Her stricken expression cut into his heart. He wanted to say that the rare and precious moment she spoke of was burned into his mind like a brand. The memory of holding her in his arms haunted him each night in his solitary bunk.

Instead, he said, "I was wrong to kiss you that day, Honey. I should have known better, but I wasn't thinkin' straight. You and me, well, we just aren't meant to be."

Her pretty eyes glistened with tears. "Why not?"

"For one, I'm too old for you. I'm thirty-five, and you're what? Seventeen? I'm twice your age."

"That doesn't matter to me."

"It does to me," he said roughly. "Besides, I can't offer you anything. No house, no land, no nothing. You belong with a man who can buy you what you're used to having in life."

"What is it I really have, Brett?" She gave a sad shake of her silvery hair. "Happiness? Love? Kristy and Chad and Lydia have left. My mother is dead. What family do I have? Just my father, and he only cares about money and land."

Tears started a slow slide down her cheeks, and she put her hands over her face. Brett felt his stomach clench like a fist. Without pondering the wisdom of his action, he drew Honey into his embrace. "Don't cry, sweetheart. Please don't cry."

He stroked the corn-silk softness of her hair, letting her sob against the leather vest covering his shirt. Her scent was fragrant and feminine. After a long moment he gently tilted her chin up. Her eyes were as blue and dewy as morning glories. Self-reproach stabbed him. He hated himself for being the cause of her weeping.

He yanked off his neckerchief and carefully dabbed at the tears dampening her face. "I don't mean to hurt you, I swear I don't," he said, his voice low and ragged. "But you've gotta see I'm just not good enough for you. A lady like you deserves better'n a cantankerous old saddle tramp with hardly more'n two bits to rub together."

Honey's fingers curled around his wrist, halting his task of wiping her cheeks. "Don't you talk about yourself that way, Brett Jordan," she said fiercely. "You're a fine man, and I love you."

His heart leapt at her astonishing declaration. How many times had he hoped and prayed she felt the same way he did? Yet he was trapped between his longing and his desire to do what was best for her.

"You don't know what you're saying."

Her chin lifted proudly. "I do. I might be shy around most people, but I know my own mind."

"You should marry a gentleman, a man rich enough to give you fine things."

"My father would give me a dowry—"

"No," Brett broke in harshly. "I won't live on another man's money."

Honey sighed. "How can I convince you that wealth doesn't matter to me? A house or land isn't as important as what I feel for you."

Her expression was so guileless that he groaned, feeling his control slipping. "Don't say things like that, Honey, please don't."

Her lip quavered, and her eyes filled. "Why not? Don't you love me, even just a little bit?"

The notion of making her weep again was Brett's undoing. "Yes, yes, yes," he whispered hoarsely. "That's the trouble—I do love you. By God, I do!"

His mouth dissolved into hers, and he kissed her with violent tenderness, tasting the sweetness he had only dreamed about for so many weeks. Emotion churned in his chest; fire burned in his loins. Half-crazed by a passion too long denied, he shaped his hands to the gentle curves and valleys of her body. She was soft and yielding, yet he sensed a certain timidity in her response. He longed to seek out a cozy spot in the barn and show her exactly how much he loved her. But Honey was no saloon girl to be tumbled in a hayloft.

Brett dragged his lips from hers, although he couldn't yet bring himself to let her go. "We shouldn't be doing this, sweetheart. I don't have any right to touch you, to kiss you."

Her sigh was a warm caress against his throat. "Then why does it feel so right?"

He smiled wistfully into the fragrant cloud of her hair. That was a question he couldn't answer. With all the females in the world, why did he have to hanker after the one who was as far out of his reach as the moon?

He held her tightly before reluctantly taking hold of her shoulders and moving her away. "I'd best walk you back to the house now. I've got some thinking to do."

"About us, you mean?" she asked breathlessly.

He nodded, warmed by the return of radiance to her eyes. Hell's bells, he had to get her out of here while he still had the willpower. "Come on," he said, grabbing his hat. "Let's go."

Her dainty fingers curled trustingly around his arm as he led her out of the tack room and through the darkened barn. The door creaked under the press of his hand. Outside, the light of a full moon pearled the path leading to the ranch house, where the windows glowed like gold. The night air was frosty. As they walked, Brett found himself using the cold as an excuse to hug Honey closely.

She stopped him beside an empty corral, lifting her troubled face to him. Her hair was silvered by moonlight, her features so lovely he yearned to do nothing but gaze at her for the rest of his life. "Oh, Brett, I'm so afraid."

A lightning bolt of rage stabbed him. He gripped her arms. "Afraid! Has that bastard Webb come back? If he's been bothering you again, he's gonna get a gut full of lead!"

Honey shook her head, her smile reassuring. "No, no, Brett, that's not it. Mr. Webb's been in Washington for several weeks now. Father received a letter from him saying business would keep him there for a while." Her expression turned wistful, and shyly she lifted a hand to Brett's cheek. "What I meant was, I'm so afraid of you deciding against me. Oh, Brett, you mustn't forget how much I love you."

His heart melted, sending liquid fire to his loins. How could he resist a woman who looked at him with such need in her eyes?

Ignoring his better judgment, he drew her into his arms again. "I won't forget, Honey. Believe me, I won't. All I need is some time to get things straight in my mind."

He shouldn't give her any hope, he told himself fiercely, even as he held her sweet body tightly against him. Just because they loved each other didn't give him the right to condemn a rancher's daughter to the life of a cowhand's wife.

Yet how could he ever give her up?

Parker McClintock splashed whiskey into a glass, ignoring the droplets that spattered the polished oak of his rolltop desk. Setting down the crystal decanter with a bang, he emptied his glass in one large swallow.

The liquor failed to ease the gnawing sensation inside his belly. The feeling had been a constant companion ever since that moment when Kristina had ruined all his plans by speaking out in Chad's defense. Parker gritted his teeth. He'd been so close to ridding himself of that bastard once and for all. Not for an instant did he believe she'd spoken the truth, that she had run off with Chad. How had that bastard won her over? Christ, she was even married to him now! Was Chad such a stud in bed that she would throw away her chance to wed one of the most powerful cattle ranchers in Colorado?

His stomach throbbed, and for a moment Parker felt old and defeated. Humiliation washed over him as he recalled the knowing glances of the posse on the long ride back to the ranch.

Irritably he shook off the debilitating sensation and began to pace the confines of his office, expending no effort to hide his limp, since he was alone. By God, he'd get back at Chad and Kristina both for making him a laughingstock! That noose he'd had left on their porch was only a warning. Somehow he'd run them off the Bar S, and money was the key. After all, Chad was just another cashpoor cowboy. If enough disasters befell the Bar S, he'd be forced to sell out and move on.

There was no time like the present to begin the attack.

Parker flung open the office door and strode out into the foyer. The room smelled of spicy pine from the garlands twined around the balustrade. He shot the decorations a look of grim humor. The neighboring ranch was about to get a Christmas present, compliments of Parker McClintock.

Fetching his beaver-trimmed coat from the hall tree, Parker yanked on the garment as he went out the back door and into the chilly night. The porch steps were icy beneath his boots. Careful of his bad leg, he walked down the snowy path and veered to the right. Ahead of him, the bunkhouse was a long, moonlit shape, its windows yellow with the light from kerosene lanterns. A faint hoot of masculine laughter drifted from the building.

A sudden squawk of hinges came from the other direction. Acting on instinct, Parker melted into the shadow of a cottonwood and peered across the deserted yard. Two figures emerged from the barn, a man and a woman, arms entwined. One of the cowhands and . . . who? Some whore from town?

Then moonlight glazed the woman's distinctive silver-gilt hair. Honey!

Rage exploded inside Parker. That cowpoke was messing with his daughter! Who the hell was the cocky son of a bitch?

The man was gazing down at Honey, his features half-hidden by his hat. Then the pair stopped by the corral, and Parker caught sight of the cowboy's face. Brett Jordan!

Violent fury propelled Parker toward them. He'd beat Jordan into a bloody pulp! That damned cowpoke wasn't going to soil Honey and ruin her chances with Horace Webb.

Yet before Parker had taken more than a few steps, a glimmer of sanity intruded. If Honey imagined herself in love with Jordan, thrashing him in front of her would only arouse her sympathy. No, Parker acknowledged, there was a better way to nip this romance in the bud. A more permanent way.

Leashing his savage wrath, he limped back into the shadows to watch, stroking his handlebar moustache, as the couple embraced. After a moment the two resumed their walk toward the house. In the gloom of the back porch they kissed briefly. Then Honey went inside, and Jordan returned to the barn.

Parker seethed with rage and disbelief. Honey was betraying him, just as Mavis and Kristina had done. By God, was there no woman in the world worth trusting?

The pain corroding his gut intensified. Once again his shoulders slumped beneath the full weight of his fifty-two years. Now that Kristina was out of the picture, he fully intended to find another woman to marry. But he had to face facts. What if the new wife failed to give him a son, as Mavis had failed?

Honey was his ace in the hole, his hope for the future. The dreams and labors of so many years would all be for nothing if he had no heirs to whom to bequeath his ranch. He couldn't put the blame on Honey. His daughter was naive; she must have been led astray, just as Mavis had led him astray so long ago. That son of a bitch Jordan wouldn't diddle with Honey and get away with it.

Parker resumed his grim march toward the bunkhouse, though now with an altered purpose in mind. First things first. His plan for the Bar S could wait a little while longer.

Yanking open the door, he strode into the bunkhouse. The place was a chronic mess, with boots and clothing strewn over the floor. The rough wood walls were papered with a haphazard collection of clippings from picture magazines and mail-order catalogues. The long room stank of sweat and manure and smoke, with a trace of licorice from plug tobacco.

A few of the cowboys lounged in unmade beds; the rest played cards at a table by the potbellied stove. Chairs scraped and mattresses rustled as every man leapt up to face Parker.

"You, Slim, get on out here," Parker snapped, jerking his head toward the door.

"Okay, boss." The lanky man who'd spoken made a dive for his boots and hat.

Parker walked back outside and paced the snowy ground in front of the bunkhouse. Damned shame he couldn't trust Rhoades with this job, but the foreman was too honest to be of much use in shady dealings. Slim, though, had no such annoying scruples.

The cowboy emerged into the night, slamming the door shut behind him. "What'd I do wrong, boss? I hung that noose on the porch, just like you asked."

"Shut up. We'll talk where nobody can hear us." Parker limped back to the shadow of the cottonwood. "I have another job for you," he said in an undertone. "You game?"

"Sure 'nuf, boss."

"I want you to get rid of Brett Jordan, as soon as possible."

Slim stared, then spat out a stream of tobacco juice. "You tellin' me to shoot him in the back?"

"I'm not saying to kill him. Just make sure he never shows his face on Diamond M range again." Parker paused, then added craftily, "Oh, and by the way, there'll be an extra couple of months' pay in it for you. Provided, of course, you can get the job done nice and quiet."

A gap-toothed grin lit the cowboy's face. "You can count on ol' Slim, boss. Yessiree."

Watching him saunter off, Parker hoped to God nothing else would go wrong. Absently he slipped a hand inside his coat to rub his belly, where the pain had subsided to a dull ache.

He wouldn't rest easy until Honey was married to Horace Webb.

With the heel of her hand, Honey rubbed a clear spot in the frosted glass of the kitchen window. Peering outside, she cradled a bowl in one arm, absently stirring the batter for sugar cookies. Her heart skipped a beat as a tall cowboy emerged from the barn. But that bandy-legged walk didn't belong to Brett.

Honey sighed with disappointment. The air was fragrant with gingerbread and pine and spices. Not once in the two days since their meeting in the barn had she caught even a glimpse of Brett. Had he come to a decision yet? His concern over money was just typical male pride. Somehow she had to convince him of that.

Excitement quivered inside her. She need only wait a few more hours, she told herself. Tonight she would have an opportunity to seek him out at the Christmas Eve party for the hired hands.

A sudden sad memory wiped away her joyous anticipation. Since her mother had died last spring, this was the first year Honey would act as hostess for the party. Mavis McClintock had been a sickly woman, able to spare scant time for her daughter, yet Honey missed what little affection Mavis had offered.

Gazing out at the snow flurries, Honey sighed again. The house seemed so lonely and empty these days without Kristy and Lydia and Jeremy. For the hundredth time she entertained a cherished dream, a solution she'd come up with after that night in the barn. If only her father would bestow his blessings upon her and Brett's marriage, everything would work out perfectly. Then Brett needn't worry about money; some day he could take over the running of the Diamond M.

Tonight at the party she intended to speak to him on the matter. If they could convince her father of how much they loved each other, maybe, just maybe, he would approve the match.

"Honey."

She whirled around, guilty at being caught daydreaming, to see her father standing in the kitchen doorway. "Yes?"

"If you aren't busy, I'd like to speak with you in my study."

Her eyes widened. His study was reserved only for momentous occasions, such as the time he had sent her off to boarding school and the time he'd announced his engagement to Kristy. "Of course," she murmured.

Honey removed her apron and followed her father into the study. Lacing her trembling fingers, she hovered near the fireplace. Somehow she'd never felt comfortable in this room, despite the homey atmosphere of oak bookcases and crimson-upholstered furniture.

Her father sat down before his massive rolltop desk. He looked at her for a moment, stroking his handlebar moustache. "I've decided it's time you were married," he announced.

Shock and joy rippled through Honey. Had her fantasy come true? Maybe Brett had come to the same conclusion she had, and he'd already spoken to her father—

"I believe I've found the ideal husband for you," he went on. "A husband befitting a woman of your wealth and social standing. You know him—Horace Webb."

The name hit Honey like a blow. Her heart stopped for an instant, then beat frantically with disbelief. No! She'd hoped Horace Webb had only been lying about her father's plans for her.

She drew in a deep, calming breath. "I can't marry Mr. Webb," she said. "I love someone else."

Her father lifted his graying brows. "Oh? Who?"

His mild response encouraged Honey. Maybe there really was hope. She lifted her chin. "It's Brett Jordan, Father. I know he isn't rich, but he's a wonderful man and a hard worker—"

"No."

"But if you'd get to know him the way I have, you'd see—"

"My dear, I hate to be the one to break this news." Her father rose and patted the back of her hand, his brown eyes sympathetic. "Jordan's no longer in my employ. He quit the other day—told Rhoades he was moving on. You know how these drifters are—can't abide hanging their hat in one place for very long."

Honey felt herself go pale with shock. It couldn't be true; it just couldn't be! Yet she remembered Brett's reluctance to marry her, his insistence that she was too good for him. Her heart sank like a stone, its weight dragging her down so that she crumpled into a crimson velvet armchair. Yes, Brett would leave, thinking he was doing the right thing for her.

The sound of her father's voice penetrated her stupor. "Best just forget about Jordan," he advised. "You're better off marrying Webb anyway. He's a powerful man, a man who can give you a good life, a happy life. He's a cinch to win the election next year. Imagine, a McClintock married to a United States senator."

Honey sat in paralyzed silence as her father extolled the virtues of the match. He would never believe her if she told him Webb had once raped her. All her life she had lived with her father's bullheaded nature, his unyielding justification of his schemes. He saw only what he wanted to see.

She could run away, find Brett somehow. But wouldn't honor induce him to return her home? A needle of pain pierced her numbness. Maybe Brett didn't love her enough in any case. He hadn't even bothered to say good-bye.

"Horace is still a young man—he'll give you strong sons," her father added. "He and I have discussed the marriage, and I'd like to telegraph him as soon as possible to tell him of your acceptance of his offer."

"Of course, Father," she whispered dully.

Her heart deadened by grief, she managed to get through the festivities that evening. Which of the cowboys she danced with, she could not remember later. The world was a cold sea of gray, and she was adrift without paddle or sustenance.

At midnight she lay in her bed, hearing the hired hands celebrate the first minutes of Christmas by firing pistols into the air and singing noisy songs. Tears rolled down her cheeks, yet inside she felt wooden. She was crushed beneath the weight of her father's will and the agony of a life without Brett. Nothing mattered anymore.

If it made her father happy to see her marry Horace Webb, then so be it. She no longer cared.

Chapter 24

Snow flurries stung Chad's face as he rode over Bar S range. He was grateful for his heavy coat and leather chaps, for the December wind was bitter and blustery. Gray clouds scudded across the early morning sky. Twice already he'd gotten down from the saddle to walk some feeling back into his feet.

His purpose today was to find a cow that had wandered away from the small herd kept bunched near the ranch house. He'd left Shake and Jeremy to the tasks of breaking the ice in the waterholes and distributing hay to the pitifully few head of stock bearing the Bar S brand. Even though today was Christmas Eve, the daily chores had to be done.

The tracks of the stray led westward to the mountains. As he rode, Chad found himself remembering the way Kristy had looked when he'd left, her cheeks flushed from the warmth of the stove, her hair curling in tendrils around her face. The memory alone was enough to heat his chilled body. He wished to God he could have succumbed to the urge to take her up to bed. But he couldn't, not after the vast wrong he'd done her. Maybe by the time the baby was born, he would have proven to Kristy how much he respected her. Maybe at last he'd have someone to share his private self, someone to confide in, to hope and dream with.

If she still wanted him. Kristy was beautiful and passionate, but he could not forget her initial refusal to marry him. She didn't love him. This marriage had been forced on her, forced by the prospect of unwed motherhood. In time she might come to hate him for coercing her into a life not of her own choosing, as his mother had grown to hate Parker.

Broodingly Chad stared at the snowswept landscape. The thought of Kristy's indifference hurt more than he wanted to admit. Somehow, without his even knowing how or when, she had become the most cherished part of his life. Although more than a week had passed since that incident with the noose, he could still feel his vivid, gut-wrenching fear on hearing her scream. By God, if Parker ever caused her or the baby any real harm . . .

Chad's thoughts came to an abrupt halt. Two new sets of tracks had joined those of the strayed cow. He sprang from the saddle and squatted down to examine the marks. Two men on horseback. A splotch of brown tobacco juice stained the snow.

The horse tracks headed off toward the mountains. The cow's trail no longer wandered aimlessly, indicating the riders were herding the animal ahead of them. A slow anger simmered in Chad at the thought of someone stealing what was his and Kristy's. They wouldn't get away with rustling Bar S cattle.

As the bleak morning wore on, he had trouble following the trail, for the combination of icy wind and snow flurries had all but obliterated the hoof marks. At last, in a draw cutting into the rocky foothills, he came upon the cow lying dead beside a barren bush. The snow nearby was spattered with tobacco juice.

Chad swung down to examine the animal. His fury flared brighter when he saw the bullet wound. By the looks of the carcass, the cow had been dead half a day at most. The iron-shod tracks of a horse led away from the cow toward Diamond M range. This was Parker's doing, Chad thought angrily. His cowhands must have spied the stray's brand and driven the animal off for slaughter.

The petty vindictiveness of the deed sickened Chad. With a half-formed plan of pursuing the rustlers, he vaulted back into the saddle. He hadn't ridden more than a dozen yards when he saw a dark shape in the scrub up ahead. A shape the size of a man.

He urged his horse forward. Dismounting, Chad saw the figure was, indeed, the body of a man, lying face down on the ground. Brown patches of blood streaked the snow, and a short distance away was another stain of tobacco juice.

Carefully he eased the man over. His heart contracted in shock. Brett Jordan lay unconscious; he had been shot, and the front of his coat was drenched with blood.

Gripped by dread, Chad thrust a hand inside Brett's scarf to feel for a pulse. His skin was alarmingly chilled, but after a moment Chad detected a thready heartbeat. Quickly checking the wound, he found blood still oozing from the blackened bullet hole in the abdomen. Hands trembling, he used his scarf as a makeshift bandage.

From the bedroll tied to his saddle he fetched a blanket to cover Brett. Then Chad set to work constructing a travois. He cut two slim young pines for poles, using the axe stowed with his gear. As he completed the primitive sled, Chad kept an anxious eye on Brett. The cold weather was both enemy and friend. Brett could die from exposure, but the chilling of his body also slowed the loss of blood.

The tracks of two horses led off toward Diamond M range. Had Parker discovered Brett's small, though unwitting, part in Kristy's kidnapping? Rage blazed inside Chad, but he forced himself to concentrate on the task of getting his friend to safety. He would deal with Parker later.

"You'll be all right, pardner," he murmured, securing Brett to the travois. Before leaping into the saddle, he took one last worried look at Brett's wan face. "By God, you'd better be."

Riding as swiftly as he dared, Chad headed back to the ranch house. A few snowflakes frolicked in the frosty wind; the afternoon sky was as gray and dismal as his mood. His insides churned with anxiety and guilt. If Brett died, Chad would be to blame, for he'd involved an innocent man in the feud with Parker.

Darkness had descended by the time Chad neared the house. The yellow glow from the windows had never been a more welcome sight. As he rode into the yard, Shake came loping up, Jeremy not far behind. "What's the trou-

ble?'' the foreman asked, with a glance at Brett's unconscious form.

"Found him up in the hills, shot in the gut.''

Shake asked no more questions and set about helping
Chad lift Brett from the travois. "Take care of my horse,''
Chad told Jeremy.

For once the boy didn't protest an order and led the tired
gray gelding toward the shelter of the barn.

They carried Brett into the house. The kitchen was warm
and inviting after the long, cold ride, and the air was rich
with the smell of spices. Kristy was drawing a mince pie
from the oven; she straightened up and stared from Chad
to Brett, her face going pale. She was all dressed up in a
fancy green gown. Tonight was Christmas Eve, Chad remembered suddenly.

"Mercy me!'' Lydia exclaimed, wiping her hands on
her apron. "Ain't that Brett Jordan from the Diamond M?''

Chad nodded curtly. "We'll put him in my room.''

"I'll get some water heating and bring up some bandages,'' Kristy said, hurrying to the kitchen pump.

Upstairs, they laid Brett on the bed. Lydia scurried to
light a lamp, then built a fire in the tiny hearth. Brett
groaned, though he didn't regain consciousness as Chad
removed the blood-stained coat. He checked the wound
and found it oozing fresh blood. Brett's pulse was er-
ratic.

"Don't look good,'' Shake pronounced, shaking his
head.

Chad refused to give in to the dread gnawing inside
him. "Just get him warm. I'll fetch the doctor.''

In the shadowy hall he met Kristy carrying a stack of
bandages. "How is he?'' she asked anxiously.

"Still alive. And by God, if he dies, Parker's a dead
man too!''

Her eyes widened. "You mean Parker shot him?''

Chad touched her cheek, aware of a fierce longing to
unload the guilt and fear weighing heavily inside him. "I'll
explain everything later. I'm going for the doctor.''

Kristy watched him bolt down the darkened steps, his
boots thumping on the wooden steps. From downstairs

came the sound of the kitchen door opening and slamming shut.

Her skin still tingled where he'd touched her. Lifting a hand to her cheek, Kristy ran her fingers over the spot, wondering how such a small action could make her feel so quivery inside.

Sighing, she went into the bedroom. Brett Jordan was lying on the bed, his face ashen. Lydia took one of the bandages and pulled back the quilt to press the cloth against the wound in his abdomen. The brief sight of the bloody injury made Kristy's stomach roll with queasiness.

She took a deep, fearful breath. "Is he going to live?"

"Only the good Lord can answer that," Lydia said.

"Depends on his grit," Shake offered as he fed wood to the fire. "I seen some men survive worse an' others die from less."

In a turmoil of worry, Kristy went back downstairs to fetch hot water from the kitchen. Why would Parker shoot Brett Jordan? Then she recalled the time back at the Diamond M when she'd seen Honey gazing out the window at Brett. Suddenly she was sure a romance had bloomed between those two. A romance Parker had discovered. She closed her eyes, feeling sick. Parker would never tolerate a marriage between his only daughter and a hired hand. And he would deal with the problem in his own brutal way.

She took the water upstairs and helped Lydia clean the wound. Then they wrapped Brett in blankets to keep him warm. Jeremy came in and sat with them, his small freckled face taut with concern. In a hushed voice he told Kristy how he'd been befriended by Brett while at the Diamond M.

Two hours passed before Chad arrived from the nearby town of Painted Rock with the doctor in tow. The rotund Doc Barlow didn't look too pleased at being dragged out so late on the eve of Christmas. Muttering grumpily, he shooed everyone out of the room but Lydia.

They trooped downstairs. On the wood stove was the supper that was to have been the start of their holiday celebration. Now the biscuits were hard, the sliced turkey dry, the sweet potatoes cold. Still, Kristy managed to salvage a meal out of the ruined fare. The men ate in pensive silence while she only toyed with her own food.

Finally Doc Barlow came ambling down the stairs. Chad thrust back his chair, the legs scraping the floor. "Is he all right?"

Barlow shrugged. "Got the bullet out—that's all I can do."

"How bad off is he?" Chad demanded.

"He's pretty durn tore up inside, but the bullet missed his vitals, and the cold slowed the bleeding. We'll just have to wait it out." The doctor's plump face brightened. "Say, is that mince pie on the table there? I got rushed off tonight before I could finish my supper."

"Please, join us." Amused that he could still eat after probing a man's insides, Kristy filled a plate, and the doctor sat down to eat with ill-concealed gusto.

Shake and Jeremy left the house. Coffee cup in hand, Chad prowled the kitchen. As she cleaned up the dishes, Kristy watched him from beneath the sweep of her lashes and recalled his angry denouncement of Parker in the upstairs hall. He was clearly upset about Brett Jordan, more upset than she would have expected him to be over a stranger. Why?

When the doctor was finished eating, Chad said abruptly, "You're not to tell anyone about the man you treated upstairs."

"But the missus will want to know—"

"Tell her one of the cowhands got hurt, but everything's okay now." Flattening his palms on the tabletop, Chad leaned toward the doctor's pudgy face and added coldly, "If I ever hear even a word of this breathed in town, I'll know who to go after. Do I make myself clear, Doc?"

"Yessir, quite clear," Barlow stammered. Pushing back his chair, he scurried to the door. " 'Night, Mrs. McClintock, Mr. McClintock." A loud belch escaped him. "Much obliged for the grub."

The door slammed shut, and Kristy was alone with Chad. More puzzled than ever by his vehement protection of Brett Jordan, she asked, "Did you know about Brett and your sister?"

He swung to face her, surprise apparent in the intense blue of his eyes. "What are you talking about?"

"Oh . . ." she said, her hand faltering on the dish she was drying. "Maybe I'm wrong."

"Wrong about what, Kristy?" he asked sharply. "What the hell does Jordan have to do with Honey?"

She hesitated. "I think she's in love with him."

For a moment his gaze was dark and penetrating, then his black brows lifted. "That would certainly explain a lot," he said musingly. "Yes, indeed, it would."

Kristy was perplexed as she put away the dish. "But if you didn't know about them, why were you so sure Parker did the shooting?"

"I didn't mean he actually pulled the trigger. That's not his style. But he paid someone else to dry-gulch Brett." Chad related a brief account of finding first the slaughtered cow and then Brett. "I have to tell you, Kristy, that Brett's an old friend of mine. He was an unwitting party to your kidnapping. I talked him into getting the job at the Diamond M so he could keep me posted on what Parker was up to." In a heavy voice he added, "I was afraid Parker had found that out."

Understanding rose in her, inundating Kristy with the urge to smooth her hands over the tired lines of his face. Instead she rested a hip against the sink and tightly twined her fingers.

"And so you blamed yourself for what happened."

"It would have been my fault, yes."

"But Brett could have left Parker's employ once you'd abducted me," she pointed out. "He didn't, so that absolves you of any guilt."

Chad stared at her a moment. "Maybe," he acknowledged. An unexpected smile caressed the hard corners of his mouth. "Who would have thought a couple of months ago that you'd ever defend a stinking polecat like me?"

"Or that we'd end up married," she couldn't resist adding.

He stared at her with eyes gone secretive. "We've come a long way since that poker game in Denver. I collected a hell of a lot more than one night in your bed."

Her heart leapt with longing. Was he, too, remembering the loving passion they had shared in the cabin? "Speaking of beds, you'll need a place to sleep tonight," she said impulsively. "Since Brett's in your room, I mean."

"Is that an invitation?"

His voice was low and gritty, and Kristy felt her legs go liquid as she imagined Chad lying naked with her beneath the quilts, kissing her, caressing her. But was that what he wanted? Doubts gripped her. Could she offer herself to him and risk the pain of another rejection? She was confused by a fog of feelings only Chad could stir up within her. Yet one thought shone clear. His emotional love might be locked away from her, but his physical love might yet be within her reach.

Heart hammering, she walked toward him, stopping so close she could feel his radiating warmth, smell his enticing male scent. Mustering all her courage, she put her palms on the hard breadth of his chest.

"You're welcome to stay in my bed, Chad," she murmured.

Silence stretched. Kristy held her breath, wishing, wanting, hoping. His gaze was intense, yet cryptic. Tossing pride to the wind, she forced herself to meet his eyes unflinchingly.

Then the hard lines of his face softened, and she knew with a wild surge of gladness that she'd won. He reached for her slowly, as if loathing himself for desiring her. But she didn't care. Nothing mattered so long as he was holding her in his arms.

Burying his face in her hair, he muttered, "God forgive me, but I want you, Kristy."

"I want you too," she whispered, running her hands over the broadness of his back.

His fingers found her breasts, rousing shuddering waves of sensation. His mouth met her lips, sparking vivid flames of excitement. Then abruptly he drew back.

"We shouldn't do this," he said hoarsely. "We might hurt the baby."

"No, we won't," she softly assured him. She touched the stubbly roughness of his cheek, fiercely glad he cared so much for their baby, so much that he would give up his own gratification. "Don't stop now, Chad, please. I need you too much."

With a groan of desire, he swung her into his arms. She felt the swift drum of his heart against her cheek as he carried her upstairs. In the darkness of the bedroom they came together in a storm of passion. Chad kissed and caressed and coaxed until the magic escaped her control and she plunged into blinding radiance.

Yet later, as she lay cuddled against him, Kristy felt a deep, troubled sadness. What had she gained by luring Chad back into her bed? Not once had he voiced even a word of affection. He didn't love her; he felt only a fleeting physical desire.

The breath came out of her in a despondent sigh. Her body was satisfied, but her heart still hurt.

The next day Kristy forgot her own troubles as a fever raged in Brett. She and Lydia took turns nursing him, laying cold cloths on the burning skin of his forehead, trying to feed him cool broth. He drifted in and out of consciousness, and once he tried to sit up in bed. His eyes dark with delirium, he gripped Kristy's arm and muttered Honey's name before collapsing back onto the pillow in a stupor. Kristy knew then she had guessed right about the reason he'd been shot.

Gloom hung over the house despite the cheery scents of Christmas. Shake took charge of the chores outside. Chad watched over Brett for a while so Lydia and Kristy could prepare supper. Even Jeremy pitched in without a fuss, keeping the sickroom supplied with water and wood.

While Shake took a turn sitting with Brett, Lydia insisted on everyone else exchanging Christmas gifts in the parlor to perk up the somber mood. Kristy had sewn Chad two shirts, but even when he thanked her, the look in his eyes was impenetrable. After last night, couldn't he see the love that had gone into every stitch?

Upon opening his present to her of an expensive set of leather-bound books by Mr. Dickens, she felt a flash of disappointment, followed promptly by a sense of shame. So what if she would have rather gotten something more intimate . . . like the lingerie he'd given her back in the cabin?

His gift to their unborn baby was more personal. Amid laughter and smiles, he wheeled in a fancy wicker baby carriage. Wistfully Kristy reflected that even if Chad cared little for her, at least their child would have a loving father.

While they were gathered in the parlor, Kristy mentioned something that had been worrying her. "If Parker found out about Brett and Honey, would he do something to harm Honey too?"

Chad shot up from the horsehair sofa, his fingers clenched into fists. "He'd damned well better not have. By God, I'm going to get my sister away from that son of a bitch right now."

"Now, don't go flyin' off the handle," Lydia cautioned. "You charge in there like a bull into a china shop, an' he's gonna shoot first an' ask questions later."

Belatedly sorry for stirring up Chad's explosive temper, Kristy said hastily, "Lydia's right. You can't just go storming over there. If shots are fired, Honey might end up hurt too."

"Anyhow," added the older woman, "I ain't never seen the man raise a hand to his own daughter, so I reckon she'll be all right. Better I should go tomorrow and see about her myself."

"I don't like waiting one damned bit," Chad growled.

"Neither do we," Kristy said placatingly. "But Parker would never let you anywhere near his daughter. At least Lydia might be able to wangle a talk with Honey."

Although Chad finally sat down again, he looked far from pleased. Early the next morning Lydia went to the neighboring ranch on the pretext of delivering a Christmas gift to Honey. Upon her return the woman declared Honey to be unharmed, though melancholy and subdued. In an outrage Lydia added that Parker had refused to leave her alone with the girl.

"The old coot bragged about her bein' engaged to that Horace Webb! Imagine, our shy little gal hitchin' herself to such a shifty-eyed snake! I smell a rat in this, you mark my words."

"Yes, it doesn't seem right," Kristy agreed, frowning.

"I could have sworn Honey was in love with Brett Jordan."

"We'll get the true story as soon as Brett regains consciousness," Chad said grimly. "And by God, if Parker thinks he can force my sister into a marriage she doesn't want, he's got another thing coming."

Brett's fever remained high for the next two days. The third morning, to Kristy's joy, his forehead felt cool to her touch. Opening his eyes, he weakly asked for water. He could barely manage to drink from the glass Kristy held to his cracked lips, but as soon as he'd swallowed a little, he muttered, "Where am I?"

"At the Bar S. Chad found you shot four days ago."

Comprehension crossed his unshaven face, and he struggled to sit up. "Four days! I gotta see Honey!"

"Lie back," Kristy said soothingly. "You haven't the strength to go anywhere. And don't worry about Honey— she's fine."

Brett sank back against the pillow, his face ashen with exertion. "You sure?"

"Yes. Lydia went to check on her."

He squeezed his dark eyes shut for a moment, then opened them. "I have to talk to Chad," he muttered hoarsely.

"All right, but first you have some of this broth. Then I'll go find him."

Brett fell into an exhausted sleep before she could feed him more than half a bowl of the soup. When he awakened again several hours later, she summoned Chad and lingered by the door.

"How are you feeling, pardner?" Chad asked quietly.

"Hell's bells—excuse me, ma'am—I'm as weak as a newborn kitten."

Chad drew up a chair. "Can you tell me what happened?"

Brett's face was pale and drawn but angry. "I got dry-gulched, by gosh. Bushwhacked by Slim Perkins!" He paused, his lips taut. "Slim said the boss wanted me to help him round up some strays, so I saddled up. I didn't notice we were off Diamond M range until we came across a stray with a Bar S brand. I told Slim, and he just laughed. Said he knew where we was, and that we had orders to lay claim to whatever critters came our way.''

Kristy took an indignant step away from the door. ''How dare Parker steal our cattle!''

''Well, I didn't much like it either, ma'am,'' Brett went on. ''But I figured it best to keep my mouth shut and send word later to Chad.'' He cleared his throat self-consciously. ''And I didn't want to get tossed off the Diamond M.''

''Because of my sister,'' Chad stated without emotion.

A trace of color appeared in Brett's pallid face. ''Yeah . . . well, anyhow, we headed that cow toward the hills 'cause Slim said some Diamond M cattle had strayed that way. We got to a draw, and I was off a little ways looking for tracks when all of a sudden Slim drew his six-shooter and nailed that cow.'' He paused to catch his breath. ''I thought he did it out of pure meanness, and believe me, I was madder than a wet hen! I hollered and started toward him. That's when he shot me.''

''On Parker's orders, no doubt,'' Chad said in a steely tone.

Brett nodded. ''That's how I figure it. Old man McClintock must've seen me and Honey together.''

A chill crawled over Kristy's skin. She had nearly married a man cold and heartless enough to order another man's death. Not for the first time, she thanked God that Chad had kidnapped her; his act of vengeance had turned out to be a blessing in disguise.

Chad stared at Brett measuringly. ''Just what are your intentions toward my sister?'' he asked in a hard-edged drawl.

''I aim to marry her,'' Brett said, meeting his friend's gaze steadily. ''I know I been the worst kind of a hellraiser, but that's all behind me now. The moment I laid eyes on Honey, I knew she was the only woman in the world for me. I never dreamed she'd want an old cowpoke like me.''

Kristy smiled in delight and surprise. ''You mean she's already agreed to marry you?''

''Yes, ma'am.'' Brett's eyes were soft, as if he couldn't

quite credit his good fortune. "Honey knows I can't offer her much, but I swear before God Almighty she'll never want for food on the table or a roof over her head." He struggled to sit up, then added hoarsely, "I gotta get her away from her pa. I don't trust him as far as I can throw a stick."

Clearly he knew nothing of Honey's engagement to Horace Webb. "Brett, there's something you should know—"

"What Kristy's trying to say," Chad broke in, turning to flash her a stony stare, "is that you should know how glad we are to welcome you into the family. And we'll keep an eye on Honey until you're well. Won't we, Kristy?"

She bristled at his untimely interruption. "Yes . . . of course. But I also have to tell Brett—"

"That he'll have a job at the Bar S for as long as he wants it," Chad finished smoothly as he stood up. "We shouldn't tire you out too much, Brett, so we'll leave you to rest up now. Come on, Kristy." Taking her by the arm, he marched her out of the bedroom and into the sunlit hall.

The instant the door was closed, she yanked her arm free and demanded, "Why didn't you let me tell him about Honey's engagement?"

"Because he'd have killed himself trying to get to her."

"That's ridiculous. He's smart enough to know he wouldn't get two steps in his condition."

"He would have made the attempt," Chad insisted. "Any man worth his salt protects what's his."

Abruptly her anger died, as she recalled how Brett had tried to get out of bed earlier, before she had reassured him about Honey's welfare. He lived by the same strict code as Chad, a code she now admired and respected.

"I'm sorry—I guess I'm just not thinking straight," she said, rubbing her forehead. "I should have known you're only doing what's best for Brett."

"You've had a hard few days, Kristy," Chad murmured, taking gentle hold of her arm to escort her down the hall. "You go lie down for a while. And don't worry.

Parker isn't going to force my sister into a marriage not of her own choosing.''

Fear for his welfare rose sharply in Kristy. She halted in the doorway of their bedroom, peering anxiously at his darkly handsome face. ''What are you going to do?''

''Find out when this wedding's taking place.'' His smile grim and wicked, he added, ''Because I just might have a plan to stop it.''

Chapter 25

Tightly gripping an ivory-bound prayerbook, Honey stood at the rear of the church. Music from the pump organ floated through the air as the bridesmaids started sedately down the center aisle of the church. The tulle veil over her face lent the scene an unearthly quality. Honey shivered. The vestibule was chilly on this February day. Despite her white kid gloves, her fingers were still cold from the ride into town.

Her heart felt just as numb. In all her youthful dreams of becoming a bride, never had she imagined she would feel so lethargic, so listless. She didn't care about her sumptuous gown of crepe de chine and white velvet. She didn't care about the fine strand of pearls adorning her throat, which her father had gifted her with that morning. She didn't care that hers was the biggest wedding the town of Painted Rock had ever seen. Inside she felt wooden, like a puppet, manipulated on strings controlled by her father.

From behind her came the sound of Parker clearing his throat. "Are you ready?" he asked gruffly.

She turned slowly, petticoats rustling. Her father looked proud and grand in a formal dove gray suit. A faint throb of emotion stirred within her lifeless heart. At least *he* was pleased with this marriage, even if she wasn't.

"Yes, Father," she whispered.

He offered her his arm. "Don't be nervous," he murmured, patting her hand. "It's a long walk up the aisle, but I'll be right there beside you."

Honey didn't bother to correct his mistaken reading of her mood. He wouldn't understand, she thought dully. To

Parker McClintock's narrow way of thinking, any woman would be ecstatic to be marrying a powerful political figure like Horace Webb.

But he didn't know the full extent of Webb's cruel nature. Or that the loss of Brett's love had left an awful aching emptiness inside her. An emptiness so absolute she no longer felt even anxiety or shyness. She felt . . . nothing.

They moved to the double doorway just as the last bridesmaid reached the altar. The stained-glass windows cast a jeweled light over the congregation. The organ music swelled, and everyone turned to face the bride. The pews were crowded with neighbors and friends, dignitaries and merchants, ranchers and cowboys. Business and political associates of both her father and her groom had come from as far off as Cheyenne and Colorado Springs. But the only people Honey would have cared to see weren't present. Parker had refused to invite Chad and Kristy.

One hand curled in the crook of her father's arm, she began the slow, solemn march up the center aisle. In the frigid fingers of her other hand she clutched the prayerbook. Her mind felt curiously detached from her body, and for a moment Honey fancied herself one of the crowd of wedding guests, seeing the perfect styling of her silvery blond hair and the demure, downcast angle of her gaze behind the transparent veil. She looked the image of the timid, scared bride clinging bravely to her father.

A sudden panic swept her back to reality. They had arrived at the altar, and she was staring into Horace Webb's pale blue eyes. He looked pompous and refined, yet she saw the lust beneath his smooth elegance . . . a lust that filled her with a dawning dread. His gaze slid downward over the curves of her body. The message was alarmingly clear. Once the vows were spoken, she would no longer have the right to lock him out of her bedroom; her body would belong to him.

Horror boiled up inside the yawning emptiness of her soul. How could she endure his loathsome touch? How could she bear to let him desecrate her, when Brett was the only man in the world she loved and wanted?

"Who gives this woman in holy matrimony?" the minister intoned.

"I do," Parker replied in a proud voice that resounded through the church.

He pressed her hand into Webb's, then walked away to take his place in the front pew. Someone coughed and a baby whined; then a reverent silence reigned.

Numbness descended over Honey like a shroud, blotting out the awful terror. Webb's fingers felt alien on hers, like the bloodless flesh of a doll. The smell of his bay rum shaving soap made her stomach churn. The minister spoke, but his words were a meaningless jumble.

She couldn't think; she mustn't think. For if she did, she would remember how she'd dreamed of standing here at the altar and speaking her vows with Brett.

Pain sliced into the numbness of her heart. Honey swallowed hard, fighting back the flood of memories. Better the bitter chill of oblivion than the fiery torment of reality. Life held no meaning anymore. Yet somehow she must endure, perhaps one day taking solace in the children that might come of this marriage—

A loud crash yanked her attention to the opened vestry door. A man strode in past the altar, his face concealed by a hood with two eyeholes. In his hands was a rope.

Several women screamed. Shocked murmurs rustled through the crowd like wind through the pines. The squealing bridesmaids shrank back against the far wall.

Honey watched dispassionately as a second masked man followed the first. Into the rear of the church sprang several more hooded men. Men brandishing pistols. Yet she felt no fear, only a vague curiosity. Why would outlaws intrude upon her wedding?

In the front pew, her father leapt up and roared, "What the hell—"

One of the hooded men near the altar swung his lasso. The rope hissed through the air and sank around Parker McClintock's shoulders. The loop pulled taut, pinning his arms to his chest.

"Rhoades!" he yelled, wrestling vainly against the lasso. "Where the hell are you?"

The outlaw yanked the rope tighter, causing her father

to stumble against the pew. "Bellow all you want," the man mocked, his deep voice muffled by the hood. "It won't do you a damned bit of good. All of your guards are trussed up outside."

Parker jerked a glare at the wide-eyed guests. "Doesn't anyone here have the guts to stop these hoodlums?"

The masked man drew a gun, pointing it at the congregation. "What do you say, folks? Anyone here anxious to be a hero?"

A woman screamed and wilted into her husband's arms. In a commotion of scuffling everyone ducked down between the pews.

"Guess not," the outlaw said with a shrug.

The other masked man started toward the bridal couple. Webb uttered a squawk of alarm. Honey caught only a glimpse of his refined face, now slack with fright, before his hands clamped down on her shoulders. He yanked her around in front of him, placing her between him and the intruders.

The outlaw stopped. His hand went to his holstered gun, though he made no move to draw the weapon. "Take your paws off the lady," he snarled. "Unless you aim to meet your Maker today."

The shrouded sound of his voice stirred something warm and familiar inside Honey's deadened heart. Against her back, she felt Webb tremble.

"Don't hurt me," he whimpered in a high-pitched voice that was foreign to his usual cultured speech. "You can have all my money—just get out of here." Still holding Honey like a shield, he flung a wad of bills over her shoulder.

The hooded man kicked contemptuously at the scattered greenbacks. "I told you to let the lady go!"

"No," Webb squeaked. His fingers dug into her shoulders like claws, and Honey gasped at the sudden pain.

Uttering a feral growl, the outlaw sprang forward and yanked Webb away by the scruff of the neck. Honey nearly stumbled as her fiancé's fingers jerked away from her skin. He went sprawling to the wooden floor beside the altar.

"Make one move and I'll shoot," the desperado warned.

Webb cowered, shaking visibly. "Don't hurt me," he repeated. "Please, I'll do anything you say."

The other hooded man waved his six-shooter at Webb's cringing form. "Take a good look at the man you would elect to public office," he drawled. "A yellow-bellied coward who hides behind a woman's skirts."

A few of the wedding guests had tentatively raised their heads over the pews to watch. Murmurs rippled through the gathering.

"Here, now," stuttered the minister, standing bug-eyed at the altar. "This is a house of worship—"

"This is an outrage," Parker McClintock snapped, furiously struggling against the rope that held him captive. "I've got a notion who you bastards are. Take off those masks and let everyone see your cowardly faces!"

He stumbled against the pew as the outlaw jerked on the lasso again. "You dare call us cowards?" he said, his steely voice muffled by the hood. "You, who would order the man your daughter loves shot and left for dead, just so you could marry her off to this mouse?"

Gasps and muttered comments buzzed through the enthralled congregation. More wedding guests came out of hiding, their fears forgotten, their eyes alight with interest.

A gust of chill wind swept in through the opened back doors of the church as Honey struggled to comprehend the outlaw's meaning. Brett, shot and left for dead? But he'd run out on her. Her father had told her so.

"Father, what is this man talking about?" she asked in bewilderment.

Parker didn't look at her. "Don't listen to these fools," he said, glaring at the masked men. "You boys have had your fun, so why don't you just get on out of here?"

"Not yet," said one of the desperadoes. "Maybe you're right. Maybe the lady'd like to see our faces."

He yanked the hood off his head. Honey caught her breath at the sight of his mussed brown hair and familiar dark eyes. "Brett," she whispered in disbelieving wonder. "Am I dreaming?"

He grinned. "If you are, sweetheart, then I am too."

Disregarding the audience of rapt guests, he took her into his arms and swung her in a circle, the white train of her gown swirling around them. The cold wall surrounding her emotions crumbled in an explosion of joy. Setting her down again, Brett reverently lifted her veil. She welcomed his kiss. The feel and scent and taste of him were so right and so perfect that her body felt alive for the first time in months.

"Get your hands off her!"

The harsh sound of her father's voice intruded on her bliss. Hurt and confused, Honey turned in Brett's arms to face Parker. "You told me he'd left town," she said accusingly. "But you really gave orders to have him shot, didn't you?"

Parker glanced at her, then looked away. "He's just a no-account drifter. He didn't have any right fooling with my daughter."

His tacit admission brought tears of pain and disillusionment to her eyes. She had known her father was a hard-headed man, but she'd never dreamed he was a killer. "Oh, Father, how could you?" she choked out, holding tightly to Brett's arm for support. "How could you do such an awful thing to the man I love?"

Parker remained stonily silent. He stared into the distance, his jaw set and his shoulders slumped. His arms were still pinned to his sides by the lasso, though he no longer struggled.

"What do you say we go on with the wedding?"

The deep voice drew Honey's attention. Somehow she wasn't surprised to see that her brother was the man holding the rope binding Parker McClintock. Chad's black hair was tousled by his discarded hood, and he had reholstered his gun.

"We'd planned on just taking you away with us, Honey," he went on, "but maybe you and Brett ought to get married right now, in front of all these witnesses. Then no one can ever say you were forced."

Brett drew her back around and tilted her chin up. "How about it, sweetheart?" he said huskily. "Are you willing to become my wife right now?"

Her heart soared at the love in his dark eyes. "Yes, I will. You know I will."

"This is highly irregular," the minister blustered. "Why, you haven't even a license—"

"Yes, we do," Brett countered, pulling out a paper. "I got it last week, just in case."

"But I hardly think—"

"Then don't think," Chad said coolly. Reaching into his pocket, he yanked out some bills, which he slapped into the preacher's hand. "Along with Webb's money, that ought to buy you a bell for the church tower."

The minister's eyes bugged out as he stared down at the wad of cash. "Ahem . . . if the bride truly is willing . . ."

"I am," Honey said softly, gazing up at Brett's handsome face.

She spared no more than a glance at Webb, who still sat sprawled on the floor as if petrified. He would gain no sympathy from her, not after the awful wrong he'd done her.

She spoke her vows in a haze of happiness. The man standing beside her wore faded denims and a flannel shirt beneath a plain leather vest, but she cared nothing for fancy clothes and elegant speech. All that mattered was that she was marrying the man she loved.

Only one moment marred her joy. When she turned to walk out of the church on her husband's arm, she caught sight of her father's bitter face. Sadness tore at her resurrected heart.

"Don't you expect one red cent from me, boy," he told Brett.

"I can take care of my wife," Brett said stiffly, sliding a protective arm around Honey's waist. "We don't need your money."

"You'll pay for this," Parker snapped. "Nobody holds me at gunpoint and gets away with it."

Abruptly Chad drew his Colt. Amid gasps and screams from the congregation, he pointed the weapon at Parker and pulled the trigger. But instead of a shot exploding, only a click was heard. Chad smiled coldly at Parker. "Then you might be interested to know our guns weren't even loaded."

Titters of laughter rose from the guests. Honey saw only a flash of the rage on Parker's face before Brett whisked her down the aisle, and she forgot all but the rapture of his love. Instead of getting into a fine carriage, she gladly shared a saddle with her new husband. Instead of presiding over a sumptuous reception at the hotel, she happily ate a simple supper in the kitchen at the Bar S.

The mood at the ranch was euphoric. Sitting close to Brett, Honey was content to listen as the men rehashed her daring deliverance. They'd been worried something would go wrong, that someone would get hurt. But the scheme had gone off without a hitch, apparently even better than planned.

"We wanted to rescue you, Honey, and humiliate Webb at the same time," Chad explained. "But we never guessed he'd play into our hands so well. He can kiss his political career good-bye. People won't ever forget he acted like such a coward."

"Serves him right," Lydia said with a sniff. "Never did like that slimy toad."

Honey basked in the warmth of their friendship. She was especially delighted to see Kristy again. Lydia had told her about the pregnancy; she was delighted to see that Kristy's stomach was slightly rounded and that her cheeks were glowing with health.

Honey felt a shock of intense pleasure at the thought of bearing Brett's baby. She wanted to give him sons and daughters. She wanted a house full of happiness and love.

The hour wore late, and everyone began to drift off to bed. Honey's blood quickened as she looked into Brett's dark eyes. "You go on up," he murmured, giving her hand a gentle squeeze. "I'll be there in a few minutes."

Her heart quaked. Tonight she would share his bed. The thought was both scary and exciting.

Love trembled inside her as she took one last look at his familiar, handsome face, weathered with lines of experience. Brett was a strong man, a kind man. His touch wasn't harsh or cruel. He treated her with respect and love. With him, the act of intimacy would be beautiful, not base.

In a flutter of anticipation, she climbed the stairs to the small bedroom Lydia had shown her earlier and donned the pretty nightdress Kristy had lent her. With shaking fingers she turned the lamp low. Then she got into bed to await her husband.

With a hand on the bedroom doorknob, Brett paused uncertainly. Honey was scared; he had seen the fear in her big blue eyes just before she'd gone up to bed. Damn Horace Webb to hell for raping her! He itched to kill the son of a bitch, but Chad had talked him out of it. Better that Webb should live with the punishment of knowing his political ambitions lay in ruins.

Brett took a deep breath. If he went slow and easy with Honey, maybe he could erase the memory of her one awful experience with sexual intimacy. He had to try. He loved her too much to forsake the right to touch her.

Opening the door, he walked inside. His blood surged. Honey was sitting in bed, her hands folded on the quilt. Her moonbeam hair cascaded down past her shoulders and over the bodice of her lacy white nightdress. A tremulous smile touched her lips. She looked sweet and shy, a fairy-tale princess who might vanish in the blink of an eye. But she was a real woman, he reminded himself, warm and alive. He could hardly believe she was truly his wife.

Half-afraid to look at her, Brett walked to the bed and sat down to remove his boots. He started to unbutton his shirt, then thought better of it. Would she be frightened by the sight of a naked man? Despite all his experience with women, he felt like an untried boy about to make love for the very first time. He knew how to give pleasure to a dance-hall girl, but Honey was a lady, gentle and trusting and virtuous. He didn't want to scare her.

He doused the lamp so only the glow of the fire lit the room. Sliding beneath the quilt, he took her into his arms. She felt small and dainty, and her womanly scent heated his blood.

"Aren't you going to get undressed?" she whispered.

He rubbed his cheek against her corn-silk hair. "In a little bit. Right now I just want to hold you."

She sighed and rested her head on his shoulder. "All that time I thought you'd left me," she said sadly. "I should have had more faith in you."

"It's not your fault," he hastened to reassure her. "You couldn't have known your pa would do such a thing."

Her eyes were like big blue pools. "Tell me what happened."

Brett hesitated. If he didn't tell her, somebody else surely would. Quickly he related the tale, glossing over the pain he'd suffered and the long weeks it had taken him to recover.

Honey shuddered. "I knew my father was close-minded and set in his ways, but I never thought of him as such a bad man."

"Don't fret about it, sweetheart. We're together again, and that's all that matters."

He kissed her forehead, his hand wandering over her shoulder. Even with the nightdress covering her, she felt soft and exciting.

"May I . . . see your scar?" she asked tentatively.

His pulse leapt. "If you'd like."

Feigning casualness, he unbuttoned his shirt. Honey's eyes skittered over his broad, bare chest to the long, pinkened slash across his abdomen. With a shy glance at his face, she feathered a finger over the mark. "Oh, Brett, you might have died!"

She bent and kissed the scar, her long, silvery hair trailing over his skin. Passion burst inside him. He sucked in his breath, fighting for control. He felt awed and humble that such a gentle lady could love him.

Desperate to express the depth of his own feelings, he drew her up and kissed her, deeply and slowly. Her willing response fired his blood. Yet he kept his fierce urges in check. By God, if it killed him, she would know the tenderness of a man's touch.

His hand roamed over her clothed body in languid caresses. Her face grew flushed, her eyes dreamy. When he could resist no longer, he drew off the nightdress and applied his mouth to the perfection of her breasts. She gasped and trembled in his arms.

Ignoring the hard desire knotting his loins, Brett pulled away. "If you're scared, just say the word and I'll stop."

"No . . . no." Smiling shyly, Honey lifted a hand to his cheek. "I like what you're doing," she whispered.

"You make me feel so quivery inside. I could never be afraid of you, Brett."

He groaned and hugged her close again, his passion raging out of control. Love burned along with the hot blood in his veins. His own hands were shaking as he stripped off the rest of his clothing. Taking care to give her pleasure, he kissed her and stroked her until he knew she was ready. When at last he entered her, he felt as if he'd gone to heaven. Nothing had ever felt so good, so right. Hearing her soft cries of ecstasy sent him over the edge himself, clinging to her, never wanting to let her go.

For a long time afterward they lay together, touching and talking. With Honey snuggled sleepily against him, Brett felt a fierce flood of protective tenderness. By God, he'd sweat and work and fight to keep her safe!

"You're my woman now," he murmured passionately. "No man, not even your father, can ever separate us again."

Chapter 26

Kristy opened her eyes to shadowy darkness. With a vague sense of alarm, she pushed herself up on an elbow and looked around. Chad was asleep with his back to her. The familiar furnishings of their bedroom were illuminated by the glow from the fireplace embers. Had she heard some noise? Some sound other than the creaking of the house or the moaning of the wind around the eaves?

From downstairs drifted the faint chiming of the mantel clock marking the hour of midnight. Then a sudden fluttering movement inside her made Kristy smile. The kicking of the baby had awakened her, that was all.

Although it was now April, the air was chilly, and she lay down beneath the quilts, snuggling against Chad's warm length. Putting her hands to the roundness of her belly, she longed for the day when she would hold their child in her arms. Since he had first felt the baby move three weeks earlier, the activity had gotten stronger, more noticeable. She wanted to share the joy with Chad, but he was exhausted from roundup chores and needed his sleep.

Leaving Brett to guard the ranch, Chad and Shake had left for two long weeks, buying a herd and driving the stock back with the help of hired hands. After their return, the work had been grueling. For days the air had rung with the bellows of cattle and the yells of cowboys as cows and calves were separated into different corrals for branding and castrating.

Chad was so busy these days she scarcely saw him. Kristy squeezed her eyes shut at a familiar spasm of sadness. Not that it would make any difference if she did see him. Outside the bedroom they might as well be strangers.

Only in the darkness of this room did he hold her close and touch her with tender passion. Even then, he reached for her almost reluctantly, as if he wanted to resist his physical needs but couldn't.

Maybe her swollen belly repelled him. Maybe once the baby was born things would change and he would come to love her as much as she loved him. Was she a fool to hope a man as cold and aloof as Chad McClintock would ever open his heart to her?

Kristy sighed and rolled over, trying to find a comfortable position. Back in the cabin Chad had spoken so scornfully of marriage and family. Now he seemed driven to make a go of ranching. Maybe once the baby came he'd let down his defenses. That hope had sustained her for so many months.

Unable to sleep, Kristy opened her eyes again. The room looked brighter. Was it dawn? Had she dozed off after all?

But something about the rosy tinge on the walls wasn't quite right. A sudden dark dread stirred inside her.

She scrambled out of bed and ran to the window. Her breath caught in horror. Orange flames were leaping against the midnight sky. The barn was burning!

"Chad, wake up!" she cried.

He shot up in bed, the quilt sliding down his bare chest. "What's wrong?" he said hoarsely. "Is it the baby?"

"No. The barn's on fire!"

Uttering a curse, he threw back the covers and jumped up to glance out the window. "Get everyone up," he ordered, yanking on his clothes. "We've got to save the horses."

Snatching her wrapper from the chair, Kristy darted out into the hall and pounded on the doors of the other two bedrooms, calling out, "Fire!" Within moments Brett and Chad were dressed and running downstairs. Kristy paused only an instant to step into a pair of shoes before following the men, Lydia and Honey close behind.

Out in the yard, Kristy stopped in shock. Flames had engulfed half the barn. Even from yards away and through the chill of the late April night, she could feel the scorching waves of heat. Smoke stung her eyes and nose. Her ears were assaulted by the roar of the fire and the frightened squealing of the horses trapped inside. Her heart constricted. Chad was in there too.

Shake and Jeremy came tearing out of the bunkhouse, trailed by several of the newly hired hands. "Grab some buckets," the foreman shouted as he headed into the smoke-filled barn.

"I'm a step ahead of you, old-timer," Lydia said, running with wooden pails toward the yard pump.

As Kristy and Honey hurried to help Lydia, a pair of panicked horses emerged from the barn and galloped off into the night, nostrils flaring and ears pricked. Then Brett came out, half-dragging their bawling milk cow.

Kristy snatched up a full bucket and hastened toward the fire. The heavy burden bounced painfully against her leg, water soaking her robe. The heat was intense as she tossed the water onto the flames.

Turning back, she saw Chad come out of the barn, yanking her brother by the collar. "Get your paws off me!" Jeremy protested, squirming and kicking.

"I've got enough to handle without worrying about you getting hurt. Now go on and help the women!" He gave Jeremy a shove toward the pump.

"I ain't taking no orders from you, and I ain't stayin' with the women!"

"You will, or by God, I'll tan your hide when this is all over."

Glancing at Chad's angry, soot-streaked face, Kristy stepped between him and her brother. "Jeremy, we need your help with the buckets. Hurry, there's no time to waste."

Chad had already disappeared into the flaming barn. She tugged on her brother's arm. Scowling, he trotted along with her. Lydia was rapidly pumping water, Honey valiantly toting the cumbersome buckets to the blaze. Enlisting the help of several cowboys, Kristy organized everyone into a line to pass the filled buckets down to the fire. Time after time Kristy hefted sloshing buckets until her arms ached with effort.

At least the work helped keep her panic at bay. The acrid smell of smoke assaulted her nose. More horses came galloping out of the burning barn. Then the crash of a rafter collapsing made her stomach twist with terror. Flames shot up against the black sky, casting an eerie orange light over the yard. Chad was still inside the inferno . . . along with Brett and Shake. What if they didn't get out in time? She saw the reflection of her own fears in Honey's worried face—Lydia's and Jeremy's too. All they could do was pray . . . and persevere.

The entire barn was ablaze by the time the three men stumbled out. A rush of profound joy washed through Kristy, and she stopped, a full bucket forgotten in her hand.

Chad headed straight toward her and gripped her by the shoulders. "You all right, Kristy?"

She could only nod, tears tightening her throat. Thank God he was safe! Even with his hair mussed and his face darkened by soot, Chad was the most handsome man she had ever seen, and she loved him.

He took the bucket from her, setting it on the ground. "There's no use in continuing," he told everyone above the roar of the flames. "The fire's gone too far. A few buckets of water aren't going to do any good."

No one protested. In silence they stood at a safe distance, watching the blaze consume the barn. The sight was awesome and awful, spectacular and sickening.

Appalled by the destruction, Kristy leaned against the solid support of Chad's arm. "I've never felt so helpless," she said. "If only I'd noticed the flames earlier."

"I'm just thankful we were able to save the animals. We can always build a new barn."

"I'm thankful you weren't hurt," she whispered low, so he wouldn't hear her over the roar of the fire. She treasured the feel of his arm around her; such moments were rare and precious.

When the flames began to die down, Lydia said, "Might as well go on inside. Mornin's gonna come mighty quick."

"We could all do with a couple more hours of sleep," Chad agreed. "Yancy, you stand watch in case the wind shifts. We don't want any sparks setting fire to the house."

"Sure, boss," spoke a lantern-jawed young cowhand.

Kristy felt bereft when Chad released her. The gathering began to disperse. Brett and Honey walked toward the house, arm in arm, heads bent close. Seeing them wrenched Kristy's heart. She was glad her friends were so much in love. Yet their happiness only served to underscore her estrangement from her own husband.

Wearily she walked toward the back porch. Chad was beside her, though he said nothing, his soot-smudged brow furrowed as if he were deep in thought. Politely he held the door open for her.

By the light of a lantern, Shake was washing his hands at the kitchen pump while Lydia searched the pantry, her graying red hair hanging in a long braid down the back of her calico wrapper. She muttered something that sounded like, "Durn old fool."

"Pardon?" Kristy said.

Lydia swung around, a jar of ointment in her hand. "The old-timer here burnt his hands gettin' them horses out. He was gonna go off to bed without even dressin' 'em."

"I don't need yer fussin'," the foreman said, though he sat down at the table and let Lydia apply the salve.

Wide-eyed with concern, Kristy turned to Chad. "Did you hurt yourself too?"

"I'm all right—"

"Let me look." Taking gentle hold of his wrists, she saw that the fire had singed the fine black hairs on the backs of his hands. His large palms were red and blistered.

"You go wash the dirt off those hands," she ordered. "You let something like that go and you could end up with an infection."

"Yes, ma'am."

His sooty face was impassive, yet as he turned Kristy could have sworn she caught a twinkle in his blue eyes.

"Nothin' worse'n a bossy female," Shake grumbled as Lydia wound a cloth bandage around his hand.

"Amen," Chad seconded from the sink.

"Humph," Lydia snorted. "An' you men call cows the dumbest, orneriest creatures on God's green earth." Tying off the bandage, she added, "You can go on off to bed now, old man."

Shake stood up. "Watch who yer callin' old. 'Less you aim for me to head on up them steps there with you and prove I ain't over the hill yet." He waggled his grizzled brows suggestively.

To Kristy's amazement, Lydia blushed like a girl. "You mind your tongue, Shakespeare Jones," she huffed. "I'll see you folks in the mornin'." Head tilted like a queen, she marched up the darkened stairs.

Kristy bit back a smile as she looked at the foreman. "Is Shakespeare really your full name?"

He ducked his weathered face abashedly. "Yes, ma'am. Reckon Ma thought if she gave me some fancy name, I'd make good. But I jist didn't take to book learnin' none."

"You don't need schooling to be a good man," Kristy said. "Why, I'll bet if your mother could see you now, she'd be proud of you."

Shake shifted his feet, obviously uncomfortable. "That's right nice of you to say so, ma'am," he mumbled. Turning to Chad, who was drying his hands, the foreman said, "Soon's it gets light, boss, I'll scout around an' see what I can turn up."

"Good idea," Chad said.

A look passed between the two men, a look that made Kristy narrow her eyes in sudden suspicion. The moment Shake was gone, she said, "You think that fire was set on purpose, don't you?"

Chad leaned against the sink and crossed his arms. "Maybe."

"By one of Parker's men, you mean?"

"Who else?"

Her throat tightened. Chad might have died in that fire. Taking a deep breath, she said, "Come here and sit down so I can take a look at your hands."

"Okay."

Chad kept his face cool as he walked to the table and seated himself. Inside he didn't feel quite so nonchalant. Her nearness disturbed him. Kristy bent over his hand, probing his palm with a light fingertip. Her brow was knit in concern, concern she would show for any injured person, he reminded himself.

Through the smell of smoke and soot, he could detect her tantalizing scent. Her wrapper gaped open, revealing her breasts swelling against her nightdress. Her unbound hair cascaded over his denim-clad thighs. He longed to thread his fingers into those silken strands and tilt her chin up so he could kiss her lips. He longed to hold her in his arms and share his most confidential thoughts—

"When is this all going to end?" Kristy asked, lifting her face to him.

He stared at her, disoriented. "What?"

"This feud with Parker," she said, smoothing salve over the blisters on his palm. "When is he going to give up?"

The memory of Parker brought a surge of restless anger. Chad shifted impatiently. "I've a good mind to end it right now."

"Don't," Kristy said quickly, clutching his wrist. Lowering her eyes so he couldn't read her expression, she added, "Retaliation will only make you as vindictive as Parker."

"Maybe, but all Parker understands is an eye for an eye."

"This vengeance has to stop somewhere. Next he might hire someone to kill you, the way he did Brett."

She made the statement offhandedly, as if it were of little importance to her. Bitterly Chad reminded himself that she didn't love him. He used to be the sort who didn't care if people were indifferent to him; now he yearned to be important to Kristy.

Though his gut felt twisted into knots, he feigned indifference. "I can't just ignore what Parker's done."

She tilted a frown at him. "Yes, you can. What'll happen to me and the baby if you're killed?"

She had a point there. He couldn't risk leaving her unprotected. "All right," he conceded. "I won't go after Parker."

Kristy drew in a deep breath, then shuddered, returning her attention to his hand. "I don't like the idea of his men creeping around here at night."

Chad didn't either. The thought of someone harming Kristy made him cold with fear. "From now on, we'll keep a man on watch," he promised. "Will that make you feel better?"

She glanced up, affording him a glimpse of her grateful green eyes. "Yes. Thanks," she murmured.

Kristy turned to his other hand, her fingers gentle as she stroked the liniment over the network of blisters on his palm. He liked having her fuss over him. She was a good woman, a woman with spirit. Helping put out the fire was something his frail mother could never have done.

"You were brave out there tonight," he commented softly.

Kristy looked up in surprise. "You did more than I. You took a big risk by going into that barn."

Tenderly he brushed his fingers against the swell of her abdomen. "I'm not six months pregnant."

A blush pinkened her cheeks, and she shifted her gaze back to his hand. "Would you like a bandage?" she asked breathlessly.

"No, it would only get in the way when I'm working."

He stared at her as she twisted the lid back on the jar of salve. God, she was beautiful. The lamplight caught the fiery strands in her mahogany brown hair. Her movements were graceful despite the gentle roundness of her belly. He longed to be upstairs, holding her in the darkness, using the act of sex as an excuse to shower her with all the tender affection he couldn't show her during the light of day. Couldn't because he knew she didn't love him. He was a fool to dream of more.

The clock in the parlor chimed three times. Chad sprang to his feet. "We'd best get back up to bed," he said gruffly.

Oh, God, did he sound too eager? He really had been making an effort to keep his hands off Kristy. How else was he to prove to her that she meant more to him than an object of lust? How else was he ever to win her love?

Kristy started to turn toward the stairs. Abruptly she stopped, her hand going to the fertile curve of her belly. "Oh!"

His heart jolted. Instantly Chad pulled her close. "What's wrong? You're not having pains, are you?"

She tipped her face up to him, her lips forming a sweetly serene smile. "No. The baby kicked me, that's all."

Chad was amazed. "You mean you can actually feel him moving inside you?"

"Yes. I started feeling movement a few weeks ago, while you were gone buying the cattle. Here, see?"

Disregarding the greasy ointment on his hand, she pressed his palm to the arch of her stomach. He was stunned and awestruck to detect a tiny pummeling sensation.

"He moves around a lot," she said, her face glowing. "We've created a strong child, Chad."

He was torn between elation and alarm. In a few short months, Kristy would endure the trauma of giving birth to their child. God, if anything happened to her . . .

Unable to stop himself, Chad buried his face in the smoky fragrance of her hair. He wanted to hold onto her forever. Between them, her body cradled their baby, the baby he had once intended to use as the ultimate revenge on Parker. A vast remorse filled him. How could Kristy ever forgive him?

A door slammed. He raised his head to see Jeremy entering the kitchen. The boy stopped, his sooty, freckled face drawing into a scowl.

"I told you before, Mister Boss-man, I don't like you pawin' my sister!"

Chad was annoyed at both the interruption and the boy's unceasing hostility. Yet he forced himself to speak calmly. "She's my wife. It's long past time you accepted that fact."

Kristy stepped toward her brother, a placating expression on her face. "Jeremy, I was just telling Chad I could feel the baby moving."

"I don't care about some fool baby. Matter of fact, I hope it dies, so we don't have another damned McClintock around here!"

Kristy gasped. "Jeremy James Donovan! How can you say such an awful thing?"

Her stricken look made Chad want to thrash the boy. But Jeremy was already running back out into the night, banging the door shut behind him.

Kristy turned to Chad, hurt etched over her fragile features. "How could he wish our baby dead?"

Chad took her into his arms. "I doubt he meant it. He

was just angry and spouted off the first thing that came into his head.''

"Where have I gone wrong, Chad?'' she asked tearfully. "Ever since my father died, I've tried so hard to raise Jeremy right. But lately he's so contrary I don't know what to do anymore.''

"He's just confused," Chad said, stroking her hair. "Maybe he needs more time to get used to sharing you with someone else.''

"How much time? You've been here at the ranch for five months now. I've tried speaking to him about it, but he just won't listen to me.''

"Then how about if I talk to him and see what I can find out? Would that make you feel better?''

Kristy looked up at him hopefully. "Would you, please?''

He didn't know what the hell he'd say to the boy, but when Kristy gazed at him with those gorgeous green eyes, he wanted to give her the moon on a silver platter. "Of course I will," Chad promised. "First thing in the morning. Now let's go on up to bed and get some sleep.''

But in the morning Jeremy was gone.

Chapter 27

"Ain't seen hide nor hair of the boy this mornin'," Shake said in answer to Chad's query. "Mebbe he's eatin' breakfast."

"Maybe," Chad mused. "I'll check in a minute."

They walked out of the yard. Here the meadows were beginning to turn into lush lakes of grass. A few scattered horses and cattle grazed in the dew-wet pasture. The sky was pearl gray; the blush of dawn tinted the eastern horizon. The day promised to be fair and warm, although at this early hour the air was chilly enough to require a coat.

Chad's blood ran cold from more than the weather as he glanced back at the blackened ruin of the barn. All that remained were cinders and a few charred timbers. Embers glowed orange in the ashes, and the smell of smoke hung heavy in the air. Anger flamed inside him. His grandfather had built the barn with the sweat of honest toil. That his work could be destroyed by one vicious act was a sacrilege.

Chad felt the savage urge to repay Parker in spades. But maybe Kristy was right. The feud had to stop somewhere. To strike back in revenge was to make himself as corrupt as Parker.

Shake bent to pluck something from the ground. "Lookee here," he said, handing a tin container to Chad. "Jist take a whiff of that."

The strong odor of kerosene wafted from the empty receptacle. "Well, if there was ever any doubt," Chad said grimly, "this proves the fire was set deliberately."

"Yep," Shake agreed. "What do you aim to do now?"

"The only thing I can do—rebuild."

Shake made no comment. As they started back toward the house, Chad issued a string of instructions. Lumber had to be ordered for a new barn, as well as tack and other supplies to replace what had burned. The horses were to be caught and corraled.

For himself, though, first on the list was his promise to Kristy. "I'll go see if I can find Jeremy," he said.

But the boy wasn't in the kitchen or in the bunkhouse. In fact, no one could remember seeing him since the fire.

"Could he have run away?" Kristy asked Chad, her eyes wide with worry. "He was so angry when he left."

"If he did, he couldn't have gone far," Chad said reassuringly. "With the horses running free, he must have walked."

Leaving the house, Chad set out on foot himself. He had a notion as to where Jeremy might have gone. When his sharp eyes spotted a small heel mark on the dewy grass, he knew he'd guessed right. The snow-capped peaks of the mountains gleamed like pearls in the early morning light. The air smelled damp and fresh with springtime. Clusters of wildflowers dotted the fertile range.

Chad walked on until he reached his destination, a stream coiling down from the foothills. Beside the water was a clump of cottonwoods wearing a vivid veil of fresh green leaves. Nestled within the trees was a huge boulder with a natural hollow on the stream side, where a boy could sit for hours and think.

Jeremy was slouched there against the rock, tawny hair tousled, elbows perched on his knees. A fishing pole lay forgotten on the ground beside him. When Chad's boot scuffed against a stone, the boy looked up, his spine stiffening.

"Go away," he snapped. "This place is mine, and you ain't welcome."

His soot-grimed face bore the tracks of dried tears. Hiding a rush of compassion, Chad sat down on a nearby rock and stared out over the trickling water. He respected Jeremy's desire to be alone, but at the same time he suspected the boy needed a friend.

"This used to be my favorite place too," Chad said. "I came here a lot when I was younger."

"Why would you come here?" Jeremy asked in a rude tone.

"This ranch used to belong to my grandparents. Guess I felt more at home on Bar S land. Whenever Parker and I got into a fight, I'd hide out here until I cooled down."

"At least you had parents," Jeremy said, his voice hostile but with the trace of a quaver. "My pa's dead, and my ma ran off when I was just a baby."

Chad glanced at the boy. Jeremy was trying hard to pretend indifference, but the pain of loneliness was clearly sketched across his dirty freckled face. What could a man say to heal a hurt like that?

"I'll let you in on a secret," Chad said. "Parker's not my real father."

Jeremy frowned warily. "He's not?"

"No. My mother was with another man before she married Parker. Do you understand what I'm saying?"

Jeremy's brown eyes were full of childlike wisdom. "You mean she laid with a man she wasn't married to."

"That's right. And that's why Parker hates me so much. When I was a kid he used to whip me, and I'd sneak off here just to get away from him." Chad paused. "I know what it's like to need a place to be alone, a place where you can think and nobody else will bother you."

Jeremy was looking less antagonistic, more interested. "Did you ever think about running away?"

"Many a time," Chad admitted cautiously. Good God, Kristy would die if Jeremy left! "I did finally, but not until I was fifteen."

"Where'd you go?"

"Down to Texas—got work as a cowhand." He gave the boy a blunt look. "You're still too young to get hired on anywhere, in case that's what you've been thinking."

Jeremy yanked at a clump of grass near his boots. "I can take care of myself," he said stubbornly.

"Can you? Life on the road is no bed of roses. You're cold and hungry 'most all the time . . . mighty lonesome too. You've got to live with the fact that you might never again see the folks you love." Chad stared out over the stream, aware of a deep regret. "Believe me, I know. My mother died while I was gone. And I didn't see my sister again for twelve long years.

Looking back at Jeremy, he added, "So you think on that, pardner. If you strike out on your own, you're leaving a hell of a lot behind. Kristy, Lydia, Shake . . . all the people who care about you. I know you won't believe it, but I care too."

Jeremy shot him a mistrustful look, although he didn't challenge that last statement. "Kristy don't need me anymore," he muttered, bending his face down as he shredded a blade of grass. "She's got you to look after her now."

So that was what had been eating away at the boy for so many months. He was afraid Kristy no longer loved him, and he was hiding his fear behind resentment and belligerence. Chad could understand how confused and alone the boy must feel.

"That doesn't mean she's stopped caring about you," he said. "She was frantic this morning when you turned up missing."

Jeremy raised his head a fraction. "She was?"

"Hell, yes. She's probably got everyone on the ranch out looking for you right now."

The boy still looked wary. "Then why's she always sidin' with you against me?"

"If she does, it's only because she wants to do what's best for you. You're the only flesh-and-blood family she's got left."

"What about when the baby comes?"

"She'll be busier, but it won't change her feelings for you. She's got enough love to go around." Except when it comes to me, Chad told himself. But what do you expect when you got her pregnant and left her with no choice but to marry you?

Jeremy was quiet for a moment. "I didn't really mean what I said this mornin'," he admitted in a low voice. "About wishin' the baby dead and all."

Chad reached out and squeezed the boy's shoulder. "I know you didn't, pardner. It was just your anger speaking."

"Do you reckon Kristy's mad at me?"

"Why don't you go ask her?"

"Maybe I will." Jeremy stood up, brushing hesitantly at the grime on his pants. "I know I ain't been too friendly to you. I oughta listen when you tell me to do somethin'."

Chad felt an upsurge of pride in the boy. "It takes a man to admit when he's done wrong. Anyhow, you've got a stake in this ranch too. Maybe you should have more of a say in running things." He rose and extended a hand to Jeremy. "What do you say from now on we're partners?"

"Okay by me," Jeremy said, shaking Chad's hand.

The boy was grinning, and something about his smile brought a poignant reminder of Kristy. Chad felt his throat knot. Swallowing the sudden swell of emotion, he clapped Jeremy on the back and returned the boy's grin.

"Come on, pardner, let's head on back. You and me've got a barn to rebuild."

Riding back toward the Diamond M, Parker McClintock took a deep breath in an effort to douse the burning lump in his belly. The fresh air didn't help. If Doc Barlow was right, nothing would help.

He was dying. As the land all around him was greening with the new life of springtime, he was withering away.

His mind was still reeling with the shock of the diagnosis issued just an hour ago. That old sawbones had to be wrong! Panic clutched at Parker, and he rubbed at the gnawing pain in his stomach. First thing tomorrow, he would go to Denver and consult the finest, most respected doctors in the city.

He couldn't die, not while he still had so many unfulfilled dreams.

None of his plans had worked out the way he'd envisioned. The plan to sire a new dynasty through marriage to Kristina. The plan to gain control of the Bar S and extend his empire. The plan to marry Honey to an influential politician.

Reining his horse to a halt, Parker adjusted his hat to keep the afternoon sun out of his eyes. Unintentionally he had ridden near the border of the Bar S. In the distance he could see a party of men digging fenceposts. Wrath flamed inside him. The two ranches should have been one, instead of being separated by some newfangled barbed-wire fence!

The one person in the world he gave a damn about lived over there—Honey, his daughter, the last of his blood, married to a common cowpoke. The knowledge hurt like the cancer eating at his belly. Yet, despite his anger, Parker admitted to a grudging respect for Brett Jordan. If nothing else, the man at least had the guts to fight for what he wanted.

After that fiasco at the church, Webb had fled Colorado in disgrace, and for weeks Parker himself had been the subject of criticism and gossip from the townspeople of Painted Rock. The situation was a humiliating blow to his pride. People who had once regarded him with respect now sniggered behind his back.

Pain corroded Parker's belly, and he longed for some soothing whiskey. This damned mess was all Chad's fault, he thought angrily. No doubt that bastard had been the mastermind behind the ruination of Honey's wedding. Wasn't it enough that he'd already stolen Kristina and the Bar S? That he'd planted the child in her that Parker had intended to be his own?

Fury festered inside him. No, none of his schemes had borne fruit. The fire hadn't ruined Chad. Neither had any of the other things: the hangman's noose, the rustling of Bar S stock, the patch of poisonous weeds planted for the cattle to graze on, the steer head left in the ranch yard.

But he wasn't defeated yet. Perhaps the time had come for bolder action. He would get his daughter back, one way or another.

You can't change an old bull's ornery nature, Parker thought as he slapped the reins and started toward home. If he was destined to die, he'd go down fighting.

And that bastard Chad would go down with him.

Sunset painted the mountain peaks crimson as Kristy walked toward the yard pump, an empty bucket swinging in her hand. The heaviness of her belly required her to move slowly now. Nearly eight months pregnant, she was aware of a serenity and contentment unlike anything she had ever before felt. Soon she would cradle Chad's baby in her arms.

The only stain on her happiness was the knowledge that her husband didn't love her. But even that she could bear. Because Chad wanted this baby as much as she did. She could only hope and pray that someday his scars would fade and he would love her.

At the pump she filled the bucket, then carried it back to the house and trickled water over the scraggly rose-bushes growing near the porch. As soon as the task was done, she turned to gaze into the distance.

Watering the flowers was only an excuse to watch for her husband. A few cowhands had already come back from their daily chores in the saddle, but Chad was always the last to return. Today he was setting fence posts, and soon barbed wire would stretch for miles, clearly defining the border between their ranch and the Diamond M.

Worry furrowed her brow. The fence was a symbol of what Parker had lost, yet other than a few petty actions, he hadn't retaliated. Maybe he'd lost his taste for revenge when he realized his neighbors weren't going to be driven away.

The smell of lumber from the new barn mingled with the succulent scents of supper. Kristy was about to go back in and help Lydia and Honey with the cooking when she spotted a pair of horsemen riding toward the ranch house. Her heartbeat surged as the two drew nearer and she recognized Chad sitting straight and tall in the saddle. The rider beside him was Jeremy.

She was glad the two were getting along so well now. Ever since the barn fire six weeks ago, their relationship had improved dramatically, though neither of them seemed willing to discuss what precisely had changed Jeremy's attitude.

The bucket swinging at her side, Kristy lifted her free hand and waved to the riders. Chad waved back and put the spurs to his horse, as if he were impatient to see her.

An instant later a distant rifle shot rent the air.

"Get down, Jeremy," Chad yelled as he ducked close to the neck of his own horse.

Kristy screamed and dropped the bucket. The horses

came galloping into the yard. Running clumsily toward them, she saw to her relief that Jeremy appeared to be unhurt. Then horror flooded through her at the sight of blood seeping down the arm of Chad's shirt.

"You've been shot!" she gasped.

As if he hadn't heard, Chad swung out of the saddle. Grabbing hold of her shoulders, he demanded roughly, "Are you all right?"

"Yes, but—"

"Then get inside," he ordered, drawing her toward the house.

Kristy tried to pull away from his strong grip. "But you're bleeding. Let me look—"

"Not out here, for God's sake!"

He half-dragged her into the house, brushing past Lydia and Honey, who were standing in the doorway. Jeremy trailed the group into the kitchen. Chad pressed Kristy down into a chair. "You stay put, and that goes for everyone here. I don't want anyone else getting shot."

As he headed for the door, Kristy rose in alarm, the hasty action made awkward with the weight of the baby. "Where are you going?"

"To get that gunman."

"But you're hurt—"

"It's only a graze. I'll be all right."

He was gone before she could utter another protest. Hurrying to the window, she watched him ride off into the deepening dusk along with Shake and several of the hired hands. Brett and the others stayed behind, apparently to guard the house.

She kept her anxiety at bay by helping Lydia and Honey finish supper preparations. Conversation was strained, and Kristy kept glancing at the door, silently entreating God to keep Chad safe. At last her prayers were answered. Hearing the thud of hoofbeats outside, she rushed to the door.

Seeing Chad dismount in the darkness, she breathed a sigh of relief and waited impatiently for him. She ached to feel his arms around her, but to her disappointment he merely gave her a weary look in passing. Brett, Jeremy, and Shake followed him inside.

"I'll see to your arm," Kristy said, hurrying to get water and bandages.

Chad sat down at the table, and she carefully peeled away his shirt. Seeing blood ooze from an angry gouge in his shoulder, she swallowed hard. If that bullet had hit a few inches lower . . .

Quickly she asked, "Did you find the gunman?"

"We lost him. Got dark too quick."

"Whereabouts do you reckon he was hidin'?" Lydia asked. "Ain't no trees nearby."

"Lots of dips and hollers out there in the grass," Shake said. "That land ain't as smooth as it looks."

"We'll head out again at daybreak," Brett added, putting his arm around Honey. " 'Course, he'll be long gone by then."

"But we know in which direction he'll head," Chad said grimly.

Kristy knew he was referring to Parker. As she bandaged the wound, she wondered despairingly when the feud would end. Burning the barn was one thing, but shooting at her husband was another entirely. Would Parker not be satisfied until Chad was dead?

"Maybe I could go talk to my father," Honey ventured. "He might listen to me—"

"Don't even think about it," Brett snapped. "He might be your pa, but I don't trust him an inch."

"Brett's right," Chad said. "I don't want anyone going near the Diamond M. Matter of fact, it'd be wise for you ladies to stick close to the house from now on."

Kristy couldn't protest the restriction, knowing Chad only meant to protect them. Yet as days passed and no similar incidents occurred, she longed to be outside in the balmy late spring weather. The men went on with their work as usual, but now no one left the yard without a six-shooter strapped to his hip and a rifle in the scabbard of his saddle.

Chad was busier than ever. When he came home at night, he was too tired to do more than eat and fall into bed. They had almost ceased their lovemaking with the advancement of her pregnancy. Chad claimed to be concerned about harming her and the baby, yet Kristy couldn't help but wonder if he'd lost interest simply because he didn't love her.

One morning as she was walking into the kitchen she saw Brett and Honey embracing near the back door. Brett kissed his wife on the nose and touched her cheek before going outside.

A lump formed in Kristy's throat at their obvious affection. That was what she wanted for herself and Chad. Swallowing hard, she entered the room.

Honey whirled around, blushing but smiling. "I'm sorry. I didn't see you. I guess you'd never know Brett and I've been married four months already."

Kristy couldn't contain a dejected sigh as she rubbed at the ache in the base of her spine. "I wish Chad cared for me even half as much."

Her sister-in-law looked surprised. "Why of course he loves you. He must. He married you and fathered your child."

"But unfortnuately not in that order." Kristy lowered herself into a chair, propping her feet on a stool. A burden of bitter despair, heavier than the uncomfortable weight of the baby, dragged at her soul. "Chad even admitted he only proposed for the sake of the baby."

"That doesn't mean he doesn't love you."

Kristy shook her head. "He's never once told me he does. Most of the time he acts as if he doesn't even want to touch me." Feeling the warmth of tears trickling down her cheeks, Kristy turned her face away, dashing at the moisture with her hand. "I'm sorry. I shouldn't be complaining. I don't know what's come over me lately. Every little thing seems to upset me."

Honey drew a chair close and sat down, her expression full of concern. "This isn't something little," she said, squeezing Kristy's hand. "I'd be in tears, too, if I thought my husband didn't love me. But you're wrong about my brother. I really do think he loves you."

"I wish I could believe that."

"I believe it," Honey said with conviction. "When I was just a little girl of five, I didn't think he loved me either. I didn't think he even noticed I existed. He was ten years older, a big man to me, and busy with his chores around the ranch. Then one day I was playing near the corral and saw a pretty white horse inside. I wanted to feed him a carrot, so I climbed inside the fence, not realizing the horse was an unbroken bronc. Chad leapt in and scooped me up before I could get trampled to death.''

''He would have done that for anyone,'' Kristy pointed out.

Honey shook her silvery blond hair. ''But it was the way he hugged me so close afterward that told me I'd been wrong, that he really did love me after all. He just didn't know how to express his love in words.''

''I realize he's close-mouthed about things,'' Kristy said, afraid to let hope rise in her. ''But during the time we were in the cabin, he always spoke so cynically about marriage. He said it was something he never wanted for himself.''

''I'm not surprised he was cynical, after seeing the unhappy marriage my parents had,'' Honey said sadly. ''He needs you to show him it doesn't have to be that way. He needs your love, Kristy, no matter how strong and tough he seems.''

As the women went about their morning chores, Kristy couldn't stop thinking about what Honey had said. Maybe her sister-in-law was right. Maybe Chad really did love her. The possibility left her shaken inside. She realized that for too long, pride and fear had kept her from voicing her love for him. Why was she waiting for him to speak of his feelings first anyway?

Even if Chad didn't love her, she could offer him her own heart. Perhaps in time she could cleanse the old hurts, soothe away his scars. But to do so she must take the initiative and make herself vulnerable to him.

Restless and anxious, she couldn't wait until evening to tell him of her love. Lydia had gone into town, and Honey was upstairs cleaning. Knowing her sister-in-law would try to talk her out of leaving, Kristy put a note on the kitchen table, then headed for the stables. The hired hand named Yancy had been left on guard duty, and she asked him to hitch up the buggy for her.

''I don't know, ma'am,'' he said doubtfully. ''Boss told me you ladies was to stick close to the house.''

"I'm only going to see my husband."

"But, ma'am—"

"If you don't hitch up the buggy for me, you'll force me to do it myself," she said with steely sweetness. "You wouldn't do that to a woman in my condition, would you?" Pointedly she rested her palms on her distended abdomen.

"All right, ma'am. But I'm comin' with you."

"No. You'll not leave my sister-in-law here alone. It's only a short distance, and my husband will escort me back."

Yancy didn't look happy, but he did her bidding. Within moments she was holding the reins as the buggy jolted over the prairie toward the place near the main road where Chad had mentioned that morning he would be setting fence posts. The late morning sun poured down from a cloudless sky. Perspiration tickled Kristy's neck. The ache in her lower back increased with the bouncing of the buggy, but she bit her lip in determination. She must speak to Chad now, before she lost her courage.

At last she caught sight of her husband in the distance. Though several other men labored nearby, there was no mistaking his tall, muscled body. Chad turned at the sound of the buggy, hands straddling his hips, his hat shading his face so that she couldn't see his expression. As she reined the horse to a halt, he came toward her with long strides. Not until he tilted his head up to her did she see the darkness of fury on his tanned features.

"What the hell are you doing out here?" he snapped.

A cold knot formed in her stomach, yet she forced a smile. "I have something to tell you. Could you help me down, please?"

Chad ignored her outstretched hand. "You drove out here alone just to talk?" he asked scathingly.

Kristy swallowed a retort. He wouldn't be so angry once he'd heard why she'd come. Awkwardly she climbed down from the buggy and put a placating hand on his chest. "Yes," she murmured. "I do want to talk—"

"You fool! Parker's men could be hidden anywhere, waiting to take a shot at you, waiting for a chance to get revenge on me!"

His harshness stung. Kristy tried to tell herself he spoke only out of concern, but her old fears resurfaced.

"Don't pretend to care about me," she retorted bitterly. "All that matters to you is that Parker doesn't steal what's yours."

She swung sharply and stumbled. Catching at the buggy wheel, she felt her knees hit the ground. A jarring pain shot up her spine. Instantly Chad's arms were around her, helping her back up. "Are you all right?" he demanded, the brusqueness gone from his voice.

But it wasn't the fall that alarmed her; it was the gush of warm liquid between her legs. Dismayed, she remembered what Lydia had told her to expect. "My water's broken," she murmured, lifting anxious eyes to Chad. "The baby's coming."

His face went ashen. "It can't be," he said hoarsely. "It's a month too early!"

Chapter 28

Kristy felt the tightness of his grip on her shoulders, saw the worried shock in his eyes. "Everything will be all right," she reassured him, though fear coiled inside her.

"I'll take you home," he said roughly.

He made a move to help her into the buggy when Jeremy came running up, his brown eyes wide. "What's wrong, Kristy? I saw you fall."

"I'll take care of your sister," Chad said quickly. "She'll be fine—I've just got to get her back to the house."

Hoisting her into the buggy, he vaulted onto the seat beside her. He snapped the reins, and the horse started off at a trot.

Kristy clung to the seat as the buggy jolted through the waving sea of grass. Her undergarments and skirts felt sodden and uncomfortable. Suddenly a twinge seized her abdomen, gathering force and squeezing the breath from her body. After a long moment the sensation dwindled and was gone.

Aware of a mingled sense of fear and excitement, she breathed a fierce, fervent prayer. Nothing must go wrong. She had yearned and waited for this birth for so long.

Chad's bronzed face was set in grim lines. Gazing at him somehow made Kristy feel calmer. Everything would be all right so long as he was with her. Surely their child would be strong and beautiful, like his father.

Another cramping pain curled from the base of her spine around to her belly. This pang was more insistent than the first. Perspiration broke out on her brow, and she sucked in her breath, digging her fingers into the leather seat.

Chad glanced at her, alarm in his eyes. "Are you doing all right, Kristy?"

The torment began to subside, and she nodded unsteadily. "I felt a contraction, that's all."

"God damn it," he muttered, and urged the horse on faster.

The bouncing of the buggy intensified the ache in Kristy's lower back. Gripping the seat, she said irritably, "For heaven's sake, slow down."

Instantly he pulled on the reins. "What's the matter?"

Her annoyance melted at the taut concern of his face. "This isn't a race," she said, touching his arm and smiling. "It'll be hours before the baby's born."

Chad gazed at her, his eyes troubled, then he turned his attention back to the prairie. "Yes, you're right," he said gruffly.

At a more leisurely pace they continued to the house. Two more contractions assaulted Kristy on the way, although thankfully the magnitude of the pain didn't increase. Still, her skin felt clammy, and she slumped weakly against the seat as the buggy finally pulled into the yard.

Honey hastened out the back door. "Kristy, I've been so worried . . . oh, goodness!" She stopped, a hand going to her throat.

"She's having the baby," Chad told his sister.

"I'll go get things ready." Honey whirled and dashed inside.

Kristy leaned into the strong support of her husband as he helped her to the ground. Her legs threatened to crumple beneath her, but Chad swung her up into his arms. "We're home now, so don't worry," he murmured, striding into the house.

She clung to his neck as he mounted the stairs two at a time. Another pain twisted through her. She clenched her teeth, burying her face against his shirt. By the time the agony ebbed, leaving her limp and shaken, she realized they were in the bedroom. Chad was leaning against the wall, holding her tightly as Honey scurried to put fresh linens on the bed.

His eyes were fiercely blue. "Ah, Kristy, if only I could spare you this."

"I'll be all right," she said, summoning a smile. "It's normal for a woman to feel pain in childbirth."

But privately she was worried. Her labor wasn't starting mildly and slowly the way Lydia had told her it would. Instead, each contraction clamped her womb in a vise so strong she was unable to think or speak. I can endure, she told herself, just as long as our baby is alive and healthy.

Lydia bustled into the bedroom and took in the situation at a glance. "Land sakes!" she exclaimed. "Let's get her out of them wet clothes."

Under her efficient direction Kristy was soon clad in a clean nightdress and lying gratefully in bed. But her rest was short-lived as another contraction began clawing her belly. She moaned and doubled over with the force of it. Through a haze of pain, she heard Lydia tell Chad to fetch the doctor.

Then the older woman was beside the bed. "Breathe slow and deep, sweetie," she said. "Slow and deep."

Gripping the older woman's hand, Kristy concentrated on doing so, and the torture seemed to ease a fraction. The next hour or more passed in a blur as wave after wave of pain pummeled her. Then abruptly and inexplicably the labor abated.

"Praise God," Honey said, rejoicing with Kristy at the respite.

Then Kristy caught Lydia's disquieted expression. Alarm stabbed her, and she pressed her palms to her swollen abdomen. She could feel no movement within. The tiny hands and feet that had hammered her for weeks were quiet now.

"My baby's going to be all right, isn't he?"

The worried lines on Lydia's face smoothed out. " 'Course he is, so don't you fret. Honey, you go fetch the baby things we've been sewin'. I'll get some towels and a basin to wash the little one in."

As the women went about their chores, Kristy lay back on the bed, trying to keep her fears at bay. Would the empty cradle in the corner soon be filled? Please keep the baby safe. Please.

Just before the doctor arrived, the pains returned, mild at first, then more excruciating than ever. Honey stayed at the bedside, grasping Kristy's hand and wiping away the perspiration on her forehead. Kristy couldn't see or hear clearly. As the doctor examined her, she caught a glimpse of Chad pacing the room, the clinking of his spurs drifting to her through a haze of pain.

" . . . too early," came Doc Barlow's voice. "Baby's turned sideways . . . don't look good."

"For Christ's sake," Chad said angrily. "Quit yammering and do something!"

" . . . can't guarantee . . ."

The words were washed away under a tidal wave of agony. Hands pressed against her belly, probed between her legs. She cried out as pain lanced her insides.

Chad's face swam before her. She felt the comfort of his muscled arms. "Listen to me, Kristy. The doc says you have to walk, so the baby'll come faster. Come, sweetheart, I'll help you." She felt him lifting her from the bed and moaned in protest. "Lean against me," he crooned. "That's the way. You're doing just fine. Think about the baby . . ."

The baby. She forced her numb legs to move. Each step was a monumental effort. Time blurred into an eternity of torment.

Abruptly came a new barrage of pain. A tremendous pressure built within her. She found herself lying on the bed again, straining to expel the child from her womb. Chad's voice was encouraging her, although she could no longer comprehend his words.

Pain tore through her loins like a hot poker. Then miraculously the anguish ceased. For a moment she lay in a fog of exhaustion until the squall of an infant rent the air.

"It's a boy," exclaimed Lydia in delight.

Kristy struggled up on an elbow, anxiously seeking out the baby. "Is he all right?"

"Couldn't be finer," Lydia said proudly, wrapping the infant in a blanket and bringing him to the bed. "He's a tiny one, but he'll grow like a weed."

Kristy took the long-awaited bundle into her arms. As she gazed down at her son's wrinkled face and solemn blue eyes, all memory of the long hours of agony vanished beneath a flood of joy. Fingers trembling, she touched the downy black hair so like his father's.

Eagerly she lifted her gaze to find Chad. But all she saw were Honey and Lydia cooing over the baby and Doc Barlow washing up. "Where's Chad?" she asked.

Honey looked around in surprise. "He was here just a moment ago."

"Prob'ly just needed to step out a minute," Lydia said. "Oh, my, ain't he gonna be a proud papa."

Kristy cuddled her son until he slept. For the first time she noticed the darkness outside. Downstairs the mantel clock chimed twice. Had she really been in labor for so many hours? Honey and Lydia helped get her cleaned up and tucked the baby into his cradle beside the bed. Kristy felt exhausted, yet ecstatic—and impatient to share her happiness with Chad. Where was he?

When half an hour had passed and he didn't reappear, distress blanketed her blissful contentment. Chad hadn't wanted a wife and a family; he was a loner at heart. Perhaps the birth had made him more keenly aware of the bonds that tied him to a life he didn't want.

Too weary to face the bitter truth, Kristy drifted into an uneasy sleep. Sometime during the night she had a vague impression of Chad's calloused hand on her brow, his deep voice murmuring her name.

But when the baby's cries awoke her at dawn, the only sign that her husband had been there was a faint depression on the pillow beside her.

Kristy named the baby James, in memory of her father. She took much comfort in the fact that Chad seemed to adore their son as much as she did. The fears that had arisen in her on the night of the birth began to dwindle, although she couldn't forget the hurt she'd felt when he had abandoned her that night.

Little Jamie quickly became the center of attention around the ranch. He grew plump and sturdy, with alert eyes and a calm disposition. When Kristy wheeled him around the yard in the fancy wicker carriage, even the roughest and toughest cowhands stopped to take a peek inside and chuck the boy under the chin. Jeremy was especially proud, taking his duties as uncle seriously, always ready to watch over his tiny nephew.

One evening, when Jamie was six weeks old, everyone gathered on the back stoop after supper to relax and enjoy the balmy July weather. Beneath a black velvet sky dusted with stars, owls hooted and crickets chirped in the darkened pastures.

"A durn shame Jamie's grandpa couldn't have lived to see his namesake," Lydia said, gazing at the sleeping bundle of baby cradled in Chad's arms.

Swallowing her own sadness, Kristy gave the older woman a hug. "But thank goodness Jamie does have a grandmother in you, Lydia."

"That's mighty kind of you to say so when I ain't his blood relation. Come to think on it"—Lydia paused to blow her nose loudly—"if I'm to be his grandma, the boy might jest as well have a grandpa too. You catch my meanin', old-timer?" Shake was leaning against the house nearby, and she gave him a poke.

"Watch that leaky mouth of yers," Shake warned. "You ain't got no lasso around me yet."

In delighted surprise, Kristy gazed from Lydia to Shake and back. "Are you two getting married?"

"Yes," said Lydia.

"Mebbe," said Shake. "If her cookin' don't kill me first."

"Quit your complainin', you old cuss," Lydia said, though affection softened her voice.

Kristy was thrilled that Lydia had at last found happiness again. Yet she was aware of a certain dejection in her own life. Sitting on the stoop, she hugged her knees and gazed wistfully into the night.

She stole a glance at her husband, who sat nearby, holding Jamie and humming a soft, tuneless lullaby. Her heart leapt when she saw Chad look at her, although in the faint starlight his expression was more enigmatic than ever. After a long moment he turned his eyes away.

Yearning trembled within her as she remembered her

purpose the day her labor had begun. Could she find the courage to tell him of her true feelings?

Chad mounted the darkened steps, taking care to walk quietly. Every night for the past few weeks he had gone to bed late, and tonight was no exception. Lying beside Kristy without touching her was rapidly becoming more than he could stand. If she were asleep, at least the torture was bearable.

In the shadowed hall he silently pushed open the door to their bedroom. And stopped, transfixed.

Kristy was propped up against the pillows, nursing their son. She was gazing down at the baby, smiling serenely, a hand gently stroking his cheek. Her loosened hair flowed around her shoulders; the front of her nightgown was unbuttoned and opened. During the night Chad was often aware of her feeding Jamie, but he had always kept his back rigidly turned away. Now he couldn't help staring. The low-burning light of a lamp on the nightstand illuminated the taut fullness of her exposed breast, the creamy perfection of her skin, the shadowy cleft between the generous swells of flesh.

Desire scorched through Chad. Instantly he was disgusted and appalled at himself. How could he feel such selfish urges so soon after the pain and suffering Kristy had endured giving birth to their son? He'd been damned lucky she'd lived through the experience. Another pregnancy might kill her.

He started to make a swift retreat, but she looked up and smiled. "Don't go," she called out softly.

"I'm intruding."

"No, you're not," she whispered. "Jamie's almost asleep anyway. Even if he weren't, I don't mind you watching me nurse our son."

But Chad minded. The hot tightness in his loins was evidence of that.

"It's late," Kristy added in a murmur. "Come to bed— you must be tired."

He might have found the strength to walk out if her lips weren't so ripe and inviting, if her eyes weren't so green and glowing. He had to go to bed sometime, didn't he?

Damning his weakness, Chad shut the door behind him. He sat down on the chair to take off his boots. Out of the corner of his eye he saw Kristy shift Jamie to her shoulder to burp him. Then, with the baby still snuggled against her, she started to get out of bed.

Chad sprang up, setting his boots aside quietly. "Don't get up. I'll put him to bed."

She smiled her thanks. "Careful—he's asleep."

In lifting the slumbering baby, Chad's fingers brushed against her breasts. The sensation was electrifying. He wished to God she would draw the nightdress back into place, but Kristy seemed oblivious of the fact that her bare bosom was exposed to his gaze.

Pivoting sharply, he took the baby to the cradle and kissed his tiny, milk-fragrant cheek before laying him inside. His eyes were soft as he looked down at his son. Gently he touched the boy's silky black hair.

"You love him, don't you," Kristy said.

He straightened and swung around. She was buttoning the front of her nightdress, although he could see the shadow of her nipples through the frilly white cloth. With effort he dragged his mind back to her statement.

"Did you think I wouldn't?" he asked, his voice low.

She looked away, but not before he caught the sadness in her eyes. "For a while, I wasn't sure. I was afraid you didn't want either of us."

Chad was silent, too taken aback to speak. Yet how could he be surprised she'd think that? Hadn't he been ready to give away his own child to Parker?

Kristy turned her troubled gaze toward him. "You've always been a drifter, Chad. I know you never intended to have a family." She sighed. "You disappeared the night Jamie was born. I waited for you to come back, but you never did. I thought you didn't want to face the reality of being bound to a wife and child."

The emotions of that tumultuous night came flooding back to Chad, forming a knot in his throat so tight he could scarcely breathe. If only she knew he'd been too overwhelmed by turbulent feelings, too convinced he was undeserving to share her happiness, too afraid to let her see his tears of relief and regret.

"That's not why I left, Kristy," he said hoarsely.

"I don't understand then." Her voice wavered; her moist eyes glistened in the lamplight. "Why else would you leave me at such a time? Didn't you want to share in the birth of our child?"

Shoving his hands into his pockets, Chad stared down at his bare feet. "I was there when Jamie was born," he muttered. "It was just that afterward . . ."

"Afterward what? Please, Chad, for once tell me what you're thinking."

Her soft, beseeching words tore at his heart. He felt a passionate urge to open up and let her into his secret thoughts. Fearful, he walked to the window and gazed out into the darkness. In the glass he could see the reflected glow of the lamp . . . and Kristy sitting in bed, arms folded in her lap, awaiting his explanation.

Whatever the price to his own pride, he at least owed her the truth. And why not? His natural aloofness had gained him no ground with her.

"All right, I'll tell you," he said heavily. "I left that night because I was ashamed . . . ashamed because I'd put you through the agony of childbirth, all for some damn-fool desire for revenge. When I saw our baby for the first time, I didn't feel worthy of sharing the experience with you." He drew in a rough breath and closed his eyes. "Christ, how could I have ever even considered giving away my own son—and to a man like Parker, no less?"

He heard the gentle pad of Kristy's bare feet; then her arms slipped around his waist from behind. "But you didn't give him away, Chad."

The warmth of her body pressed against his back was more comforting than any words. She was a good woman, a forgiving woman, yet the burden of his sins weighed heavily on him.

"I can't absolve myself of guilt so easily. I used you. How can I ever forget that I forced you into this marriage?"

She curled her small fingers around his forearm. "Chad, look at me."

He turned slowly, afraid, yet desperate to breach the chasm between them.

"You never once had to force me to make love with you," Kristy said softly. "I'm glad of what happened. If you hadn't kidnapped me, we wouldn't have our beautiful son."

Her gentle eyes made his blood leap with longing, a longing he couldn't yet indulge. "You didn't want to marry me. You agreed only because of the baby."

She shook her head, smiling. "If I refused at first, it was only because I thought . . . Chad, remember that day I came out to see you, the day I went into labor? I had something to tell you—"

"How can I forget that day?" he broke in. "If I hadn't yelled at you and gotten you all upset, you wouldn't have had the baby early."

"For heaven's sake, stop blaming yourself for everything that's happened. No one can tell a baby when to be born."

She was so warm and close he couldn't stop himself from touching the silken hair cascading past her shoulders. "I thought you were going to die having Jamie that night," he murmured raggedly. "I was so afraid I was going to lose you before I could tell you how much you mean to me." He drew in a deep breath to ease the ache in his throat. "I was too shaken that night to say what I felt inside, but I'll say it now. I love you, Kristy. I'll understand if you can't feel the same about me—"

She put a finger over his lips, her eyes soft and misty. "But I do, Chad. I fell in love with you months ago, while we were still back in the cabin."

His heart thumped with wild hope. "You did?"

Kristy smiled. "Yes. But I never told you because I thought you'd only married me out of obligation. I let fear and pride keep me from voicing my feelings. That's what I was coming to tell you the day I went into labor."

"And all I did was snap at you." He plunged his shaking hands into her hair, bringing her face up to his. "My God, Kristy, I've been a damned fool."

His mouth melted against hers. He felt her arms twine around his neck, her soft body strain against his. Driven by hungry desperation, he kissed her deeply and thoroughly, letting her warmth wash away the scars of a lifetime. The emptiness inside him filled with the wonder of holding her in his arms again.

Kristy drew back a little, her eyes sparkling. "You might be interested to know the doctor told me I'm fully recovered now." Smiling, she pressed her hips against him. "It's been a long time for us."

Passion seared Chad's blood. Yet his concern for her well-being was stronger. "Are you sure that's what you want, Kristy?" he asked hoarsely. "You might become pregnant again."

"I'd like us to have more than one child, wouldn't you?" she asked softly.

His hands gripped her shoulders with the force of holding back his hot desire. "Yes, but Jamie's birth was so hard on you. How can I let you suffer through that again?"

"Oh, Chad, the birth was only difficult because he was turned wrong. It isn't likely to happen again."

He tried one last time. "I don't want to see you spend your life the way my mother did, always pregnant or recovering from a miscarriage."

"I'm strong, Chad. And I want you too much to deny myself the fulfillment of our love."

She arched up on tiptoe to press a gentle kiss on his lips. With a groan deep in his chest, Chad enveloped her in a fierce embrace. "God, I love you," he whispered into her hair. "I love you so much."

Kristy's heart soared at his impassioned words. To feel him holding her, to hear him speaking his heart, seemed almost like a dream. Eagerly she lifted her face to his kiss, welcoming his taste, his touch.

He unbuttoned the front of her nightdress, then eased it off her shoulders. The frilly white garment slid to the floor. She was naked beneath, but Kristy felt no shame as Chad drew back to gaze at her; instead she thrilled to the passion darkening his eyes.

His palms curved gently around the full swells of her breasts. "I'm almost ashamed to admit I've envied our son these past few weeks," he said with a rueful smile.

"He's had the privilege of feasting himself where I couldn't."

Chad feathered his lips over one breast, his tongue circling the peak. Her skin tingled beneath his kisses, and the place between her thighs began to ache with anticipation. His hands drifted lower, slowly seeking out every curve and valley, touching her waist, her hips, her thighs, until she was burning with need.

"I want to see you too, Chad."

With trembling fingers she unbuttoned his shirt, then spread her palms over his firm muscles. As she brushed her lips over the black thatch on his chest, his exciting male scent enveloped her. Her hand trailed down the line of dark hair that disappeared into his waistband. Slowly she undid the buttons of his pants. Then she reached inside to stroke the rigid length of him, glorying in the magnificent proof of his love for her.

"Ah, Kristy," he groaned. "I want to lose myself in you."

Quickly he removed the rest of his clothing and drew her over to the bed, pressing her against the coolness of the sheets. His palms cradling her cheeks, he kissed her long and hard. Her fingers curled into the thickness of his hair; her heart beat faster at the feel of his muscled male body. A turbulent yearning began to build inside her, a craving for the act that would be the ultimate celebration of their love.

His hand slid down over her breasts and lower, over her waist and belly. For one endless, tormenting moment he caressed her intimately, then eased a finger into her moistness. She gasped out his name and opened her legs to him. The stroking pressure of his hand caused her to writhe beneath him, arching her hips as a wild need seized control of her body. The storm gathered force until the excitement exploded within her, leaving her exhausted, yet awash with wonder.

Half-dazed, she opened her eyes to see Chad smiling at her. "How could you think I'd prefer the life of a drifter," he whispered, "when I have you to come home to?"

The intensity of emotion in his voice warmed her heart.

"I was afraid of losing you, Chad. And afraid you didn't love me the way I love you."

"I do love you," he said huskily. "By God, I do."

His mouth met hers in an impassioned kiss. Kristy felt drained of the ability to feel, yet when his skillful hands began caressing her body, the erotic sensations began to build inside her again. His hardness probed her entrance. She gasped as the tight passage was invaded; then the pleasure of feeling him inside her was so great, she cried out.

He drew back, his eyes dark with concern. "Am I hurting you?"

"No." She shook her head and smiled shakily, too consumed with rapture to say more. Groaning a response, he thrust his hips against hers in a natural rhythm that wrested a moan from her lips. The fiery feelings inside her climbed to a peak, then erupted into glorious satisfaction. She felt a violent release quake through Chad before he relaxed atop her, breathing hard.

Contentment flowed in her veins like warm honey. After a moment he rolled off her but held her close, and she knew that he, too, wanted to savor the sweet aftermath. He ran his fingers over her face, following the shape of her jaw, the line of her cheekbone.

"I never knew a man and a woman could find any lasting happiness together," he murmured. "When I was just a young boy, I swore I'd never let myself get tangled up in a marriage. I was better off alone, avoiding all the arguments, all the hatred, all the tears."

Kristy tilted her head to see his eyes. "You didn't have a very good example to go by," she said softly.

"I know that now. I loved my mother, but I never knew her very well. Looking back, I can see she was a weaker woman than you, too absorbed in her problems to pay much attention to her children. She'd been hurt once in love and never risked it again." His face hardened. "And God knows I never had much in the way of a father."

Kristy gently touched the faint scarring on his back. "I wish I could erase all the pain you suffered as a boy."

He kissed her nose. "You have. It doesn't matter anymore, now that I have you."

Her hand moved to caress the whitened scar on his shoulder, and she shivered at the memory of him being shot. "I wish Parker could put vengeance behind him too. But maybe he's given up, since he hasn't done anything to us lately."

"Yes, maybe," Chad agreed.

But Kristy felt the sudden tensing in his arm muscles, and suspicion made her rise up on an elbow to study his face. "Parker *has* done something, hasn't he?" she asked accusingly. "Something you haven't told me about."

For a moment his bronzed features were set in closed lines; then Chad admitted, "The fence we strung was cut last night and some of the cattle stolen, that's all."

"That's all?" Rage sparked in her, both at the act and at him. "And you weren't going to tell me?"

He touched her cheek in apology. "I didn't see the need to worry you. You've got enough on your mind right now, what with taking care of the baby."

Her anger died down. "I have a right to know what's going on, Chad. Especially when your life is involved."

"Nothing's going to happen to me." He paused. "We might not have to worry about Parker much longer anyhow. I heard talk in town today that he's sick, so I paid Doc Barlow a visit. The doc admitted Parker has a cancer in his stomach."

Stunned, Kristy didn't know how to react. "Will he die?"

"Doc didn't give him long, but Parker's a stubborn old bull. He won't give up until the bitter end."

Kristy fell silent, shaken by the news. She would be thankful to see an end to the guns and violence and glad when she could know her husband was safe. Yet there was a certain sadness in seeing the fall of such a proud man as Parker.

"Does Honey know?" she asked.

"Brett was going to tell her tonight."

"Poor Honey," she whispered. "I remember how I felt when my own father died. He wasn't always the best of fathers, but I loved him anyway."

Chad hugged her close. "Trust you to think of someone else's grief instead of your own relief at the ending of the feud," he said huskily. "Darlin', you're the most tender-hearted woman I know."

"That's not what you told me back in the cabin," she couldn't help saying teasingly. "You said I was greedy and selfish."

"That was before I knew you." He lifted her palms to his mouth. "Before I fell in love with you."

His lips met hers, filling Kristy with radiance. She was fiercely proud of her husband. Proud that he could overcome the destructive power of vengeance. And most of all, proud that he could at last open his heart to her.

Early the next morning Kristy sat in a rocking chair in the kitchen, nursing her son as Lydia and Honey finished washing the dishes. With a frown of concern, Kristy noted the glow was gone from Honey's cheeks, leaving her pale and somber. Lydia broached the topic that had kept the atmosphere subdued at breakfast.

"We all heard about your pa's sickness," she said bluntly. "I ain't gonna pretend I like the man, but I know how grieved you must be, and I'm sorry for that."

"Thank you," Honey murmured. "I know he did an awful thing to Brett, but he's still my father. I can't help worrying about him."

Lydia patted the girl's hand. " 'Course you can't, sweetie."

Tears shone in Honey's blue eyes. "He'll die without even seeing his grandchild."

"You and Brett are going to have a baby?" Kristy asked in surprised delight.

Honey nodded, her lips curving into a tremulous smile. "I think so, come February."

"Mercy me," Lydia exclaimed, giving the girl a hug. "Ain't that fine. We're gonna have us another little one to love."

A baby would help heal Honey's hurt, Kristy thought as she smiled down at her son. Jamie had fallen asleep at her breast, and she stroked a finger over his plump, velvety cheek. Nothing in the world could match the joy of holding Chad's baby in her arms.

An hour later Kristy discovered the note. The small square of paper was lying on her bed when she went upstairs to change Jamie's diaper. As she read the message, her eyes widened with worry. Clutching the baby in her arms, she went hurrying back down the narrow flight of stairs to the kitchen.

The fragrance of baking bread suffused the air. Lydia was bent over, pulling a loaf pan out of the oven.

"Honey's gone," Kristy said breathlessly, waving the paper. "She left a note saying she was going to visit her father."

"Land sakes!" The oven door squawked shut, and Lydia straightened, anxiety in her brown eyes. "Well, I don't like her goin' off alone, but her pa's never raised a hand to her. Likely she'll be all right."

Kristy tried to convince herself that Lydia was right, but a sense of unease nagged at her. When several hours had passed and Honey failed to return, Kristy couldn't wait any longer.

"Lydia, I'm going to fetch her. Will you watch Jamie for me?"

"Now, hold your horses, girl. We'll send for Chad or Brett."

"We can't," Kristy said urgently, placing the baby in Lydia's arms. "Parker would shoot to kill if he caught either of them on his land. I'll go bring her back, and no one will be the wiser."

"It ain't safe—"

"Please, Lydia, don't say anything to Chad. I won't have his life endangered."

Before Lydia could argue further, Kristy headed out the door and hurried toward the barn. The building was dim inside even on such a sunny day. The smells of grain and manure and new lumber scented the air. At the far end of the barn, she could see Shake forking hay into an empty stall. Knowing the foreman might try to stop her from leaving, she slipped quietly into the tack room.

Minutes later, she was out in the corral, struggling to

put the cumbersome sidesaddle on her roan mare. As she led the horse out the corral gate, the clatter of hoofbeats drew her attention.

She shaded her eyes against the bright sunlight and gazed at the trio of riders coming into the yard. Two of them hung back at a respectful distance from the first. Her breath caught in a startled gasp as she recognized the man in the lead.

Chapter 29

Parker McClintock sat erect in the saddle, shoulders squared proudly. Yet as he drew nearer, his illness was perceptible in the pallor of his weathered skin and the gauntness of his broad build. Kristy felt only the briefest stirring of compassion before her heart turned to stone. This was the man who had tried to hang Chad, who had ordered him shot by a sniper.

The hooves of Parker's horse kicked up clouds of dust. The two cowboys riding in the rear must be guards, she thought, for they glanced around nervously, as if expecting gunfire at any moment. Stopping before her, Parker swung down from the saddle, his movements as slow and studied as an old man's. Yet when he spoke his voice was as strong as ever.

"Good morning, Kristina. You're looking well, considering you just gave birth to Chad's brat." Flipping the reins to one of his subordinates, he looked her over insultingly. "I knew you'd be good breeding stock."

Kristy was too wary to take offense. Why was Parker here if Honey was at the Diamond M? Unless he didn't yet know his daughter had gone to see him.

The roan danced impatiently, and Kristy clutched the reins tightly, staring at Parker. "Why have you come here?" she asked cautiously.

"Just paying a neighborly visit, that's all."

"There's nothing neighborly about you, Parker."

He merely stroked his graying handlebar moustache and glanced at the large building behind her. "Quite the fancy new barn you have there," he said. "Must have cost you folks a pretty penny."

Kristy controlled an upsurge of anger. "We won't be driven off our land. You might as well give up this pointless feud, because you won't win."

The pretense of civility vanished from Parker's face. "Don't be so sure about that, Kristina." He limped toward her, stopping a scant foot away. "There are other ways to win."

Alarm raced through Kristy's blood; she was thankful Jamie was safely in the house. Lifting her chin, she refused to show her fear. "Chad will kill you if you dare touch me."

"You think I'm scared of that son of a bitch?" A hand pressed to his belly, Parker let out a bark of bitter laughter. "Maybe I don't even care if he shoots me, so long as I can take him with me when I die."

"Mebbe you oughta die now, mister."

Kristy turned to see Shake standing in the shadowed doorway of the barn, a rifle in his hands.

"Don't make idle threats, old man," Parker snapped. "You wouldn't dare shoot with the woman between us."

"You gonna hide behind her skirts jist like that Webb feller did with your daughter?"

Parker's pale face darkened with fury. "If you're calling me a coward—"

"He's not calling you anything," Kristy broke in, anxious to defuse the explosive tension. "Why don't you just get on your horse and ride off, Parker? You're not welcome here."

Shake aimed the rifle at one of the mounted men behind Parker. "That goes double for you, Slim Perkins," the foreman said threateningly. "I oughta blast you to kingdom come for what you done to Brett Jordan."

The lanky cowhand shifted uneasily, saddle leather creaking. "Now don't get riled," he said, a trace of alarm in his voice. "I don't want no trouble—"

Parker turned to scowl at the man. "Shut your mouth."

Slim fell silent and spat a stream of tobacco juice onto the dusty ground.

Parker looked back at Kristy. "I'm not leaving until I see my daughter."

"Honey isn't here," Kristy said quickly.

"You lying hussy," Parker growled, taking a menacing step toward her.

Shake cocked his rifle with a snap of his wrist. "Stand back, mister," he warned.

"Yes, you leave her be," Lydia called from the doorway of the house. Hands astride her hips, she walked down the steps and across the yard. "Honey went to see you, you old buzzard. Don't rightly know why, but the girl was grieved to hear you was ailin'."

Kristy frowned. "I wonder why you didn't pass her on the way."

"I stopped off in town first." Parker's eyes narrowed. "If I don't find my daughter back at the Diamond M, you folks will be hearing from me. And next time I won't be so polite."

Wheeling around, he limped back toward his horse.

"I'm going with you," Kristy said decisively, turning to the roan. "Honey might be foolish enough to trust you still, but I won't let her be alone with you."

Stopping beside his horse, Parker glowered. "She won't be alone," he said. "Horace Webb is waiting back at the ranch for me. He's far better company for her than that cowpoke husband of hers."

"Webb!" Lydia exclaimed, fingers twisting into her apron. "You mean you let that snake back into your house after what he done?"

"It's no concern of yours whom I choose to entertain," Parker snapped. "Now that the scandal's died down, there's still hope for his political career. He might be a coward, but at least he's no dirt-poor cowpoke."

"You're the sorriest excuse for a father I ever did see!" Lydia stormed. "You'd give your only daughter to a man who'll"—she glanced at the mounted cowboys who were listening with ill-concealed interest and lowered her voice to a hiss—"who'll probably rape her like he done before."

Parker's face turned ashen. "What the hell are you talking about?"

"Honey told me what that snake done to her," Lydia went on in a low, accusing tone. "Imagine! She was afraid to tell you, afraid her own pa wouldn't believe her! And now you're fixin' to hand her over to Webb again like a lamb to slaughter.''

"Dear God," said Kristy in horror. "And she's pregnant. He could hurt her and the baby."

Parker looked stunned; then fury convulsed his haggard face. "Goddammit!" he roared. "I'll kill him if he touches her! By God, I will!"

Half-stumbling in his haste to mount, Parker heaved himself into the saddle and kicked his horse into a gallop. The two cowboys followed in a trail of dust.

"I'm going too," Kristy said, even as she was stepping up onto the corral rail to seat herself in the sidesaddle.

"I'll ride for the boss," Shake said, hurrying into the barn for a horse.

Kristy didn't argue, although her heart contracted with fear. They might need Chad's help in getting Honey away from Webb. She mustn't let herself think of the danger her husband would be courting by invading Parker's domain.

"Take care of Jamie," she called out to Lydia before snapping the reins to urge the roan into a trot.

Kristy rode as fast as she dared across the grassy plains. Far ahead she could see Parker and his men riding toward the Diamond M. The wind whipped her skirts and hair, and the pounding of her horse's hooves jarred her spine, yet she didn't dare slow the roan's swift pace.

Anxiety clenched her stomach. Chad and Brett had done serious damage to Webb's political aspirations. Unlike Parker, Kristy didn't see how the man could ever overcome the humiliation of that day. The knot of apprehension inside her squeezed tighter. By scorning Webb and marrying Brett, Honey had completed Webb's fall from grace. What would he do to her in retaliation?

Kristy rode for what seemed like an eternity. The late morning sun shone blindingly, and she wished fervently for a bonnet to shade her eyes. The gently waving grasses stretched before her; to her left rose the snow-topped mountains.

After a time she reached the fence Chad had erected along the border of the two ranches. Anger simmered in her when she saw a place where the wire had been cut, enabling cattle to wander through at will. Or to be driven through by rustlers. Kristy slowed the roan to a walk, not wanting to injure the horse on the twisted barbs. Once beyond the fence, she rode quickly after Parker and his men, now mere dots in the distance.

At last she saw the white, two-story ranch house with its fancy gingerbread trim around the porch. The double front doors stood open beneath the fanlight window of leaded glass. Dread snaked through Kristy. Parker was nowhere in sight. The only signs of life were the three lathered horses cropping grass near the yard.

She slid down from the roan and hastily looped the reins around a slat in the railing. Abruptly the blast of a gunshot came from inside the house.

Fear for her sister-in-law sent Kristy racing up the steps, hands lifting her heavy skirts. The foyer was dim after the bright sunlight and cool with the breezes wandering in through the open doors. In the parlor doorway she stopped in horror.

A cowboy was sprawled face down on the settee, his blood staining the rose-and-silver fabric and dripping onto the floral rug. Parker and Slim Perkins stood nearby, their gun belts tossed to the floor, their hands held high.

Though Kristy had never before met him, she knew the feral-eyed madman in front of the fireplace was Horace Webb. With one arm he held a struggling Honey before him. In his other hand he brandished a six-shooter.

The bodice of Honey's striped gingham gown was ripped open, revealing her lacy chemise. Her silvery hair was tumbled around her shoulders; her blue eyes were wide with terror.

Kristy took a step into the parlor, and Webb shifted his gaze to her. "You must be Mrs. McClintock—how nice to meet you." The lustful smirk on his face belied his gracious words. "I can see why Parker wanted you so badly."

"Get out, Kristy!" Honey cried. "He'll kill all of us!"

Webb swung the gun barrel toward Kristy. "A capital notion, my dear. After all, I mustn't leave any witnesses."

Seeing the wild look in his dark eyes, Kristy realized belatedly that she'd been a fool to rush in here. Horror coiled inside her. Somehow they had to get Honey away from Webb. But how?

"You let my daughter go this instant!" Parker shouted.

"Why?" Webb said, sneering as he aimed the gun at Parker again. "Just a few hours ago you were ready to talk her into annulling her marriage to that cowpoke so you could hand her back over to me."

"That was before I found out you'd raped her. Nobody soils my daughter and gets away with it, by God!"

Suddenly through an opened window Kristy caught a glimpse of Chad's face before he ducked down out of sight. Her heart surged with mingled relief and alarm. Curling her fingers into her skirt, she forced her eyes back to Webb, not wanting to alert him to Chad's presence.

"And nobody humiliates *me* and gets away with it," Webb returned coldly. "This little hussy is responsible for everyone laughing at me."

"Horse shit," Parker spat. "You did it yourself by acting the coward, by hiding behind my daughter's skirts, just as you're doing now."

The politician scowled. "If she'd renounced Jordan at the altar, she could have saved my career."

"I'm thankful now she didn't." Parker brandished his fists. "Why don't you let her go and fight me, man to man?"

Webb laughed scornfully. "Why should I, you sick old bastard? I'm the one holding the gun. No, I'll just be on my way and take your lovely daughter along . . . as insurance. We're going to have fun together, aren't we, Honey?" Keeping his arm taut around her slender waist, he reached up and fondled her breast.

Uttering a roar, Parker lunged like an enraged bull. "You filthy son of a—"

A shot exploded from Webb's gun. Parker staggered as the bullet tore a blackened hole in his sleeve.

"Stay back!" Webb cried hysterically.

Parker surged onward. Panicked, Webb fired again.

Parker swayed. Disbelief was etched on his ashen face as he looked down at the bloody wound in his chest. Slowly, like a mighty oak falling, he toppled to the floor, barely alive.

Honey screamed and jerked free. She started toward her father, but Webb grabbed her skirt and caused her to stumble. Kristy darted toward them and seized the distraught girl by the arm, dragging her away. The gingham skirt ripped out of Webb's hand.

"Bitch!" he snarled. "Stop, or I'll kill you!"

"Like hell you will," came a deep voice from the other end of the parlor.

Webb whirled. Chad stood inside the opened window, the draperies stirring in the summer breeze, the long-barreled Colt leveled at the politician. Kristy drew Honey toward the safety of the foyer.

"Drop the gun," Chad added coolly. "Unless you'd prefer the grave to jail."

Webb froze, his pistol lowered. "Prison?" he whimpered, his eyes rolling in fright. "You can't lock me away!"

He whipped up the gun, aiming it at Chad.

Kristy cried out in terror, hands paralyzed around Honey's arm. Parker came to life at the same instant. Using a weapon drawn from one of the gun belts lying on the floor, he fired at Webb.

Webb retaliated, but the bullet went wild, smashing into a group of china figurines on the mantel. Blood bloomed on the pristine front of his shirt. His face contorted with shock, then agony. Clutching at the fast-flowing wound, he crumpled to the carpet, his eyes glazing over with death.

Chad was at her side before Kristy was even aware he'd moved. "Are you all right?" he demanded, hugging both her and Honey close as if to reassure himself.

Kristy nodded shakily. "Yes, thank God, we're fine."

Chad pulled back to look at his sister. Honey choked out a sob and wrenched herself away to kneel beside her father's prostrate form. Her heart constricting with compassion, Kristy followed, Chad at her side.

Parker's fingers clung loosely to the butt of the smoking pistol. His skin was pasty gray, the breath rattling in his throat. His dark eyes fluttered open and sought out his daughter. "Shouldn't have trusted him," he gasped. "Forgive me."

"Of course, Father. But don't talk, save your strength."

Lifting teary eyes to Chad, Honey said, "Send for the doctor, Chad! He's losing too much blood."

"No . . . time," Parker gurgled, groping for his daughter's hand. "Is it true . . . you're going to have a . . . baby?"

Honey nodded, a sob tearing from her throat. "In February. I was coming to tell you—you're going to be a grandfather."

The pale lips beneath his sweeping moustache softened with satisfaction. "Promise me . . . you'll come live here . . . keep the ranch going . . . you and Jordan . . . the child."

"We will, Father," she vowed in a quaking voice, clinging to his hand. "We will."

Parker closed his eyes as a spasm gripped his bloodied chest. Then his body went slack, and his breathing ceased.

Honey's hand drooped, and her shoulders shook with silent weeping. Kristy crouched down to put a comforting arm around her friend, murmuring words of sympathy. She glanced up at Chad's grim face and silently communicated the need to get his sister out of this death room. With his help she drew Honey up and led her out of the parlor.

Brett was hurrying into the foyer, forcibly marching Slim Perkins before him. Slim's face was battered, and blood trickled from a corner of his mouth along with brown tobacco juice. Shake followed, gun drawn and ready. On seeing Honey, Brett shoved his captive at Shake and rushed to take his wife into his arms.

"You all right, sweetheart?"

"Oh, Brett . . ." She buried her tear-stained face against his shirt.

He glanced into the parlor at the dead men, his eyes widening. "What in tarnation happened here?"

Chad gave a brief accounting of the events.

"God Almighty!" Brett breathed, hugging Honey tighter. "Let's get you out of here."

When they were standing in the warm sunshine, Brett muttered, "If Shake had found me sooner, I'd have pumped that lead into Webb myself."

"I'm glad it's over," Kristy said with a shudder, leaning against Chad's strong supporting arm, "but I'm sorry about Parker. He did the right thing in the end."

"Well, at least I caught one of the varmints," Brett said, steely satisfaction in his voice as he jerked a thumb at Slim. "That bushwhacker was slinking out the back door when Shake and me rode up here. It figures he'd try to save his own skin instead of staying to protect the women."

"Lemme go," Slim whined through a bloody gap where his front teeth had been. "You ain't got no call to hold me."

"Sheriff'll decide that," Shake said, poking the gun barrel into the cowhand's gaunt ribs. "He'll be mighty interested to hear how you dry-gulched Jordan."

"Why take him into town?" Brett asked angrily, stepping away from Honey with his fists clenched. "I'll be glad to even up the score in a fair fight."

"Don't, Brett," Kristy said urgently. "You'll not rectify one wrong by committing another."

Chad put a restraining hand on Brett's arm. "Kristy's right. There's been enough violence today—and in the past. It's all going to end, right here and right now."

A cool night breeze, fragrant with the lush scent of grass, wafted through the open window of the bedroom. Shadows darkened the corners and flitted over the walls, although the full moon cast a luminous, silver-blue veil over the bed and its occupants.

Content to bask in the afterglow of their lovemaking, Kristy idly explored her husband's naked chest, tangling her fingers in the silken black hair. Beneath her palm she could feel the steady beat of his heart. Praise God he was alive. Even now, the thought of what had transpired that afternoon had the power to make her tremble.

"Cold?" Chad murmured, fitting an arm around her to nestle her closer to his heated body.

"Only when I think about what happened." She tilted her head to gaze at him, drinking in his beloved face. "Oh, Chad, Webb might have shot you. How ironic that Parker ended up being the one to save your life."

"Parker wasn't trying to protect me—he wanted vengeance on Webb for Honey's sake," Chad pointed out. "Anyway, if he hadn't pulled the trigger, I'd have killed that scum myself. Any man who'd rape a woman deserves to die." He paused, then looked away, letting out a self-deprecating laugh. "Listen to me talk. Rape is what I intended when I kidnapped you."

Kristy put her palm to his stubble-roughened cheek, turning his face so she could gaze into his eyes, dark and haunted in the silvery moonlight. "Forget about the past," she said softly, her hand drifting to his belly. "I'd rather look to the future . . . to a life with you and Jamie."

Chad glanced at their son, who was sleeping peacefully in the cradle near their bed. The look he gave Kristy was profoundly tender. "You're right," he murmured huskily. "For so many years I was alone . . . and I never even knew what I was missing. I love you, Kristy. By God, I'll cherish your stolen heart forever."

His lips met hers in a deep and satisfying kiss. Kristy twined her arms around her husband, awash with love, feeling that special, wild need for him grow inside her, the need to share her life, her heart, her body.

After a long time, he lifted his mouth from hers. Letting his hands glide down to her lush, milk-taut breasts, he said, "Bet you can't guess what I'd like to do right now." His gaze was teasing.

The feel of his hot desire against her thigh sparked a rush of fire inside her. "Bet I can," she shot back. "And speaking of bets, there's only one thing still puzzling me."

"As long as I don't have to think too much, I'll answer."

Trying to ignore the breath-stealing movement of his hands down her spine, she aimed a suspicious look at him. "Did you cheat in that card game?"

His expression was innocent . . . too innocent. "Who, me?"

"Yes, you."

He grinned, caressing her bare bottom. "Let's put it this way. From the first moment I laid eyes on you, sitting so prim and proper in that bank, I knew I'd lie, cheat, or steal to get you into my bed."

Kristy rose to her knees, hands on her hips. "Why, you

sneaky polecat! I was right all along!'' She attempted to glare, but a smile broke through and ruined the effect. "How did you pull off that trick? I was watching you the whole time, and I never saw you make a single wrong move.''

Still grinning wickedly, Chad feathered his fingers over the slim length of her leg. "That's my little secret.''

"We're married—we're not supposed to keep secrets from each other,'' Kristy said indignantly.

His hand wandered up her inner thigh. "Well . . . maybe I'll tell you someday.''

"When?'' she asked, pouting as she gazed adoringly at his handsome features.

"Oh, on our honeymoon, maybe. We never had one, you know.''

Kristy sighed as his fingers found her most sensitive spot. His languid stroking liquified her insides, yet she managed to hold onto a thread of rationality.

"I want to hear more about this honeymoon,'' she said breathlessly. "When . . . and where . . .''

Chad flashed her a rakish smile. "Soon,'' he murmured, drawing her down beneath him. "As for where . . .'' He paused to kiss her again, briefly but thoroughly. "I happen to know of a secluded little cabin up in the mountains . . .''

BARBARA DAWSON SMITH

Even as a girl, BARBARA DAWSON SMITH spent long hours writing poetry, reading romances, and dreaming of becoming a published author. Numerous creative writing classes during high school and college deepened her love for storytelling. A native of Michigan, she moved to Houston after graduation and worked as a technical writer for an oil company.

Years passed; the hope of seeing her own books in print was shelved but never forgotten. She kept writing, kept dreaming. Winning the 1984 Golden Heart award, a nationwide competition sponsored by Romance Writers of America, unlocked the door to her long-awaited first sale. Since then, Barbara has published several romance novels, with many more to come. Her husband, two cats, and two-year-old Jessica often entice Mom from the computer, but she is diligently at work on another novel for Avon Books. She likes hearing from readers and wants to continue writing the kind of stories they enjoy.

If you enjoyed this book, take advantage of this special offer. Subscribe now and . . .

GET A *FREE* HISTORICAL ROMANCE
—— NO OBLIGATION(a $3.95 value) ——

Each month the editors of True Value will select the four best historical romance novels from America's leading publishers. Preview them in your home Free for 10 days. And we'll send you a FREE book as our introductory gift. No obligation. If for any reason you decide not to keep them, just return them and owe nothing. But if you like them you'll pay *just* $3.50 each and save at least $.45 each off the cover price. (Your savings are a minimum of $1.80 a month.) There is no shipping and handling or other hidden charges. There are no minimum number of books to buy and you may cancel at any time.

send in the coupon below